if you're
not the one

BOOKS BY LAURA BRIGGS

One Day Like This
One Winter's Day

LAURA BRIGGS

if you're not the one

bookouture

Published by Bookouture in 2019

An imprint of StoryFire Ltd.

Carmelite House
50 Victoria Embankment
London EC4Y 0DZ

www.bookouture.com

ISBN: 978-1-78681-808-9
eBook ISBN: 978-1-78681-807-2

Preface

Eight Years Ago

Natalie's cell phone, a clunky older model left over from her high-school years, rang persistently, but she ignored it. Her open textbook on American history partly covered the stupid phone as it buzzed to life every few seconds.

She was definitely moving on from her past. Fashion shows, Manhattan design houses, and Milan runways awaited her if she was dedicated and kept her nose to the grindstone—childhood was over, and so were summer vacations working at Icing Italia and relationships with stupid high-school boys who cared more about hot rod cars and hot models than they did girls with talent and brains. And no more enduring the crush a certain someone had on her, which had been hanging over her since second grade.

"Aren't you going to answer it?" her friend Tessa asked, lying sprawled across her dorm-room bed beneath a poster of a very chiseled-looking Russell Crowe. In her hands, an issue of *Bridal Today*, through which she searched for material for her composition essay on new trends in the event-planning world.

"No." Natalie's answer was curt.

"Why not? It's been ringing for ten minutes, Nat. It's probably your mom. Maybe she tried to call your room and found out you weren't there."

"It's not Ma," said Natalie. "She knows I'll call if something's up—besides, my annoying roommate probably told her that I was visiting a friend's room."

"Maybe it's your brother. Don't you have a brother—Bob?"

"Rob. And it's not him, it's…" She hesitated. "It's this guy who's friends with him. He's just weird, and he's probably trying to call to see if I'm okay."

"You have his number in your phone?"

"Just so I know it's him to avoid the call." Natalie glanced over her shoulder. "He won't take no for an answer. But I *told* him that I would be way too busy to talk after I left for college."

"Is he cute?" asked Tessa, whose definition of this wasn't exactly broad but made allowances for every boy with a cute smile and a good sense of humor. Natalie could answer this one safely.

"No," she said.

"But he has a crush on you?" Tessa abandoned her magazine and rolled over on the bed, crawling closer to Natalie's seat at the desk. "Oh my gosh, he does. You have a high-school sweetheart. Is it anybody I know?" Although they had grown up in the same city of Bellegrove, Tessa and Natalie's high-school years had been spent in separate schools. Childhood bonding over plastic teacups and imaginary friends might have faded, but Natalie had been grateful to find at least one familiar face in the newness of college life, especially in the same dormitory.

"You don't know him," said Natalie. "He's just a nerd named Brayden who has been hounding me for years to go out with him.

He wanted to go to the prom with me, and I barely escaped *that* experience." She shuddered. Memories of prom were less than magical anyway, now that she was free of the high-school scene, and she couldn't imagine how terrible they would be if she had actually been forced to dance with Brayden that evening.

"Wait—wasn't there a boy down the street from you named Brayden?"

"Aren't you supposed to be clipping articles for your paper?" asked Natalie.

"I want to hear the story about your prom first," said Tessa. "Was it better than mine? I went with a group of girls who hadn't been asked out either, and the football team threw a frozen football right into the punch bowl while we were standing in the drinks line. It ruined my dress, and I was going to wear it to a formal here before I got rid of it for good."

"I'll make you a better one," said Natalie, who would rather talk dresses than review her prom night.

"So what did this Brayden guy do that nearly roped you into prom with him?"

Natalie rolled her eyes. "Everything," she said. "He begged, he sent me a card, he wheedled information out of my mom that I didn't have a date already, then he showed up with flowers at school to formally ask me... I found out later that he'd planned all this stuff behind my back, like nobody was going to ask me instead."

"Somebody did, obviously?"

"Of course." So it was at the last minute, and a member of the track team who had only recently broken up with his cheerleader girlfriend. It had still been a better evening than the one Brayden had pictured for them. One which she would have resorted to only if she had become too desperate to live.

"Will you two *please* be quiet so I can study?" Penny, Tessa's room-mate and a girl Natalie vaguely remembered as an unpleasant third grader with Marcia Brady's hair, lifted her headphones off and gave them each an annoyed glance. "Some of us have a future to think of, all right? I'm an honor student, hello?" She turned the page in a book on the history of diplomacy, crossing her ankles behind her as she lay across the dorm room's second bed.

Natalie and Tessa exchanged looks. "You ever think maybe our brains are faster than yours, since we can process social exchanges and academic information at the same time?" said Natalie to her friend's roommate.

"Coming from one of the girls whose homework includes reading *Cosmo* weekly?" Penny shot back.

"Hey, I needed a lighthearted current event. It was my first day in that required Health and Wholeness 101 class," said Natalie.

With a smirk, Penny popped her headphones in place again.

"I wish I had known you were coming here," said Tessa, more quietly than before. "We could have shared a room."

"Me too," said Natalie. "Maybe in the future, right?" She turned the page in her book, and the phone beneath its cover began ringing again. She buried it under one of Tessa's issues of *Perfect Planning*.

She could ignore the ringing phone, but she knew Brayden would never just stop at trying to call her.

A few weeks later he appeared in the flesh in her dormitory's televi-sion lounge wearing an ironed button-down, and having made an attempt to comb his lank, reddish-brown mane. He rose from the chair by the window, that semi-geeky smile on his face and a dessert carrier in his hands as he moved to greet her.

"Brayden," she said, trying not to sigh. "What are you doing here?"

He shrugged, his smile falling into place. "I happened to be in the neighborhood," he said. "Thought I'd stop by and make sure you're settling in okay."

Natalie didn't believe it for a second. This was just like Brayden to show up at her new school and make some big scene as if they were friends or childhood sweethearts. Didn't he know that girls liked a bit of mystery in guys? *A little subtlety goes a long way*, she thought wryly. *Try playing hard to get for a while.*

"My mom sent these, by the way," he added, holding out the dessert carrier. "Cupcakes, a half-dozen or so. They're cherry chip cream cheese. Your favorite."

Brayden knew all her favorite foods, probably. He'd memorized everything about her over the last decade of her life, it seemed. A stalker could take tips from Brayden. For all she knew, he kept a shrine to her in his bedroom closet with Polaroids of all their times on the playground and school events where Brayden always managed to edge his way into her social sphere before the evening was over. The thought exasperated her.

Still… he looked so hopeful standing there in another effort to win her approval. She knew deep down that he wasn't a bad guy—in fact, he was more like the ultimate nice guy. The kind who would help her move her dorm fridge without a grunt of complaint, or drive cross-country to give her a ride home for the holidays. Brayden might have even been the friend she relied on for those things, if he wasn't so intent on pursuing her romantically. Really, *really* intent.

Natalie caved, accepting the dessert container with a half-smile. "Thanks, Brayden," she told him. "These look good. I've kind of been missing home-cooking since I got here. The food here is… well, let's just say it makes our high-school cafeteria seem like gourmet and makes me wish Uncle Guido's pasta dishes could survive the ride in traffic over here."

Most of Natalie's family worked in the food industry. Her uncle ran an Italian restaurant, her mom a bakery, and her cousins worked kitchens and waited tables in restaurants across the whole of Bellegrove, the southern city with small-town heart. Cozy enough with its historic buildings, but with a fashion house or two among its local artisans. Maybe she would work for one of them someday, she imagined.

"You should come home for dinner more often," Brayden suggested. She knew he was hoping he'd be there too, sitting across from her at the big table in her mom's dining room. Since he pretty much had a standing invitation to dinner at the Grenaldi household, Natalie knew that he probably would be.

"Not with my homework load," she said, trying to brush him off with what sounded like a joke, albeit a flat one. "Maybe after I get settled." She hesitated to shoot him down completely, in the face of that age-old disappointment in Brayden's green eyes for the distance between them. She had a heart, despite her brother Rob's repeated assertion she must have been born without one. Even tough-as-nails Natalie could weaken a little beneath the hurt that Brayden tried to mask.

Until she spotted a group of fashionably chic girls from her Fabric 101 class on the other side of the dorm building's glass, that was. They were watching her and Brayden, whispering to each other as they passed by. Probably saying, *Isn't Natalie's boyfriend such a nerd? What a loser she must be ending up with someone like him.* Or, *Can you believe a fashion major would date someone with such awful taste in clothes? She must've been reaaally desperate back in pokey old Bellview, or wherever it is she lived.*

She couldn't take their stares, or the snicker one of them wasn't bothering to disguise. Hoisting her backpack onto her shoulder, Natalie cast a lukewarm smile of farewell toward Brayden. "Gotta run now—lots to do before my next class. Say thanks to your mom for the cupcakes, okay?"

She didn't have to turn back as she beat a retreat to know the look on his face. She knew it was there even as she climbed the stairs to her dorm room, her own face burning with shame. If only he would get the message so she wouldn't have to feel so bad about turning him down over and over, and putting up barriers between herself and a friendship that had probably peaked when she was eight.

Wouldn't Brayden *ever* give up on liking her?

Chapter One

Present

Natalie's suede boots clipped down the sidewalk in Bellegrove at a steady pace, avoiding the wet patches left over from the New Year's snow flurry. One hand clutched the funky tote bag sewn from scraps of her favorite fabrics while the other held a peach and praline bagel fresh from her mom's bakery. Breakfast on the run, since Natalie's steps were taking her to the historic heart of the city and the business she ran with her old pal Tessa and her much newer but equally loved friend Ama.

Wedding Belles. That was the name Tessa had chosen for the bridal agency they'd opened together last summer, housed in a century-old brick-and-sandstone building with lots of wear—or "character," as Tessa chose to think of it. Natalie was seamstress and fashion consultant to the brides, Ama oversaw the cake and food prep, and Tessa pulled together all the little details that made a ceremony special for each new client.

Together they had already planned more events than Natalie ever dreamed would come their way, and for the first time since picking up a needle and thread, she had gotten to see her creations appreciated by someone besides herself and her immediate circle. It still amazed

Natalie to see a client's face light up whenever they wore something she had sewn. Be it the bride herself or the four-year-old flower girl, Natalie had designs for all ages and sizes. Passion for fashion ruled Natalie, and her talent lay in finding just the right fabric and style for each one.

True, it wasn't the glamorous career she set her sights on back in college. Life had taken some detours since then, with Natalie helping out at her family's business and deciding to pursue graduate studies in fashion and design. Wedding Belles was yet another unexpected path, but not an unwelcome one thankfully.

And the new year already held an even brighter possibility for showcasing her ideas: the Magnolia Fashion Revue.

The Magnolia Revue was a big deal in Bellegrove for anyone who worked in fashion, and thanks to her experience at Wedding Belles, Natalie finally had the confidence to enter it. Even though it was still months away, her work for the show had already begun, which was why her phone chirped with a message from Cal, her friend and former co-worker at a local fashion house that had been more like a dungeon of horrors until Tessa had offered her an escape.

Meeting at 10!!

Cal's text held dramatic urgency, as usual.

A little drama never hurt when it came to your dreams, in Natalie's opinion, especially since her dreams were on track, as far as Natalie was concerned. At least when it came to fashion—everything else was still up in the air, including her feelings about romance. A certain handsome rock climber named Chad showed every sign of being "the one" according to Natalie's nearest and dearest, although Natalie herself believed that concept belonged with other myths like the Tooth Fairy and Santa Claus. She didn't buy into the intensely romantic concepts of soul mates and happily ever after, even if her fingers spent most of their time creating dresses for those who did. That's just the way it had always been for her, even back in the days when a boy with a crooked, homely smile had offered his heart—and a plate of cupcakes—in the desperate hope of changing her mind about those ideas.

A step up from the dandelions he'd offered her in second grade, true. But even a dozen red roses wouldn't sway her heart when it came to Brayden Carmichael. The fact he was *still* trying to get her attention after all these years—almost as frequently as his package delivery truck stopped at her family's bakery—just proved that hopeless romantics were always destined for heartache.

But the less said on that subject the better, as far as Natalie was concerned.

*

"So, what have we got so far?" Natalie set her coffee cup on the table and took her seat in the old leather office chair behind it. "Are the alterations finished on that lace tunic top or should I take it home with me tonight?"

"I finished them last night," said Cal, who laid the portfolio on the worktable beside the light-as-air summer garment, its sheer panels made to serve as an overlay to a solid camisole top.

Cal's plans to rent a cool loft for working on their runway project had disintegrated due to lack of funds, so, for now, they were working out of Natalie's Wedding Belles office. It had plenty of space and added an interesting element to both sides, Natalie had to admit, seeing fake tiered cakes, vintage-inspired businesswear, and books of floral arrangements jockeying for shelf room amidst volumes on the history of fabric. On the other hand, it also meant that wedding business and fashion business tended to mix with each other in ways that were sometimes a little distracting.

"What about the pinstriped suit?" she asked, glancing at the portfolio. "Was it you or Nella working on that one?" Nella was the cheery intern and aspiring designer helping Cal and Natalie compile the line of summer garments. She was also late for this meeting, which wasn't too unusual, since she was coming from classes at the university all the way across town.

"It was Nella," said Cal, "so you'll have to ask her about it when she gets here. Which is… now," he added, at the sound of high heels furiously scaling the metal spiral staircase in the Wedding Belles' lobby.

"Sorry I'm late," called an upbeat southern accent from the doorway. Nella hurried inside, her bouncy blonde waterfall of curls trying to escape her scarf headband. "Did I miss anything?" she asked, glancing around eagerly.

"Nat was just asking how close you were to finishing the pinstriped suit," said Cal.

"Oh, it's finished all right, except for the jacket's buttons 'cause I forgot to bring them home," said Nella, who pulled out the dark navy trousers and matching jacket to add to the table's half-finished garments.

"We need to let out the waistline in that eyelet skirt with the ribbon-trimmed beltline," commented Natalie, who was searching for her seam ripper underneath a copy of *Weddings Today*. "Remember, curves are our thing—we want to flatter anybody and everybody's shape, not squish it. Cal, you did a great job on that tunic, by the way, so no more changes there, obviously."

"Thank you," he answered, with a little bow. "A friend of mine is already dying to buy it. She says she can't find anything that fits her at the local boutique except for some shapeless muumuu fashions."

"Our first customer already!" Nella clapped her hands. "This is so exciting! Oops, I forget—let the skirt out. Right." She seized the garment from the table and went digging in her corner of Natalie's studio for supplies, on a shelf that Nella had decorated with glittery cat stickers.

Ama poked her head inside the office doorway. "Coffee, anybody?" she asked, cheerily. "I'm making a midday snack run to the Java and Julip down the street if anybody wants anything." The Indian-American baker's short dark hair was pinned back with a barrette, a festive winter scarf tucked inside her coat collar. Her green skirt was decorated with fancy beadwork that was part of her mother's cultural tradition, although Ama had shortened it from the ankle-length style to a trendier knee-length.

"Can you grab me one of their mocha cream delights?" Nella dug through her bag for a few dollars, accidentally knocking a ream of beaded fabric and a stack of nuptial invitation samples to the floor, where they mixed with some scraps of fabric and thread snips.

"Can do," answered Ama. She glanced at the dresses. "Nat, is that the new line?" she asked. "It looks *amazing*."

"Thanks," said Natalie. "That's exactly the kind of compliment we need. Of course, hearing it from the fashion judges would be better, but after working our fingers to the bone, we don't care who says it, so long as they're human."

"Not having your full dose of morning coffee makes you extra bitter," joked Cal, poking her in the shoulder.

"Yeah, it does. Ama, can you get me something strong with a little vanilla in it? Anything's fine, really." She handed her business partner a few dollars, too. "Just to take the edge off my witty personality?"

"Sure," laughed Ama. "So are you guys going to give us a little fashion show preview?"

"Yes," declared Nella at the same time Cal and Natalie answered, "Maybe." Natalie's eye was on the unfinished hems and problematic layers in the skirt she was altering. Could they be ready in time, even with weeks of work behind them? Summer would come faster than any of them imagined.

"Two coffees coming up," Ama called as she descended the stairs, leaving Natalie alone with her crew.

"So… how's things with the guy?" Cal asked as he refolded the blouse. "I notice there's no more fake ring being worn around the office."

He asked questions carefully about Natalie's long-term boyfriend. Hunky Chad had defied the odds this winter by becoming Natalie's longest-running relationship to date. Jokes had long circulated about Natalie being hard to catch—a non-romantic who dated for fun and not forever, as per her philosophy. But she and Chad had impulsively shared a pact before Christmas to make each other's families happy by appearing as a steady couple—right down to the "fake" engagement ring Natalie sported on her finger as a joke a few times—but that temporary relationship still had steam at the beginning of the new year, against the usual odds.

"The ring is staying in the drawer from now on," said Natalie. "I think that joke went a little too far, since my cousins were practically Instagramming my impending nuptials. But Chad's fine." She shrugged. "He's great, as always. We're just taking things easy. And now that nobody is nagging either of us about finding the right one, we can take it easier around our families, which is way more relaxing."

"And honest," Cal pointed out. "I think your mom was ready for a church wedding by Easter."

"Does your mom like him?" asked Nella, perhaps wondering if there was any truth to Cal's joke.

"In moderation," answered Natalie. Nella's face fell. "No, she likes him fine. She'd like anybody I dated for more than five minutes who might at least try to persuade me to marry them someday."

"I'll bet your brother thinks he's cool."

"Rob has weird taste." Natalie stuck out her tongue. "But I've heard him say worse about my dates."

"I've never heard your friends say better things, though," said Cal, as he searched for the fabric shears in Natalie's desk drawer. "I think this guy has done the impossible: won you over *and* won over everybody in your crowd."

Seeing each other a few nights a week and on weekends, they were drifting routinely into each other's social lives. While that made him sound more like a habit than the love of her life, that was fine with her because she didn't believe there was such a thing as true love. As for what she did believe in, Chad checked those boxes nicely. The fact that she didn't feel happy was totally her fault, as far as she knew.

Maybe this was how it worked, Natalie thought. You fall into a casual rhythm, then you tie the knot and it doesn't feel any different from before. Maybe that could be her and Chad's destiny after all.

"You guys are so cute together," said Nella, who thought everything about Chad was cute, as far as Natalie could tell. It was the hunky muscles and confident chin.

"Nobody has called me cute since I had Band-Aids on both knees," said Natalie, with a snort.

"Oh—speaking of cute—you will *not* believe what I dreamed up last night," said Nella, leaping from one topic to the next. "It is so *gorgeous* I just went lickety-split straight to its creation and didn't even bother with a sketch." She'd dropped her shoulder bag to the floor and was busy untangling a huge pile of fabric from within it.

"Let's see it." Unlike Natalie and Cal's former boss, Kandace, she believed in encouraging input and creativity from budding designers, especially those who weren't consumed snottily by their own talent. She remembered what it was like to have no one care about her individual thoughts: Kandace had never cared what any of her junior designers thought about fashion, and had never taken so much as the meekest, tiniest hint from a much-restrained Natalie about possible improvements to the clothes she sold.

"Be honest," Nella said, albeit with mollified courage for these words. "Tell me if it's totally awful."

Out came the evident pride and joy of Nella's creativity: a dress sewn from light ivory paper taffeta in multiple layers, a sleeveless, strapless bodice, and a spread skirt in a series of wide panels which were lifted and frozen upwards slightly along their edges, like the hemline's bell was curling both inwards and outwards delicately in turn. It took Natalie a moment to realize the effect: that of an upside-down flower, its petals not quite open to a saucer's shape.

"I call it 'Sweetbay,'" said Nella, proudly. "After the magnolia blossom. What do you think?"

"It's like… Marilyn Monroe's Seven Year Itch got hitched to a gardenia," said Cal. "I think I love it."

"I think it's fantastic," said Natalie. "Sew a label inside it, make a sketch and sign it—I think it should be part of the line for the show."

Nella's eyes widened "You want it in the show?" she squealed "Seriously? It's, like, that good?"

"We're only offering the best, right?" said Natalie. "You're a designer for this house, right? Then do it. Come on, chop-chop—we only have until summer before showtime, and every second counts. Let's get busy before we all go back to our real jobs."

She lifted the suit and reached for her sewing basket and a set of antique red porcelain buttons from New Orleans. Grenaldi's Couture's public debut was on the line, and she planned to give it her very best.

Chapter Two

Ama hummed along with the song on her laptop as she packed decorative cookie tins into postal boxes. These were the latest round of specialty orders through her baking website Sweetheart Treats. A side business of sorts, it had been her only way to fully explore her culinary passions before last summer had landed her the job of chief baker at Wedding Belles.

Of course, not helping out at her family's restaurant wasn't really an option, so Ama had three jobs these days. But since all three involved her most favorite thing in the world, it didn't seem to make her feel too overwhelmed.

She swept some receipts into a folder, her fingers brushing against an open gift box in front of the mirror. Her lips formed a smile as she lifted the item inside it: an adorable cookie cutter in the shape of an elaborate crouching tiger, one of a set of five artistic cookie cutters based on antique woodcut illustrations of Asian animals. A gift from Luke, her unexpected crush-turned-boyfriend, just in time for the holidays.

She hadn't expected him to get her anything, not really. After all, they had only started dating a couple of weeks before the holidays. It seemed like a good omen, this gesture on his part, although he was full of moments of touching, impulsive gestures from the very beginning of their relationship. Dating someone like that was too good to be true, just like in the sappy Hollywood romances she loved.

Secretly dating, she reminded herself. She sighed a little bit inside as she wrapped a bow around one of the cookie tins and pictured breaking the news to her family that she was involved with someone who bore all the hallmarks of a classic bad boy: motorcycle and leather jacket, just to name a few.

The list could go on, but Ama knew even the first two would be enough for her traditionally minded Punjabi father to rule him out as a possible match for her. And her auntie Bendi, too, who wanted a boy in a suit, a tie, and a suitable white-collar career. The very fact he didn't share their culture or background was enough to keep the oldest members of her family from even considering him in the first place. Despite thirty-something years of American citizenship, Ama's parents, especially her father, were still very much in tune with the old way of doing things, it seemed.

If her father could only look past the stereotypes, maybe he would see the Luke that she already knew. Someone who was kind and sensitive and cared about Ama in ways she had only dreamed about in the past.

Her sister Rasha and her two brothers would understand. And her sister-in-law, Deena, had practically pushed her into Luke's arms that first day they encountered him among the stalls at Bellegrove's food market. She would be over the moon if she knew they had officially become a couple. But Ama still cringed for the memory of her parents' first encounter with Luke, for their barely concealed looks of confusion and worry that December afternoon he had dropped by the restaurant. Afterward, she heard her family arguing about her possible connection to this stranger, one her father obviously viewed with suspicion.

Of course, in the weeks before she had met Luke, her father had his heart set on making a match between Ama and a very eligible young Indian businessman named Tamir. Someone perfectly successful and polite—and perfectly dull in Ama's book. All the spark and color that was missing from her relationship with Tamir became present almost instantly when she met Luke. Not just because of his swoon-worthy looks, either (although she couldn't help going a little weak in the knees for that muscular physique and unruly dark hair at times).

No amount of good looks would earn Luke points with Ama's parents, however. So it would have to be his infectious smile and heart of gold that won them over, right? If they gave him a chance, things could be different. They could be happy for her—even if her happily ever after wasn't exactly the one they envisioned for her.

This had better be true, because no matter what they thought, she was going to tell her family about her and Luke tonight. It was her one and only New Year's resolution, to tell the complete truth about the boy she'd been secretly seeing since before Christmas, and as the clock in the hall chimed the dinner hour and the beginning of another evening in the family kitchen, Ama forced herself to stay committed to this plan.

What's the worst they can do? They won't disown you, will they? So Papa growls and mutters for a few weeks… and gives you those injured little glances whenever your boyfriend's name comes up… and shuts down any talk about you and Luke being in love by abruptly changing the subject…

Just remind him that he *liked motorbikes when he was younger, too. Right?*

Okay, so it could make life unpleasant for her. But surely that was worth enduring to spend time with someone like Luke.

She heard footsteps pounding up the stairs, and her sister Rasha burst in. "Ama, you have to see this," she said, turning off the music and pushing a DVD into the side tray of Ama's laptop.

"What are you doing?" Ama tossed aside her spool of ribbon. "That's my computer, you know."

"Sanjay and I bought this movie," Rasha answered, referring to her husband. "It's from the director of that awesome Bollywood romance I couldn't stop watching for weeks, about the silk merchant's daughter, remember? Anyway, look at *this*." She skipped past several scenes of moonlit terraces and crowded city streets until a dance number appeared onscreen, an upbeat Indian pop song providing the beat for some wedding guests to break out their moves beneath a shower of petal blossoms.

"Isn't it awesome?" said Rasha, triumphantly. "It's so much fun! I love this song. Sanjay and I actually did part of this dance when we watched it for the umpteenth time since buying the DVD. Come on, it's easy."

"Rasha, I'm a lot of things, but I'm definitely not a dancer," said Ama, who was resisting the infectious rhythm and movements onscreen which looked intricate and graceful compared to her usual ones. "I don't gyrate well, or whatever." Wanting the romance of the most sappy of love stories was one thing, but imagining herself in a street crowd bursting into song and dance was almost enough to embarrass her without so much as twitching a foot.

"You're in your *lungi* skirt—we have to do it," teased Rasha, referring to the brightly printed Indian-inspired fabric of Ama's outfit.

She pulled Ama along with her until even Ama's feet found the right rhythm, the two of them giggling as they followed the moves of the performers. In the bedroom mirror, Ama's skirt became a flash of orange and glittery metallic beadwork, while Rasha's showy earrings and embroidered blouse were like little twinkling lights.

"Can I come in?" Deena poked her head inside the room, her tone that of curiosity until she saw the scene on the laptop. "Oh my gosh,

I love this song! You are *not* doing the routine from *Silk in Simla*, are you? I want to join the dance party, too," she pleaded.

"Come on, then," demanded Rasha, between smothered and escaped laughs with Ama. Their sister-in-law, a better dancer than both of them together, had all the right moves and the right costume for it, given she was wearing her hostess's sari. She danced with a mock seriousness and concentration that made Ama laugh even harder as her body and feet finally memorized all the right moves from the movie sequence.

In some ways, maybe life is like a Bollywood musical, Ama thought— at least, it could be, if you imagined it right. Her semi-traditional, semi-Westernized Punjabi family bundled energy, loyalty, and craziness into every day like the cast of this movie probably did… meanwhile, she was filling the "star-crossed lovers" portion of the story that was supposed to find a happy ending before the final dance number.

Peppy love songs and smooth dance moves can't cover up the reality of what waits downstairs when the dance is over, the sober part in the back of Ama's mind kept telling her. She was going to tell her family the truth about her feelings for Luke.

Deep breath, calm mind, happy thoughts. Maybe a little moment of unreality snatched before the evening's waves of rising *gulab* dough and boiling rice was just what she needed to summon up the courage for tonight.

Chapter Three

New Year's Eve, Tessa had elected to drive home from Florida rather than stay for her mother's mah-jong night featuring the best of Dick Clark and lots of snacks selected from the latest issue of *Southern Sampler*. After a morning layering sweet-and-sour three-bean dips and rolling bacon around cheese-and-apricot-jam-stuffed peppers and figs, she loaded her bags and latest Christmas presents into her borrowed car and ejected the Perry Como CD from its player after starting the ignition.

Christmas cheer had been hard this year, and she was glad the season for it was almost over.

Darkness blanketed Bellegrove's winter streets as she returned the car to its rightful owner and walked home, wheeling her suitcase and holding the oversized gift bag containing the perfume and argyle sweater from her mom and the desk calendars and candy boxes from her mom's various friends and neighbors.

The streetlights were still wreathed with little circles of greenery and bright red berries that looked frosty in the chill night air. The window to her right was festooned with New Year's party decorations: glitzy pink-and-silver striped hats and noisemakers, a big silver banner wishing everyone good luck for another 365 days.

Tessa remembered one of the dips she helped layer contained black-eyed peas, the old southern staple for guaranteeing good luck in the new year by eating a big portion. Each bean represented a day of good luck; that had been her problem this past year, maybe, passing on a can of good-luck beans for a frozen gourmet grilled chicken pizza.

Maybe this year would be better, since things were looking up for Wedding Belles and her bank account finally had a tiny bit of money in it instead of an OVERDRAWN notice in bold red letters. Natalie was finally dating somebody for longer than two weeks, Ama had been brave enough to take a motorcycle ride with her dream guy... All Tessa needed was a positive outlook to see that things weren't so bad.

She was telling herself this with a firm and perky inner voice as she neared the front door of Wedding Belles, and she might have believed it by the time she found her keys if not for the New Year's Eve party guests exiting the hot little night cafe on the opposite side of the street, its electric blue ceiling lights and tiny white candles hiding all but the shadows of bodies crowding the tables within to listen to the band. The exiting guests were pausing for air, sending clouds of white-vapor breath skywards in the cold night. Among them was a figure Tessa would recognize anywhere, even without his carpenter's belt, wearing a nice dark wool coat that reminded her just how good Blake looked in stylish clothes.

Blake Ellingham, the master craftsman in charge of restoring the historic charm of Wedding Belles' headquarters. He was more like their unofficial business partner, though, having lent them a helping hand in more than one client-related crisis. Over the past few months, Tessa had come to think of Blake as a friend and then, unexpectedly, something more.

But that had been a mistake. She had let one tiny, accidental kiss between them last summer go to her head. A lip-lock so incredible it had made her wonder if Blake was worth risking her heart for, even though past attempts at love had always left it broken. But Tessa had never confessed those feelings to him… and the chance to do so slipped away with the realization of Blake's holiday engagement to the beautiful and talented interior designer known affectionately as Mac. The moment he introduced Mac to the Wedding Belles, a sinking feeling in the pit of Tessa's stomach informed her that her own chance was lost.

Tessa had only known Samantha "Mac" MacNeil for a few weeks, but Blake must have known her for years. And she must have been more than a colleague to him for at least part of that time, perhaps even when Tessa had shared that kiss with him, she acknowledged with a twinge of guilt. Then again, it might have been a case of longtime friendship suddenly turning to something more. A very serious something if the engagement ring she saw Mac sporting on Christmas Eve meant exactly what Tessa feared it did.

As if she needed any more confirmation than seeing them together at this moment. She knew one of the people standing closest to him was Mac, even before the woman in the white winter coat and hat turned around to glance at him and say something. The group of friends they were with were laughing and talking, having a great time on the last night of the old year, judging from Mac's smile, and the sound of Blake's laugh—audible to Tessa, even over the noise of a passing car and the din of a blues band playing "Happy New Year, Baby"—which was carefree and relaxed.

Mac met Blake's eyes beneath the glow of the streetlamp, then pointed upwards to some ornament dangling below its lantern, causing him to laugh again. He leaned toward her and she shoved him away, her laugh mingling with his now. He offered her his arm and escorted her off the curb to a car parked parallel to the sidewalk, opening its passenger door for her. More people emerged from the restaurant—a man holding two takeout bags now tagging Blake's elbow to say something—then a box van drove past, and the car was pulling out behind it, apparently guiding Blake and Mac to another party spot for the evening.

Tessa stood there, watching the vehicle drive away, watching the remaining guests waiting for a ride across the street, though all the others were strangers. Something was wrong with her eyes, little diamonds glinting in her vision like the glow from Mac's engagement ring. Tears, she realized. She glanced up above her head, seeing an ornament like the one that Mac had been pointing to, dangling from the bottom of the lantern. A sprig of mistletoe.

She only thought she couldn't feel any worse at this moment. Heart sinking in sadness, she unlocked the door to Wedding Belles and let herself inside. Upstairs, a dark apartment awaited her, without even the comforting twinkle of Christmas lights left plugged in. It was cold, too—the stupid radiator was clearly on the fritz again. She sighed and tossed the presents on the side table.

"Happy New Year to me," she muttered, dropping into the nearest chair. At least this side of the building didn't have a view of the neon cafe with its noisy blues concert and happy customers.

She had to get used to this. Blake was with somebody else, and was evidently happy. Tessa had spent the past week trying to deal with the fact that she had to forget about him. And since it was her own stupid fault that kiss remained unaddressed between them, what right did she have to be upset?

Deal with it, Tessa. Lots of people in the world are having a rotten holiday, but they'll have to face the world on January 2, just like you. Think of how much you already have. You're lucky to not be unemployed and homeless in the new year; forget about having love on top of that good fortune.

So what if she was spending New Year's Day alone with another frozen pizza and a stack of unopened mail?

*

Blake hadn't returned to work the day after New Year's, but the rest of the Wedding Belles' official partnership had—Natalie bearing leftovers from her mother's brunch, including praline crunch cake and some sort of Italian fruit bread that made Tessa think for a moment that heartache was bearable. Ama brought a basket full of goodies, including snowflake sugar cookies to die for, and a new set of cookbooks, almost entirely devoted to petit fours and chocolate work.

"Happy New Year to us, right?" said Natalie, filling three champagne flutes with fizzy white grape juice cocktail. "May we have the best year ever after one of the weirdest ones ever—at least, mine was weird. I never thought I'd quit Kandace so soon, or be a partner in a business."

"I think it's amazing," said Ama, her eyes glowing. "Good for you. Your dream is finally coming true."

"What about yours?" said Tessa. A slight change in Ama's attitude for this question, as she tilted her head. But maybe she imagined that.

"I think I have everything I want right now," Ama answered, after a moment's thought. "I'm a baker for a living, my family is healthy and safe. I have somebody special in my life, which is what I always wished for." The sometimes-shy baker's dreams of true romantic love: nothing could have come closer to them than motorcyclist Luke sweeping up like a knight on a Harley-Davidson.

"How is the gorgeous Luke?" asked Natalie.

"He's great," said Ama. "He and I didn't get to see each other much over the holidays, but we did have some time together afterward. We spent the day in this great little Germantown district, where I bought some amazing gingerbread."

"And what is your family saying about him now?" Tessa asked.

"Well... my family wasn't *exactly* thrilled when I told them about him." Ama toyed with her champagne flute. "I'm pretty sure my mother cried after I left the room, and Papa didn't say too much, but I could tell he was upset in the kitchen later that night. When cooking sounds like a storm, you know something's bothering him." She sighed, then her face brightened a little, as if optimism was forcing its way to the surface. "But I had to tell them eventually, and at least my brothers and sister were happy. I couldn't go on keeping it a secret, not with how I feel about him."

"Families have a way of sniffing out secrets," said Natalie. "Ma has a lie detector installed in one eye. I swear, all she has to do is look into mine for five seconds and she can tell I'm not being honest." She tucked her feet underneath her on the parlor's sofa, draped in a velvet winter shawl.

"What are you not being honest about now?" Ama asked. "You have a great guy. Your mom must be thrilled."

"Sure," said Natalie, but in a vague manner that edged away from committing to real emotions for this reply, although they all knew her latest paramour met the perfect checklist for Natalie: smooth charm, individualistic, and with a relaxed dating style that complemented her own.

Tessa wasn't actually sure what she thought about him, personally. Something about Chad didn't seem like "the one" for her friend—not that she could pick the right person for herself or anybody else. He was too smooth, too polished. Like someone who had practiced hard to become an effortless, casual person.

"I hear wedding bells," teased Ama.

"Shut up," said Natalie. "No, you don't."

"I think I saw a ring on Instagram. Was that real?"

"What do you think?" answered Natalie, but coyly, despite her sarcasm, which a friend less astute than Tessa might've missed.

What is going through Natalie's mind? Tessa's gaze narrowed, shrewdly. She couldn't be sure these days.

Tessa and Ama had exchanged several texts on the subject over the holiday break, when Tessa was willing to discuss anything that would distract her from thoughts of Blake. Lots of Instagram photos of Natalie and Chad at holiday parties were scrutinized; lots of wild theories about how intense they really were became part of their silly back-and-forth exchange, ending with Ama texting a picture of the "perfect" wedding gown for Natalie's upcoming nuptials.

Ama's teasing about Natalie's wedding would become the running joke in the office for the next few weeks, with new clippings added to a special folder for it on Ama's desk every time she spotted something tempting. Even Tessa added one or two, though she could see it annoyed Natalie slightly, these casual references to her supposedly impending matrimony.

Client appointments were rare in January, but there were two potential ones scheduled to meet with Wedding Belles in February. Valentine's Day, the day of love, inspired lots of engagements, and interest in wedding planners to help arrange just the right details. The new window display featured a white dress and red rose bouquet studded with mint-green buds. Natalie had made a garland of glittering red roses, succulents, and green carnations to festoon the window.

"I have something for your folder." Ama dug into her oversized shoulder bag, one sporting a very glitzy purple sari design that clashed with her baggy red corduroy trousers and embroidered white eyelet shirt. "I saw it yesterday in a baking mag and thought it was perfect." A clipping emerged of some cookies iced to resemble designer bridal gowns.

Another item for the folder labeled NATALIE'S DREAM WEDDING, with little wedding stickers decorating the cover. Tessa could see Natalie grimace.

"You mean that horrible joke you've been displaying prominently on your desk for the past couple of weeks?" corrected Natalie.

"Or maybe a prediction for the future?" hinted Ama. "Shall we put another item inside?" She danced the clipping between both hands, hinting for its acceptance.

"How about putting this thing in a vault sealed for a hundred years?" answered Natalie. "I have no interest whatsoever in picking out a chocolate groom's cake or a white tulip centerpiece. Not yet, anyway. Chad and I haven't even talked about the idea."

"Come on, Natalie. You said you and Chad are serious. Don't you think you could at least *think* about what a possible future with him would be like? You must have a few wedding dreams of your own tucked in the back of your mind. Doesn't everybody have a secret wedding fantasy?" persisted Ama.

"Chad and I fantasize about dinner dates right now, and lazy weekends hanging out together. I'm not into tulle, bunting, and long guest lists. You know me." Natalie sipped her cup of coffee. "I'd sooner transform myself into a total romantic sop who… I don't know… ran after Chad in the rain, like lovers in a movie, than start planning my so-called dream wedding." She set the mug down on the table.

"So call it a joke and leave it at that," said Tessa, trying to bring back the lightheartedness, sensing Natalie was going to turn into a romantic grump if pushed.

A strange pain had pricked Tessa for some inexplicable reason, at the sight of a wedding folder with one of their names on it. It wasn't as if Natalie and Chad had really reached that stage yet... but it reminded her that even skeptical, romantically carefree Natalie was in a relationship. Something she, reformed hopeless romantic that she was, now envied in a way that made her feel a little ashamed of herself.

"Chad might be the one," teased Ama. "You never know."

"Remember what I think about 'the one'?" said Natalie, archly. "You'll find him in the same place as the unicorn, the dodo, and Elvis and JFK's secret underground bunker."

"*I* think you're going to change your mind someday," said Tessa. "We should look at dress designs, too."

"Let's face it, girls. In life, nothing's predictable." Natalie tossed the cookie clipping inside a random folder on the table. "Thanks for the confidence, though, Tessa."

*

Beautiful Mac hadn't come around since that fateful day she sported Blake's ring, but her texts had kept coming to Tessa's phone over the Christmas break, since sealing the deal had become official, apparently.

Love for u 3 to plan for me. U r recommended by the best!

This was Blake's ringing endorsement of their work, Tessa knew. Naturally, he would have suggested that Mac look to them to plan the wedding. Who else but the three event planners he'd worked with so closely for the past year?

The one sent the day after Christmas said:

Still thinking a fall wedding. Do u have a venue list?

And in the middle of January Mac asked:

Can u hire a classical quartet for a reception?

Today's was a question about caterers, and whether Tessa had one to recommend. Short answers were all Tessa ever supplied. She breathed a sigh of relief every time new messages buried the thread between herself and Mac, even though no painful references to Blake were ever made, not even to his name.

In March, Mac texted that she was planning a late-spring engagement party with her family, something Blake hadn't mentioned on any of the afternoons he spent whistling and sawing lumber in the spare room under construction.

Setting the date. U r still my top pick 4 planning. We r excited to talk plans for fall vows!

We'll make an appointment soon. Can't wait to sit down with u!

Tessa had been avoiding answering them, much like she had been avoiding Blake since she returned to work. Pretending she was swamped with work now that she was back at Wedding Belles, pretending he was too busy with carpentry work to bother with conversation. There were lots of emails for her to answer, lots of new contacts to be considered, who might be just what future clients wanted for their caterer or their musical entertainment. Who could blame her if she was remiss in answering personal messages from Mac right away? Especially for a fall wedding—what's the rush in talking about something months away?

The truth was, she couldn't handle the thought of setting a date for Mac to officially become her client. Answering detached questions about ceremony sites and centerpieces was one thing, but doing it face-to-face was another. Having Mac sit across from her in the parlor, Blake in the groom's seat, holding his fiancée's hand…

She couldn't face it. She just couldn't. She could tell herself every day that the mature thing to do was to forget about him, but it was easier said than done. It was one thing to lose him to her own stupid mistakes, but to lose him to another woman—to realize that all the time she liked him, Mac had been in the background, the perfect choice for him. While she, Tessa, had only been a brief ripple of doubt for him on the road to proposing to his ideal match.

With a sigh, she reached for her phone and texted back.

I'll let u know when we can meet.

Any time was fine, but she didn't say that. She would work her way up to that part.

Chapter Four

"It's been kind of fun, actually," said Chad, over his green beer at Mc-Gilly's Pub on St. Patrick's Day. They had gone to Natalie's favorite spot to celebrate, due to its over-the-top shamrock decorations and twinkle lights. "Pretending to be serious with you."

"Agreed," said Natalie. "Seeing Ma's face that first time we walked in together was priceless. And the look on my cousin Janet's when she saw the ring and thought it was real. Did you see that? It was hilarious!"

"Are you wearing it tonight?" He glanced at her hand for the first time since they had sat down to an appetizer of pretzel bites and melted cheese for Natalie, and some kind of hummus spread for Chad.

"No, I took it off," said Natalie. "If I wore it all the time, they'd think—" She stopped here, in order to skirt using the dangerous word "engagement," second only to "marriage" in Natalie's book. "Well, you know what they'd think."

He nodded. "Makes sense," he said. "Don't want to go too far, right?"

Tonight was originally agreed upon as the official end to their "serious" relationship. They had decided it months ago, before they'd spent weeks dating each other in earnest to get through the family scrutiny of singlehood and the holidays.

Tonight they could opt out. No strings attached, no blame for either side if someone wanted to call it quits. It was the perfect casual romantic connection.

"Still," said Natalie, "it really has actually been fun, having everybody think I gave up my carefree ways and settled down." She grinned. "Not at all painful and torturous, like I thought it would be."

Chad nodded. "My mom actually liked meeting you. She's kind of fond of you now. I think it doubled the number of invites to come by her apartment. She knows I'm busy, so she doesn't ask a lot. Maybe she just wants to see you," he added, as a joke.

Natalie rearranged the pretzel bites on the side of her plate, thoughtful in the conversation's pause. "Do you want to take a step back, or go on with this?" she asked, lifting her gaze to Chad's. "I want an honest answer, which makes sense given how we both are romantically. Nobody's going to cry or storm out of here if the answer's no, right?"

Maybe he would say yes to be polite, though he didn't have to. Maybe he wanted to keep exploring their relationship, curious to see if something deeper was happening between them. But if either of them was ready to move on, now was as good a time as any to say it.

He shrugged. "What do you think?" he asked.

"Truthfully? I'm not sure it has to be tonight when we decide how we feel. We've put in time together, and we're still pretty comfortable with each other," she said.

"We're kind of in the zone," Chad mused. "The ground rules are laid about basic things, like food, entertainment, pet peeves. It seems wrong not to enjoy the basic chemistry between us, doesn't it?"

It was playfully put, but a little serious at the same time. Natalie could appreciate that, even if it was devoid of the deeper sentiments that made the likes of Tessa or Natalie weak-kneed.

Chad had been a good boyfriend, nicer than a lot of guys she had dated. Her family had accepted him, which was a bonus. They fit into each other's lives better than either of them expected, without inspiring any dramatic changes that couples usually experience, emotionally or philosophically.

"I wouldn't mind going on for a while," he continued. "Being fake engaged was a little much, we both agree—"

"Yes, we do," said Natalie, with a wry grin for the memory of her mother's mixed disappointment and relief when she found out Natalie was only teasing Rob and her cousins with the ring. "I definitely agree we're dropping that part."

"But outside of the joke, I enjoy being with you as a person. Our time together has been really good," said Chad. "We'd probably even miss it a little if we stopped now. I would, since I know I like you, and I can definitely see myself spending more time with you in the future."

"I wouldn't mind it," agreed Natalie, being playful in return. From their first flirtation to the time they spent together through the holidays, there had been a mutual physical attraction. "It's a pretty new experience for me, truthfully, but... I like it. Being serious with somebody."

She had to admit, deep inside, that it was actually pretty lovely to have someone to hold her hand on those family occasions, instead of being on her own the way she had always preferred. Being part of a couple was nice, no matter what she said to Tessa and Ama. That was just her opinion about the soppy seriousness of romantic love. And she wasn't head over heels for Chad, wasn't going to be either—not for ages, at least. Not with her philosophy on love.

"Plus, everybody says we make a great couple," she added, teasingly. "It'd be a shame to waste that, I suppose."

"So maybe we shouldn't disappoint them, huh?" said Chad, continuing the joke.

"Let's set a new date for reevaluation," said Natalie.

"How about the Fourth of July?" said Chad. "Let's stick with holidays. It makes it easy to remember. Independence Day we declare our freedom from seriously dating, or we decide to move to the next stage. Simple."

"To Independence Day." Natalie clinked her glass with his.

Of course, Natalie knew her mom would die of shock if she didn't see a permanent ring on her daughter's finger at the family's July picnic after eight months of courtship—but that was just her mom being dramatic as usual when it came to opinions about serious relationships. The odds that her heart would be anywhere near head over heels by summer were slim by even the most generous bookie's odds.

Chapter Five

The Blue Moon Travel Agency had changed its window display to posters of the Mediterranean for the beginning of May: See Athens in five days, dine in style in Monte Carlo, take a week-long cruise around the Spanish coast. Tessa paused to watch the energetic travel agent in her official blue blazer paste up the latest one of the cruise ship gliding across sunset waters.

Maybe a weekend getaway would be nice. It would take her mind off a busy season of weddings and blushing brides. Summer would usher in one whose western-themed wedding had required finding a venue that looked like an old red barn for the reception, while a supposedly small spring ceremony had blossomed into an Indian wedding requiring a Taj Mahal-like setting. Didn't anybody want simple elegance with gardenia blossoms on tables in a dignified white summer tent? Must it all be stylistic drama?

Then again, it would probably help her attitude if she had something to do besides plan weddings—for instance, a social life to pursue. It had been over a month since Natalie's last offer to set her up. Or had it been longer? Not that she had been tempted to say yes, anyway. Keep the hopeless unromantic shtick from now on, she reminded herself. Even now, if she pictured Blake with his arm around Mac's shoulders, she felt the fresh sting of pain, though the decorator had yet to make good on her threats to drop by soon.

But not the sexy contractor. True to his word, he was still remodeling the rooms upstairs, ones Tessa had begun to envision as the future parlors and showcase rooms, with the downstairs transformed into a space attractive enough to host a ceremony, maybe even a reception, making the historic Wedding Belles' headquarters a wedding venue in its own right. Blake wasn't back at work full-time yet—thank goodness he had a couple of other projects vying for his attention that kept them from crossing paths too often—but he was there enough of the time to make Tessa painfully aware of his presence with every saw's growl or drill's whir.

She should be happy Blake was back. Thanks to his carpentry skills, the Wedding Belles would truly become a one-stop location someday… if they ever found the time and the money to pull its partly historic, mostly eclectic self together the way she envisioned it. That was what made Blake's eye and expertise so vital to keep close at hand. That, and the fact that as their unofficial fourth partner, he still had a habit of stepping in to help save them from sticky problems. Blake had no idea how truly valuable he was to them.

Them, not her. *Stick to that truth and you'll be fine*, she reminded herself.

Only a couple of weeks ago, he had found the perfect photography site for bridal photos – a rustic old wagon in a field of spring flowers – which he had suggested to Tessa at precisely the moment she had been dealing with one of her brides insisting that the photographer's suggestion of the local state park just wouldn't do. If Blake hadn't stepped in, she would have had one angry wedding party.

If I hadn't been so stupid all this time… if I had told him that that kiss between us wasn't an accident… would he have liked me instead of Mac?

That question just wouldn't leave her alone after all these months. No matter how hard she tried to escape.

With a sigh, she crossed the street and walked past the western-wear clothing store and the southern-fried catfish to-go shop. One more block found her in the chic district where the Wedding Belles' headquarters remained the elegant-but-crumbling cousin of the historic buildings around it, which had been semi-modernized as chic bistros, wine shops, and specialty professional services. Tessa didn't care if their building was still slightly shabby in terms of its edifice's carved sandstone trim or the interior's most unusual choice of spiral staircase to access the upper stories; she still loved it despite the expense and heartache that owning it tended to bring to her.

Home at last. She thought this now, as she pushed open its front door and entered the foyer.

"I dropped off the price quotes for the potential client on Sawmill Street," she announced as she laid her satchel on the "reception desk" that the three of them seldom occupied. There was no answer, so her partners were probably all upstairs in their offices—or, in Ama's case, in the kitchen, cooling down the latest batch of Sweetheart Treats' mail-order cupcakes.

Tessa's office was next to her private living quarters. It had a nice view, since it was originally intended for the traitorous Stefan, a popular wedding planner who would have been a senior partner in their business, if he hadn't chosen to ditch them last-minute for the high life in Paris. Its walls were adorned with enlarged photos of events Tessa had helped plan over the past year. The latest one, of the bride in a simple white gown and pink ribbon standing in a weathered old wagon, revealed a sea of clover and small pink flowers rippling in the breeze in the same manner as the bride's ribbon. It looked perfect right next to the shower of petals falling on the very first couple whose nuptials she planned, Paolo and Molly.

Opening a book on summer wedding ideas, Tessa tried to envision what the next client might want for a ceremony. A tea garden wedding? Something antebellum? A simple, modern reception?

"Knock, knock." Natalie stood in the doorway, an envelope in hand. "We got the final check for the Gellar–Wright ceremony today. Six thousand dollars for bridesmaids dresses with southern belle skirts."

"Who will ever wear one of those again?" Tessa wondered. "Do you keep it, dye it, and go as Scarlett O'Hara to a Halloween party? Donate it to a debutante ball society?"

"Beats me. All I know is three full skirts in spring green with crinoline underneath, and matching parasols and posy bunches in hand," said Natalie. "I had quite a time finding parasols without giant sheer ruffles or tacky fake pink roses, let me tell you."

"At least we pulled it off," said Tessa, sliding the check inside the bank bag in her desk drawer. "I have something for you in exchange," she added, reaching inside her tote bag on the floor. "I ran into Molly Fazolli on my errands today and she had those business cards printed off to give you."

Their first-ever client, a shy bride with a digital graphics business, had stayed in touch with the Belles, who recommended her printing services to clients for their invitations. The cards she printed for Natalie were meant to be handed out at the Magnolia Fashion Revue later that summer. Natalie's name and contact email shared a space with those of Cal and Nella, along with the tiny silhouette of a glamour-girl figure in an evening gown beside the words *Grenaldi's Couture*.

"Cute design," Tessa remarked, seeing the card in Natalie's hand. "Simple but effective. Did Molly come up with it or was it your idea?"

"Mine," said Natalie. "Sort of. I got the idea from a greeting card someone gave me once." She didn't elaborate on this statement as she popped the business card back in the box. A second later, Tessa jumped at the sound of a Skilsaw firing up on the lower floor. A guilty jump, she realized, rather than a surprised one—Natalie would be able to tell the difference.

"So I take it our loyal handyman is on the premises today?" Natalie asked, archly.

"Hmm? Yeah, just for a couple hours." Tessa was suddenly busy perusing a folder on her desk. "He's got some other projects to finish up before he tackles that dry rot in the old powder room. Which is fine, obviously. It's not like we have an emergency need for a second powder room or anything—we're not *that* popular yet."

Tessa was taking the denial route on this one. Big surprise.

Natalie's gaze was perceptive. "If you want to talk about it, let me know." A voice that left no room for doubt as to what she meant. "Or you can vent to Ama. She's a little better at understanding the deep romance stuff probably."

"What about you and Chad? That seems pretty romantic. Going out to dinner every week, scaling cliffs together on the weekends." Tessa poked a finger in what she knew was Natalie's sore spot: serious commitment.

"We have a nice thing going, true," Natalie replied, not letting herself be goaded this time. "But I don't think we'll be riding off into the sunset anytime soon."

"You could find yourself head over heels before you know it's happening." Tessa's tone became wistful by accident, as if the sound of a drill whirring to life in Blake's construction zone reminded her of lost chances.

Natalie chose to say nothing, deciding it was wiser to leave Tessa to her thoughts for now. She scooped up her business cards and made her way to her sewing studio down the hall. The desk was littered with patterns and sketches for upcoming projects, as well as some fabric swatches she kept as samples for showing prospective brides. Sweeping aside some spools of thread, she plopped the business cards beside the desk phone.

Maybe Tessa was right. Maybe love could sneak up on you out of the blue. She could wake up in love with Chad and not even know how it happened. Or she would just look at him across the room and know in a heartbeat that he really was the one. Wasn't that how it happened in love songs, anyway?

A summer breeze fluttered through the window, catching the edge of the top business card in the stack as if lifting one to admire it. The inspiration for its silhouette figure had been inspired by a greeting card from her last birthday. A card that Brayden gave to her, no less. She had run across it buried in a desk drawer a few weeks ago, the cute glamour paper doll he once said had reminded him of her.

He would be flattered beyond anything if he knew she had used it for part of her business. He would probably think it was a subconscious sign she really cared about him or something. The first step to a deeper tie between them after nearly twenty years of knowing each other.

But he would be wrong, because no amount of cupcakes, cards, or other romantic gestures could just *make* someone fall in love with you. Natalie was just grateful he hadn't turned up on her doorstep on Valentine's Day bearing chocolates and dressed in a tuxedo, which he had done more than once in her life but which Chad's presence had probably prevented.

Brayden hadn't even sent her a card this year. Which was really strange come to think of it, since he had never missed a chance to send her something, even after that ill-fated heart-shaped romantic note when they were kids. Maybe it got lost in the mail, or maybe he, too, finally decided that silly sentiments were a waste of time and stamps.

Whatever the reason, she shouldn't be pondering the state of Brayden's feelings or the nature of an odd friendship that she had outgrown years ago.

Chapter Six

"Happy birthday, baby sister!"

Ama pushed up her sleep mask and scrambled onto her elbow as she felt herself and her comforter squashed beneath Rasha's weight. According to the alarm clock on her bedside table, it was one minute past midnight, as she expected.

"Rasha, what are you doing?" she said, in her froggy sleep voice.

"Being the first person to wish you happy birthday," Rasha answered. "I've been hiding in the hall for a quarter of an hour now. Mama will probably be here any second, so I had to be fast if I wanted to make it."

"Doesn't Sanjay care that you're wandering around in the middle of the night?" Ama flopped back against her pillow.

"He left for a conference a few hours ago," said Rasha. "I told you yesterday he was leaving. Anyway, you don't have to be at work early tomorrow, do you?"

"No, but I still want my sleep," said Ama, with a laugh.

"Come on and open your birthday gift—I can't wait to give it to you."

A little gift box lay on Ama's stomach now as her older sister sat cross-legged expectantly at the foot of the bed. Ama untied the ribbon and opened the lid. Inside, a beautiful new necklace with a pale-blue turquoise stone in a silver setting, and two matching silver flower buds and leaves linking it to either half of its chain.

"It's beautiful," she said, sleepily. "Is it western? Like, from the Old West?"

"Sanjay bought it from an artist's store while he was attending that workshop in New Mexico," said Rasha. "But *I* picked it out from the photos he sent."

"Thanks," said Ama, with a half-hug for Rasha—one arm around her sister while the free arm's hand fumbled to put the lid back on the box.

"Happy birthday, little one." Pashma's kiss landed on the top of Ama's head. "I cannot believe you are a year older already. You were a little girl only yesterday." Ama caught the scent of coconut oil and faint lavender from her mother's cotton robe and hair.

"Thanks, Mama."

"I beat you to it this year," said Rasha to their mother, triumphantly. "Did you see the adorable gift Sanjay and I bought her?"

"Can't this wait until morning?" said Ama. Tradition or not, she never liked being awake before 6 a.m.—mornings in the restaurant always found her yawning and slightly crabby, hunkered over the first cup of coffee while her dough slowly rose in its covered bowl.

"See you then." Rasha kissed Ama's head then crawled off the bed. Pashma tucked the blanket around Ama, who had slumped beneath the covers again. "I'm bringing a new mango dessert bar recipe for you tonight, by the way," her sister called out in farewell before disappearing into the hall.

"Sleep well." Pashma closed the door behind them.

Ama's droopy eyes snapped open. *The dinner.* It came back in a rush, that her birthday dinner was tonight, and Luke was coming. His first time to eat with her family, and meet with all of them in one room. She had been looking forward to this with a mixture of nerves and anticipation for weeks, while planning the special menu down to the Punjabi dessert and the Western-style Georgian pecan birthday cake recipe she'd paired together for the final course.

But it was the thought of what conversations might unfold, how her family would react to Luke's presence at an official family dinner for the first time, that had occupied her imagination the most ever since she'd announced to her family that she had invited him. And he, of course, leaped at the chance; after nearly six months of dating, he had only had casual encounters with the rest of the Bhagut relatives.

Sleep was gone, suddenly. Ama lay awake, staring at the ceiling. *Please, please let everything happen perfectly.*

*

"I work nearby, so I walk past your building every day, and I thought, 'That's the exact place I need.'"

The Wedding Belles' newest prospective client was named Harper, a smile on her face as she told them this. "You had that beautiful bouquet in the window, with all these orchids and pink roses, and I was totally in love with it. So I thought, 'I'm gonna give them a call and see if they can do the wedding.'"

"I'm glad you thought of us first," said Tessa as she set the silver coffee pot back on its tray, beside the decorative lace cookies that Ama was still rearranging in perfectionist fashion. Tessa handed Harper one of the decorative coffee cups—almost a china teacup in pattern, which was what Tessa loved about this set, used strictly for entertaining possible clients.

"I figured anybody in a building this nice can't be outclassed too easy, right?" said Harper. "You know what you're doing if you're on this street. Where I work, every other building's got a tattoo parlor or a bail bondsman on it. How do you lose so much class over two streets, I ask?"

"Where do you work?" Ama asked.

"Travel agency. The one on Cypress," said Harper.

"Really?" said Tessa. "The Blue Moon? I always love looking at your posters. Do you travel a lot? See the world in between planning others' trips?"

"Have you planned a wedding for yourself?" Harper asked, bluntly.

"No, I'm not married… at this time," said Tessa, hastening to add the last bit, in case there was some misunderstanding—for instance, that she was totally hopeless at relationships.

"And I don't get to travel. Much. You know what they say, always a bridesmaid, never a bride. That's what it's like when you own your own business, am I right?" said Harper. "It's all business when I do it, too. I've only been running the place a few years. I started out small—I took some college courses at night before that, I spent spring break in Puerto Rico looking at hotels for a friend who did it part-time, then worked at a big firm for a while. I got to know the airlines, the hotel people at the big conferences; I read all the restaurant menus and reviews; I know how to talk out a problem with just about anybody… but I don't know the atmosphere in Athens from that of the airport in Annapolis, Maryland, when it comes to the firsthand stuff like breathtaking views and describing tranquil little hideaways."

"Touché," said Natalie, knowingly. "The joys of workaholism. How do fictional playboys ever find the time to play the field and run those multimillion-dollar companies?"

"They have assistants who do the work," said Harper, knowingly. And jokingly.

Harper Lucas was unique among their clients, Tessa sensed immediately. There was an unusual fire and independence in her, like untapped passion that had channeled itself into sensible, logical, and purposeful resourcefulness. She was tall and slightly athletic-looking, with long legs, a trim waist, shapely hips, and slightly broad shoulders, her physique of curves and strength possessing an easy, natural grace that was the complete opposite of a delicate ballerina type.

Thick, almost kinky, black hair touched with a few threads of premature white, stunning green eyes, medium skin tone like a latte's foam, only the faintest lines anywhere from careless afternoons in the sun: their client was in her early thirties but no older, Tessa estimated. Although she was wearing non-designer high heels and a skirt which had been re-hemmed more than once, her finger was sporting a diamond engagement ring that was easily two carats.

"So, tell us a little about the big day." Tessa lifted her own coffee cup and stirred in the cloud of creamer on its surface. "Tell us about the groom. Was it love at first sight?"

A faint laugh from Harper. "It was kismet," she said. "He works on the other side of town—he was planning this getaway package for his secretary as a Christmas present, didn't want to use the big travel agency who plans his yearly getaway… so he walked into my place. Two months later, he gives me a ring at dinner for Valentine's Day. What can I say? He's everything I never thought I would have: successful, handsome, a big-time executive. Me, I didn't finish college. Didn't even really start college, to be truthful."

"Who cares, if it's love?" said Ama.

"True," said Harper. "Only I figure his family cares a little. They're a tiny bit… well… snooty. You ever heard of the Winship Plastics Company?"

"The people who make every plastic thing known to man?" answered Natalie.

"That's them," said Harper. "Only they just make kitchen storageware these days, and some fixtures for faucets. Anyway, he's kind of taking over for his father, gradually... I guess maybe I'm a little worried that I'm not what they had in mind. Not that they'd ever say it. They were nice when we had brunch. Once." She placed her coffee cup on the tray again.

Ama spoke up. "Not to suggest that this is a mistake... but are we what he has in mind for a wedding planner?"

In the cake baker's eyes, Tessa could see the look of perplexity that the rest of them must surely be wearing after hearing the name of one of the most illustrious manufacturing families on the southeastern seaboard. Eyes wide as saucers, the three Wedding Belles' employees gazed across at the soon-to-be millionaire bride.

"He says I should be the one to plan it." Harper shrugged. "I guess his parents don't have a problem with that. But I would like to have their blessing for it, so to speak. To include them in part of this, even though I don't want to call up some really snooty, exclusive place—I'd have to use his name, throw around some details like that. It would make me feel cheap."

She snapped a piece from one of Ama's biscuits with a delicate precision that kept any crumbs from escaping her plate. "So if it's all right, I would like you to meet with them before we really seal the deal. See, I was going to pay for the wedding myself, 'cause I saved up money... you know, in case I ever got to take a real dream trip of my own. But now, Brett says he wants to pay for the whole thing. He picked out this place that's kind of grand—some friends of his parents own it, apparently. I guess it feels like they should have a say in part of the planning because of that."

"I see," said Tessa, with slight dismay. Nothing led to trouble quicker in the wedding planner world than having too many opinions on hand.

"Anything goes for the wedding, Brett says; it's a special day after all, so no holds barred. There's a lot to plan, but then again, I figure you've done that kind of thing before, so it won't be a problem. Will it?" She glanced at each of the three partners in turn. "You plan big weddings all the time, right?"

"Right," said Tessa before anyone else could answer. "Society weddings and ordinary weddings have one thing in common: they have to feel special to the people involved, and bring to life the vision of the couple sharing them. That's what we do best, no matter the budget size."

Harper opened her purse, a funky red-leather one that Tessa thought was secondhand, since it still had the residue from a recent sticker tag on one side. "This is the place Brett and I are getting married at," she said, laying a brochure on the table. "It's a hotel, so you can stay while you're working. Don't worry about travel expenses—it's no problem to pay for that either."

The three of them leaned forward. The brochure depicted a veritable mansion with Palmetto Isle Resort printed above a breathtaking photograph. All three exchanged long, meaningful glances in return.

Chapter Seven

"A member of the Winship family? That name is huge," said Natalie. "I don't know, Tessa. I don't know if we're ready for a society wedding. Are we?"

"Why not?" Tessa pulled three books from her shelf, all on beach- and seaside-inspired weddings. "I think our reputation precedes us now. We have a pretty long list of happy clients after being in business for a year. No complaints yet, right? Plus, we have a breathtaking ad in the very center of *Southern Brides* magazine—"

"Which was twice as expensive as that huge billboard you paid for," pointed out Natalie, with a touch of disgust.

"—and we've built trust between ourselves and a couple of the best vendors in the city, like Accented Creations and the Garden Catering Company," continued Tessa, ignoring her business partner's remark. "With a wedding like this one on our client list, there's no end to future possibilities. It opens a whole new door for us. Our clients will span from the financially modest to the Fortune 500 types. What could be better?"

"Are the Winships *that* successful?" Ama asked, dubiously.

"They make faucet spray nozzles and spill-proof plasticware," said Natalie. "It's not the Apple Macintosh empire we're talking about."

"We're going to impress them, trust me," said Tessa. "And if for some reason the interview doesn't go great, at least we get a free weekend out of it at one of the most glamorous spots in the state."

"Can't argue with that," said Ama.

Palmetto Isle was privately owned, the site of the exclusive resort named for it. The brochure had stunning color photos that promised fine dining, relaxing spas, sandy beaches and lush tropical gardens. If the Winship family friend who owned it also lived there, they probably felt as if every day was spent in their own tiny version of the Caribbean with a southern twist. Lying on snowy sand, watching the sapphire waves wash ashore, with the breeze whispering through the weeping willows and towering palmettos behind them.

"There's the Cyprus Trail leading to the outdoor Wedding Grotto," Natalie read from the resort's website. "The Willow Walk Gazebo, where the open ground 'charms visitors with clear skies and the gentle murmur of the sea in the distance.'"

Just like Tessa's fantasy.

"Do they have a menu posted?" Ama asked. She had been leafing through one of Tessa's books on summer events, studying a "beach wedding cake" that wouldn't be grand enough for a society wedding.

"I'll text it to you. Spoiler alert: it involves seaweed crêpes and organic cucumbers for the first appetizer."

"Sounds very hip," said Ama. Her phone buzzed, and she checked the time as she opened Natalie's message. "I have to go," she said. "I have some market shopping to do today."

"If your birthday present needs alterations, I can fix it on Monday," Natalie called after her.

"Thanks, but it fits perfectly." Ama twirled for a demonstration before she grabbed her cardigan and shrugged it on over the medium-blue tartan printed with soft thin magenta-and-yellow stripes, its spread skirt and sleeveless bodice with scoop neckline old-fashioned in both cut and style. Natalie had seen the fabric online two weeks ago and known instantly that it was a perfect choice.

"I sent your present to your home. It'll arrive by tomorrow at the latest," said Tessa, who had decided at last on a DVD anniversary copy of *Pride and Prejudice*. "And if you need reinforcements for tonight's dinner, feel free to call us."

"We'll be your impromptu extra guests seated at the kids' table," added Natalie.

"I wish." Ama groaned. "Sometimes I'm not sure *I* want to be there. But there's no time like the present for leaping ahead in life, right?" With a brave smile, she made her exit.

"So how do you plan to impress our fancy new clients?" Natalie asked Tessa.

"With assuredness, dignity... and sheer force of presence," she answered. "We'll pull out all the stops." One of those stops would require an Armani suit... but she thought she would mention that part later.

"Where are you going?" Natalie watched as Tessa loaded her books into her overburdened shoulder bag and lifted it from the table.

"I have an errand to run. We don't have any other clients needing our attention, at least until Harper's ready to begin," said Tessa. "And I thought I would take a working lunch at the Peach and Praline after I introduce myself to that new caterer who opened on Maxwell Lane last week."

Tessa's real reason for leaving early wasn't to sit in the aforementioned tea shop and bistro, sipping chamomile mint tea while reading chapters on seaside flowers and driftwood centerpieces. Instead of driving downtown, she turned off at the third exit leading to the outskirts, a less populated and less industrial zone a few miles away from the city, where dirt roads appeared at intervals, and trees belonged to occasional fruit orchards or wooded lots instead of the state park.

She turned off on a roughly paved drive, winding through the trees a short distance to a large clearing with a gravel parking zone. Outside a weathered, towering old barn, gray face turned to the distant road, a work truck was parked near the shade of some massive water oaks and elderly black walnut trees, antique furniture and fixtures lashed into place in the back of the pickup. She knew that truck on sight, although the items in the back changed frequently, except for the chipped, red-painted toolbox just behind the cab. She didn't know this place, which seemed wild and antiquated yet intriguing.

This was Blake's warehouse, where he once mentioned he stored everything for his contracting business. There was an office to one side in an added-on shed which had once been painted white, its entrance marked by a small sign above an old-fashioned Victorian storm door, but Tessa noticed the barn's large double doors were slightly ajar. Blake was probably inside, making room for his latest acquisitions, or doing something in his workshop.

Tessa pushed open the first door and stepped inside. The hinges emitted a low, creaky groan as the door opened wider. The smell of sawdust, old paint, and musty furnishings filled the high-ceilinged space inside, along with more random objects than Tess's imagination could conjure on its own. Sideboards, hutches, cabinets, mantelpieces, and piles of things with names that Tessa knew only from her association with Blake: sconces, corbels, facings, and wainscots among them.

"Hello?" she said. "Anybody home? Blake?" He couldn't be out on a job somewhere, not unless he was riding with a member of one of his hired crews. She heard the sound of a motor rumbling faintly somewhere in the building, and a soft thud.

She glimpsed what must be his workshop on the other side of a half-wall of decorative old radiators and fireplace inserts. A long worktable coated with fluffy, white wood shavings, with a row of various saws on platforms or anchored stands. A shadow moved away from some sort of lathe, where one of those decorative corbels that Blake loved so much lay in a pile of wood chips, its scrolls and feathered design half-finished.

"Blake?" She turned down a veritable aisle formed by stacks on either side: sheets and rolls of ornate wall coverings, old chandeliers and Tiffany-style light fixtures, a bookshelf facing with Gothic revival carvings. "Are you here somewhere?" She peered around one end, then turned the opposite direction and ran straight into Blake's torso.

A shriek of surprise escaped Tessa.

Blake held up his hands. "Easy," he said, with a half-smile. "I didn't mean to scare you."

"I didn't mean to be scared," she answered, a hand against her chest. "I thought I heard you—"

"I was fixing up a piece for that apartment building I'm renovating," he said, at almost the same time. "I thought I heard somebody at the door." He tucked his hands in his pockets. "So, what are you doing all the way out here?" He glanced around. "In need of a few extra fixtures?" he asked. "Something to replace that ugly modern lamp upstairs in the bathroom?" He wasn't being serious, although Tess knew he wasn't a fan of the old seventies-era green and orange crackled glass globes currently installed there.

Worn blue plaid shirt, denim jeans faded and marked with dirt from furnishings—how was it possible that he looked as amazing in these as he did in formalwear? It was something about those rather intense blue eyes and his attractive chiseled features... even in need of a shave and a slight trim, as usual.

"Looking for you," she answered. She tucked aside a strand of hair. "Actually, I've come to offer you a sort of vacation," she said. "As our official fourth partner, you qualify to come. And we could use your help, maybe." Nothing said sophistication like Blake in a suit, as unusual as it seemed. But when the handyman donned one of Natalie's borrowed designer labels, he exuded a certain confidence and sophistication that clients tended to find irresistible—even when he wasn't doing anything particularly sophisticated or assertive while wearing one—which they could definitely use in the setting of a private island.

She showed him the brochure from her purse. "Our latest would-be client is planning to have a ceremony here," said Tessa, indicating the resort on its cover. "We're supposed to visit next Saturday for the interview with the family and to give them a sort of pitch for the wedding. If they like us, we're hired. And if they don't, what do we have to lose?"

He opened the brochure's folds, releasing a slow whistle as he admired the aerial view of the glamorous, plantation-style hotel. "I guess I've never said no to a free vacation," he said. "But I can't cheat your client. All I'll be doing is standing around while you do all the work."

"We might need an extra hand," said Tessa. "If we're hired, then we'll spend the weekend picking out the site for the reception and the ceremony. That'll entail lots of different tasks and we could use all the help we can get." She hesitated. "It could be the most fantastic fee we've ever earned... We might even be able to pay you what you're actually worth, for a change," she added, jokingly.

She touched his arm, carefully, afraid to linger too long because her fingers might actually tremble a little. "What do you say? It's just one tiny plane ride from the coast."

He was thinking about it. Or, probably, thinking about what sort of change the Wedding Belles could make to their building, with a handsome fee to fund it, if Tessa knew him at all. "All right," he said. He folded up the brochure. "You've got yourself a fourth partner. One more time." He smiled.

She smiled back, partly with relief, partly with a deeper feeling that she tried desperately to hide by turning the other way. "So, this is where you work?" she said, by way of changing the subject. *Why are you stalling, Tessa?* "I always pictured the address on your card as part of a warehouse on the other side of town, not a... feed storage lot."

"I had an office in town for a while, it just got inconvenient to store stuff there. Then a cafe moved in next door, and they didn't like the noise from the tools, so I moved. There's more room for the crew, too. This place is too crowded with stuff I don't need at this point but can't bring myself to throw away. Like I'm a packrat for antique fixtures."

"It could be worse," suggested Tessa. "You still have floor space."

"Oh, yeah?" he said, with a laugh that told her there was more to this story.

"Sure," she said, turning to face the nearest wall of decorative ironwork. "If you moved a few things closer to the walls, and maybe hung a few things from the ceiling that weren't too heavy—"

She felt a strong pair of hands wrap themselves around her shoulders from behind. "Look up," instructed Blake's voice, close to her ear. Tessa lifted her gaze to see that high above, a half-loft had been constructed in the warehouse. More furniture and fixtures were piled in it, while dozens and dozens of different light fixtures were bolted to the open ceiling above. Between old chains and pulleys hung Tiffany-style lamps, corroded chandeliers with dangling crystals, and rusty cast-iron lantern globes straight from a foggy Dickensian night.

"Wow," she said. "You really *do* need more space."

"Told you." Blake released her shoulders. Tessa wondered if he felt the shiver that had traveled through her body in response to his touch.

"But I thought you used it all," said Tessa, bringing her thoughts back to their conversation. "In restoring places like ours."

He laughed. "I couldn't use it all if I tried," he said. "And not just 'cause the rest of my clients are as stubborn as you when it comes to making changes."

"I *like* the spiral staircase."

"So you've informed me," said Blake, smiling. "So… want the grand tour?" he asked.

Love one. That's what she might say, if circumstances were different. If he wasn't engaged to Mac for instance. But things were different now, and being alone with him just wasn't an option if she wanted to start getting over those feelings she'd harbored for him ever since their kiss last summer.

"Sorry, but I should probably get back to work," she told him. "Another time?" Meaning never ever, but she kept that part to herself.

"Sure. I'll see you back out, then. It's easy to get lost in this place," he added, with a slightly sheepish grin for their crowded surroundings.

Blake led her through pathways formed between stacks of trim and pieces of molding detached from houses long torn down or remodeled. "Some of this stuff comes from odd places," he admitted, catching her quizzical look at the array of antiques. "I get calls from people who want to unload everything from garden statues to stained glass."

"Carousel horses, too?" Tessa ran her hand over the worn paint on the neck of a prancing gray-and-white mare on a gold carousel pole, forgetting she was supposed to be leaving as she stopped to admire it.

He grinned. "I picked that up at an auction," he said. "Somebody salvaged it from an old one, I guess. Looks like it was probably replaced by another animal. Wish I could find the others. Look at that craftsmanship—carved in the 1800s, the original paint still on it. Though it's mostly worn off from the saddle and the sides, and anywhere people have petted it in decades past."

Tessa, who had been doing exactly that, moved her hand, but not before it made contact with Blake's, which had been smoothing the surface of the gold-painted saddle and the pony's dappled paint. Fingers brushing fingers, feeling the rough skin and assured strength of his own... Tessa's moved aside only because she made them obey her after a quick second of electricity.

"I always loved carousels," she said, covering for her flustered reaction. "As a kid, I begged to ride the one just down the street at the corner mart. But it was one of those little metal ones with only three tiny little painted horses. You put a quarter in and it went around five or six times before it stopped."

"I think I have one of those," said Blake.

"Really?" She glanced at him with surprise.

"Auction for storage buildings," he said. "Some vendor abandoned it. There was a gumball machine, too."

"Is this thing on a stand?" Tessa asked, finding the pole anchored to the base of the carousel horse in what she had mistaken for the base of an old column lost in this pile of stuff.

"Yeah, the former owner mounted it—probably to let kids pretend to ride it," he answered. "It's safe, it won't fall over. I've had a couple of people test it out."

On impulse, Tessa put her hands around the pole and hopped up on the saddle. Riding side-saddle wasn't as easy as it looked in the movies, she discovered, and the worn surface of the carousel horse's back was slippery beneath her business skirt's fabric. "How much do you want for it?" she joked. "I might like owning my own carousel horse. I think it would look good in the corner of my office. Don't you?"

"For only three thousand dollars, your dream could come true."

"Three thousand?" she repeated.

"Ballpark. I'm open to negotiations." He held out his hand to help her down, and Tessa made the mistake of accepting it. Blake might have felt her trembling in his hold because he didn't let go right away, even when she slid down. For a moment, their fingers remained clasped, his warm hand surrounding hers. Tessa didn't pull away.

She cleared her throat. "I'll have to think about it," she said. "That's a big deal."

"What?"

"The horse." Her brain had momentarily clicked to an empty track of thought, its space occupied purely by the sensation of Blake's hand.

"Oh." He laughed. "I wouldn't worry about that. I'll give you the bargain price reserved for friends and family." He let go of her—and was his face slightly crimson with a blush, or was she imagining it? Wishful thinking, perhaps, although she felt it was more than that as she studied his expression for a moment. But no… he loved Mac, right? So he couldn't be having second thoughts, even if there *was* some kind of chemistry at work in this moment, and not merely in her imagination.

"See you next Saturday, then?" she asked. "At the airport?"

"Next Saturday," he agreed.

Chapter Eight

For her birthday dinner menu, Ama had chosen tandoori chicken and seasoned rice, with steamed vegetables and a sweet sauce that her brother Jaidev had created for tempering dishes that were too spicy for some of their customers. Her father cooked the main dish, her mother cooked the sides, and Ama herself frosted the three-layer pecan cake, its sides covered in crushed nuts.

"Is that what you're wearing?" Rasha asked, surveying Ama's birthday dress from Natalie. "You have a dressy dress upstairs—that orange one I loaned you for the last wedding, remember? The one with the silky fabric and all those cute little tucks?"

"I don't want to be dressy, I want to be me," said Ama, for what felt like the thousandth time in her life. "But I'll put on a little jewelry when I spruce up before dinner."

Upstairs in her room, she slid a little antique-looking hair comb to one side of her short hair, its tiny crystals catching the light from its tarnished silver setting. Her birthday gift from Luke.

The doorbell downstairs buzzed. "I'll get it!" she shouted, taking the stairs swiftly to beat her father to the main foyer connecting the restaurant and the upstairs quarters of the Bhagut family. On the other side of the glass, she could see Luke waiting, a bottle of wine in hand.

She opened it. "Hi," she said, breathlessly. "Come on in."

"I'm not late, I hope," he said, shrugging off his jacket. "This guy came by the shop late to drop off his bike and we had to talk about its paint colors before he left." He kissed her cheek. "Happy birthday," he said. "You look beautiful, by the way."

"Thanks."

From beneath his arm, he shrugged a small bundle. "I brought this for your mom, as a hostess gift," he said. "It took me awhile to find something."

"I'm sure it's great." She took his arm. "Ready?" she asked. "It's not too late to back out," she joked.

Despite his smile, she could see he was a little bit nervous, though he had been coaxing her for weeks to invite him to a family gathering. "Ama, they're your family. You're not embarrassed to have me around them, are you?"

"No. No, of course not," she said. With emphasis. "Just… don't give it another thought. I only want to be sure you have a good time."

For her birthday, her siblings had decorated the private dining room with brightly colored crepe-paper streamers, paper lanterns, and a glitzy "Happy Birthday" pennant sign that her other brother Nikhil had strung across the windows. Usually her family ate meals at one of the main dining tables, in "shifts" as everyone worked, but this was the only table where everyone could be seated together. White serving dishes were in the middle while Ama's cake and a tray piled with *gulab jamun* waited on a serving table used for wedding parties at the Tandoori Tiger.

"Everybody remembers Luke, obviously," said Ama, as they walked in. She set the bottle of wine on the table, though she knew it would go untouched.

"Nice to see you again," he said, waving his hand at all of them. "Mrs. Bhagut, this is for you," he said, holding out the package to Pashma, who tried to hide her quizzical expression.

"Thank you," she said. She opened the brown paper wrapping. Inside was a piece of blue pottery with tiny mirrors decorating its surface.

"I read that Rajasthani culture has a long tradition of pottery-making, especially blue pottery," he said. "A friend of mine is a potter. He made this, actually. I saw it in his shop and thought maybe you would like it."

Ama smiled. Pashma did, too… politely. "Thank you," she said, setting it carefully on the table.

It was nothing like Indian-style pottery, really—it should be brighter and not studded with sparkly bits—but Ama didn't see the need to point this out, even though the southwestern style of this pot's shape and color was clearly nothing like the traditional handicrafts of her mother's native culture.

"Let's eat," said Ama, with a bright smile.

Her whole family was here, except for Rasha's husband Sanjay. Rasha, Nikhil, Jaidev and Deena, and even Ama's other sister Nalia had come for the week, bringing her toddler with her. And, of course, Aunt Bendi was there, seated a few places away from them at the table. She had been scrutinizing Luke with a disapproving stare from the moment he walked through the door to greet them, and it wasn't because of the pottery's inaccuracies, Ama knew.

He stuck out by comparison, even though her siblings were all dressed in typical Western clothes. It wasn't the fact that he was the only non-Indian at the table, and it wasn't the tattoo, which was hidden beneath the sleeves of his white shirt. It was like Luke's carefree spirit somehow… *exuded* itself, albeit invisibly. Spiky hair, scarf, faint grease stains under his fingernails—how these things added up to make him seem like a complete alien sitting cross-legged at their long restaurant dining table, Ama simply couldn't explain. But her auntie's sharp eyes remained suspicious despite his general politeness and cheerfulness as he made conversation with her family.

Was it wrong that Ama wished her aunt had some sort of emergency appointment at the hairdresser's tonight?

"How is the motorcycle business?" her father Ranjit asked. True to form, the only thing he ever remembered about her boyfriend was his work. Ama suspected he mentally blocked all other details.

"It's great," said Luke. "Lately I've been rebuilding the shell on an old Harley-Davdison, but my next customer has a forties-era English bike he wants rebuilt. That'll be something new for me. I've never done this model, so I'll have to do some research on it."

"I think it's cool what you do," said Jaidev. "Maybe I should get a mechanic's certificate and give up spices and sauces. What do you say?" He glanced at Deena.

"It's your life," she answered. "But given the state of *our* garage, I don't trust you to finish anything except leftovers in the fridge."

"Jaidev has a good job already," said Ranjit. "Why quit to do something that might not be as good?" A risk like that was the kind her family never took. Why do something different with your life when three generations had already been successful at one thing? Ama could recite this argument without hearing it yet again.

"I think everybody's born with something they were supposed to do," said Luke. "Kind of like a built-in destiny, so to speak. We just shape it out of our experiences. Some people rebel against it, of course, and they're never really happy with their lives, I don't think, because they're not authentic to themselves."

He had spoken German at the dinner table, as far as Ranjit and Pashma were concerned, Ama knew. The way he glanced around the table and smiled in his open way was proof he didn't have a clue. She lifted the bowl of snow peas. "More vegetables?" she asked.

"Sure," he said. "These are great, by the way. And I love the chicken. You're as great a cook as Ama said, Mr. Bhagut."

"Ranjit will do," her father answered, in response to a long, pleading stare from Ama to remind him of his promise. "That is my secret recipe you are eating. I made my first restaurant famous with it."

"He says that every time someone eats it," said Pashma, with a near-hidden smile at Ranjit's evident pride for his so-called secret recipe.

"It's delicious," said Luke. "This is Punjabi, right?" He glanced at Ama. "Ama's been trying to explain the differences to me. Twenty-something states, different languages, different backgrounds—I had no idea there was so much diversity. It's actually kind of like here."

"It's nothing like here," laughed Jaidev. "Unless you mean the part where everybody always thinks their way of doing things is totally right."

"Jaidev," came Pashma's warning, though uttered in a calm and quiet tone—their mother had learned that this worked best on reining in her older son's jokes.

"I saw pictures on the internet of some of the places you're from," said Luke. "It was beautiful in your state, Mrs. Bhagut. Or Pashma— may I call you that?"

"Yes," she answered. "Of course you may." Ama didn't think her mother was particularly a fan of this idea, though.

"I liked the handmade dolls that were topsy-turvy style—the 'up-down' dolls. Another artist friend of mine was really interested in them because cultural crafts really appeal to his customer base. It's Brody—the one who was selling the kites when you and I were there last weekend?" he added to Ama.

"Right," she said, although she didn't remember this friend offhand. Maybe they could talk about something besides India right now, she thought. It felt weird, hearing Luke try to relate to her parents, who certainly didn't seem impressed by the internet encyclopedia facts her boyfriend had memorized.

"Until I met Ama, all the facts I knew about India could pretty much be counted on one hand," he said. "Sitar music, saris, the Taj Mahal, coconuts and banana leaves and curry. Did you ever see the Taj?" he asked Ranjit. "While you lived in India? The pictures I've seen are great."

"Wrong part of India for Dad," said Jaidev.

"I spent most of my life in Himachal Pradesh before I came to America," said Ranjit, shaking his head.

"It's just a day's drive away though, right? I thought you would have seen it at least once," said Luke.

"I did not have the time for the bus that drove people to Agra," said Ranjit, sounding impatient. "I had a restaurant and I had a family. Tourists go to the Taj Mahal, but I had too much work to waste time traveling."

He sounded dismissive about it. Ama felt irritated, for no other reason than she knew her father was making a big deal out of it because of Luke's ignorance. Couldn't he see that Luke was at least trying? At least he didn't ask if they were descended from the emperor or any rajahs, or make any jokes about *Bride and Prejudice*—unlike the girl Nikhil dated for a while, who thought arranged marriages were barbaric and assumed all Indians were vegetarians.

"What do you think of the rice?" Jaidev asked. "That's my special blend of seasoning, not Dad's. I think it's better than the fast-food version at the Punjabi Express. Do you ever eat there?"

"Don't answer that question if you don't want to hear an hour-long lecture from either of these guys about why it's so horrible," Deena chimed in. "And I happen to like their masala fries."

"I don't eat much Indian food, actually. There's a Polish cafe near the apartment I rent above this all-night drugstore, and most nights I grab a bite there," answered Luke.

"You live above a store that isn't yours?" Bendi already sounded disapproving. "Drugstores are so noisy, the ones that are open at night-time." She frowned. "I hope this apartment of yours is big."

"More like a couple of rooms," said Luke, with a laugh. "The last place I shared with a friend of mine. He got his own place in back of his tattoo parlor, though, so I had to find a cheaper place so I wouldn't spend all my profits on rent."

If Bendi could see the part of town where he lived, she would be horrified, Ama knew; she suspected her auntie already had an inkling of what it was like, thanks to her boyfriend's few but colorful remarks on the subject.

"Of course, we owe the menu mostly to the birthday girl," said Jaidev, coming to her rescue. "Ama's the one who picked the dishes, and even made her own birthday cake."

"Like she'd trust any of us to do it instead," said Nikhil.

"I trust you," said Ama. "I just think I'm better." A series of groans and laughs for her remark.

"Ama picked the recipe, of course," said Rasha. "Very sweet, very southern, and made to perfection—exactly like all her favorite desserts."

"Exactly like her," said Luke. He caught Ama's eye, and small butterflies released themselves inside her. Her right hand sneaked beneath the table, searching for Luke's, until she brushed against the fingers of the one resting on his left knee.

"Aww, that's adorable," said Deena. "You guys are so cute together. Aren't they adorable?" she added to Ama's sister Nalia. "I should've waited longer and I would have found a cute motorcycle guy instead of getting stuck with your brother."

"Hey, watch it," said Jaidev. "I have feelings too, you know."

"You are a lucky girl," said Bendi, half-scolding Deena. "Jaidev is hard-working and from a successful family—he'll run a restaurant someday, not run around the city on a noisy motorbike."

"*Bendi*," hissed Ama.

"What did I say that was untrue?" her aunt demanded.

"I think anybody is lucky when they find the right person," said Nalia, in her usual quiet way. "That's why I'm not in Bellegrove anymore, after all. I chose someone whose life took them somewhere else… but it was worth it. Look what I have now." Here, she proudly tousled the hair of her one-year-old, who was flattening the rice on Nalia's plate with one hand.

"I still think I got stuck with a raw deal." Deena stuck her tongue out at Jaidev, who did a poor job of hiding his smile in return.

"None of you are as lucky as me," said Rasha. "Even Mama and Papa. Sanjay and I are perfect together. I don't care what Ama says about matchmaking, the moment we laid eyes on each other, we knew we would be an amazing couple. Whereas she's getting stuck with some devastatingly handsome guy she met on the street," she added, teasingly.

"Ama is not stuck with anybody," said Ranjit, firmly enough that it was evident he didn't approve of the idea of Luke being Ama's destiny. For a few seconds, there was awkward silence before Pashma spoke up again.

"I think it is time to light the candles on Ama's cake. Jaidev, will you do it?" she asked.

"Sure thing, Mom." He scrambled up from the table as his mother and aunt began clearing away room for dessert.

Ama felt awkward. Her hand was holding too tightly to Luke's, she realized, not that he was complaining.

The number of candles that spelled out Ama's name matched her age in years, a twenty-something number that she knew she should enjoy before she reached Rasha's stage of protest for its public exposure. The two flames danced above the surface of her buttercream icing decorated with whole candied pecans, creating a warm glow equal to the bright lanterns above them.

"Make a wish," Nikhil reminded her.

"Wish for Mom to say yes to that second restaurant," supplied Jaidev.

"Jaidev," said Pashma, in her mild-but-warning tone of voice.

"It was just a suggestion," he said. Deena elbowed him, forcing a guilty grin to his lips.

"I'm not wasting my birthday wish on a second restaurant," answered Ama.

"I think you should wish for a good husband," muttered Bendi, who was in turn given a warning look from Rasha.

"Or to be declared world's best baker," suggested Nalia.

"Oog!" declared Nalia's toddler.

Luke leaned closer to her, his lips almost brushing her ear. "Wish for something that makes you alone happy," he said, soft enough that no one else could hear it.

Ama closed her eyes. *I wish all of my family would like Luke*, she thought. *I wish they would see our relationship as something worth pursuing, not just a temporary phase.* Desperate words for desperate times, and she knew there wasn't a chance that this would happen, at least not for her father or her auntie. She opened her eyes and smiled, however, before she blew out her candles. Little wisps of smoke drifted upwards from the two waxy pink-and-white candles.

"Yay!" said Nalia, clapping the baby's hands together.

Pashma drove a cake knife with precision through the layers of fluffy pecan cake and sugar frosting, cutting the first slice. Jaidev had already stolen one of the sticky *gulab* balls from the platter.

The cake was delicious, although Ama wished she had chosen a slightly different filling, maybe with the candied nuts in a thickened syrup. Luke ate two pieces, however, and complimented it between servings.

"It's certainly better than her first cake," said Jaidev. "Even your dolly wouldn't eat that one."

"Shut up," said Ama, blushing at the memory of an Easy-Bake Oven disaster from her grade-school past. "I didn't know what I was doing. Besides, I didn't even want to be a baker then."

"You never told me about that cake," said Luke.

"She frosted it in chocolate ice cream syrup," said Rasha.

"I was trying for Boston cream pie," protested Ama. "I—I wasn't exactly a culinary artist at eight, clearly. The Easy-Bake Oven I used to make it belonged to a friend, anyway, so it's not like I was practicing my culinary skills a lot back then. I probably wouldn't even be baking if the restaurant hadn't called for it."

"What would you be doing?" Luke asked, curious.

"Ama would be right here," said Ranjit. "In a restaurant, there is always something to do. You don't have to cook to be part of one. Sanjay worries about the expenses and the investments—he never cooks a pot of rice for customers."

"I'm a waitress and seating hostess," said Deena, smirking. "They wouldn't trust me to flavor the food."

"Do you know anything about restaurants?" Ranjit asked Luke. "You waited tables in college, maybe flipped burgers, as they say, in the restaurant at the end of the street?"

"I've never worked in one," said Luke. "I cook a little, some Polish recipes from a friend of mine, and some Spanish ones in a cookbook I bought at a bookstore sale. I didn't go to college, so I never had to wait tables for money."

"No college?" Bendi repeated.

"I studied mechanics in a vocational program. I always had an interest in the artistic side of repairs, though—I studied art in some night classes, then took some courses in bodywork."

No college. Bendi was probably ready to faint by now.

"I think if she wasn't baking, Ama would actually probably be off backpacking the country," said Jaidev. "You could have been a wanderer in the right conditions, sis."

"Like the homeless people who walk on the roadside?" Ranjit's brow knit together with worry.

"You like the thought of exploring the country?" Luke asked her. "A free spirit on the road?"

"I have a slightly restless streak, but I think Jaidev's exaggerating," she answered, shaking her head. "I admit I would like to see more of the world than just this city, and the one I saw in Mexico."

"It's not so good as it looks," mumbled Ranjit, who had only eaten half his cake, preferring the heavier confections among Ama's recipes. She knew this was not about pecan cake.

"Remember when you talked about backpacking Europe?" Rasha said. "I thought you were crazy."

Crazy is relative, Ama thought. Reflexively, she squeezed Luke's hand again before remembering to let go.

By the time the cake was down to a single slice, her sisters were arguing over which one of them would take home the leftovers, while her mother was trying to hush the baby, who had begun crying because bedtime was well past.

Ama saw Luke to the door after his farewells as her father argued with Jaidev over whether yesterday's curry had been overspiced.

"You worried for nothing," said Luke. He kissed her cheek. "I think it went great. Your family is really nice. Your dad's starting to warm to me a little."

"Mmhmm," said Ama, who thought this probably wasn't the case. "I'm glad you enjoyed tonight," she answered, not agreeing openly and eagerly with his previous statement, though he didn't notice. "It was really thoughtful of you to bring the pottery, too."

He had both of her hands in his, stroking the right one softly with the tips of his fingers. "Lunch tomorrow?" he asked. "At that little barbecue stand near the park? Or maybe breakfast at the cafe."

"I'd love to." She rose up on the tips of her toes to kiss his lips goodnight. Quickly, in case her father was watching. She then watched from the windows to wave goodnight again before he started his motorcycle.

The fight over the curry was over when she returned, and the table was cleared of part of its dishes. "Did you see the boyfriend home?" joked Jaidev.

"I saw him to the door. He said he had a really great time with all of you."

A snort from Ranjit.

"I thought it was great having him come," said Rasha, quickly, in order to make peace.

"He's a polite boy," said Pashma, mildly. No real enthusiasm for this statement, but at least it was nicer than Ranjit's usual reaction.

"I don't like him," said Bendi, firmly. "He is a wild boy, you can see it with only one look. All he talks about is motorbikes and running around without doing anything."

"And the Taj Mahal," muttered Ranjit.

Customarily, Ama ignored remarks like these, but tonight she spoke up. "What's that about?" she asked, uncharacteristic anger creeping into her tone. "Luke was a perfectly behaved guest tonight. Why do you have to point out every flaw every time you see him?"

"Why does he try so hard?" Ranjit asked. "Talking about things he knows nothing about—"

"At least he's trying to appreciate my culture," Ama answered, quietly. "You didn't seem interested in asking about his heritage, though."

"I asked him about motorcycles. That's all he is interested in, as far as I can see," said Ranjit, dismissively. "Boys like that do not have cultural ties. They are all mixed up—free spirits who believe in destiny and adventures and hiking along the road like hobos."

Deena squeezed Ama's shoulder. "I think he's great," she whispered softly in Ama's ear. "He looked fantastic in those jeans, too." With a teasing smile, she slipped on her jacket and linked hands with Jaidev. "See you all bright and early tomorrow morning."

"You could find a better boy than this one." Bendi shook her head as she gathered the last plate from the table.

Ama's birthday candle wish clearly wasn't coming true anytime soon.

Chapter Nine

The Bertha Blossom Seed Company had been in operation in Bellegrove since 1904, but several years ago its metal waterfront factory building had been converted into a bluesy country-and-western dive open Thursday through Saturday. The club was labeled as "the Cannery" on its neon sign, one with a Mason jar drink tipping to one side, sending a waterfall of white lightning into a simulated foamy pool.

Inside the building's brick walls, the atmosphere was smoky beneath the pink glare of stage lights, and a country band with a rock edge was playing a loud set on the stage located opposite the main bar. The tables were crowded with patrons enjoying a Saturday on the town, and the dance floor was equally crowded with enthusiastic concertgoers and impromptu line dancers alike.

A friend of Chad's from work had recommended this place, although it was a bit noisy compared to his usual hangouts. Chad was waiting in line at the bar for their drinks while Natalie found a table for them on the crowded floor. Stifling a yawn, she checked her cell phone. Another hour and this would be the latest she'd been awake and not sewing a garment in weeks. So why wasn't she having a great time?

"Look who the cat dragged in." Cal's voice reached her ear before her friend pulled up a chair at her table. "What are you doing sitting here alone and beautiful?"

"Chad's at the bar, ordering something for us," she answered. "I was just sitting here thinking the amps for the band are kind of loud… or maybe I'm just really tired and not in the mood for lively music."

"It drowns out conversation on the dance floor," Cal joked. "Seriously, though, are you all right? You look really glum for someone who's out on the town."

"I'm not glum," said Natalie. "Just tired, like I said. I'm practically working three jobs you know," she joked. Dress designing, consulting at Wedding Belles, helping her mom at the bakery—all things she loved for different reasons.

"So the boy of your dreams is really here?" Cal glanced around. "I haven't seen him with you in weeks."

"Don't call him that," said Natalie, with a short laugh. "It's so… not me."

"Be frank. Are you and Chad still… 'you and Chad' in reality?" asked Cal, for lack of better words. He had been partly in the know on Natalie's secret pact with Chad at Christmas.

"We're still together, aren't we?" answered Natalie, somewhat flippantly.

"I've been dying to have a heart-to-heart with you, Nat. You've set a record in steady dating with him. So is he the permanent thing?" The noise died down between songs, so she could hear him more clearly over the club's noise. "This is serious stuff for you."

"I know." Natalie shrugged. "But it's still me we're talking about, Cal. And I don't think he's on the verge of proposing either, if that's what you're hoping. One day at a time."

"Maybe not hoping, but predicting. He seems like your perfect choice," said Cal. "That's just a surface impression on *my* part, but he's definitely the whole package when it comes to the Natalie checklist: looks, brains, athleticism, sensitivity, not too clingy."

"True, true," said Natalie. "I can't argue that he's practically the combination of every guy I've ever dated." And with none of the qualities of guys she hadn't: the type who went in for true love and tenderness, mushy romantic sentiment, and deep, passionate attachments between human souls. As Tessa might put it, really.

Cal frowned. "Don't say 'yes' to him at first proposal to get your mom off your back," he said. "You should only commit to this guy if he makes you happy. Something about him must be making you happy, though, or you'd have dumped him. I know that much about you."

"Being a fun date made me happy until recently, so I'm not an expert at knowing my own mind," said Natalie. "But Chad is nice. And fun, as you aptly put it. And we have good chemistry and interesting conversations, so you're right about him meeting all the right criteria." As always, she put Chad's qualifications into succinct words. Why did she have to keep justifying him, she wondered? What was it about their relationship that had people still asking questions about its legitimacy even while they popped jokes about the big day? It was as if they could still smell the pretend seriousness of its past clinging to the fibers.

"So what's this about not knowing your own mind, huh?" said Cal, jokingly.

Natalie smiled back but didn't laugh. Something about it wasn't funny, as if some piece was missing that would explain the universe of this relationship emotionally, to herself if no one else. Her problem was she had never tested herself emotionally before by remaining in a long-term relationship. It's not as if it revealed a giant hole in her life that needed filled, did it?

Chad returned with their drinks, and Cal sidled away after a polite greeting to Natalie's boyfriend. The rest of the evening was spent in small talk about work and future outings which included a compromise: a trip to a fabric store to make Natalie happy, and a trip to the climbing wall to get Chad in shape before an upcoming endurance weekend.

When she got home, she shoved aside the pile of garments on her bed and listened to a long message from her mother reminding her about her agreement to help out at the bakery this weekend, before going to bed without remembering to text Chad goodnight.

"I'll be at the bakery Sunday afternoon, Ma," she said over the phone in the morning as she gathered up a few things that she needed to take to work to finish—a light blue caftan-esque casual shirt dress of chiffon with white embroidery, a belt of white Chinese silk with a rosette chain for its buckle—and a new issue of *Today's Bride* to peruse. "I can work Tuesday afternoon, maybe… I'll have to check with Tessa." Lately, Tessa had been noticing her absences from Wedding Belles' matters, favoring the piles of alterations for Grenaldi's Couture instead.

"No, I won't forget the chocolate. Yes, I will call you from the resort when I'm there for work. Bye, Ma." She hung up before any questions could be asked that she might not want to answer—for instance, how her date with Chad had gone.

"How was your birthday?" Natalie asked Ama Monday morning at work, as she dropped her stuff on the fainting couch in her office and glanced in the direction of the baker's open office door. She'd remembered her business partner's big dinner was last week, a full-blown gathering to assess Ama's relationship, in other words.

Pinned on the dressmaker's form was a leftover swatch of white sateen from the last wedding's designs. Natalie removed it and slipped the chiffon dress over the shoulderless figure.

Ama appeared. "All right." She held the notebook labeled "Best Cake Ideas Ever." "I mean, Luke thought it was great. And nobody directly insulted him at dinner, except my aunt, so that's something, right?"

"Your family's still not enamored with him, huh?"

"Jaidev really likes him, and so do Rasha and Deena. My siblings are great, and my mom is really trying. But my dad? Not so much." Ama sighed. "I won't even bother talking about my aunt's feelings when it comes to him. She talks about me and Luke like a phase of life issue, not a relationship. He doesn't see it, lucky for me. Or maybe he's just nice enough to ignore her rude comments." No amount of polite cultural reserve or friendly restaurateur training had ever restrained Bendi's opinions.

Natalie *tsked* with sympathy. "Maybe they just need more time," she suggested.

"I don't think time is going to make my auntie love black leather and motorcycles," said Ama. "She's never going to see Luke for the person he is, and the person I really care about… and my dad probably just wishes I would stay a spinster rather than run off with a boy like that."

"How about running off, period?"

"Don't tempt me." Ama borrowed a book on French fabric design, one she sometimes used to create imprints for decorative cake collars, or to mold unique cupcake toppers for Sweetheart Treats' more elegant events.

Natalie's phone beeped—a text message from Cal about a missing link in the paperwork for their runway registration. She texted him a quick answer as she went downstairs, hearing Tessa in conversation with someone else in the foyer.

A deliveryman was picking up a package, loading it onto a handcart as he and Tessa chatted in a friendly fashion. A familiar green uniform, rumpled reddish hair in need of a trim, a voice with a warm, slightly husky southern drawl. It had been months since she'd heard that voice, but she would still know it anywhere.

"Brayden?"

He glanced in her direction. A brief smile followed. "Hey, Natalie," he said.

"What are you doing here?" she asked.

"I'm working DeMilt's route while he's on vacation," he said. "Just for a week." He reached for his clipboard as Tessa handed it back. "Thanks," he said. He glanced at Natalie. "How've you been?"

"Fine," she answered. "Just fine." She crossed her arms, as if it was suddenly cold in the building. Stupid drafts from the uninsulated windows, she imagined. That, and she hadn't had her morning coffee yet. That totally explained this strange reaction to seeing her unwanted admirer face-to-face again.

"Good." He nodded. "I, uh, guess I'll be going. You ladies have a nice day." He tipped his hat to her and Tessa, offering them both a polite farewell smile, then maneuvered his cart to the front door, which closed behind him.

Tessa looked at her. "That was *Brayden*?" she said. "*The* Brayden? The guy you talked about when we were in college, the one who wouldn't leave you alone?"

"That's him." At least she was pretty sure it was, unless his body had been snatched in an alien invasion. "I didn't expect to see him here. He used to work a delivery route north of the city." She glanced at Tessa. "Why do you sound shocked that was him?"

"I don't know. I was picturing something different all these years, I guess," said Tessa. "Somebody... odious? Somebody repulsive? Not anybody like the guy who just dropped off this package."

"He might seem that way if he'd been asking *you* for a date since he was ten and you were eight years old," pointed out Natalie. Which was exactly when her childhood friendship with Brayden began to go wrong, though it wouldn't sour altogether until they were teenagers.

"Still. He seems nice and normal," said Tessa. "Not that five minutes is enough time to judge anybody. And he didn't mention you even once." She seemed puzzled. "Doesn't he know this is your building?"

"He does. Did," she said. Maybe he forgot, although she couldn't imagine that. Brayden's ability to memorize details about her life had been legendary. After all these years, it wasn't possible that his brain had started deleting them at long last.

"*That* is the guy who has a crush on you?" said Ama, who was standing at the halfway point on the spiral staircase.

"In the flesh," answered Tessa.

"Now you see what I mean," said Natalie. "You can actually put a face to the person who hounded me to go to the prom with him, who tried to wheedle invitations to my junior high birthday party because he thought we would all play 'spin the bottle.'"

"Actually... I thought he was cute," said Ama. "He had that boyish look that makes certain guys seem so endearing. And just a little bit nerdy—but in a good way."

"You're talking boy-next-door kind of cute?" Tessa suggested. "I'll second that. Especially his smile. And his eyes—I noticed those first, actually."

"Me too," said Ama. "They were really striking. Sort of an emerald green."

Natalie couldn't believe what she was hearing. Did her friends actually think Brayden was *attractive*? That his smile could set off butterflies in someone's chest or cause their cheeks to flush crimson under that quiet gaze?

"He was just so far from what I pictured," Ama told her. "I thought he'd be horrible, from the way you described him in the past."

"Well… he is, sometimes," said Natalie. This statement fell flat, despite mounds of evidence to make her point after years of dodging Brayden's unwanted attention. Her friends looked as if they didn't believe her, not faced with the real person. "Maybe you just failed to notice."

She laid the bridal magazine from her apartment on the low coffee table in the parlor. Behind her back, she knew her partners were exchanging glances. "At least today he was too busy to be his usual annoying self."

Brayden was probably just in a hurry today, since he was driving an unfamiliar route—no time for chitchat, or asking her a long line of questions. Maybe he and Rob had a falling out that she hadn't heard about; maybe Rob had finally taken her pleading to heart and stopped updating Brayden on every little thing that happened to her, too. There were any number of explanations for why he had seemed perfectly normal, and hadn't seemed the slightest bit interested in her.

It was weird to realize that she hadn't seen him since before Christmas until today; Brayden had seemed to cross her path every other week since she had returned home from college. But he hadn't stopped by Icing Italia in a while, so he must've changed routes some time ago, come to think of it.

"So how was the birthday dinner?" Tessa was asking Ama now.

Ama groaned. "Let's talk about something else," she said. "I don't want my love life reviewed, given present tensions between my father and my choice of boyfriend."

"So, Natalie," said Tessa. "Does Brayden *still* have a major crush—"

"I don't want *mine* discussed, either," answered Natalie, before Tessa could finish. "Let's talk about yours instead."

She knew Tessa's face would change color as quickly as those words were uttered. That was the end of Tessa teasing anybody else. The blush cleared her face quickly, however, restoring her business self.

"I think we should talk about something more pertinent," Tessa announced. "How about the many virtues of the Palmetto Isle Resort?" She turned the desk monitor around and the first image on the website's photo album splash page of blue waters and stunning plantation hotel greeted them.

"Are we allowed to use the spa?" Natalie asked, as the picture became that of a serene woman in a cotton robe receiving a facial.

"Oooh, is that blueberry Italian cream cake?" said Ama.

*

"Did you bring your whole wardrobe?" Tessa asked Natalie, who was struggling with a bulky carry-on, trailing behind Tessa and Ama as they waited outside the security line.

"No, but I have to finish a couple of alterations this weekend. A photographer is coming in on Monday to photograph them for Magnolia Revue's catalog, and Nella and Cal are both working this weekend." She shrugged her purse higher on one shoulder. "So that's what I'm doing when we're not traipsing around the grounds of Tara!"

"I'm only bringing a book and a swimsuit," said Ama, ignoring Natalie's reference to the famous house from *Gone with the Wind*. Tessa gave her a look. "But I am hoping to sneak into the kitchen to get a feel for the place, in case we're hired."

"Does anybody remember what flight number we are?" Natalie asked, searching for her ticket on her phone.

"Flight 415." Blake dropped his overnight bag on the floor beside their luggage. He was wearing a designer suit that Natalie's friend Cal had "scrounged" from his job at a garment rental emporium. He pushed up a pair of sunglasses and greeted them mutually with a smile.

"I feel underdressed," said Ama. "Should I have worn my sister's formal?"

"Is it too much?" Blake asked. "This is what you wanted me to wear, isn't it?"

"I didn't know you took requests," said Natalie, before Tessa elbowed her, sharply.

"You look fine," said Tessa. "More than fine" was not a verbal option here. He had sounded confused by their reaction to his appearance, as though he had never drawn some lingering stares in the past at weddings and parties. Blake might as well have stepped out of an advertisement for some rugged cologne brand, like the billboards spaced yards apart from Wedding Belles' own.

Tessa realized she was staring at him. She caught herself and fiddled with the arms of her sunglasses to give herself something else to do. "It's a really nice suit. I think the client will probably be impressed."

"I know *I* am." Natalie pressed her smile inwards while Tessa pretended not to notice.

"Shall we?" Blake lifted Natalie's overstuffed carry-on.

"Paradise awaits," said Ama, who lifted the handle of her own and wheeled it along behind the contractor, giving Tessa a moment to recover from her lapse of judgment.

The plane ride was only an hour long and landed them at the tip of the coastline, where the tiny cluster of private islands known as the Palm Rock Islands were reachable only by ferry. Palmetto Isle's private boat was waiting for guests of its resort to emerge from the airport; its pilot held a sign for the hotel. Beneath the bright sunshine, the motorcraft sped along toward the dock on the opposite side of the island from the ferry's platform.

"Are you newcomers to Palmetto Isle?" he asked Tessa over the noise of rushing water and whirring engine blades.

"We're planning a wedding there, hopefully," she answered.

"It's a beautiful place for weddings," he agreed.

The boat was in view of the private dock, where small watercraft and brightly painted sailboats were tied. Striped sails and vivid hulls were floating on the sapphire waters. In the sunlight, the water sparkled like a jewel—and so did the vibrant colors of the garden surrounding the Palmetto Isle Resort. They could see the sand of the white beach the resort's owners had created, nestled below the steep gray walls of the island's natural rise.

At the top, at the end of a curving, tree-lined drive, stood a mansion of white elegance gleaming like a pearl in the sun, its gardens like gem-stones adorning the smooth green ripple of a perfectly trimmed lawn.

"Look at it," breathed Ama.

"It's got columns, porches, windows taller than me, mansion gables…" Natalie ticked them off, one by one. "What doesn't this place have?"

"Is that a *lighthouse*?"

"That's the lighthouse tower wing," replied their boat pilot. "A 365-degree view of the harbor from there. It's the tallest story of the mansion, but the most popular wing was based on some of the architecture of Monticello. The Jefferson Garden is near the Willow Tree Walk, which is a pretty spot if you want to just wander around the grounds and see some natural beauty… but the Paradise Garden is the most popular spot among guests, I hear tell, because it has a view of the water. Best view in the south, I say, when the water's just the right color of blue."

His engine idled as they drew to the docks, and he helped Blake lift out the bags. "Just up those little tile steps or the concrete rail and you'll see what I mean," he told them. "Happy stays at Palmetto Isle Resort, y'all." He tipped his cap, then sped out to sea again.

They climbed up the steps, reaching the terrace outside the mansion. A lush garden of tropical blossoms greeted them: vivid red, pink, and tiger-stripe cannas in antique, glazed pots, buds of magenta and wine blush peeking open on thick green stems amidst the lilies and the broad hibiscus flowers. The scent of gardenia was heavy in the air; water burbled from a stone fountain in the garden's courtyard, which gazed out at the water, and the tip of the distant mainland shore.

"There's the 'stairstep rocks' between this island and the smallest one, Cleft Island," said Natalie, climbing the tiled steps to the view and pointing in the distance. "There's a couple of chain bridges connecting them so you can walk out there and feel like you're standing on a rock in the middle of the sea. They had to rebuild the trestles after a hurricane a few years ago."

Tessa touched the rough bark of one of the nearby palmettos, which dotted the garden at intervals. She gazed upwards, where lace curtains fluttered in the breeze from one of the upper rooms. Luxury suites, the brochure promised, complete with all amenities, including breakfast delivered at the hour of your choice.

"Guys, come look at this!" Ama had disappeared down the tiled garden path leading to the other side of the mansion's grounds. "The pool has Grecian tiles *and* the water is Caribbean blue!"

"They hauled in white sand for the beaches," said Blake, brushing a little from the stones along the massive flower beds. "Guess that way it matches the house."

"Now *this* is paradise," said Natalie, with a sigh.

Like the patios outside, the hotel's lobby was decorated with summer furnishings of white wicker and nautical stripes, while a bronze sculpture of a sailor seated on a rock was surrounded by a ripple of tiny blue and white flowers like sea spray. The walls were mahogany paneling, papered above by a pale blue-and-white damask-style wall cover that was real linen, Tessa discovered, when her fingers touched it. The desk clerk gave them keys to their rooms—not the lighthouse tower one, of course—and directed them to the elevator.

"We're meeting with a party at eleven," said Tessa. "The Lucas–Winship party. Are they here yet?"

"They checked in last night. They'll be waiting for you in the Orchid Meeting Room, which is to the right of the grand staircase," he answered.

"Ms. Miller?" A chirpy, confident voice spoke, not that of Harper Lucas but a young woman in a short business skirt and tiny jacket cut in the trendiest fashions, her brown hair in a princess twist pinned into a chic knot. She strode confidently toward them despite the pencil-thin stilettos she wore, which elevated her two or three inches above Tessa and clicked staccato-style on the grand foyer's marble floors.

"That's me," said Tessa.

"I'm Ashleigh, Mr. Winship's personal assistant. Welcome to Palmetto Isle. I'll be joining you for lunch with the family, and for your tour of the resort's grounds to get a feel for the place." She was shaking hands with the Wedding Belles now, each in turn.

"Nice to meet you," said Tessa.

Ashleigh's hand lingered when she reached Blake's grip, and the assistant's stare was not unlike Tessa's at the airport.

"This is Ama, our culinary expert, and Natalie, who's our designer and assistant coordinator. And this is Blake," Tessa added lastly, and strangely reluctantly. "He's assisting me in planning the event."

"A pleasure, I'm sure," said Ashleigh. "We'll be seeing a lot of each other in the coming weeks, since I'll be helping you with Mr. Winship's side of things." She meant all of them, judging by her words and voice, but her eyes never left Blake.

"I'm sure we will," said Blake, with a polite smile.

At last, Ashleigh released his hand. "I'll see you all soon," she said, and tripped off lightly toward the other side of the hotel.

Tessa caught herself glaring after the assistant and turned her head away, quickly, feeling embarrassed. After all, this was her client's assistant, probably a perfectly harmless and thoughtful professional who simply had a natural reaction to Blake's good looks. What right did *she* have to be annoyed by it?

"Let's go see our luxury rooms," said Ama, pressing the elevator's button. "You know the view has to be incredible."

Harper was waiting in the Orchid Meeting Room with a big smile to greet the girls. Her frizzy hair was pulled back by two large rhinestone strawberry clips; the rest of her ensemble—a white sundress with a bold floral spray print and a pair of strappy sandals—was slightly dressed down from the cheap red leather shoes and the outdated business jacket of their first meeting. Meanwhile, the older couple sitting to her left appeared pale, drab, and dignified in casual "summer sporting" wear that retailed for several hundred dollars per garment, as Tessa knew from catalogs that sometimes arrived by mistake at the Wedding Belles, and that were usually pitched straight into the garbage.

The woman had a pale-blue cardigan paired with a white blouse and pearls, her professionally tinted hair somewhere between red and brown, and her neutral lipstick adding to her general paleness. The man wore a pullover and summer linen trousers, with a pair of slip-on boating shoes with natty sailor's knot tassels that Tessa remembered from the catalog's cover, actually. They were introduced as Myra and Terrence Winship: Brett's parents, and Harper's future in-laws.

"I'm so glad y'all could come for the weekend," said the hotel's activities director, Norris. "The gardens are only now entering their first stages of summer glory, so you'll get a little taste of what this place'll be like in June. We've got several sites that would be just perfect for both the ceremony and the reception, so we'll be touring them all today."

"I think the gazebo would be a nice choice," remarked Myra, sipping one of the sparkling waters with lemon wedges the hotel provided as complimentary beverages. "Polly and David's daughter was married there one, no, two years ago. I remember well. She and Brett dated for quite a while. I really thought they might be engaged before it ended."

"Harper should choose, of course," said Terrence. "It's always the bride who cares the most where she stands for the ceremony. I couldn't even tell you anymore what the church looked like where we were married." He squeezed lemon juice into his water.

"That's because you're not sentimental, dear," said Myra. No real affection for the "dear," Tessa noted, as if everything Brett's father uttered possessed equal emotional value, regardless of meaning.

"Sentimentality kills you in my business," he answered. "Brett has the same instincts when it comes to nailing down profit instead of chasing after risks for the sake of some bold horizon somebody or other envisions."

"Where is Brett?" Tessa asked. "We were eager to meet with the groom so we can confirm that our approach is exactly what the couple needs for their big day."

"I did suggest to you that you should call the Perkins' planner," sighed Myra to Harper, who, for only a moment, flashed crimson in both cheeks.

"Brett won't be able to come this weekend," said Harper. "He works a lot. He's got this business deal in Charlotte that was going down on Monday, so he said he couldn't make it back in time to meet with you. But he loves the work your agency has done," she added, quickly. "I sent him pictures and everything. He thinks you'll be great."

"That's why I'm here," piped up Ashleigh, the assistant. "I'll be representing Bre—, Mr. Winship's interests in this process. He's given me *carte blanche* with regards to last-minute details, and a complete list of suggestions to refer to regarding ceremony details, little things for the reception that would appeal to his personal friends and clients, and so on. Not to mention a complete list of clients, contacts, and other associates he wishes invited to the wedding." This, she handed to Blake, not Tessa. "In alphabetical order." She locked eyes with him for a long moment, in which Tessa was almost sure the contractor blushed.

"How… nice," ventured Tessa, after a slight pause. Blake handed her the sheet, which she tucked with the rest of her notes, switching to her businesslike self again with a second breath. "So, Mr. and Mrs. Winship are clearly interested in helping secure this location for the wedding; will any members of the Lucas family be participating in the planning or the wedding itself?"

"No." Harper shook her head. "No one from my family will be part of the wedding. My father's busy, Mama's sick, and the rest of my relatives—who knows where they are these days, right?" She shrugged her shoulders but there was a trace of discomfort in her voice for this admission. "They've got lives of their own to live, they don't care about seeing me in a white dress, riding off into the sunset with my prince charming."

The Winships exchanged glances—subtly but not entirely nicely, Tessa noted.

"We'll need a guest list for you as well," said Tessa. "If you and Brett will select your invitations, I can have them mailed by the end of next week. We have several good graphic designers on our list of contacts, including a very promising new artist whose work has really impressed us." She was thinking of Molly, the bride from the Wedding Belles' first wedding.

"Our family always prints theirs at South Station's Printing Company," grunted Terrence.

"Harper's wedding, dear," Myra reminded him.

"Of course. I was only thinking of the company's bulk rate agreement. She'll pick the place she wants, of course." He set his glass on the table and checked his watch. "I have a tee time on the mainland with an old friend," he said to everyone present. "I'm sure you don't need my input in this matter any further, since I've already had a word with Freddy about booking this place."

"I suppose it's time to begin our tour," suggested Norris.

*

"Isn't this the most beautiful place ever?" Harper asked them. "This is how I picture all those island vacations when you have a full suite in one of those exclusive resorts only the *Lifestyles* crowd ever visits—the big blossoms, the perfume in the air, the water blue like those drink packets you love when you're a kid. *This*," she declared, "is my version of a perfect world." She spread her arms out as she spoke, head thrown back and lifted to the sun, as if drinking in all its energy.

"Then I think this is the spot where you should say your vows," said Tessa. "You and Brett can be married right where you're standing. Your guests seated below… a full spread in the glass conservatory party room…"

"It's called the 'glass dining hall,' actually," contributed Myra. She was sitting on the fountain's edge, still sipping water from one of the hotel's complimentary bottles, and looking slightly bored—or maybe that was her natural dullness shining through.

Tessa ignored this snooty correction. "Of course, we'll need Brett's opinion before we can make this possibility a certainty in your plans," she added.

"Oh, he'll love it," said Harper. "He knows I always dreamed about getting away to some private tropical island, having a real vacation of luxury there. That's how I ended up in the travel agency business in the first place, though I had a chance to make a dollar an hour more by managing the night shift at the pizza parlor one street down. I guess I was dreaming of the day I'd get some breathtaking experience in some spot of paradise—though real life turned out to be about following around managers on routine tours, and checking the softness and hardness of mattresses in regular hotels where people usually stay."

She sighed deeply. "I still can't believe all this is happening to me." Her voice softened. "He keeps saying I can have whatever I want, however I want it. It's like he made me into a princess or something. An island princess whose wedding is a dream come true."

"Island Princess it is," said Tessa, smiling as she made a note. Behind her, Ama was examining one of the bright canna blossoms up close.

"Do either you or Brett have a favorite tropical flower?" she asked.

The bride-to-be snapped back to the present-day world. "Brett is a roses' guy," said Harper. "That's what he always sends me: eleven red and one white in a box on Tuesdays. Me, I like the bold stuff."

"Brett's favorite flower is the white carnation," said Ashleigh. "It's not very tropical, is it?"

"That's his favorite?" said Harper. "I've never heard him say that. We go to the florist up the street together sometimes, he never picks those for a bouquet or anything."

"He has two delivered every week to his office for the bud vase on his desk," said Ashleigh. "Every week. And it says so on this sheet he provided for me to use on his behalf." She held up a neatly typed list of items with categories like "color," "wine," and "spice," Tessa noticed.

"So… that's a no on favorite tropical flowers?" said Ama. "What about tropical flavors?"

"I love mango, coconut, kiwi. Passion fruit, that's just the stuff to die for, in my opinion," said Harper. "I like fruit around the house, and I order all those flavors when I'm at a restaurant. Brett not as much—he keeps a little bowl of apples at his place. He always orders the fancy plain stuff, the crème brûlées and those little chocolate mousses."

"Strawberries," said Ashleigh. "He likes them domestic, preferably. Blueberry parfait is his favorite dessert."

"Blueberries?" repeated Harper.

Ashleigh checked the sheet, as if confirming this fact, but said nothing else.

Harper shook her head. "I'll ask him, I guess," she said. "He never mentioned anything about them before. But I'm sure he likes something besides white carnations and domestic strawberries, which I've never seen him buy, even when we stopped by one of those swanky organic food stalls."

"Let's move on to the possible reception site," suggested Norris.

The "glass dining hall" was the obvious choice, since its conservatory-style construction would allow guests to watch the sunset without the direct glare of a full west view. More lush tropical plants decorated this space, though Norris assured them it could be "toned down" if so desired.

"Now, there's a lovely spot out on the south lawn where we can pitch a big marquee, if that's what y'all prefer," he said, indicating a place on a map of the grounds on his phone. "One of those big silky tents with some very nice little lanterns—we have some of those torches that keep away the bugs, so don't worry about them. Just think of all those pretty little paper globes lit up. Or we have some very chic new ones, made like those big old Edison bulbs, only as sweet little miniatures."

"I'd love to see some photos of previous events here," said Tessa.

"I think I like this room," said Harper. "We could put a big dessert table for the cake right over there, couldn't we? There's room for tables all through here."

"It's probably sufficient to hold Mr. Winship's guests," said Ashleigh. "He only has 200 listed—only his closest associates."

His closest associates number at 200? Tessa didn't think she herself knew 200 people distantly, much less closely. "Can we put a temporary dance floor on the lawn for the reception?" she asked the director. "In case the bridal couple would like to hire a DJ or a band?"

"We can do that," he assured her. "Or we can throw open these doors to this little room here that leads to the ballroom. Big enough for a small orchestra, I always like to say."

"There's a ballroom?" said Natalie. "Wow. You *do* have it all." She pushed open the pocket doors in question behind a large marble statue, revealing a tiny conversation zone, its pocketed double doors opening to a large ballroom with wainscot walls, a heavy chandelier, and a polished marble floor.

"I think it's perfect," said Tessa. "How do you feel, Harper? I assume you and Brett have discussed the possibility of providing entertainment at your wedding?"

"Sure," she said. "Maybe a nice jazz band, or something people can dance to. I want them to play our song. You know, the song you hear with that person for the first time and you just fall in love all over again?"

"Not that I'm trying to interfere," said Myra, who was studying the label on her bottle as if it contained an important message, "but we *do* have several contacts in the music business who might be able to provide an entertainer of actual fame to sing at your wedding."

"Really?" Harper looked amazed.

"I think Brett has already mentioned Enrique Imerez," said Ashleigh. She consulted her sheet. "Or the classical singer Pablo Montova."

"Pablo Montova?" repeated Natalie. "That guy who sings love songs to sold-out stadium crowds?"

"The one and only," said Myra. She checked her watch and sighed, quietly. Maybe she had a tee time for this afternoon as well.

"I have one of that Enrique guy's CDs," said Ama. "He's that 'Latin Beat Hearthrob,' isn't he?"

"That's who Brett has in mind for the wedding?" Harper sounded as disbelieving as the rest of them. "Oh my gosh. I can't believe it. He never said anything to me."

"I'll let you know as soon as I hear a reply from his booking agency," said Ashleigh, to Tessa more than Harper, and only because Blake had stayed behind at the gazebo earlier, in conversation with one of the groundskeepers about the history of its construction.

Harper fanned herself. "See what I mean?" she said to Tessa. "He's amazing. How does he think of this stuff?"

"Are they your favorite singers?" asked Tessa, sitting beside the bride on a marble bench near the windows. Brett must be taking his "anything goes" policy for his bride very seriously.

"No, but... but they're famous," said Harper. "I've never had anybody famous serenade me. It's like one of those episodes of *The Bachelor* where they go to some ballroom and there's a Frank Sinatra impersonator singing just for them, or something. Only bigger."

"He must be quite a guy," said Tessa. "I can't wait to meet him." Mostly because it felt weird to have the groom represented by a facts sheet in this process, although she was also feeling curious about the apparent prince who swept Harper off her feet, no doubt to the consternation of his parents.

"You'll love him," said Harper. "He's such an incredible guy. I'm still making myself believe that he really wants to marry me. You know, I laughed when he opened the ring box. I thought it was a joke, I swear. He had to propose twice, just so I would believe it. Can you imagine?"

"I suppose so," said Tessa. "If you weren't expecting someone to declare they loved you that much, it would be sort of a shock." She could imagine it, although she would never admit who was making that declaration in her fantasies, especially not within Natalie's hearing.

Tessa clicked her pen. "Tell me a little about him," she said. "Sometimes knowing a little about a person helps us come up with ideas for the wedding that will matter to them."

"Wow." Harper took a deep breath. "He's... he's really focused. He's calm and cool. It's really hard to rattle him. I've actually never seen him angry. Or upset. He just keeps his eye on whatever the goal is, and does it. But he's sensitive. I mean, he sends me flowers every week. He opens doors, stuff like that."

"He likes romantic movies? Romantic music?" suggested Tessa. "He's the knight in shining armor type, who likes to sweep in when someone's in trouble?"

"I don't know about that last part," said Harper. "I mean, I imagine he would help anybody who needed it. He's just such a stable, reliable person... he's so... put together," she finished, after a long pause of searching for words. This one seemed to satisfy her.

Tessa's pen doodled a little flower in the corner of her notebook.

The Wedding Belles dined alone that evening, since scheduling conflicts had called away the bride and other members of the wedding party. The Palmetto Isle Resort's restaurant promised a "culinary palette of modern, fresh, and flavorful dishes," which Ama was eager to try.

"I'll handle booking the photographer if you want," said Natalie. She buttered one of the restaurant's famous southern buttermilk rolls and took a bite. "Mmm, that's really good. We couldn't do better, and Ma's been collecting bread recipes for years."

"You can also handle the wedding favors and the confetti for the departure," said Tessa. "And maybe contact someone about fireworks and permits—something tells me Harper and her groom want a grand finish for the ceremony, or maybe the big moment of departure. We need some ideas to show Harper by the end of next week. And Brett, if he ever appears." She checked her notes. "Ama, of course, will talk to the kitchen about catering and handle the cake as soon as we're sure of our theme."

"I'll go through some of my old sketches so I have a few suggestions to throw out when Harper's ready for that decision," promised Ama.

"I'll get on the invitations, and call Accented Creations and try to book an appointment for Harper to see their showroom presentation in a couple of weeks," said Tessa. "I'm pretty sure we've seen the ceremony site and reception site today, if the look on the bride's face is our judging point."

"Sorry I'm late." Blake pulled up a chair at their table, his back to the view of the balmy mansion grounds. "The guy tending the grounds showed me the path down to those rocks connected by bridges. There's a pretty sweet view from the far point." He opened the menu, scanning the selections. "So, how'd the rest of the tour go?"

"We're hired," said Tessa. "So really well."

"What do you need me to do?" he asked, grinning. "Book the band? Carve an ice sculpture for the buffet?"

"You can take off your tie," said Tessa. "You're off duty now. Unless you want to help us lay out seating arrangements in the glass dining hall."

"I can do that," he said. "I was thinking… if your couple is fond of island stuff, why not have something kind of unique at their reception, instead of a standard chocolate fountain? An ice fountain for fresh fruit or something. I saw one before that was basically a three-tier serving tray."

"That sounds pretty cool, actually," said Natalie. "No pun intended."

"Thanks." Tessa made a note of it in her book. She tried not to notice as Blake loosened his tie and shrugged off his suit jacket. He rolled his sleeves back. *Do not think about him differently from any other co-worker*, she reminded herself. For the hundredth time today alone.

"If you ran a clear plastic beverage hose through it, you could pump champagne over the top and into the tiers instead," suggested Blake. "Fresh chilled, and with strawberries standing by for the glasses."

"Why don't we invite him to more of our meetings?" asked Ama.

"Because he has a real job that pays better than working with us," said Tessa. "And we still haven't paid him for fixing those windows upstairs so they actually open."

"You will," said Blake. "I have confidence in you." He buttered one of the rolls from the bread basket. "Sorry I interrupted, by the way," he added, apologizing to them collectively. "You were probably in the middle of discussing big plans when I walked in."

"I think we've already discussed them," said Ama. "We start next week when Harper and Brett pick their theme and colors, and we'll go from there. Flowers, cake design, table arrangements." Her eyes lit up as the waiter set her dessert in front of her, the coveted blueberry Italian cream cake. She dug a fork in eagerly, a little moan following her first bite.

"No dress for me, though," said Natalie, knowingly. "I feel in my bones that Myra Winship has the name of some premier designer up her sleeve. Just wait."

"She seems pretty hands-off," said Blake. "I wouldn't be too sure. I heard Harper asking her about something, and she just threw out an answer like it didn't matter."

Too hands off, Tessa thought, privately: not in a way that respected Harper's right to decide these things, but in a way that suggested resignation. Had Brett warned his parents about interfering? It was a precaution worth taking in some cases, as the wedding they planned last December proved. Maybe that's why the Lucas family wasn't planning to be involved with the process, either.

"We'll make this event as special as possible, and not because it has an impressive budget that would run any other we've planned under the table," said Tessa. "Because Harper deserves to have her dream come true."

"Here's to that," said Natalie, lifting her glass. Four water goblets clinked together, as Tessa vowed quietly that this wedding would be as perfect as possible. The best wedding ever planned by the Wedding Belles, that would draw new clients to their doors and signal a whole new era for their business.

How could this wedding be anything else, with a dream like Harper's behind it?

Chapter Ten

"Anything you have that looks like a miniature Triton's trumpet would be great," said Natalie. "What colors? I see… Can you send me a price quote for 400? Thanks." She hung up and made a note about the large seashells on her list of possible wedding favors and table decorations, next to a price quote for tiny folded paper boxes shaped like orchids.

She lifted the blouse lying across the counter and added another stitch to the cuff's buttonhole. This afternoon the photographer would expect to see two models dressed in outfits from her sketches; better not disappoint if she wanted the juicy exposure the Magnolia's runway catalog offered prospective buyers.

Balancing everything was tough. A part of her wished Tessa understood exactly how much so, and didn't think she was simply shoving Wedding Belles in the background. Maybe she should talk to her, Natalie reflected. But only when Blake wasn't around to provide a distraction.

The front door bell jingled as a customer entered, and Natalie hastily stowed the blouse out of sight. Looking up with an expectant smile, she discovered the prospective customer to Icing Italia was only her brother Rob.

"You know, Ma's probably tired of picking little pieces of thread out of her cannoli," said Rob. "Two dozen crullers, by the way. I have some hungry guys waiting on my shift."

"You could serve yourself," Natalie said, although she assembled a bakery box at the same time. "You don't have broken fingers."

"Yeah, but I'm not in an apron. It ruins the effect." He stole a strawberry turnover from one of the other glass bakery cases. "Don't take all the leftover raspberry Danishes, okay? I want to take some on this picnic I'm planning for Kimmie."

"Now that you finally have working transportation at the ready, after two years of hitching rides off everybody else?" Natalie slid three crullers into the bakery box. "You could have replaced that truck's transmission a year ago."

"Yeah, well, live and learn."

She fastened the folds for the box's top. "I saw Brayden the other day at work," she said. "Weird, actually. I hadn't seen him in months. I guess I thought he quit the delivery business."

"Nope. He changed routes back… end of January, I think." Rob stuffed the rest of the turnover in his mouth. "Got a cushy one from some guy who moved or something."

"Good for him." Natalie closed the box lid. That explained why he didn't deliver the bakery's specialty ingredients anymore.

"I haven't seen much of him myself," said Rob. "He's got other friends, stuff to do. I'm crazy busy these days, now that Kimmie's transferred closer to the city."

"Brayden has other friends?" said Natalie, only half-joking. Brayden had always been teased as having only Grenaldis for friends. "Somehow I can't imagine his mom cooking dinner for a whole table full of delivery guys."

"He doesn't live with his mom. He has his own place," said Rob. "Didn't you know?"

She didn't, actually. Odd, because her mom usually told her everything about Brayden's life, along with a half-dozen other people in whom Natalie had very little interest. Something as big as Brayden—the perpetual homebody who mowed his mom's grass and bought the weekly groceries—finally getting his own pad should've made the list of interesting tidbits at Sunday brunch.

"Wow. That's a big step for Brayden," she said, somewhat impressed. "I figured he'd make over the basement into a bachelor pad eventually." Not that she'd ever thought about Brayden's future with that much detail, truthfully.

"This was ages ago. Keep up with the world, will you?" Rob took the bakery box as she set it on the counter. "Tell Uncle Guido when he comes in that I want some of that pasta salad he's making for Renny's deli."

"Hey, you didn't pay for those crullers," said Natalie. "You're eating Ma out of house and home, now you're taking her business goods?" Rob had the appetite of a bear. He had once eaten an entire box of powdered doughnuts in one sitting on a dare.

"I'll catch her later," said Rob, with a grin.

"You need to take this place more seriously, Rob. You think it runs on ingredients left to us by Italian bakery elves?" she asked.

The door closed behind him. Natalie rolled her eyes. Why didn't Rob ever volunteer for bakery duty? When he did, it was always minding the pastry ovens in the back while he read old paperbacks and watched movies on his phone. He didn't have to read off ingredient lists to picky customers who didn't like almonds, or explain why they didn't have Italian Christmas bread in stock today. No wonder the Grenaldi family never wanted her to move to a big design house outside Bellegrove—it was probably because they knew secretly that Rob would eat all the stock from the shelves in one afternoon while minding the store.

*

While Natalie was serving two of Icing Italia's cheerful regular customers their morning pastries, on the other side of Bellegrove, Ama was taking her morning break with a new twist on eggs Benedict at a bistro near the light rail station. Across from her, Luke sampled some of the restaurant's famous pepper jelly, shaking his head a little before Ama could try it.

"Save yourself," he said.

"That bad?"

"That stuff your brother made for that curry dish was a lot better," said Luke. "I think they need more sugar to offset the spices or something."

He settled forward, meeting Ama's gaze. "I got some tough news the other day," he said.

"What?" She paused while squeezing a sweetener into her coffee.

"My shop's building is for sale," said Luke. "The owner thinks he has a buyer—some guy who wants to put in a pawn shop. I figure I'll have to close by the end of the month."

"Luke, that's terrible." Ama's jaw dropped slightly. "No warning or anything?"

He shrugged. "They made him an offer he can't refuse. I can't blame him, since the building's pretty old. It needs a lot of work that he can't afford to give it."

"What are you going to do?" He couldn't paint bikes on the streets. Luke's room above the drugstore was on a street where rental space didn't abound. "Can you find another place?"

"This short notice, probably not. I'm going to have to rent a garage locker to park my bikes, and tell my customers I'll probably be closed for a while. But that's life, you know. We don't know when things like this are going to happen, but we have to roll with them afterward." His smile was lopsided. "Fortunately, I have some marketable skills, so I won't starve."

"Still… I'll miss your place," said Ama. "And I don't want you to be stuck doing something temporary after building a business you really love."

She knew what that was like from experience—cooking curry and rice at the Tandoori Tiger would never be as exciting for her as the thrill she felt for perfectly frosted cupcakes or discovering candied fruit sprinkles existed. In Luke's shop, with the exciting pungency of fresh paint, diesel, and hot metal sparking beneath a welder's torch, she had sensed something of his personality in the air. Part artistry, part hands-on labor, and an air of gritty adventure that fought its way between the cracks of the real world.

"I'll find a new building somewhere, with a little time to search," he said. "Of course, I'll have to make some more money first so I can make the deposit. I thought maybe of piggybacking off a mechanic friend's garage business, if he has some space and needs an extra pair of hands to help with the mechanical side of things." He stuck a fork through his fried eggs. "Or I could always wash dishes at an Indian restaurant," he added, as a joke. "If your dad would have me."

Ama's smile became a little dimmer. "I'm sorry," she said. "I know that he's not trying very hard—"

"It's okay, Ama," said Luke. "It takes time. I think maybe he likes me a little better than when we first started seeing each other."

That probably wasn't the case at all; he didn't know that Ama had all but twisted Ranjit's arm to get him to move to a first-name basis with her boyfriend. "It's hard for my parents, especially him, to accept anybody into our family at first," she said. "But maybe he only needs more time. I mean, my brother thinks you're one of the coolest people on the planet. That must count for something."

"Hey, if that's a compliment, I'll take it," said Luke, with a faint smile. "Don't worry about the rest, Ama. We'll get there." He touched her hand, fingers softly tracing her own.

She met his eyes. "I really do love that confidence," she said. "You always see the bright side. One of my favorite things about you. That, and your philosophies, which are *so* the opposite of everything I've ever known."

"And the tattoo?"

"I mostly love it," she said. "But… I think I would have to think about it before I decided if I would love any others—like that really long sleeve-style one your friend Jenkins sports."

"I won't get one of those, promise," said Luke. "Not without asking." He kissed her lips, lightly, as he rose from the table. "I'll grab some extra creamer and see if they have some hot sauce for your eggs."

"Thanks," she said, and waited at the table with a long sigh of worry for what Luke was going to do. Luke as a responsible businessman had been the only part of her so-called "wild boy" that Ranjit liked. He definitely wouldn't be thrilled to know that part was about to be gone.

*

As Ama spiced her lackluster hollandaise with a little red pepper sauce, Tessa was on her way to a modern high-rise far from this eclectic little railway diner, to meet with perky Ashleigh the assistant. The assistant had phoned to see if Blake was available instead, since it would be "so much trouble" for a planner like Tessa to come.

"Mr. Ellingham's busy," Tessa explained. "It's no trouble for me to swing by your firm and pick up the package, so don't worry." She knew that Ashleigh was probably deeply disappointed by this fact.

Winship Plastics Company headquarters was on the fifth floor of the glass high-rise in the newest business district in Bellegrove, a zone that smacked of too much modern, sanitized industrialization for Tessa compared to the city's traditional architecture. She pushed the elevator's button and rode to the reception desk. Behind a simple glass rectangle, Ashleigh was speaking into a Bluetooth phone mic as she rearranged files on a tablet computer. She offered Tessa a toothy business smile.

"Mr. Winship wanted me to deliver this to the wedding agency," she said, pushing a box across the desk. "He said a friend of his designed it, and that he'd like one ordered for each guest as part of the wedding favors. It's sort of a charity thing," she added, in a whisper.

"You mean it's for charity?" asked Tessa.

"No… that is, the artist is really poor… sort of a naturalist handicrafts type… and Brett felt cornered when they approached him in the cafe to catch up on old times," said Ashleigh. "Anyway, there's a card in there. Just take care of it however you think best. Oh, and say hello to your partner Blake for me, will you?" Another smile, then she answered her latest call with a trilling voice. "Winship Plastics Company HQ, this is Ashleigh speaking."

Outside the elevator, Tessa unfastened the tape on the box, one which Ashleigh clearly could have mailed to their office address with an email of explanation sent first. It was just a maneuver to see Blake again… Then again, her coming down here had partly been in hopes of seeing Brett the groom in person to make her first assessment of the elusive second half of her current client, since he hadn't made it to the meeting at the resort. So maybe she couldn't fault Ashleigh for using work as an excuse to appease some form of curiosity.

Inside, she found an odd-looking miniature parrot made from pieces of bark and natural wood, with mismatched seed eyes and a tiny beak of dried nuts. *Made from all recycled park maintenance materials*, proclaimed the tag dangling from its little claw feet made from some kind of twig. It was whimsical and eccentric, and, apparently, would be distributed by the hundreds to Brett Winship's friends and family so he could escape having a conversation with an old friend.

Is this really the right platform for escape, Tessa wondered? But since it wasn't her place to question it, she tucked it back in the box. At least a starving artist would eat their next meal knowing it had a place next to the celebrity wedding singer's CD and the expensive hand-painted shell-shaped chocolates Natalie had located from an online shop.

Chapter Eleven

"Icing Italia, how may I help you?" Natalie answered the phone, cradling it against her shoulder as she shifted her attention between the ages-old schedule daybook for the bakery's shifts and the question Cal had emailed her earlier in the day.

"Is Maria there?"

"Sorry, she had a doctor's appointment and won't be back until tomorrow," said Natalie. "Can I take a message?" The voice on the other end was familiar, and Natalie's brain placed it in a lightning-fast realization before it spoke again.

"That's all right. It wasn't anything important."

"Brayden?"

"That's me. But I still don't have to leave a message. If you think of it, just tell your mom later that my mom wants to change her order to three dozen cupcakes."

He had recognized her voice at first word, probably. "I can do that," she answered. "Um, can I do anything else for you?"

"No, not really." A long pause. "How's your work?"

He was making awkward small talk, an equal attempt at politeness. Natalie shifted gears, trying to respond in a like manner. "It's great," she said. "Same stuff as always. Lots of sewing."

"I saw your business cards. They look pretty snazzy," he said.

"You did?" Natalie said. "Did Ma give you one?" Her mother had passed them out like candy, pride for Natalie's venture outweighing the usual skepticism for her choice of career.

"Rob did. He said you were doing a fashion show pretty soon. Guess it's probably that big one that's been advertised in the papers, isn't it? I saw its billboard out by the old town exit the other day."

"I didn't realize you followed the fashion news." She was kidding a little bit, since everybody knew about Brayden's attempts to follow along with her life from a distance.

"Guess I pass it on the way to the comics," he answered.

She laughed, which was usually hard for her in conversations with Brayden. "Yeah, it's the same one," she said. "But it's not a big deal to anybody who's not part of the local fashion clique. We're just testing the waters to see if anybody likes our brand."

"You've got good taste. I don't see how anybody could dislike it," he said. "The guy you work with posted a picture online the other day, of something you were working on. It's got class, from what I can see."

"We're hoping so," said Natalie. "My goal was to create something for everybody, inspired by vintage couture—make it timeless, make it flattering, so everybody feels like they have a little bit of glamour in their wardrobes. I want to do it for all sizes, because the picture we have of beauty and glamour has changed so much... there was a time when curves were great, then suddenly they weren't, and when the fashion era forced everybody who wasn't super-skinny to wear tents rather than expose the fact that they didn't have society's notion of the ideal body size or shape."

"Sounds like what my mom says every time she tries to find a blouse that looks good without doing that thing they all do when they're kind of fitted," said Brayden. "You know, outline the muffin top."

"See what I mean? There are ways to make things fit without highlighting issues people are self-conscious about," said Natalie. "It's about picking the right fabrics, the right garment cuts and seam structure... all while creating something that feels like it won't go out of style and could've been in the closet of any glam girl in the past, whatever size she was."

"There were Hollywood stars and models you see in some of the old pictures who couldn't squeeze into a size zero," said Brayden. "So is this for your online shop?" he asked. "All these designs you're working on?"

"It will be. I mean, if we get some interest at the show, and we can come up with enough creative designs to feel confident about trying to retail them. We'll be rolling out our first plus sizes, and presenting some accessories that Nella is designing."

She had been chatting forever about this, she realized, babbling on and on, as if Brayden actually cared what they were doing with their work or how she planned to launch the sale of their couture. Given his crush, he'd probably listen to her babble about cheese varieties if she chose that topic, but that wasn't an excuse. She didn't do this to Chad, after all.

She cleared her throat. "So how are things with you?" Back to politeness, a quick switch from personal topics that she never dared go into with Brayden before. "You must be pretty busy these days yourself."

"Good. I have been pretty busy actually. You know, all the stuff with work. A friend's restoring a hot rod, so I've been helping him on the weekends. And I've got practice with the softball team from work."

Brayden *did* have friends who weren't Grenaldis. Natalie was relieved to hear evidence of this, and not just from Rob's anecdotes. The image of Brayden engaged in masculine activities like engine repair and athletic sports was also new to her. Of course he wasn't a scrawny kid anymore, and hefting big packages around all day for the delivery company had probably resulted in some muscles beneath that green uniform, though she hadn't bothered to wonder before now. Discussing Brayden's hobbies with him had been taboo, since she was always so intent on dodging conversations that might give him the wrong impression of her feelings.

"I guess if I order a package this week, you'll be the one who delivers it to my building," she told him. "Driving somebody else's route for a change?"

"Change is good, they say," he answered. "I've been trying to make some lately. It's not easy." He hesitated. "I guess when you've been used to life being a certain way, you feel like you're losing something when you move in a different direction. Kind of like you're losing a part of yourself, even if you're moving on to something better. Makes it kind of hard to know at first if you're doing the right thing."

There was a seriousness somewhere deep in Brayden's voice that Natalie wasn't sure how to interpret. She used to practically read his thoughts, but that was because he always wore them on his sleeve. Along with his heart, though Natalie had always done her best to avoid reading that part of him too deeply.

"Uh, Natalie? I have to go, actually. If you could just tell your mom—"

"I will," she answered, quickly finding her voice again. "I'll let her know."

"Thanks. Bye."

*

"Here's something that's been begging to see you." Luke pushed a little beribboned box across his kitchen table, next to Ama's chopsticks and a vase of two slightly wilted dandelions.

"Luke, you already gave me a birthday present," she protested.

"I wanted to give this to you then, but it hadn't arrived yet," he answered. "Go on. It's the real present; the comb was just something extra." He folded his arms as he waited.

Ama opened the box. "Oh... wow... where did you find this?" From inside, she lifted a little wooden mold. A hand-carved gingerbread mold from Europe, to be specific—something she had only seen in books until now. A little peasant woman, hands on hips, surrounded by stalks of grain with a bird flying above. It reminded her of old illustrations in German storybooks.

"My friend who's a baker. She had a friend in Hungary who inherited a bakery a while ago. It's closed now, and the friend doesn't bake much, so she sold the molds to collectors."

"Luke, you shouldn't have. Especially now, since you're losing your shop. This must have been so expensive," she said, laying it gently in the box again.

He shrugged. "I bought it before I knew for sure it was happening," he said, dismissively. "Listen, don't worry about it." He lifted the skillet from the stove, spooning fried rice onto two mismatched plates from his cupboard, as Ama opened the box of sweet-and-sour chicken from the Kung Pow Express on Luke's street.

He sat down across from her again, placing a glass of water beside her plate. "I got a job offer today," he said. "That's what I want to talk to you about."

"Someone offered you a place? That's awesome." She lifted her feet off the neighboring chair, feeling surprise and relief. "Is it a space for your shop?"

"Not exactly. A friend of mine who's been working as an art dealer here owns a hotel and needs a guide to operate a simple boat tour along the coast for the summer and autumn seasons. The pay would be enough for me to save up money for another garage. Downside…" He paused, trepidation in his voice. "It's overseas. In Portugal."

The world had stopped spinning momentarily; Ama felt it freeze beneath her very feet. "What?" she said. "You're leaving?"

"Maybe. I know." He smiled, wryly. "I know it's pretty crazy. But it's cool at the same time. I've never been there before. He's got a place he can let me have for the tourist season, kind of a bungalow on the hotel grounds. The job's easy to learn, fairly safe, and there's time off. I can see part of Spain, maybe backpack across Morocco—there's a lot of places to go that aren't on the beaten path for tourists. I can even take my motorcycle, or maybe I'll find a vintage model over there in need of fixing up. I could do some work on European bikes on the side, since I know my way around foreign models pretty well."

Her heart was beating like a drum as she listened to all this. "You're really taking the offer?" she asked. No more boxes of sweet-and-sour chicken or pea pods opened. Her appetite for Chinese food was gone.

"I'm thinking about it," he said. "I could work for change in a garage or two here, or find some other job that's just a job… but this would be something special." As he spoke, he reached across and took Ama's hand. "So, what do you think about coming with me?"

"To Portugal?"

"Sure," he said. "The hotel has a kitchen, and they always need new staff. My friend says there are plenty of staff bungalows available. You could learn Portuguese baking traditions, and see part of the world at the same time. You've always wanted to see it, to have adventures. Take a chance and come with me. We can spend the rest of the year just exploring and hanging out. It would be incredible."

She didn't know what to say.

"Come on." He squeezed her fingers, gently. "Your brother's right about you—there's an adventurer's heart in you that wants to explore new places. That's the first thing I noticed about you. The part of you that's dying to take a chance on new things."

Ama could feel his heart beating through his fingertips. She could feel the reassuring warmth of his touch, that of the first and only person she had ever loved romantically. Before her was a proposal to see the world. Collect snapshots in her mind of unseen places, unforgettable moments, with Luke wrapped up in them. No more mornings of mixing sticky dough to rise, of boiling sugar syrups as she waited for her coffee to perk, and Ranjit yawning over the morning paper. The scent of the wood-fired grill for cooking the meat, of saffron and turmeric in the air. No more wedding cakes for the Wedding Belles—not for months, maybe longer. Wanderers like Luke didn't always come home just because one adventure ended.

"I don't know," she said, softly. "Jaidev wasn't completely right. I dream of things… but I don't do them, Luke. I don't go places out of the blue, or see sights just because they're there. Imagination is one thing… but I'm used to a smaller world than you. My dream of baking fits in it, and so do most things I want."

"But you want things that don't too," he pointed out. "Everybody does. If you come with me, you could see if you're missing anything worthwhile."

"But this is… this is home for me. I've never planned to leave it, not really," said Ama. "There's a lot to leave behind if I do. It's sudden. I… I would have to think really hard about it."

She wouldn't just be leaving her online business and Wedding Belles, but her family, of course. Maybe a life of working at the Tandoori Tiger wasn't her goal, but it would be strange not to have her family around her like a constant heartbeat in the background of life. In fantasies, yes, she had run away with a knight on a horse to escape the tedium of chopping vegetables, minding rice pots, and listening to yet another customer's engagement party in the dining room. But in reality? She had never truly envisioned what lay in store for her on the other side of a happily ever after. What future she wanted most in life. That hadn't been a question she really faced until this moment, when someone asked her about it directly.

It would be easy for somebody like Natalie, who had dreamed about big fashion houses and exotic cities since she was a child. Not for Ama, whose dreams had finally come home in the form of sugar pastes, sweet syrups, and the romance of someone else's hand, the gentle routine of her own tiny world.

"Not even for me?" Luke asked.

This wasn't a question just about a few months in Portugal. Ama sensed this immediately and felt a strange shiver pass through her. Life with Luke would never be about settled locations and safe spaces, but about embracing the future, the world, the unknown. He lived for the open road, the open possibilities in life, and the part of Ama that loved adventure loved that part of him.

Was Luke asking if she loved him enough to become the same kind of person? Was this some kind of ultimatum on his part, about whether they would go on dating?

"Are you saying that we'll break up if I don't?" she asked. Quietly, but seriously.

"I'm not saying that. Of course not," said Luke. "But I don't want to have to miss you. I don't want to take a chance on a long-distance relationship if we don't have to. So I thought maybe we could find another way."

"I really love you, Luke," she said. "I want to be with you. These months we've spent together… they've made me happier than anything else I've ever known."

Her time with him had been incredible, to put it mildly. It changed the world to have a hand in hers on every train ride in the city, to have a person who wasn't related to her care deeply about her feelings and life. Sometimes she felt as if it simply changed things to know another heart beat for hers, in a manner of speaking, just like it changed the rhythm of hers to encounter the merest suggestion of Luke's presence. If that wasn't the first sign of love, then all the movies of Ama's youth had been totally erroneous in their depiction of romance.

"I know how you feel about me," said Luke. "You don't have to say it. That's not something I have to ask you to put into words at this point, except for maybe one."

He reached into his pocket and took out a gold circle, a miniature frame between his fingers. The stone set atop it was small, but Ama's breath still vanished at the sight. No huge diamond like Harper's could possibly shock her any more deeply than this one.

"Marry me," he said. "That's what I want, Ama. It's not about Portugal, or about where either of us is, or what we do for a living. But whatever I do in the future, whatever I'm going to do… I really want you to be with me for it."

Her eyes filled with tears. "Luke," she said, when her tongue actually found the ability to speak.

"It's sudden, I know. But I feel like we have such a strong connection. When we're together, it's like we have this harmony in our diversity. We fit, we match, even though we have different tastes and experiences, like the way the different angles of two puzzle pieces lock into place. We become whole. And it's a feeling I'd like to keep. I may never know anybody else who can make me feel complete that way."

Shock reeled through Ama. *Luke is proposing to me.*

"I want to say yes…" she began. The words were having trouble finding a way to the surface. "I want you—I want to stay with you, and have it last forever." *Just like in the movies. Just like the fantasies and the fairy tales… but I never saw this coming, not now.*

"That's what I was hoping for," he said, and tried not to grin.

"But—but this isn't just about Portugal, or where we are or what we do together," said Ama. "It's not even about what we do apart. This decision, it's about making a leap of trust. Not just in each other, but trust that we're right for each other."

Are you the one? That was the question in her head. It was so sudden, so soon—they had only known each other a few months. Believing in love at first sight, in spontaneous romance, should make her feel more certain of her powerful connection with Luke, but it didn't. It made her feel terrified. What lay on the other side of the sunset ride with her fairy-tale knight had never formed itself in her mind until now, when, suddenly, all the romance of it had to become reality.

Me and Luke forever? Backpacking the world, defying my father's last hope that I'll change my mind. Would it truly be the right thing? Is what we have really and truly a love worth challenging and changing everything we both know? How can I be sure?

"I told you, it doesn't have to be Portugal," he said. "Doesn't that help? We'll pick a whole new option, the two of us. Or when I come back, we'll decide what to do together then." He laid the ring on the table beside the little vase of dandelions. "I have never told anyone I've felt this way, Ama. I've never offered anybody a commitment like this one. This would be a whole new life for me—for both of us, together."

"I'm not sure I'm ready," she said. For any of it, though she didn't want to tell him about her doubts because that would only hurt him. "For adventures that just... sweep people away into new places and new dreams," she said. "For taking steps forward that would change our lives that much overnight. Or for anything," she added. Trusting herself that much suddenly seemed impossible.

"Why not?" he asked. "In your heart you've always dreamed of love. And adventure, too. I can't count the number of times you've told me that. What's wrong with now?"

She shook her head. "I can't tell you," she answered. "Maybe because I don't know myself as well as I thought I did." Her voice trembled. "I love you, I know that... but I never thought about what it would be like to face these decisions. I never thought about the reality of falling in love. Or what the future would be—what it really means to be with someone forever."

That was as close as she could come to saying what she felt. She loved Luke. That much was completely true. Why did she think that her choice could be the wrong one, or that her feelings could lead her to a mistake? Why think only about the problems it triggered with her family, her life, and any future feelings she might have... or think that the heart of a romantic like herself could suddenly turn fickle, or melt its deepest feelings to nothing in the face of a little conflict or trouble, especially given the way she asserted herself just to have this relationship with him.

I can't look him in the eye and make him a promise for a lifetime right now, not while I'm so confused. There's no taking back that first promise—that's what I've always hoped for in love, and I could never risk hurting Luke in the worst way by giving him one if I can't keep it and build a life with him.

"I can't imagine we'll go on like this forever, though," he told her, gently. "Us having lunch and dinner, just hanging out on weekends. I may be pretty casual, but I take my heart seriously. I take you seriously. I want you to believe that. I'm not just playing around, Ama, waiting to grow tired of you, you know."

He was so caring, so good at trying to ease tensions and untangle problems. Even now, when he was obviously having a difficult time understanding what was happening, he was still gentle, and still trying to make her smile.

"The big questions about where we go in the future and what we do, together and individually, it'll settle itself with time," he said. "I only want to know what's in your heart right now. That's the part that matters to me."

She nodded. "But what if I'm not ready to answer yet?" She lifted her eyes with this question, aware that the rim of tears in her own was making it difficult to see clearly. If she couldn't answer this question right now, would he understand? "It's so soon, Luke. It's so soon, and I…"

I have to be sure that I'll love you the way you deserve to be loved for a lifetime… and the way I've always dreamed of feeling about someone, even when we're old and gray. Somehow, she couldn't say those words aloud without losing control of her emotions and her voice, although she wanted to, and although it was the right thing to do so he could understand fully why the ring wasn't on her finger. The one thing that was stopping her was the idea that doubts would somehow drive him away. Losing Luke would be unbearable, and even a doubting Ama was firm about this fact. If he thought there was even the slightest chance she didn't love him, she had this wild idea he would say goodbye to her with all the suddenness of this Portugal job's acceptance.

In Luke's eyes, she saw a look of sadness that told her he didn't understand. Not really.

"What do you want me to say?" His voice was quiet. "I can't answer questions when I don't know the future, or who we'll be when it comes. If you want me to be part of it, I need to know. I don't want to make you choose between things you love, though. If you think being with me means you're losing your life and your family, then I get that you'd say no." He lowered his gaze as he stated this. "I don't want that for you. But things can't stay the same way forever for us, can they? I mean, we should start building a life together that we're both part of."

"I don't expect you to be part of the restaurant," she said quickly, shaking her head. "I never did. You know I didn't expect you to fit your life to mine or my family's."

"But what about you?" he asked. "Is it what you want, the life you already have? The city, the bakery, your business—would leaving them for even a little while be too hard? If you think there's a way to compromise, then let's talk. We'll figure something out together."

Here, in this moment, when everything was spinning out of control, she had no answers or ideas for Luke. Reality was getting the better of this moment, the one she had waited for all her life, and her silence was hurting a person who was more special and amazing than anyone she'd ever known.

She wanted to be with him. To keep life frozen at this point before it escaped her, or time somehow changed what she loved most about it. But that was impossible, because Luke was right: time simply changes everything.

Don't leave, Luke, she wanted to beg him. *No matter what, don't give up on us, not yet, please.* In Portugal, he would send postcards and emails, then maybe disappear forever in the coming months. And if he stayed—if she put on that ring to keep him here, and something happened to break the magic between them apart—he would be just as gone. How long would he wait for her answer? Days? Weeks?

"I want you to take this." He pushed the ring toward her.

"I can't. Not unless I say yes to you," she said. "Luke, please."

He didn't take it back. "I mean it," he said. "As much as I think you feel for me, I want you to have it. When you know what you're going to say, you can…" He paused. "You can give it back, if that's what you have to do."

"I don't want you to doubt how I feel about you just because I'm not sure right now what the future should be," she said. "Do you?"

"That's the last thing I want to do," he answered. His voice was quieter than before, however; Ama noticed this right away.

He lifted his plate and set it by the sink. He gazed out the tiny window above it, saying nothing. Ama felt horrible. Clearly, this wasn't how he envisioned the evening going. He thought she would leap at a chance to see another part of the world for a few months, and to be with him forever. That's how she always imagined it, too… until the moment actually came.

Forever was what she always dreamed of, wasn't it? Her perfect, spontaneous romance had reached impossible levels of feeling in mere months, if Luke was proposing to her. Could she say no to that for any reason? Even when it came to facing love's topsy-turvy effects on life? Surely her routine in the city didn't matter as much as the dream of sharing her life and all her passions with someone special. And no one as special as Luke had ever offered to be part of it until that day in the market.

"I, uh… have to leave the city for a while," he said, without turning around. "A friend has a friend in Georgia who needs a rebuild and wants me to do it for them. I wasn't going to take them up on the gig… but now I'm thinking maybe I should."

He didn't have to say why, but it was obvious he thought they needed some space to think. And maybe they did… but it still hurt. Ama swallowed hard and asked, "How long will it take?"

"From the end of the week until late June, probably. It'll be enough money for my ticket overseas. Two, maybe." He glanced at her, briefly. "In case you decide by then, and you want to come."

"Will I see you before you go?" She didn't want this to be the last conversation between them before Luke left, even it was only a temporary absence. And it was… right?

"Come to the station with me?" he asked. "Say goodbye?"

She nodded again. "I will."

She didn't touch any of the takeout boxes on the table. Neither of them was hungry anymore. Ama didn't even open her fortune cookie, which was her favorite part of Chinese takeout. She couldn't imagine what message tucked in that crisp little shell could possibly make all of this better. Love was messy, complicated, and chemically mixed up. In the movies, it always sorted itself into a perfect ending, but not in real life. In real life, you could make a tremendous mistake and screw up everything for good. Every question came with good possibilities and bad, and you couldn't see which ones would win the day until you were on the other side.

She rose and lifted her sweater from the neighboring chair. She looked at the ring on the table. Hesitating, she lifted it and closed it between her fingers and her palm. Luke shouldn't think that she didn't want it. Even if somehow, for some terrible reason waiting to define itself, she couldn't keep it in the end.

He looked at her again. "Call me when you get home," he said, softly. "So I know you're okay."

"Maybe we can talk some more," she said, wanting him to feel that this discussion wasn't over yet, though she had no words of explanation she could give him.

"I don't think you'll have made a decision between this rail stop and home," he answered, with a halfhearted smile. The truth of this statement hurt, for Ama knew he was right. She would probably agonize over this conversation the whole ride home without knowing if she was right or wrong to wait. She touched his shoulder then leaned up to kiss his cheek.

She had never thought about the day she might not be able to do that anymore. It could be here already, after four months of happiness. Why did things have to change, and reality have to come so hard so quickly in this romance?

Briefly, Luke's fingers laced with hers. He was upset, she sensed. He let go of her, and she shouldered her bag and opened the door to the stairs leading to the street below.

Leave the Tandoori Tiger, leave my family. They would be shocked if she actually did it. It was so sudden and so dramatic—exactly the thing they feared and dreaded about her falling for Luke. Off to foreign parts with a boy she hadn't even known for half a year. Her whole life would turn upside down, a steady job suspended for a culinary fling overseas, a quick promise binding her forever to another, and it could be either wonderful or horrible, depending upon how she and Luke made it work together.

But if she sidestepped this question and lost Luke in the process, what would she do afterward? Even with all her romantic imagination, she couldn't imagine loving anyone else this way, not now. To rip him out of her life would be like ripping off a piece of her own flesh: a grotesque idea, but the closest she could come to picturing that pain.

And all so she could roll a thousand more balls of sticky *gulab jamun* as she yawned over her morning cup of tea, and pursue her passion in the same two kitchens forevermore? Was she so afraid of change that she would cling to familiarity forever?

"You're back early," said Rasha, who was ironing restaurant napkins in the main dining room. "Didn't you and Luke have a nice time?"

"It was fine." Ama knew her voice sounded odd, so she kept her replies short. "I have to call him. Goodnight." She went upstairs before any sisterly gossip could follow—say, questions about whether she and Luke had been growing more serious as of late.

She dialed Luke's number. It went to voicemail. "It's me," she said. "I'm home safe. I love you. I'll call you tomorrow, okay?" There wasn't anything else to say. She knew he was probably staring at the screen of his phone, but not answering it. Being so careful not to say anything that would hurt either of them more than what had been said already... and left unsaid.

Sitting on her bed, she stared at the ring lying next to a pile of mini cupcake toppers on her bedside table, destined for Sweetheart Treats' next order of Cupcake Doll-inspired ones for her eighties-style dessert line. It twinkled a little next to the glittery half-dolls. It wasn't anything impressive in the jewelry world, but Ama felt as if a whole universe was encapsulated in that diamond. Her universe, as defined by everything she knew, loved, and dreamed, represented by one tiny stone.

What am I going to do? What if at the end of Luke's absence, he didn't come back, but bought a ticket to Portugal and flew straight to his friend's hotel? What if she decided her hesitation meant there was no way she could make the leap into the future this soon or ever—and she wasn't waiting for him at the station when he came back, but hiding from that truth, too ashamed to face him and admit it?

She had to answer him. And hide this ring in the meantime, so no one would find out about any of this.

Chapter Twelve

"I'll bet the salads here are wilted," said Chad. "I think I'll order the fish and some grilled vegetables." He laid aside his menu. "So how many garments do you have left to finish for the show?"

"Most of them," said Natalie, with a short laugh. "That's how it is. You alter everything until the last minute. I'm used to it, though, thanks to my time in Kandace's fashion internment camp." Her old boss had been a tyrant when it came to producing a fashion line… and pretty much everything else about her work. She treated her assistants like dirt and belittled every design that Natalie ever attempted to make for her boutique of supposedly avant-garde clothing. And yet, she had been positively livid when Natalie left to work for Wedding Belles.

"Maybe you should ask her to the show," said Chad. "It might show her what a good thing she lost when you quit."

"Me, invite Kandace somewhere?" said Natalie. "I don't think so. If I can avoid seeing her for the next two years, I'll consider that time well spent. She seriously hated my guts, my ex-boss. Trust me, we are never going to be buddies in the fashion world."

"I have a couple of ex-bosses like that," said Chad. "At least now I'm in a comfortable place where I don't have to worry about it anymore. I'm feeling confident that I'm looking at a promotion in the next couple of years, and a raise, too."

"Exciting," said Natalie. "What are you going to do with it?"

"Start saving for my future home in Ecuador," he said. "You know, invest in a mutual fund or something."

"Wait, what? A house in Ecuador?" Chad had never mentioned actually living in Ecuador, not that she could remember. "You're kidding, aren't you?"

"No, I'm serious. I think retiring there would be great. I love the culture, I could hike, climb, and raft to my heart's content. I'll still be in great shape if no accident happens to me, so I could be looking at twenty years of adventures."

"I can't see myself living in a foreign country full-time," said Natalie. "Even Europe would be a stretch for me." She did not have to say that most South American nations would be low on her list of choices for the wildlife alone.

"But what if you have a chance to work at a Paris fashion house?" said Chad. "You'd probably move then, wouldn't you?"

"I'd have to think about it," said Natalie. "If it happened, which it probably won't. Those chances are pretty rare in the fashion world. I don't know what I'd do, truthfully." Time and experience had altered some of Natalie's youthful aspirations, since reality didn't match the dream she'd held as a college freshman. She could admit this without feeling the sense of regret she would have expected, though.

"Don't tell me it's just because of your family?" he said.

"That's part of it, of course," said Natalie. "But I like fashion on a small scale—it gets really pretentious in a lot of the bigger houses. A lot of them wouldn't have the same goal as I have for my line, since they tend to focus more on unrealistic body types. And you have to be really thick-skinned, and willing to accept that they may crush your dream just to do it."

"I can't believe you'd pass on a major fashion house," said Chad.

"I'll cross that bridge if I come to it," said Natalie. She was being coy on the subject all of a sudden, as if the honor of a major fashion house's invitation wasn't anything that would rock her world to its core after working hard to emulate the individualistic style of labels from Milan to New York.

She surprised herself by saying any of this; it wasn't as if she was known for devotion to her hometown. Loyalty to the Grenaldis was one thing, but staying within arm's reach of them had always been something completely different in her book. Yet here she was, pretending that any career move that pried her away from her life and her experiences in Bellegrove would do just that: pry her away.

Maybe it was because of Chad's suggestion that he wanted to build a life elsewhere in the distant future, a life technically incompatible with hers. Clearly, this dream of Chad's existed separately from their relationship, since he knew she found Ecuador vastly less exciting than he did. Knowing her better hadn't altered his vision of the future, of the solo adventurer exploring the wilds of South America.

Had Chad ever pictured an alternative life, one with a dream they shared? Truthfully, she had never pictured Chad in her future either, though they were dating steadily, and everyone expected them to grow closer.

"What if, hypothetically, you married somebody who didn't want to retire to Ecuador?" she asked, trying to be playful in this hypothesis.

"I guess we'd talk about it," he said. "Try to find a compromise. But I can't imagine I'll end up with someone who doesn't share my passions, at least enough so that they won't mind living that life with me. At least part-time," he said. The movement of his head suggested a dismissal of all other ideas. "Look how far you've gotten, learning to appreciate a new culture. It falls into place if it's meant to."

"Mm-hmm," said Natalie. *She'll have to be a more outdoorsy woman than me*, she almost added, but caught herself in time. It would be weird to confess that she saw somebody else in that future with him, maybe. She should be picturing herself there, at least for the sake of this conversation.

Suddenly, Natalie felt tired. She reached for her glass of wine and sipped it carefully. She tried to picture herself in South America after years of fashion design, and found that it didn't work. Somehow it was easier to picture herself back in Icing Italia instead. Maybe teaching a grandchild how to sketch garments, or sew their first seam, and showing them one of the many dresses from her closet that had begun her own career.

Maybe that was an omen in their relationship, but Chad didn't seem worried about it, so she shouldn't be, either.

At work the next day, she pushed open the door to Wedding Belles and went upstairs to her office, the door between hers and Ama's held open currently by the prop wedding cake from the "Violets are Blue" window dressing a few months ago. One of the fake violets had fallen from the plaster frosting, leaving a gap in the topmost cluster.

"Is it just me, or are men incredibly hard to understand sometimes?" Natalie asked.

She leaned in the doorway between the two rooms, where Ama was sitting cross-legged before an open cupboard of craft supplies and Styrofoam layer cake shapes, one half-assembled for next month's window display. "Maybe it's just me that's the problem," Natalie continued.

"Do you think I expect too much? Is there anything between clingy and 'don't care' waiting out there, or am I expecting the impossible?"

That's when she noticed that Ama's eyes were red and puffy. Instantly, the petty problems of her love life evaporated. "Ama, what's wrong?"

*

Downstairs, Tessa put the finishing touches on her presentation outline for today's meeting with her client. Accented Creations had agreed to a showcase with one of their artists, and Tessa had already worked out three potential floor arrangements for the glass dining hall and the seating in the Paradise Garden—if these were the choices of her clients, that was. But she had received no indication from Harper that her fiancé would be there today to weigh in. Probably perky Ashleigh would contribute his opinions via satellite phone.

Don't be sarcastic, Tessa. She couldn't give any special reason for resenting her client's personal assistant, at least not one related to the job. If this was how Harper and Brett wanted to conduct their wedding plans, who was she to question it?

A screech from Blake's Skilsaw in the adjoining room brought her thoughts back to reality. The contractor was replacing some sort of moldy ceiling material in the bathroom, which he had informed her was a hazard to both health and safety, so Tessa hadn't tried to argue. The door was open, revealing a plywood-covered claw-foot bathtub serving as a makeshift workbench, and a pile of ruined ceiling tiles that looked soggy and gray. Blake stood on a ladder, stretching a measuring tape between two ceiling joists.

No suit today. Just his regular clothes, a faded pullover of gray cotton and a pair of jeans with a hole torn through one knee. Various fantasies of Blake's muscles involved in moving furniture, lifting heavy sheets of wall covering, and—occasionally—catching her once more after an errant stumble on a ladder had crowded Tessa's mind whenever she watched him working. Not anymore, though. Tessa was determined not to let her thoughts stray into wishful thinking when Blake had chosen someone else. Someone who wanted her to plan their wedding, no less.

When he glanced down and noticed her, Tessa knew she blushed. "How's it coming?" she asked, by way of covering for her presence.

"Great. I'll have all this out by tonight," he said. "I'll bring some period stuff I have in the back of my place that'll probably match what these tiles were like in their heyday. Of course, I'll have to make sure that leak in the roof is fixed first. Do you want a roofing guy, or do you want me to tackle it sometime this weekend?"

"Whatever you think," Tessa answered, nonchalantly.

"I'm cheaper. Does that help?"

"I guess I would have to pick you, then," she answered.

Blake on a roof in the hot Saturday sun, possibly shirtless... She could see this scenario as clearly as if it were a scene in a movie, only playing in her head instead. An image she quickly banished in favor of concentrating on the old tile that was chipped and worn on the countertop. Her face was hot enough to boil water if a kettle touched her cheek right now.

"You okay?" Blake gave her a funny look as he climbed down the ladder.

"Never better," she said.

"Are you going somewhere?" he asked, noticing her shoulder bag.

"Lunch meeting with a client," she said, remembering now that she was meeting Harper shortly. "We have to grab a couple of color charts and some sketches to show her."

"Say hi for me," said Blake, as he placed the board underneath the saw's blade.

Tessa's thoughts were firmly back on wedding stuff as she walked into Ama's office. "You know, I think we should tell Harper…" she began, but didn't finish. A sad and quiet version of her baker partner was sitting in an office chair, with Natalie's arm around her comfortingly.

"What happened?" Tessa asked. "Did someone die?" Her mind flashed to Ama's long list of family and extended relatives, thinking of emergencies and crises involving the sister who lived out of town, the brother-in-law at the conference, even healthy, hearty Ranjit, though he was well past his prime

"No," Ama answered, foggily. "Everything's okay." She shook her head.

"No, it's not," said Natalie. *Luke*, she mouthed silently to Tessa.

"Ama, what is it?" Tessa sank down on a footstool in the office. "Did Luke break up with you? Did you have a fight?"

"Not exactly," said Ama, vaguely. "I'm just in the process of maybe breaking my own heart. It happens." She shrugged her shoulders. "You can't be sure that love's fated by the stars, right?"

"Are you breaking up with him?"

"No—no, listen, everybody, it's not Luke. Luke is great as ever. I really love him… I have since we met." She dabbed her eyes with a tissue. "This is about me, not him. I'm mixed up, and I don't know what the right thing to do is. About anything in my life, really."

"That's my role, not yours," said Natalie, hugging her shoulders. "You're not the person who changes their mind about what's right every two minutes. Unless someone switched our personalities, I think this is just a case of quarter-life crisis, or some relationship jitters. It gets serious, you ask some questions, then you get past it one way or another and everything turns out fine."

"Think so?" Ama sniffled, trying to smile again, although it wasn't quite successful—maybe because one of her solutions could involve deleting Luke from the picture. "I'm taking things too seriously, I know. I'm not good at confrontation, or standing up until I'm pushed into a corner and there's no other way out. I mean, a proposal's just a question, really—"

"He *proposed*?" Tessa echoed, in utter surprise.

"What?" said Natalie, whose jaw had dropped momentarily. "Could you *not* lead with that information in the first place, thank you very much?"

"But I didn't answer him," said Ama. "And I keep asking myself why. Is it because everything changes? Or because I can't be sure this feeling can last the rest of our lives?"

"Listen, Ama. Everything will be fine. Obstacles come up, but they can disappear too," Tessa soothed, although she was still reeling slightly from Ama's casual reference to taking the plunge. "I don't know what the problem is, exactly, but I know that you'll figure it out because I've seen you fix situations here that *I* thought couldn't be fixed. You're the peacemaker between us, the calm person who always knows the right thing to say…"

Tessa's phone beeped just then, sucking her back to what had been transpiring moments before. "I'm so sorry," she said, helplessly. "The client—we have to be at the travel agency in ten minutes."

Ama didn't look like she was in any condition to talk about potential cakes and catering menus. Natalie sent Tessa a worried glance, traveling pointedly from Ama to the nearest tissue box. Clearly, someone had to stay, or else leave Ama alone in crisis.

"I've got this," said Tessa. "I'll take care of things with Harper. You two hold down the fort here and I'll be back as soon as the meeting's finished, I promise."

"I'll help Ama finish the cake for the window display," said Natalie.

Tessa squared her shoulders and tried not to feel distracted and worried as she watched Ama quietly brush away the latest tear that had escaped.

You've got this, right? she thought to herself, as if she had any choice in the matter.

*

The Blue Moon Travel Agency's windows were all but papered over with new and exciting travel prospects. A South Seas Island getaway in a retro sunset-pink image of tropical flowers and a floating cruise ship faced Tessa as she pushed open the door to Harper's office.

Her client was sitting behind her desk, clicking computer keys like mad as she chatted through a Bluetooth headset. She waved briefly at Tessa but kept talking.

"… then we could arrange a car so you can drive along the Amalfi Coast. There are three lovely hotels I know in Positano, any of which would make you happy, I'm sure. I'm emailing you the links and some photos that a couple of very happy customers sent me. Right. Call me when you decide, okay? Bye."

She pulled out the earpiece and laid it on the desk. "That's lunch," she declared, leaning back in her chair. "Another wedding anniversary couple. That could be me in a couple of years, I keep telling myself, but I still feel like I'll be saving my pennies in a big jar for a weekend in Atlantic City."

"When you're married to Mr. Industrial Enterprise himself?" Tessa laughed. Harper did, too.

"See what I mean? I'm crazy," said Harper. "Okay. Do you want a sandwich?" She opened a mini-fridge behind her desk. "I've got two here, one of those 'buy one, get two' deals. I can't resist a deal, if it saves even a buck or two."

"No, thank you," said Tessa. "I'm not that hungry." She opened her portfolio on Harper's desk, her gaze scanning the travel agency's little office space. It was smaller than she had pictured it from the outside in this past year of walking by at least once a week. Shabby carpeting on the floor, pea-green walls literally papered in old travel posters.

Harper kept a corkboard with postcards and printed photos from happy clients, featuring smiling faces with Caribbean seas or Eiffel Tower views in the background, and foreign postmarks on cards from Germany's Romantic Road and safaris in Kenya. Kind of like herself, Tessa thought, only hers were less exotic, and kept in a photo album.

Tessa discussed the possible details they were building around the island paradise theme, the work of the artist creating Accented Creations' upcoming "showcase" for Harper, and the wedding favors, lightly touching on the contribution made by Brett, who, of course, was absent again today.

"Now, according to the pertinent details on the fact sheet, you have five bridesmaids, right?" said Tessa.

"Is that what it says?" Harper's chair clicked upright as she leaned to confirm this fact. "Five it is, I guess." She caught Tessa's perplexity. "I... uh... don't have that many friends, actually," she explained. "That is, most of them live out of state these days and are too busy to be a bridesmaid on short notice. So Brett kind of filled in this part with some of his connections. A couple of friends from college, his best friend's fiancée... this exchange student his mother's hosting for a year from a university in Australia... and this girl he's been friends with forever, so she's practically like a sister." Something in Harper's tone conveyed a tiny bit of doubt for this last one.

"I see." Tessa added a note to the sheet in pencil: *bridal party = strangers*. "Dinner, not hors d'oeuvres, right?" she said. "For the reception?"

"Me? I like finger foods," said Harper. "But Brett kind of thinks it's improper. You should have everybody sit down, eat something fancy off china plates. I figure that's the way to go, since his family's kind of the focus when it comes to the guest list."

"What about yours?" Tessa asked. "Will we be meeting them at some of the planning sessions?"

"Probably not," said Harper, dismissively.

"At the wedding?" joked Tessa.

"Oh, they're coming," Harper assured her. "Probably. They just have other stuff, like I said before. But my parents will probably be there at least." Vague tone for this reply. "I figure I have time to fill them in on the wedding details later."

"Okay," said Tessa, making a note of this also, and finding it extremely odd. "But Brett's family will be involved?"

"Well… I think they'll have more ideas for it," contributed Harper, after hesitating. "But Brett keeps saying it's my big day, that all the decisions lie with me. So I guess this is it, huh?" She spread her hands, as if gesturing to both herself and Tessa in one.

"I hope we'll be seeing him at some of the meetings, at least," said Tessa, pretending she was joking a little, even though she was still a little serious—after all, she had never planned a wedding where half the couple was a mere shadow.

"Oh, sure," said Harper, nodding emphatically. "Next one, he'll be there, I promise. Unless he can't be, of course." She smiled. "So, can we look at those flower pictures? I'm excited about the idea of lots of tropical colors. That just feels exciting. Flower wreaths, leis—I've seen them all in cruise ship posters and in clients' pictures. Do you think I could go with a flower garland instead of a veil?"

"I'm sure that would be perfect," said Tessa, who could see the stars in Harper's eyes for this idea. "The bridal party could wear them, too." She made a note. "What about your dress? Where are we on that topic?"

"The designer's a friend of Brett's mother," answered Harper. "It'll be ready in a couple of weeks. I think maybe the bridesmaids should be in a tropical color. You know? Coral, maybe... or magenta. Is that something you guys could handle if I get you their measurements?" She studied the bright pictures from an Accented Creations' floral showcase entitled "Bold as Love" from last year. "The groomsmen could have little pocket handkerchiefs in that color or something."

The dinner would be three courses of exclusive plates created by the hotel's chef, followed by a dessert buffet featuring a towering five-layer cake at its center. Tessa took notes on all of these things, planning to ask Natalie if she wanted to offer couture bridal party gowns or simply help Harper select them from one of the city's more exclusive boutiques. Ama would be interested in knowing about the colors, of course... and while the buffet leaned toward fine chocolate, there might be room for Blake's suggestion about a frozen fruit fountain.

She stepped outside the agency, waving goodbye to Harper before the postered-over door hid her view of the agent answering yet another phone call. She turned in the direction of Wedding Belles, taking a few steps past the line of Mediterranean shores and London landmarks.

"Want to buy a piece of art?" asked a voice belonging to a man sitting on the fender of an open van parked at the corner, its compartment filled with small, funky-looking sculptures of metal displayed in packing crates.

"No, thanks," answered Tessa, stepping closer to the crosswalk sign's pole.

"How about one for free?" he persisted, having scrambled to his feet, a piece in hand. "Just for answering a couple of questions."

"I'm in a hurry. I'm not the kind of person who answers surveys or fills out questionnaires, I'm afraid."

"Just one question," he said. "The lady inside the travel agency: do you think she really loves the guy she's marrying?"

Tessa paused in the act of edging to the curb. "What?" she said.

"Humor me. Does she really love him?"

"Who are you to ask?"

His body language was that of someone considering how to answer. "Let's just say I have a strong curiosity on the subject," he said.

"Stay curious."

"Look, just give me a hint. Why are they getting married? Is it money? Is it looks? He's a workout buff or something, right? And she's very beautiful, that almost goes without saying."

"None of my business, I'm only here to plan the wedding, not explain the couple's chemistry," said Tessa. Her short tone of voice deflated the stranger a little. "The lady in question seems very happy and very excited."

"I'm telling you now, something is wrong with that wedding," said the artist. "Don't go through with it. Quit while you're ahead, but don't be sucked into the idea there's going to be some magical happy day at the end of it."

"Who are you to say?" demanded Tessa, incredulously. *Who is this weirdo?*

"You'll see," answered the artist. Tessa noted his appearance: rough clothes, dark hair in need of a trim, semi-attractive features despite a somewhat intense undercurrent to his personality. Not a friend of the groom, clearly, unless this was the parrot artist whom Brett was avoiding. Was this simply a crazy person who had chosen to fixate on another's situation? A semi-dangerous stranger she should be moving away from as quickly as possible right now?

She moved to cross the street. The artist stepped off the curb.

"Hey, deal's a deal." The artist put something in her hand, pressing her fingers around it. He turned back to his street corner, where a couple of shoppers leaving a music store were looking at his artwork.

The item in her hand was paperweight-size, a cluster of pointy layers gathered tight like a close, multi-petal flower blossom. It had a coppery sheen in places, a patina over its metal imbued with hues of pink and blue. It was pretty but an odd thing to give someone in return for the questions this stranger had asked her. On its bottom was taped a card with a name and studio printed on it, which came off in Tessa's hand.

Should she mention this to Harper, she wondered? To the other girls at Wedding Belles? Or just keep this weird incident to herself?

Chapter Thirteen

Harper's wedding plans had progressed as far as a date chosen at the resort for table arrangements, and a meeting booked with the chef for the plate tasting for the menu. Tessa received the texts the previous night, as well as a picture of the bride's gown for Natalie.

"We have a lot to do," said Tessa as she tapped her pen against her notebook. "Obviously, bridal couture for the rest of the party is still on the agenda, as is finalizing the flower arrangement after the showcase; and table centerpieces are still undecided."

"Brett's mother sent me a link to a gift bag vendor she thought would be suitable," said Tessa, texting it to the others.

"Hand-woven sheer silk?" Natalie raised an eyebrow. "Pretty impressive."

"I like the little pearl handles," contributed Ama. "Very elegant."

"So, Nat: sewing dresses or consulting this time?" Tessa asked.

"Consulting. I'm not sure I could meet the Winships' expectations, and I still have tons to get done for the runway show anyway," said Natalie. In a way she was relieved, although it felt as if she was letting Wedding Belles down by not having a role in their biggest job to date. *And you've been letting them down a lot more lately*, the little voice in her head accused her.

"Cake, Ama?"

Ama took a deep breath. "There's a lot of possibilities," she said. "But there's one that comes to mind that would be perfect." She opened her folder of original designs. "I've been waiting for the perfect wedding for ages. You can probably guess. It's—"

"—'Birds of Paradise,'" said all three girls in unison.

"I can't believe you finally get to create it for someone," said Natalie. "Talk about luck."

It was Ama's favorite sketch in her book: a multi-tiered creation of stunning white frosting and fondant flowers as vivid as their namesake. It held the very center of Ama's sketch board most of the time and had a close shave with a beach wedding last summer, but the bride and groom had decided sand dollars and starfish were a better fit in the end.

"I can't wait to make a layer for the cake tasting," said Ama. "Of course, that's only if Harper approves it."

"She'll love it," said Tessa. "How can she not? It's your best original design, and no one has ever appreciated it. She'll be the first—what could be grander for a society wedding than the debut of an original cake?"

"Did anybody notice we didn't bother to ask how the groom might feel about it?" said Natalie, with a laugh. "I mean, the bride's always first when it comes to approving things, but we don't even mention his name most of the time, like he doesn't exist."

"I know," Tessa said.

"It's kind of weird, isn't it?" said Ama.

"Comfort-wise, I'm not thrilled about it," said Tessa. "Even one meeting would be helpful. We're going entirely by what Harper says, and by the fact that even his parents seem pretty indifferent when it comes to the wedding, so long as it plays by society's rules."

"Maybe it's true that he only cares about marrying her," said Ama. "It means a lot, making that commitment. To some people, that's the only part they want. No big ceremonies, no big family weddings."

She realized both of her business partners were staring at her, clearly thinking of what had transpired in her life a few days ago. A deep flush appeared in Ama's cheeks. "Not that I would know anything about that," she added.

No talking about the Luke thing yet, apparently.

Tessa released a quiet sigh. "There's nothing we can do about our no-show groom, obviously," she said. "So we'll make the best of things on our own. Nat, what's the latest word on table decorations? Did you talk to any of those wholesale vendors? Polynesian Palace, or the Caribbean Souvenir Company?"

"Both," answered Natalie. "I like some of their seaside merchandise. I was thinking sand and shells would be nice, if she wants to go understated. But let's face it, big flowers in tropical colors would impress, and I think Harper means this wedding to lean toward glitz."

Tessa smiled, going over her to-do list. "I think we're doing great so far," she said. "This wedding will be our best, hands down."

"You say that about all of them," said Ama.

"I do. But I mean it this time," said Tessa. "How could it possibly fail?" She pulled out the sketches she had made over the weekend. "Here's my thoughts on the flowers, which I've emailed to Accented Creations to give the artist an idea of Harper and Brett's general wedding theme."

A *tap tap tap* of knuckles on the doorframe behind Tessa's two partners. "Hello," chirped Ashleigh. "It took me ages to figure out where everybody was—I waited downstairs in that little foyer for a while, then I thought I would come up here and try my luck. I hope it's not a bad time to discuss the seating chart for the reception?"

They exchanged glances. "Please, come in," said Tessa, testing the measure of her bright-and-businesslike smile. "Join us—we're actually talking about Harper and Brett's wedding right now."

"Perfect." Ashleigh seated herself in the wing chair near Tessa's desk. "Shouldn't... everybody... be here for this discussion?" she asked, glancing around the room. Thinly veiled hopefulness for catching sight of another. "I have the suggestions from Mr. Winship here, and the recommendations of his mother right here; those are the most helpful when it comes to putting the right people at the right tables," said Ashleigh, removing two laminated sheets from her bag.

Laminate? Tessa lifted one and scanned the little circles representing tables, the rectangular lines for the glass dining hall's floor plan. Little numbers for all the socialites and wealthy clients invited to the Winship–Lucas nuptials.

Natalie scanned the guest list. "There must be thirty tables here," she said. "That's before Harper's guests are seated.

"Oh, I think you'll find Miss Lucas's list is very small," Ashleigh assured them. "She'll need... one table, maybe? Two? Hardly any, really. I think the dining room will be able to squeeze them in with Mr. Winship's sizeable number nicely. There's a Post-it note listing them, stuck to the back of the sheet in Miss Grenaldi's—Natalie's—hand, actually. I had a few spare minutes, so I jotted them down when Miss Lucas called a few weeks ago."

Natalie glanced at Tessa, as if reading what this patronizing and offhand tone for the bride-to-be was doing to her. Tessa managed to hold onto her smile, albeit with effort. "That's a lot of people," she ventured. "Good thing it's a big room."

"There's a list here also of guests who will receive the top-tier wedding-guest favors," said Ashleigh, removing a second memorandum from her bag. "Mr. Winship would like something special for these people. Top clients, the members of his company's board of directors… you get the idea."

Tessa accepted it, dropping it in the pile of paperwork to one side. At that moment, Blake appeared. Not in his suit from the resort's meeting, of course, but in his faded denim and a worn blue cotton shirt. "Tessa, did you write this note about the leaky faucet downstairs? Because I can't read—" He paused when he realized they were in the midst of a meeting.

"Mr. Ellingham—Blake," corrected Ashleigh. "A pleasure to see you again."

"Likewise," he said. "Sorry, I didn't realize a meeting was in progress."

"No apology necessary," said Tessa. "We've got it under control." She smiled.

"Good." He held up the slip of paper. "When you get a chance…?" he said, then stepped out again.

Ashleigh looked perplexed. "Does he do all the building repairs too?" she asked.

"He's a man of many talents," contributed Natalie. "That's why we say we only hire the best."

"Let's get back to business, shall we?" said Tessa, clearing her throat.

*

Ama's mind was far away from Indian desserts even as her knife chopped the nuts for garnishing the Rajasthani dessert known as *pheni*. Her thoughts were constantly orbiting the problem in her universe: the tiny engagement ring concealed in her pocket. She couldn't leave it in her room for fear Rasha would find it while searching the bedside table and dresser drawers for batteries or spare earbuds, for instance—or that Bendi would find it while snooping around for evidence about the status of Ama's relationship with her unsuitable boyfriend.

What would she do if they found out? Especially if something happened, and she and Luke weren't together… but that didn't need to be thought about, not yet. Why ruin the last day she would see him with thoughts about a time when it might never again be possible?

I love Luke. These feelings, those butterflies in my stomach at the beginning and the way I feel so warm and safe with him—I've never felt them for anybody else but him. Of course, that might not mean anything, since Luke was her first boyfriend, after all. She could trust nothing she felt, really. Not if she was only desperately clinging to straws, and still a coward when it came to the hard decisions.

Round and round went the dilemma as Ama scraped the chopped nuts into a canister. Jaidev plopped down a bag of rice flour on the counter. "Ama, is that your syrup boiling madly over an open flame?" he asked.

"What?" She looked up. "My syrup?!" With a yelp, she rescued the hot pan and turned down the flame's gas. "Stuck. Great. I'll have to start over." A smell of scorched fruit and sugar as she scraped out the ruined contents that were meant for drizzling over the sticky milk dough balls that were a staple on the restaurant's menu.

Jaidev *tsked*. "What's gotten into you lately?" he asked. "You're walking around like you're half-asleep most of the time."

"I'm fine," she said. "I have a lot on my mind. Work and the online business, and the new recipe for the fall menu that Papa asked me to find."

"I think it's more than that," said Rasha, who was cracking open the seal on a new jar of pungent, yellow turmeric powder. "You didn't have an argument with Luke, did you?"

"No," said Ama. Emphatically, although she should watch her tone when it came to this subject, since her family was good at sensing each other's little secrets. "We're fine."

How many times was she going to give out this line before it was really the truth again? If ever, that is?

"That wild boy. I still think you should stay away from him," said Bendi, who was washing banana leaves in the sink. "He's only going to lead to trouble."

"Bendi, stop," said Rasha. "He makes Ama happy. Can't you be happy for her?"

"Not with a wild boy who has tattoos. Gangs have tattoos in America," insisted their aunt, stubbornly.

"Prisoners have them in Russia," pointed out Jaidev, less than helpfully.

Ama glared at him.

"I think you should stop saying negative things about him," said Rasha. "So if it's not something with you and Luke, then what is it?" she asked Ama.

"There is a problem between you and the boy you are dating?" Pashma had entered the kitchen now, carrying a series of baskets for today's naan bread.

"There isn't," insisted Ama, who felt as if she was lying with every word.

"There is," asserted Jaidev.

"Good," grunted Ranjit, who had emerged from the pantry with a bottle of vinegar for the rice.

"Papa!" said Ama, who added her pan to the basin of dishes with more force than necessary.

"I am sorry. But if you leave him, I think it is good news. It means you can find somebody better. More suitable," reasoned Ranjit.

"Someone who doesn't talk about motorcycles all the time, and thinks Indian cuisine is only curry with chicken."

"He's trying, Papa. He reads Indian cookbooks, I'll have you know; he reads novels by Indian novelists," said Ama. "Did you know he actually learned to order food in Punjabi?" One of the rare times that Ama had suggested they eat Indian food, he had tried to impress her by doing it.

Another grunt from her father. Ama pretended not to hear it, although she was seething inside. So this was what she had to look forward to if she put on Luke's ring: comments about how he simply didn't try to fit in according to Ranjit's rigorous standards. Seizing a sponge, she began wiping charred fruit bits from the pan's sides.

"Don't listen to him, Ama," said Rasha. "He just doesn't appreciate the fact that you could be dating some weirdo vegan setting fire to the market's meat sections, or someone who hates sitar music."

"Serial killers. Terrorist bombers. There are probably plenty of single people in those categories," pointed out Jaidev, as he began dicing onions.

"I don't want to talk about it anymore." Ama's tone was short. "Everyone stop talking about Luke and me, all right? Not another word. I'm sick of hearing about it, and this is the last time I want to say it."

Her tone was so forceful that it produced stares from all her family members, even the supportive ones. Ama silently scolded herself for losing her temper

"Are you okay?" Deena was the first to speak up, probably because she was the last person to join the number in the kitchen, standing there with the rest of the bread baskets pressed against the folds of her yellow hostess sari.

Ama shrugged. "Just stop picking on him," she said. "That's all I ask." She turned away and began scrubbing her pot again. The stuck sugar was not budging, but she kept at it, as if a little sponge could cut through the solidified syrup basting its sides and bottom.

"You heard her," said Jaidev, looking pointedly at their auntie.

Bendi released a huffy breath as she turned back to her simmering pot of masala on the stove. Ranjit said nothing. A moment later, they were talking about a problem with the roasting fire, but Ama kept on with the problem of the burned sugar syrup all the same.

*

Luke set his bag by his feet on the station platform, amidst the crowd of travelers waiting for the next light rail to the airport. Ten minutes to arrival, his smile a sadder one than usual as he faced Ama.

Two people in a crowd, saying goodbye, she thought. In the romance movies, from Bollywood to Hollywood, they were always standing apart from everyone else, the only two people in the world, it seemed—but here she was, being elbowed by a man with two big suitcases, and a couple of teenage girls arguing over a movie they had both watched recently.

Luke took her hand, and Ama held tightly to his. "Listen," he said. "I know you'll be thinking about what I asked you while I'm gone. But... I want you to know that you're free to choose. You're not tied to anything right now. If you think about it, and you can't..." He paused. "I'll understand."

He folded her in his arms, and Ama held tightly to him. "Don't be gone too long," she said.

"Call me," he said. "Especially if you need to... to tell me something before I come back," he said. "If plans change, I'll let you know."

There was a terrible subtext in all these lines, Ama felt. If she made her decision before he returned, he didn't want to be in suspense. Probably he wouldn't return but leave the country from the airport closest to his friend, as she feared all along. And, if sometime before then he decided he wasn't coming back, he would tell her, too.

Maybe he would change his mind about having asked her this monumental question, since its answer wasn't the immediate one he dreamed it would be. Another terrible probability in the mix. Could they really go back to the way things were, never thinking of how close they had been to a permanent decision?

"I'll miss you." She held him tighter. "I'll be thinking about you every day. I really care for you, Luke. It won't change that... I don't want it to change that, no matter what."

"Maybe it would be better if we made sure we have a real goodbye, if something happens," he said, softly. "However long it takes, whether it's good or bad in the end, I want you to tell me to my face what you decide. We'll have our moment to say anything that shouldn't be left unsaid."

"Promise." Ama's arms didn't let go until Luke drew back. In the distance, they could hear the train rumbling closer.

"Take care of yourself," he said. He kissed her forehead then cupped her face and kissed her lips, lightly and softly. Behind him, the train's rush slowed as it came to a halt in the station, its hydraulic doors whooshing open to release its passengers. Ama felt the breeze across her face, ruffling her hair and the fabric of Luke's loose button-down pulled over his T-shirt. She looked up into Luke's eyes for a moment then buried her face against his shoulder. She felt his arms tighten before he released her.

He lifted his bag. "Until next time," he said.

"Be careful," said Ama. "I love you."

He nodded. "You, too." He boarded the train, along with the passengers who had been shoving against Ama. The doors closed a moment later, and the train was ready to leave.

He had never failed to say those three words before; it was different now, she thought, because of her hesitation. It would hurt to say that line to someone whose actions expressed latent uncertainty; it would remind him how quickly he could get hurt by a simple reply from her.

She felt lonely as she watched the train speed away into the night. No hand holding hers this time as she emerged from the station to the street outside. She slipped it into her pocket, touching the ring which lay there, and wondering why there was once a time she let herself imagine love's heartache could be both wonderful and terrible like in songs and novels, instead of just terribly sad and empty.

Chapter Fourteen

Natalie fumbled with the keys to her apartment building in one hand and a latte from the Pecan Grove coffee shop in the other. Twenty minutes of precious free time upstairs would allow her to finish getting the quote for table decorations for Harper's wedding before she raced to help Cal finish fitting their runway models into the newly finished garments for their runway line. In other words, a rush pit stop in her hectic life.

The keys were all locked together in an impossible tangle, and she dropped them just as someone on the inside opened the door and emerged. They bent down to pick them up at the same time she maneuvered her armful of grocery bags to the sidewalk—and Natalie found herself face-to-face with Brayden again.

"Natalie." He offered her a polite smile. He scooped up her keys and held them out to her as she mastered a standing position again with her burdens.

"Brayden," she said. "Are you—"

"Package to 3B upstairs," he said.

"Mrs. O' Dell, who orders specialty cat food," said Natalie. "The handcart probably comes in handy for that."

Brayden smiled again. Not the familiar one that she knew so well, but one that Natalie, were she speculating on its general use, would have guessed was for classmates he didn't remember very well but met occasionally on the street. "Guess so," he answered.

Awkward small talk. Since when had their small talk been awkward for anybody but her?

"So, Rob told me you changed routes permanently," she said. "I mean, not just for your vacation."

"Yeah. I got Cooper's old route—he retired. It's a couple of small blocks, a few cul-de-sacs. Kind of easy, and no vicious dogs to worry about." He rubbed the back of his neck, ruffling the edges of his overly long, lank, reddish hair emerging from beneath his delivery uniform's ball cap.

"Lucky you," said Natalie. "But you deserve it, you've been working there since…" She didn't know, so she trailed off. Probably sometime after she went to college, when she tried terribly hard not to keep up with any details of Brayden's life, planning to escape all annoying reminders of her high-school years.

"A while," supplied Brayden, for lack of better—or any—words from either of them. "I guess I should go," he said, jerking his thumb toward the delivery truck parked along the sidewalk. He hesitated. "Do you need some help with all that?" He was glancing at the shopping bags and homework from her graduate classes in Natalie's arms. Not hopefully, but kindly. Natalie didn't shrink away from his offer as usual, though she was prepared for that reaction.

"Me? No. I'm fine," she said. "I'm just going upstairs to grab a few things. You go on. Great to see you, though."

He smiled—this time with less apology and more relief, Natalie noticed, with surprise. "You, too," he answered. He then opened the truck's rear door to load his handcart, and walked around to the driver's side. Had he been hoping to avoid her here, she wondered? Had he actually been relieved to think he'd missed an opportunity to see her until this unfortunate run-in outside her building?

Natalie managed to free her door key from the jumble and let herself in, struggling through the door after it tried twice to crush her between itself and its frame. The grocery bag with the torn paper strap managed not to break until she reached the second-floor landing, where it spilled pasta and a bundle of celery everywhere. Natalie groaned aloud.

In her mother's kitchen, later in the afternoon, she found equal obstacles to a smooth afternoon, as well as unwanted personal commentary. "You look like death on rye toast," said Rob, as he rummaged behind the leftover pasta containers and the cream cheese and lox until he located a jar of marshmallow paste.

"What does that even mean?" Natalie answered. She slammed closed her textbook. "Tell me, do you spend your time dreaming up weird insults for me as your sister, or is it a natural gift?"

"Take a guess." He closed the fridge. "I'm just saying. Put on a little makeup so Ma doesn't think you've been doing drugs all night or something."

Natalie regretted her decision to study for her upcoming exam in what she assumed was the privacy of her childhood home. Her mother was busy at work today with Natalie's aunt Louisa, since it was cannoli day at the bakery, and Guido was baking bread this week. Rob was *supposed* to be at some sort of training day, not hanging out with Kimmie, who was off work and taking advantage of the time with Rob to binge-watch some vampire detective series they both liked. *He could be helping Ma out*, Natalie thought. Then again, maybe that was just her own guilt talking, trying to shove responsibility onto others since she was so busy herself these days.

"I'm just tired," said Natalie. Old sarcastic habits die hard, especially when Rob was raiding the kitchen. "First, I had to drop off my paper, which will automatically be docked a half-grade for being late, then I had to help hem trouser lengths and tuck a problematic waistline on a dress, and now I have to study to pass this exam on interest rates, and I haven't had time to call back my wedding supply vendor about the cost of thirty giant triton's trumpet seashells." Someone from their florist had apparently suggested they hollow them out and use them as centerpiece vases for stems of bold multi-blossom flowers.

"Clearly, you need an awesome job like mine," said Rob. "So long as no one sets fire to a city block around here, I can enjoy grisly mayhem and mystery on television while eating a Rob specialty: peanut butter, marshmallow cream, and cocoa puffs on cinnamon bread."

"Ew," said Natalie, turning the page in her book as Rob unscrewed the lid to the peanut butter. She pretended her mind was on the analysis of long-term effectiveness of short-term business loans, and not elsewhere. She cleared her throat. "I saw Brayden today. Weird to run into him twice in such a short amount of time, since I haven't seen him in a while. My apartment building wasn't on his new route, so I didn't expect to see him there."

"Good ol' Brayden," said Rob. "Probably counting down the days until he goes back to his sweet new route instead of delivering to dumps like the place where you live."

"It has walk-in charm," Natalie retorted. Another pause, as she turned the page. "Good for him. Getting a new route, I mean." Brayden deserved it, and she really meant it. He had been a loyal employee for years without reward. Knowing him, he probably covered people's packages with his waterproof jacket when it was pouring rain, and hated using those supersonic whistles to deter aggressive dogs.

"Not for long though," said Rob. "He's transferring." He smeared marshmallow cream over his layer of peanut butter, as Natalie's fingers froze in mid-turn of her page.

"He's transferring?" she said. "Another route?" But that wasn't what Rob meant, she already sensed.

"His big promotion. You know. He's been taking classes for the past year or so through that training credit program the company offers. Now he's moving up to a manager's position or something. Ma was talking about it last week—I missed part of it, but they're basically gonna pay for him to get some kind of associate's degree or whatever it is, at some training college in Virginia, then to work supervising one of the big depots."

Natalie was stunned. "Brayden's leaving?" she said. "Leaving Bellegrove? This is Brayden Carmichael we're talking about—the kid who used to live down the street from us, right?" It was unbelievable, like being told Uncle Guido was giving up cooking, or that Tessa had just decided to sell her part of Wedding Belles.

"You think I mixed him up with some other Brayden you know?" scoffed Rob. "Nat, I'm not pulling your leg. Give me some credit, I don't lie all the time." He took a bite from his sandwich. "Did you think the goodbye party invite was for a weekend trip?"

Goodbye party. This was news to Natalie, although Brayden's life was a mystery that had only recently presented itself to her thoughts. She shouldn't be surprised. "I hadn't heard about it," she said. The page between her fingers had drifted its corner to touch the book again.

"I'm taking this little wind-up delivery truck that Kimmie found online," said Rob, between mouthfuls of marshmallow cream. "Can't go with the conventional and give the guy a set of towels for his new pad, can I?" He pressed the layers of sandwich together between his bread, crunching a few of the cocoa puffs in between.

The invitation was tacked to her mother's fridge, right next to the shopping list, one of those fill-out invitations from the store, with balloons and a party hat printed at the top. The date was three weeks from now, at eight o'clock at Brayden's mom's, not at his place. No gift necessary.

So that's why he needed three dozen cupcakes from Icing Italia.

"I hadn't heard about the party, either," said Natalie.

Rob swallowed his latest bit of sandwich. "Yeah, well, I think he probably figured you didn't want to come," he said. "You know. Awkward and everything, after him chasing you for years. This way he didn't make you uncomfortable. Lucky for you, huh?" He plopped the sandwich on a plate, licked his fingers, then grinned at her as he exited the kitchen, leaving her alone at last with her books.

Natalie turned the page in her book and tried to concentrate on the figures printed in the time versus interest graph on its back. From the living room came the sound of screams on television from the latest rampage of the episode's vampires.

"It's just weird," said Natalie, over the phone to Cal several hours later. "He's never *not* invited me to something. That's all." Time to let go of this subject, yet she didn't. Weird, how it persisted in her thoughts like this.

"Aren't you relieved?" said Cal. "You've been dodging this guy for years, Nat. Maybe he finally got the hint and did the smart thing for both of you."

"True," said Natalie. She propped her feet against the wall of her apartment as she sank deeper into her Indian-style floor pillows, a gift from Ama by way of her sister's passion for shopping online at international warehouses.

There was no one else in whom she could confide this nagging feeling under the surface of her skin with regards to Brayden's circumstances, however, except for Cal. Certainly not Rob, who had never treated her concern over the crush with the seriousness she felt it deserved. Or her mom, since Maria had chosen to turn a blind eye to Brayden's puppy love years ago—and, frankly, took his side in long-ago arguments with Natalie over her disinterest in him. As for the girls at Wedding Belles… Natalie wasn't so sure they needed to know about this development after their first impression of Brayden. Clearly, they thought she had been making a big fuss over nothing all this time.

They had used words like "cute" when they'd met him. "Boyish." "Endearing." Was that right? Was his smile a charming one, and not really shudder-worthy, as her fourteen-year-old self had decided whenever it was directed at her?

Natalie tried to imagine she was meeting him for the first time, as an adult, and not as a four-year-old in her childhood sandbox. Brayden passing her in the hall to her building as he wheeled a stack of delivery packages on his cart. Tipping his hat with a polite smile or holding the elevator door for her when she had an armload of books and unfinished garments. Would it be different if she could see him without seeing the past, she wondered? As a nice guy who was genuinely interested in who she was?

"But… he's still an old friend," she continued. "I don't want him to think I wouldn't come wish him *bon voyage* before his big move." Guilt washed over her for… what? Being mean and undeserving toward Brayden their whole lives? For being too much of a coward to simply tell him goodbye on her own?

"Do you really care about it that much?" Cal asked.

Natalie paused. A moment's reflection to decide what the answer really was. "Yeah," she said. "I kind of do. It's weird, but it's the truth. Maybe I owe him something, I don't know… Maybe I just think knowing somebody for twenty-something years is something you can't cut off in a couple months' time."

"So absolve yourself of guilt or whatever and send him a gift," said Cal. "And a nice card. Tell him there are no hard feelings. How's that for a release trigger?"

"Better than nothing?" said Natalie. It didn't feel like it, though.

"You don't want to go to this party. You said you're uncomfortable every time he asks you out. Spare yourself anything but the joy of freedom, Nat. Maybe he's doing the same."

"It's not like I can blame him," said Natalie. "Who wants to ask somebody who's openly snubbed them to come to a party? I wouldn't. Me, I tried so hard to get out of inviting him to my birthday parties when I was a kid that my mom threatened to cut off my access to chocolate in junior high if I didn't behave better."

She wouldn't know most of the guests, if they were from his workplace. A few Grenaldis would be there, a few old high-school friends. Brayden's mom would probably invite some of her friends—people who used to babysit Brayden, for example. She wasn't missing anything by not going except for a dull evening, and was probably saving them both a lot of discomfort by letting Brayden leave town without any attempt at an awkward goodbye. She owed it to him, really, didn't she?

When Natalie hung up, she opened the top on a box of chocolate-covered cherries, a stash she reserved for emergencies only. Her first free night with only her aching fingers and sore feet for company seemed like a good use of her secret weapon.

Popping one in her mouth, she fumbled for her phone beneath one of the pillows as she heard its standard ringtone. A number she wasn't expecting appeared on its screen. Hesitating, she answered it. "Hello?"

"Hi. Natalie? I didn't wake you or anything, did I?"

It was unmistakably Brayden's voice. "No, I was up," said Natalie. "Um… is everything okay?"

She knew Brayden had her latest phone number, though he had never dialed it or texted her. She had accidentally called his cell once when they were in the same room, revealing that his chosen ringtone for receiving her calls was the Lionel Richie song "Hello." Of course, she had talked him into changing it, but that was the last time her number had popped up on his screen probably. It surprised her to hear from him at this moment.

"Yeah." A pause. "It's just… earlier, when I ran into you, I thought about… well, about inviting you to this party," he said. "I didn't, 'cause I thought it might make you uncomfortable. But then I felt kind of guilty. So I thought I'd let you know in case you want to come. No obligations or anything, you understand."

"A party. Sounds nice," said Natalie, for lack of anything better to say that wouldn't give away the fact she'd been overanalyzing this situation.

"It's at my mom's. Rob can tell you the time and the date," he said. "It was my mom's idea, since I'm leaving after this, and I couldn't say no when she suggested it."

"I heard about your promotion," she said. "Congratulations."

"Thanks. Guess I don't get to enjoy that cushy route I worked my way up to, though," he said. "Classic me, huh? Never wanting something if it's easy."

Natalie almost laughed. When did Brayden learn to tell a halfway decent joke? He'd always been so earnest and so eager that he had a tendency to stumble over his words when he tried to joke around her. Maybe this meant he didn't need her approval anymore. He was actually relaxed in conversation with her, instead of trying to read his chances with her in every word or nuance in reply.

"I'll let you go," he said. "I just… thought I owed you an invitation. Just in case."

In the past, that hopeful note would have been hanging in the air between them, even on the phone, as Brayden waited for her to accept the invitation in absolute terms. It was gone now, and this pause was more for the sake of searching for the right goodbye, Natalie sensed.

"I'll be there," she answered, softly. "Thanks for inviting me, Brayden."

"No trouble," he said. "See you then, I guess. Oh—no present or anything. It's casual, so you can come late, leave early if you want."

"Okay," said Natalie. "Bye, Brayden."

"Have a good night," he said. "Bye."

She tossed her phone on the nearby pillow afterward and stared at the colorful Klimt poster on the wall, trying to decide if it was too weird or too rude to show up at Brayden's party with some kind of gift in hand. It was the sort of thing Brayden would do if he was going to someone else's party. Say, one of hers—not that she'd invited him, not since her final rebellion against family politeness while in high school.

It was unbelievable that Brayden was about to relocate himself hundreds of miles away from her: the one thing she had secretly, fervently hoped for all through university. Ironic it was happening now, when there wasn't any need for it. Ironic that she felt as if some sort of hole would be left in the city when he was gone, though countless people moved away every year.

Then again, was she thinking of life in the city being absent another soul, or of her own life being absent one?

Good for Brayden, she thought, forcing her mind elsewhere firmly. *His life is finally becoming normal.* All he needed, now that she was rooted out of his life emotionally and physically, was to find a nice girl who could appreciate him. If only she had some nice friend to fix him up with, Natalie reflected. He deserved someone who was a good catch.

Now I sound like Ma, she thought. *It must be genetic, or something you come down with at a certain age.* With a groan, she buried her head under the pillow as if to block further thoughts like this one from finding her brain.

Chapter Fifteen

Tessa recognized the smooth, chocolate waterfall of Mac's hair and those elegant suede leather boots even before the interior designer turned around on the upstairs landing. An immediate knot formed in her stomach. Was Mac finally here to talk wedding plans? Cornered, she had no escape, not if Mac intended to drag her upstairs to the office, and there would be Blake, waiting to discuss saying "I do" to Mac, while wearing his old flannel shirt sprinkled in wood shavings from his work...

"Tessa, how great to see you," said Mac, greeting her with a friendly handshake.

"You, too," said Tessa, lying with a beautiful smile.

"I was hoping to run into you. We still need to make that appointment to talk about the wedding," she said. "We're still planning on late fall unless we move it to early spring next year—of course, we'll have to wait until the groom has time to sit down and talk." She laughed.

Tessa laughed, too, although she felt as if a sharp needle had been jabbed into her chest at the thought of Mac and Blake across from her. "In the future, we'll have to make an appointment, won't we?" said Tessa, without enthusiasm.

"I just stopped by to see how Blake's coming along with those remodels upstairs. He keeps texting me pictures, asking me if I can help him find something a little more period for replacing the hardware." She shook her head. "That man is obsessed with his work when he's here."

"I don't know about that," said Tessa, though it was probably true. "Sometimes your personal life and your work just sort of... go together." After all, shouldn't a contractor and an interior decorator be a perfect match on both counts?

Then again, would Mac think her words meant that Blake's personal and professional lives crossed here? For a moment, Tessa felt a rush of guilt and embarrassment. The interior designer didn't seem to notice.

"Maybe you're right," said Mac. She checked her phone's screen. "Whoops, I'm going to be late for my next appointment. Catch you next time, Tessa. We'll talk then."

"Sure," said Tessa. She watched the decorator descend the staircase and exit the Wedding Belles' headquarters. She managed not to sigh—with both relief and despair—until the door was safely closed.

Why couldn't she accept the inevitable: that she was going to have to plan this wedding? If that's what they wanted, that's what she would have to do. No crying off because of old feelings or stupid mistakes, like letting Blake think she didn't care about him romantically. He was a friend, and this was what friends did for each other. It's not like Blake quit when she let distance fall between them after that kiss.

Her phone buzzed with a text, pulling her out of her thoughts again. Time to meet Harper about the dress details. Squaring her shoulders, she finished climbing the stairs to her office, where she grabbed the necessary folders before striking off in the direction of The Blue Moon Travel Agency.

*

"Isn't it gorgeous?" Harper held up the picture with evident pride. "I have never seen anything like it. Nothing this beautiful has ever touched my body. I don't know if I can wear it to walk down the aisle or if I'll just die in it and have to be buried in it."

It was gorgeous, judging from the photograph of the dress on a seamstress's form. Natalie was every bit as talented, however, Tessa reflected. If only Mrs. Winship hadn't had a friend from one of the top design houses.

"I think it's gorgeous," said Tessa. "I can't wait to see it in person."

"She's fitting me at Mrs. Win—, I mean, Myra's place," said Harper, in what was obviously a new state of corrective thought. "But the final fitting will be out at the resort before the wedding. The designer's a friend of the family—she does this kind of thing all the time for big weddings. You know, coming to the wedding, making last-minute adjustments. I was flattered 'cause she's so famous I figured she would be too busy to come."

Seeing her dress in the society column's pages was part of the reason the designer agreed, Tessa thought, but since Natalie would've been just as impressed, it would be petty to say so. "I have some possible bridesmaids dresses here," she said, opening her tablet computer.

"Wait—I thought Natalie was planning to show me those next week," said Harper. "She said we'd look online, then I could go shopping with the girls. I'm doing this thing out with them. Day with the girls," she said, as if trying to sound eager. "I figure we need to get to know each other better."

"I take it that you and Brett haven't spent much time with each other's friends?" said Tessa.

"We were just so busy when we first got together," said Harper. "We wanted to spend all our time together. He is always saying that he prefers having me all to himself. Plus, you know what business people are like. His friends are always working all the time, so they aren't exactly available."

"Natalie would be happy to go along for your shopping day," suggested Tessa. "If you feel like you need the support. For picking out dresses, that is." She crossed her fingers that the madness that was Natalie's fashion show prep would die down long enough to make this possible.

Despite Harper's enthusiasm, Tessa couldn't help thinking that Harper might feel just a tiny bit intimidated by the candidates chosen to be her bridesmaids. Everything she'd heard about them so far suggested they were a posh sort of crowd and not too eager to mix socially with Brett's future wife.

"That's okay," said Harper. "I think it would feel more natural if I just spent some time with them on my own at first. Just to see if we click, you know?"

"Of course," said Tessa, trying to sound as if she thought this was a real possibility. Checking her folder, she asked, "Has Brett given any thought to the colors for the groomsmen?"

Harper's face changed slightly. "I don't think he's decided," she said. She checked some papers on her desk, rearranging their order. "He's had a lot to think about. But, hey—the moment he decides, Ashleigh will call you. She's very punctual." Harper made a slight face that betrayed her real feelings about her groom's assistant.

"I noticed," said Tessa, with a smile that didn't commit to any real liking for Ashleigh, for more than one reason. "I'll touch base with her soon. We have to work together on the seating chart this weekend."

"I'll ask him about the colors next time I see him, I swear," said Harper. "I feel like I'm not real helpful when it comes to his side of things. I guess I don't know them as well as I should. It takes time—they're hard people to get to know. But Brett said they really like me. In no time, I'll fit in… you know, after I've gotten used to things. Check out the new shoes," she said, pointing downwards. "Brett picked them out for me. He said I need to stop wearing the ratty old secondhand ones I have."

Trim, slim black leather high heels. They were very fashionable, but also not quite Harper in taste, Tessa noted, aware that her client liked things a bit more colorful. Red shoes with her navy travel agency blazer, then hot-pink open-toed pumps… but those were nothing like the sedate designer footwear that Mrs. Winship wore to the resort.

"Nice of him to be so thoughtful," ventured Tessa.

"Isn't it?" said Harper. "He almost died when he heard that the last new pair of shoes I bought was three years ago—and off the rack of some weekend market vendor. He says used goods are a health risk; that's why he doesn't want me buying them anymore."

"When you're saving money, it's easier to buy secondhand stuff," said Tessa. "That's where all my furniture comes from, shops like those. My favorite is this old chair with a bad spot on its upholstery that I keep covered with a knit throw."

"I just love flea markets and charity stores," said Harper. "I always did. As a kid, I thought of them like treasure hunts… you know, like you could buy anything in the world in them. I still like browsing through them, though as a grown-up I know there's some limitations to what you're actually gonna find—but it's like a museum of real people's lives somehow. The thrill of finding a bargain, or just coming across something kind of special in one… I guess maybe it does for me what a winning scratch-off ticket does for some people."

"You play secondhand markets instead of the lottery," surmised Tessa, with a smile. "Probably a better deal a lot of the time."

"I don't like stores where they only have ten pairs of shoes and they're all the same shade of beige," said Harper, shaking her head. "But I guess sometimes I'm a little much for him," she admitted, and the light from before dimmed slightly in her facial expression. "He says that, sometimes, there are some aspects of me that are a little loud for his parents' tastes. Not that they said anything," she added. "I'm sure they'll adjust. But I figure I should be nice in the meantime."

"I'm sure they will," said Tessa, reassuringly, though doubtful that Brett's real concern over Harper's shopping taste was for the possibility of cold germs clinging to those garments.

The phone rang, and Harper lifted the receiver. "Blue Moon Travel Agency," she said. Her chipper tone changed. "Look, can we talk about this later?" she said. "I'm with a client. Look—no, I don't want to talk about it while I'm working…"

She glanced at Tessa, who sensed this conversation was something personal, and one that Harper wanted to have alone. Tessa waved at her client as she rose from her chair.

"Pa, honest, I am thinking of your feelings. I swear. But this is something I gotta do—" Harper waved goodbye distractedly as Tessa slipped out the front door, then swiveled to face the other way to hide the worry furrow which had been plowing itself in her forehead seconds before. "I know you don't approve, but see facts on this one, Pa. What am I waiting for if I don't? And maybe if you'd give somebody a chance, it wouldn't *seem* like a mistake to you…"

At the corner Pig's Whistle Cafe, Tessa ordered the house specialty lunch of pulled pork on a bun with sweet cabbage and carrot slaw, and a glass of sweet tea with a lemon wedge. Through the parted chintz curtains across its railroad car windows, she watched the passersby flowing from the direction of the light rail station.

"Is the sandwich as good as it looks?" It was the strange artist from the other day, standing at her elbow again. Tessa gave a little jump, and her gaze whirled away from the foot traffic outside.

"What are you doing here?" she asked, suspiciously. And uneasily.

"Having lunch," he said. "Mind if I join you?"

"Maybe?"

He sat down across from her without invitation. "I think I gave you the wrong impression before," he said. "I'm not a crazy artist or a street psychic." He extended his hand, which Tessa shook only after a long hesitation. "Danny Reynolds. Sculptor, born and raised in the city, very trustworthy and likeable person in general, though I know I seem a little strange to you at the moment."

"A little?" She raised one eyebrow, Natalie fashion.

"Okay, maybe more than a little. But I have my reasons. I don't just go around predicting doom for people's relationships in my neighborhood block. Truth is… I have a history with the woman whose wedding you're planning. In case you hadn't guessed it already."

Hmm. Tessa had considered the possibility of a random crush before now, and maybe that was the case. "By history, I presume you mean you actually know her?" she asked.

He laughed. "Know her," he repeated. "Yeah. I guess you could call promising eternal and undying love to each other twelve years ago a form of knowing each other. But it sticks in the minds of some folks longer than it does for others. In my case, twelve years. Maybe until I die." He shrugged his shoulders.

"College sweethearts?" guessed Tessa. This was a lot of drama for writing each other's names surrounded by hearts in advanced geometry textbooks.

Some of his grin erased itself. "Something like that." His voice was slightly gentler. "I made a mistake. I took off after we had a slight bust-up—not to leave her, but because I had this chance worth taking for my career, and 'cause Harper wasn't ready for a life with me if things stayed the way they were, so something had to change. I tried to make it happen: I offered her anything in the world if she would wait for me. But sometimes promising the world isn't enough."

"Didn't you think maybe she could fall in love with someone else while you were gone?" Tessa asked. "A twelve-year-old promise between two people who were practically kids isn't binding."

"Do you think she loves him?" Danny leaned closer. "Harper may not carry a torch for me, though I find it hard to believe, given the way we felt about each other back then. It hasn't been twelve years, it's been five, since I left the city. I came back a year ago, but she wouldn't see me. And then she met what's-his-name, with the Mercedes, the Rolex, and a dozen roses delivered like clockwork every Tuesday, which shows no imagination, in my opinion."

"How could you possibly know all of that?" Tessa asked, concerned just how much time he might have spent hanging out near Harper's workplace.

"It's not exactly a state secret," Danny replied. "The guy has a reputation for glitz. Everybody thinks it's so impressive but you have to wonder just how genuine it is beneath all the flash. Specifically, how genuine his feelings are when it comes to Harper."

"I think it's time you leave so I can enjoy my dessert roll," said Tessa.

"Okay, I put that badly. Let me try again," said Danny. "Harper is... is a rare and beautiful person who thinks she's not. A lot of people don't see it, or they think of those aspects as being a little rough or a little tacky. They don't see that if they tried to turn her into someone else, everything that makes her alive and unique would just disappear. A shell would be all that was left. They would snuff the light that shone through it."

The beige shoes, Tessa thought. "What makes you think Brett can't see how special she is?" asked Tessa. "He thinks enough of her to marry her, after all."

"You can buy a Victorian house and remodel it into a hideous modern duplex inside and out, right?" said Danny. "That's what he'll do to Harper. He'll make her over, and he won't realize that he's erasing all the reasons he was attracted to her."

"You mean liking loud, bright colors, wearing secondhand clothes, being talkative and opinionated," said Tessa. "The outdated hot-pink faux leather high heels."

"Does she still wear those?" Danny's smile reappeared. "She bought those back when we were still together. Coming out of the city tunnel one day when I was hunting scrap metal, I caught a glimpse of those on the street above, and I knew it was her." He shook his head fondly. "Even without seeing the rest, I just knew."

"Did you think maybe Harper wants to change?" Tessa asked this softly, and very carefully. "Maybe she's tired of gaudy-colored shoes and purses that smell like other people's perfumes and hairsprays."

He rested his forehead against clasped hands, a pose of deep thought. "The woman I knew and loved wouldn't want that," he said. "But the woman she is now... maybe she thinks that you can compromise anything for a new life."

"That sounds suspiciously like gold-digging," said Tessa, who was beginning to like him less for this suspicion alone. She could have the same one herself, however, if she let herself think it, but Harper seemed genuinely connected to Brett, money or no.

"No. Not Harper," he said. "But... maybe she's a little blinded by the glamour of his life, though she won't admit it. He's a big shot in the city, from a big, wealthy family. Harper... she's lived most of her life from hand to mouth. And she has big dreams, and wants them to come true. You must know that. All those posters in the windows are places she wants to go. That's why we didn't make it before, her and me. She never thought those dreams could come true with me."

There was regret in his voice; for a moment, Tessa pitied him. The ghosts of that past were strong for him, and he seemed to genuinely care about her client.

"Coffee or tea, darlin'?" a waitress asked Danny, pencil and pad in hand.

"Nothing for me," he said. "Thanks, though. I'm leaving this lady to enjoy her dessert alone." He rose from the table. "When you see them together, maybe you'll see what I mean," he told Tessa. "It doesn't take much to realize she's not her real self with him. If he wants to deserve her, he has to look at her the way I do, and I don't think he can."

He laid a couple of folded bills in the tip dish on the table. "Thanks for hearing me out," he said. "Tip's on me." He smiled then collected his ratty cap from the table and left.

"One honey praline roll, fresh from the oven." The waitress placed the dessert plate before Tessa, along with her check. "Anything else, you just let me know."

Chapter Sixteen

Round tables covered by silk cloths filled one section of the glass dining hall's space, a miniature version of the floor plan designed for Harper and Brett's wedding. Tessa adjusted the napkins and silverware belonging to the formal place settings on either side of the gold-rimmed china and crystal stemware.

"If we seat ten people per table, we'll have enough room left for the dessert buffet at the far end of the dining room," she said, consulting her chart. "It's going to be tight if everyone RSVPs."

"Do you expect everybody to?" Blake asked.

Tessa shrugged. "One is supposed to assume," she answered. "Part of the job. Help me move these two tables a little further apart, will you?" she asked him. Blake seized one side of the neighboring tables as Tessa did the other, putting another hand's width of space between the two dining spaces.

"How's that?" asked Blake.

"Better," said Tessa. "Guests won't be bumping between tables like a pinball, at any rate."

Blake smiled. "Nice analogy," he said.

"Thanks." Tessa turned the page of her table chart. "So... the only thing missing is centerpieces, which is Accented Creations' department. We'll have to envision the big shell and flowers in the middle."

"If we need overflow space, we can always move the champagne station to the patio," suggested Ashleigh, who stood by with her copy of the lengthy Winship guest list. "Or maybe we can create an overflow guest dining space in the small drawing room between here and the ballroom."

And banish the Lucas side of the guest list, Tessa imagined. "I think we'll try moving the champagne station first," she said. "Let's see what kind of illusions of space we create if we open those doors to the patio."

"Let me help." Ashleigh moved smoothly to unlatch the door adjoining the one Blake was now opening. She smiled at him—too eagerly in Tessa's opinion. Surely Blake could read through this and must be at least a *little* annoyed by these obvious attentions. Why not just drool on his shirt and be done with it?

The fork between Tessa's fingers fumbled, almost landing on the floor. She caught it in time, though she hadn't caught her train of thought with similar efficiency to keep from mentally sniping at Ashleigh for no valid reason.

"So… you do the repairs on your building as well as plan weddings?" Ashleigh was saying to him.

"I have a background in architectural repair and service contracting," he answered as he pushed down the door's stop foot to keep it from blowing shut in the breeze. "So I do a lot of repair work. A lot more than wedding planning these days."

"I try not to keep him too busy with flower arrangements," said Tessa as she tried a swan-fold napkin on one of the plates. Ashleigh barely glanced her way.

"Let's move these urns and see if it looks roomier," suggested Blake, who took hold of one of the ornamental flowerpots stationed near the doors. Tessa moved to help him, but Ashleigh was there first, weakly tugging her side of the pot as Blake rolled it aside. Tessa didn't roll her eyes, although petty thoughts were practically screaming to be let into her mind.

"Strong arms," commented Ashleigh, whose admiring glance was sweeping Blake again. "All that construction work pays off."

"Mostly in smashed thumbs," answered Blake. "Fortunately, no severed fingers." He wiggled his own as proof. Ashleigh giggled. Tessa's fingers dropped a spoon on one of the plates, where it clattered loudly, not that either of her assistants noticed.

"Tessa, are you ready for the menu tasting?" Harper appeared in the dining room doorway. "He says the kitchen's all ready to bring out the dishes."

"Coming," said Tessa. "I think we're finished in the dining room, except for taking some photos for reference."

Blake turned away from Ashleigh's eager gaze to glance at Tessa. "I can do that for you," he said.

"Are you sure?" She lifted her bag—reluctantly—although there was no logical reason to linger in the dining room, clearly. Task finished, next one waiting; that should spur her to leave this room with her usual energy for the job.

"No trouble," said Blake. "I'll text them to you so you have them first thing."

"Thanks," said Tessa. She glanced at Ashleigh, who finally noticed her with a polite smile.

"You go ahead," said Ashleigh. "I'll catch up. I just have a couple of things to finish first."

I'll bet you do. With this indulgence in personal pettiness, Tessa exited the dining room.

*

The chef's creations for the wedding consisted of artistic dishes like chicken breast wrapped around arugula leaves and pancetta bacon, with a vegetarian alternative of marinated grilled zucchini with artichoke hearts. The salad was a green palette with a delicate vinaigrette dressing, and the vegetables were fire-roasted roots with some sort of ancho chili sauce.

"Pear stuffed with feta and wild goat cheese, served in organic honey syrup," announced the waiter, setting the latest course before them. A whole pear, de-cored, its cavity stuffed with lightly herbed cheese, sitting in a caramel pool. It was delicious, as Ama's rapturous expression indicated at first bite.

"It looks too good to eat," said Harper, who was hesitant to poke hers with a fork. "Like it should be on display in a bakery window or something. You know, like those luxury chocolates in Paris and Germany that look just like real shoes, or old hardware tools."

"It's the chef's specialty, apparently," said Tessa. "I think it'll make a nice presentation. It would be nice to have something a little more tropical, I suppose."

"I know," said Harper. "I feel like I need more mango and kiwi or something. But I guess the whole wedding can't be like that, can it?"

"Only if you want it to be," said Ama. "Maybe I'll suggest that the cook can add something tropical to the sauces. Like pineapple, or mango, or pomegranate, for example. It would marry some of these dishes to the wedding's theme a little better." She made a note on her pad. "I'll find out if they can add some grilled fruit to the vegetable course, too." She rose and headed eagerly in the direction of the kitchen.

"This thing is pretty tasty," admitted Harper, who finally made herself cut into the perfect pear. "I could grow used to this. At home, pears were brown things you bought for a quarter apiece from the overripe fruit bin. I never eat an apple unless it has a big mushy spot on one side."

"That sounds like frugality to the max," said Tessa, who was the kind of person who didn't eat bananas once their peel had too much brown on the yellow.

"I'm used to frugal," said Harper. "It's been my life. When you live a certain way for thirty years, it's hard to be any other way. You know what I mean?"

Danny the artist had claimed that Harper was blinded by the idea of Brett providing everything she could ever want, Tessa remembered. Of course, he might well be delusional or lying, although he didn't seem as crazy as the first time she met him.

"Something odd happened the other day," she said to Harper. "I met a guy named Danny who claimed that he was your ex. He wanted to know if you were really going to marry Brett, because he thought it was a terrible idea."

At the mere mention of this name, Harper's face had changed. "Danny spoke to you?" Her voice held a sharp note of dismay. "How could he do that?"

"Then he really is your ex?"

"Ex." Harper snorted. "That would imply that we ever had a future and not just a bunch of dreams. We never could've worked, and don't let him tell you that malarkey that we were one step away from the altar. Danny's a dreamer who sees the world the way *he* wants to see it." She laid down her fork, pushing aside the pear. "Let me guess—he's trying to sabotage things between me and Brett somehow. How low and petty is that?"

"In fairness, he didn't try to do anything but ask me questions," said Tessa. "He just wanted to know if you really loved Brett, that's all."

"Why? Because he thinks I'm still in love with him? What good would it do if I had waited around for someone like him?" asked Harper. "I would still have been living paycheck to paycheck at that little corner stop in worldwide travel, and he would have been backpacking across New Orleans like a tramp."

"Backpacking?" said Tessa.

"What did he say he was doing?" Harper said. "He's a bum, an artist. He went off to work on some sculpture he claimed was going to put his art on the map, and I stayed behind. All because I wasn't happy with a future of starving while living in a van, while he played with fire in an old steamboat shed. He knew I couldn't leave the city. He knew how I felt about taking risks that probably won't pay off and all that stuff. All those promises that he was going to build a life for us somehow were just hollow; everything he did was proof."

Danny hadn't been forthcoming with these details of his life, Tessa thought, wryly. "He didn't tell me what the career opportunity was, only that he accepted it," she said.

"Career opportunity. A nice name for playing around with scrap metal for a while, then coming home when nothing panned out," said Harper. "Ignore what he says. I used to listen, when I was stupid enough to still care about him and his crazy ideas. To think he would somehow…" Harper paused here, looking momentarily lost in thought. She shook her head, however, as if to dislodge whatever idea held it.

"I told him the connection between you and Brett wasn't imaginary," said Tessa. "I think he's just feeling regret for having lost someone like you. He thinks you're really special."

"He would say that," Harper muttered in reply. "If he comes around again," she added, "tell him to get lost, all right? I don't want to see him anymore." Her mouth set itself firmly in a line after this, without a hint of a smile.

Maybe she had some latent regrets about the end of their love affair, but there wasn't any evidence of her giving into any ghost of a feeling, if that was the case. And given what Tessa knew about Brett, he was the kind of person with whom anyone would have a hard time competing, even someone's first real love.

"I'll tell him, if I see him," Tessa promised. "Don't worry."

"Good," said Harper. She checked her watch. "Look at the time. I have to call Brett. I promised I'd tell him if the menu was good. Especially since his assistant didn't make it to this one."

"I think Ashleigh was detained." Tessa managed to keep her tone in check for this reply.

"Can't say I'm that broken up over that, actually," confessed Harper, with satisfaction. "Finally, I get to be the one who fills him in on a decision."

"Do you need the chef's menu?" Tessa held out the card as Harper stepped away from the table.

"No need." She covered the mobile phone's receiver. "His mom gave him a copy. Brett? Sweetie, it's me..." She continued walking, leaving the dining room in search of privacy, no doubt.

Tessa picked at the last remnants of pear, her fork tines drawing little lines in the syrup pool. It was hard to compare Brett to Harper's old flame. Brett was rich, sensible, and sophisticated, obviously, while Danny was persistent, overconfident, and weirdly charming, if one put it nicely. Judging from Harper's photos of the groom-to-be, Brett was extremely good-looking. Breadbox jaw and toned, well-defined muscles—maybe eyes the same unusual green as Myra, his mother. Not that Danny had been unattractive, in a somewhat endearingly nerdy, masculine sense.

Unlike Brett, however, Danny had made Harper feel doubtful in some manner or another instead of reassured by their relationship. Offering her the world in words alone had been his big mistake.

Chapter Seventeen

Between a mix-up at the fabric store and a traffic jam downtown, Natalie was running late to dinner at her mom's house. Fashionably late—or at least fashionably dressed, in an ecru blouse and tailored charcoal-gray slacks she had designed for part of her summer business-casual line. Climbing the steps to her childhood home, she reached for the knob only to have her mother pull it open from the other side.

"You had your phone turned off," Maria scolded her, one hand on hip for this greeting. "I was worried something happened to you, but your brother kept insisting you must've forgotten about us. We had to start without you."

"Sorry, Ma, I forgot my cell battery ran down this afternoon," Natalie said. She held up a small tray covered in cling wrap. "I brought some biscotti for the dessert table. Gram's old recipe, so it has cranberries and pistachios instead of chocolate."

"You made biscotti?" Her mom looked as stunned as if she had just announced the treats were laced with arsenic. "But I didn't ask you to bring anything this time. I know how busy you've been."

"Who says you have to ask? I'm a Grenaldi, and we never come to dinner empty-handed." She followed her mom into the hallway, the sound of animated conversation drifting from the dining room ahead. It was a full house tonight, judging by the sound of it.

"Nice of you to remember," said her mom, but without sarcasm. "And making your grandmother's recipe too." She bestowed a kiss on her daughter's cheek. "You going through all this trouble for a reason?"

"It was no trouble, Ma. Really. I had some extra time last night, so I thought why not?" protested Natalie. Digging through her recipe box had been fun for a change, a welcome distraction from everything else in her life, including the unfinished garments piled on her bed.

Maybe baking could turn out to be the hobby she never knew she wanted, the way people suddenly appreciate a shade tree in their yard, or a bookshelf perfectly sized for their tall art books.

"No Chad with you tonight?" Her mother craned her neck, as if expecting Natalie's boyfriend to appear behind her with a bottle of wine and a charming smile.

"He had a Skype meeting with his boss," Natalie said. He had texted her about it last-minute while she was changing. Before she could text him back, the battery had given out. But he probably hadn't expected a reply, knowing Chad. What could she really say, anyway? It's not as if she had told him this was a do-or-die family event, the kind that qualified for Chad's attendance these days. Which it wasn't, truthfully.

"Oh, too bad," said her mom without a trace of surprise in her voice, and not much disappointment, either. "Maybe next time, right? Go on through to the table—Guido's opening some of that wine his son Tony bought in Tuscany last summer. I'll just put this biscotti with the other desserts in the kitchen."

"Thanks, Ma." Natalie made her way to the table, where her uncle was prying the cork free from a bottle of red wine. His son was seated next to him, chatting with their cousin Gabby, who waved to Natalie as she slipped into the only available spot left at the table. Rob was on the opposite side, one arm draped across the back of Kimmie's chair, his other hand sneaking a breadstick from the basket in the middle of the table. Beside them, Brayden was passing the salad bowl to Natalie's other cousin Carrie.

Brayden. Natalie hadn't realized he'd been invited, too.

Faded jeans and a button-down shirt, his reddish-brown hair brushing against the collar in its usual scruffy style. Nothing could be more natural than the sight of Brayden at her family's dinner table. He practically *was* family, after all this time. So why did seeing him there in this moment seem so... unexpected? Surprising, in the way it felt to walk into a room and see a long-lost friend?

"Hey, Natalie," he greeted her. His tone was friendly but casual. "I, uh, didn't know you were having dinner here too," he added. A little of the discomfort was back, the kind she had sensed in his attitude from days ago when he met her outside her building.

"I was running late," she said. "There was a traffic jam on Magnolia Drive... Well, you know how rush hour is around here."

"Delivery men know something about traffic," he agreed, taking a breadstick from the basket in front of him.

Natalie followed his example, sliding one onto her empty plate. The salad bowl had disappeared somewhere further down the table, one of her younger relatives groaning as part of its contents were heaped onto their plate by an insistent parent.

"Here," said Brayden, passing her the dish for the main course. "Grab some of this before it's gone," he advised. "The sauce is your Aunt Louisa's Parmesan and spinach recipe."

"Mmm, that's a really good one. She makes that one for Christmas dinner sometimes," said Natalie. "I think it might be my favorite of all her specialty sauces."

"I can't decide that easily," said Brayden, shaking his head. "Her three meatball marinara and roasted red pepper ones are pretty stiff competition."

"The chicken Alfredo," said Natalie. "Can't forget that one." They both laughed at this remark, however —it was an old family joke that Louisa's Alfredo was the worst in the Grenaldi clan.

Natalie paused, winding a forkful of pasta tightly in place. "So, thanks again for inviting me to that party," she said. "Even if you did take a while to get around to it."

She was teasing him now, a little, but not meanly as in times past. Not the way she used to, when it sometimes felt like he was a shadow following her around.

His gaze deftly avoided hers, moving instead to the bowl of pasta being lifted between them. "Sorry if I seemed distracted that day," said Brayden. "Things have been pretty crazy lately, especially at work. But I'm glad you'll be there."

"Me too," she said. Nodding, as if to confirm it against possible doubts. "And congratulations again, by the way. It seems like your ship has finally come in."

"I think it might be more like a row boat in my case." Brayden grinned in that humble style she had grown so used to seeing. She laughed; so did he. Laughing with Brayden twice in a row was a record, something that probably hadn't happened since they were both in grade school.

"Who knows?" Brayden said. "Maybe it's the beginning of something bigger. Like your fashion show. That's got to lead somewhere exciting for you."

"We'll see," said Natalie, vaguely.

"What do you mean?" He looked surprised. Puzzled might be the better word, as if he couldn't understand how Natalie could doubt it.

"My intern is over the moon about things, of course. Cal's convinced we'll have our designs on the Milan runway someday." She shrugged. "I'm just hoping it will get us a foot in the door with more of the local retailers. It's a start, like you said."

"Hey, Nat, my friend Macy said thanks again for the formal dress you made for her," her cousin Carrie interrupted. "She sent a pic of her wearing it, if you want to see your handiwork in action." She was holding up a tablet from across the table, its screen showing off a picture of a young woman in a pale-blue gown, its seashell bodice and paneled skirt designed to complement her above-average height and slightly gangly build.

"She looks great," Natalie agreed. "But I think it's the smile that really sells it. See how confident and happy she looks? She just needed the right dress to bring it out. The attitude is what makes the outfit perfect; no matter how good an outfit is tailored, it looks lifeless and boring without a good smile to complement it."

"Is that what the posters are gonna say in your boutique?" asked Brayden.

Her boutique. Natalie shivered a little. "I'm just calling it how I see it," she answered. "Women aren't comfortable in their own skin all the time—frankly who is? But in the right outfit to bring out their best qualities instead of just hiding their less ideal ones, they can finally appreciate themselves."

"That's what you see in the picture," said Brayden. "The way she's smiling tells you that you found the real her when you sewed that dress."

A simple enough statement, but uttered with a profound gentleness that took Natalie's words for a moment. She blinked. Before she could say anything, her cousin spoke up instead.

"Be all modest about how good you are if you want, but Macy says it earned her tons of compliments. She recommended you to a friend of hers that's getting married next spring, so maybe you'll have another wedding gown to sew," said Carrie.

"Who needs Paris when you've got Carrie selling your clothes to every woman she's ever met?" joked her cousin Tony.

"I know Natalie. She'll take Paris if she can get it," asserted Maria, in the voice of one long-resigned to this idea.

"I wouldn't say that." Natalie's vague, faraway voice had returned once more for this topic. She poked at a dried tomato among her uncle's sweet sauce ingredients.

"Maybe Natalie will be busy making her *own* wedding dress." This hint came from Rob's girlfriend, Kimmie, a mischievous smile in place. "She and Chad are heading for the big six months. I'll bet she's at least started a folder for inspiration just in case."

A few chuckles greeted this prediction. Natalie rolled her eyes, trying not to think about the one that Tessa and Ama had already started on her behalf. "Kimmie, we're not engaged. Dating is about testing the waters, not a marathon swim to the other side."

"You've tested enough waters to be an Olympic swimmer by now," scoffed Rob. "Face it, sis—there comes a time when you have to make a decision and stick with it for better or worse. That's what I plan on telling Kimmie the next time she tries to break up with me anyway."

His girlfriend delivered a smack to his arm. "Don't end up with a joker like this, Nat. Play it safe and pick Chad with his hunky build and sense of adventure. You won't regret it, trust me."

"I'm not picking anybody for better or worse." Natalie's tone sharpened suddenly. Anger, she realized. That's what it was. Was that a healthy emotion to be spawned by thoughts of her and Chad being together forever?

Brayden had kept quiet through all of this. She glanced at him, half-expecting to see a little misery in his eyes at the subject of a long-term future for her and Chad. Instead, he offered her a smile. A supportive and sympathetic one, if she wasn't mistaken.

Maybe Brayden really *had* changed. And changed his mind about her in the process.

"Stop needling your sister," Maria scolded her son as she began to collect the empty plates around the table. "You two are always fighting, always criticizing. Can't you act like flesh and blood?"

"That's what flesh and blood do act like, Ma," Rob insisted. "Besides, I'm just kidding around. Everybody knows Natalie isn't going to pick any of the guys she dates. She'll probably wind up on old maid, holed up in that apartment, trying on all her old dresses in front of a big mirror. Wearing a designer wedding gown around the house like that crazy old lady in some Charles Dickens' book."

"Since when do you read anything besides the sports section in the newspaper?" Natalie shot back.

"Cliff notes, sis. It's a guy's best friend in English class. What's for dessert anyway?" he asked, turning to their mom again. "You said you were making that blueberry cream cake earlier…"

Conversation shifted in a new direction after this, to Natalie's great relief. Everybody forgot all about the possibility of her and Chad getting hitched, the discomfort she expressed for the idea, and the fact that she showed no interest whatsoever in a glamorous career in Paris.

After dinner, Natalie helped her mom wash the tons of dishes that accompanied a Grenaldi dinner, drying the last pan as the summer sunset turned the sky to a deep rose. Stepping onto the back porch, she hugged herself as she gazed at the horizon, only to realize that someone else had had the same idea as her.

Brayden stood by the porch rail, cell phone in hand as he looked at something on its screen. He hadn't gone home as she had assumed a half hour ago, but must have stuck around to talk with her brother and cousins.

Texting a friend? Or returning a missed call? He would probably be the world's most chivalrous date, she imagined. He never answered his social media messages at the dinner table.

She started to ease back through the door, but its hinges groaned, giving her away. Brayden's smile was one of surprise when he glanced up. But not dismay.

"Trying to find a cell signal," he explained, holding up the device in his hand, a meager single bar visible on its tiny screen. "My provider's crappy coverage makes service spotty a lot of the time."

"You should probably switch," Natalie said. "You might as well. As long as you're making so many other changes, I mean."

Brayden laughed. "Yeah, probably. After I move I'll have more time for little stuff like that."

They both fell quiet for a minute. "Nice night," Brayden remarked. "Your mom's gardenia is in bloom. It doesn't feel like summer officially until I catch a scent of that. Must be nostalgia."

Natalie grinned. "It makes me think of this air freshener Tessa just bought for the office. She said it infuses the place with the scent of southern charm."

"Makes me think of camping." He had leaned back against the porch post now, hands resting in his pockets. "Remember all of us camping out here in the summertime? Me, you, Rob, a few of your cousins. We were—what? Six, seven years old?"

"Something like that," Natalie said. It had been ages ago at any rate, and sometime before Brayden's crush became like a giant immovable wedge between them. Back when they were still friends, at least mostly friends, even though there had always been a couple years' difference in age between them. Brayden was her big brother's friend, the only one willing to be nice to her when she was only the annoying kid sister who wanted to tag along.

"You and Rob had to use Uncle Guido's old tent, right? The one with that big tear in the roof."

"The skylight," Brayden grinned. "That's what we called it. Good thing we weren't scared of bugs, since it was full of them most of the time."

"Bugs weren't the problem," Natalie said. "The problem was anytime Bilbo escaped from the yard next door and raided our stuff. Remember the time he ran off with that mini cooler of sandwiches?"

Bilbo was the semi-vicious dog belonging to one of Natalie's neighbors. He was never allowed out without a leash, but every so often he would dig his way out to terrorize the neighborhood children and steal stray possessions in other yards.

"Good ol' Bilbo." Brayden shook his head. "I always liked him, even if he was kind of a menace to the neighborhood. I was glad he lived to a ripe old age."

"The neighborhood hasn't been the same without him," Natalie said, wryly. "Or his owner, since they decided to move to that retirement village in the new part of town."

"How come their place is still empty?" Brayden wondered, glancing toward the darkened house on the other side of the fence. "They could probably get a good price for it. Seems like it has a nice-sized yard."

She shrugged. "I've never seen it up-close," said Natalie. For obvious reasons, when the big grumpy dog was still its occupant.

"I have," said Brayden, and grinned.

Natalie did the same, blushing slightly. The memory of Brayden going over the wall for her favorite doll—while terrible at the time, and embarrassing for most of her adolescent and adult life—had a certain humor in it.

As if by silent agreement, their steps had moved from the porch in the direction of the old fence in the distance. Some of its slats had been damaged where a tree branch had landed on it in a recent storm. Natalie wished the owner's realtor would suggest they get those fixed, since it bordered her mom's yard where she liked to grow plants.

Brayden rested one hand against the fence, peering upward to the rooftop and tree line visible on the other side. "I guess I've only been back there that once," he said. "I was too busy at the time to really look at the place."

"Don't remind me," Natalie said, cringing slightly at the memory. "My family will never, ever let me live that down—how I almost got you killed as a kid by letting you rescue my favorite doll from a doghouse."

"It was just a tiny little nip on the arm. Not that much blood and only twelve—"

"—stitches," Natalie finished automatically.

They looked at each other. Brayden was the first to laugh, though it had a sheepish sound. "It was pretty crazy of me to go after it," he admitted. "But kids do crazy things, right?"

You did crazy things for me, Natalie almost said. It was true. Then, and until now, there wasn't anything he wouldn't do for her. Even keep his distance to make her happy. No one else in her life would ever do those kinds of things for her again, gestures as cheesy as the ones in all of Tessa's chick flicks, as unreal as all the larger-than-life moments in one of Ama's favorite Bollywood love stories. He was everything she had disbelieved and mocked when it came to love in real life.

"They do," said Natalie. Brayden probably thought he'd win her heart forever by snatching her princess doll back from Bilbo's clutches… and he probably would have done it anyway if he had known how it would end, she reflected.

An old ladder was leaning against the fence where Rob had trimmed some of the storm-damaged branches away at their mom's request. To her surprise, Brayden scaled its rungs, leaning over the top of the fence to look at the yard below. "Wow," he said. "This place looks exactly the way I remember it. I think some of Bilbo's stolen goods are still down there even."

"Ugh," said Natalie, making a face. That could be why the house wasn't selling maybe—old piles of junk had a way of discouraging prospective buyers.

To her surprise, Brayden swung a leg over the fence, then another. Natalie watched in astonishment as he dropped out of sight a moment later. A sound like something colliding with metal reverberated, followed by some scuffling sounds that made her apprehensive.

"Brayden?" She stepped closer, her arms tightening around herself. "What are you doing?" She tried to peer through the broken slats on the fence, but all she could see were mimosa blossoms and some bricks that might have been part of a flower bed once upon a time. "You didn't fall and crack your head, I hope. Ma will kill you if you hurt yourself doing something stupid." Her tone was joking, but inside she was slightly on edge. There was still something menacing about the thought of Bilbo's yard, and for Brayden to just brazenly trespass on it seemed a little dangerous. Maybe she was getting sucked back into her childhood self at this moment.

"It's okay," he called back. "I'm just looking around a minute. There's some interesting stuff back here. That noise was just me landing on the metal trash can under the fence, by the way."

She stood a moment, debating whether she should go back inside. A part of her was curious to see what he was doing. After a moment, she placed a foot on the ladder and started climbing.

This was nuts, though. Why would two grown adults climb an old fence to sneak into an abandoned backyard? It was the kind of thing teenagers did when they were bored, but Natalie couldn't help feeling a strange sort of thrill as she hoisted herself over the fence into forbidden territory. At least she was wearing flats today, her shoes hitting the metal trash can below with a soft thud.

Brayden was crouched beside the old brick doghouse, where the "treasures" from Bilbo's collection remained. Dandelions sprang from the neglected earth around them, a series of tangled vines crawling from the brick flower bed nearby. *This place could definitely use some TLC*, Natalie thought.

Brayden lifted a broken plastic sword from the pile and brushed its dirt off. "This is like the ones we used for playing pirates back then. Rob always got to be the captain. He'd clip a stuffed parrot to his shoulder and wear that eye patch he got from the drugstore."

"You got to play the stowaway, right?" Natalie asked, knowingly. "Forced to walk the plank by my rotten brother." In real life, it was the teeter-totter in the park. "You should have told Ma and made him switch with you." Brayden ended up with more skinned knees from gravel that summer than in the entirety of his childhood.

"He used to let you play the kidnapped princess," said Brayden.

"Only to shut me up," she said. "But I was the crew's cook sometimes too."

"He knew you could steal cookies more easily, that's why," laughed Brayden.

She remembered donning a castoff apron from the restaurant's kitchen. "It was better than being a damsel in distress all the time, wasn't it? At least I could wield pretend knives and use pirate talk like 'avast ye matey' and 'shiver me timbers.' Besides, there was no point in being a princess since—" She caught herself here.

"Since there was nobody to rescue you," concluded Brayden.

She swallowed. "Pirates aren't the most charitable and chivalrous bunch," she said. "Besides, they'd already made the only person who would've done it walk the plank."

He could have come back in the game as a swashbuckling prince, though they both knew the reasons why that wouldn't have worked.

She took a deep breath. "Remember when I pretended to be a victim of the 'scurvy' outbreak?" she asked. One of Rob's geekier friends had pretended to be the ship's doctor, prescribing her chewable vitamin C while using a lot of scientific lingo he'd memorized from old episodes of *Star Trek* or something.

"Those chewable vitamins made you throw up," he chuckled. "That's what I remember."

"Thanks," she said, sarcastically. She picked up the pieces of an action figure that Bilbo had chewed to bits. One of Rob's, probably.

"I doubt I would even have been allowed to play with you guys if not for you," she said. "I'm still not sure how you convinced my brother to let his annoying little sister tag along, but I know it definitely wasn't his idea. I don't think I ever thanked you for that. I just took it for granted that you would always let me play."

He shrugged. "What can I say? I wasn't afraid of getting cooties, I guess." A slight grin followed this statement. Quiet, but ever so sardonic, to Natalie's surprise.

Was he really teasing her? Brayden Carmichael teasing *her*, Natalie the queen of sarcasm? It would seem impossible if it wasn't happening before her eyes. And it caught her so off guard that she actually forgot to think of a comeback. Instead, she gave him a playful little shove on one shoulder, fingers making contact with him for the briefest of touches.

"Easy, there. I'm armed, remember?" Brayden waved the plastic sword in mock defense. "I guess I could rescue you now, if you still want to play princess, m'lady."

"M'lady?" She grimaced at his awful pirate impersonation. "Wouldn't a pirate be less formal? More like, 'wench' or 'lass,' or something like that?"

"Yeah, probably. Guess I'm out of practice."

He let the sword drop, and they glanced over the other lost treasures in the pile. "Hey look," he said, fishing a roller skate from the rubble, its strap hanging by a thread. "This was probably yours. You skated all over the neighborhood back then."

"I was *the worst* at skating," Natalie said.

"I know. Always falling down or breaking a strap. I must have fixed your skates for you a hundred times…" He trailed off, getting lost in a memory. Or maybe he was just tired of reminiscing about all the nice things he'd done for her.

Brayden had always managed to put her straps or wheels back in place. And helped her up and put his arm around her when she wouldn't stop crying after a fall…

Natalie's gaze met his, and she felt certain that he was remembering the same thing. A shiver passed through her, stronger than either the guilt or the regret. Before she could think of what to say, another voice broke through the silence. Her brother Rob was peering over the fence at them with a knowing grin.

"You know, I thought I heard someone talking back here," he said. "You two will be so busted when Ma finds out you're trespassing. By the way, Nat, she wants to know how much dessert you want boxed up to take home."

"Just a slice of cream cake," said Natalie, getting to her feet again. She glanced at Brayden. "Don't worry, he'll never rat us out to my mom. He knows I have way too much dirt on him to ever sell me out for something this minor."

"Thanks," said Brayden. He climbed to his feet as well. "I wouldn't want a lecture from your mom. They're pretty tough if I recall from grade-school days."

"Even tougher now," she said. "But you're safe this time."

On the drive home, Natalie found herself pondering an unexpected question: could she ever be friends with Brayden again?

Really and truly friends, and not just two people who shared a bond for old times' sake, for instance. A few weeks ago, she would have said it was unlikely, maybe even impossible. But now, it was different. Brayden was different. So was she.

Seeing him tonight had been like seeing him for the first time. Well, maybe not that dramatic, but it was definitely different than any time she'd spent with him since their awkward years began in pre-adolescence. Being around him was almost comfortable, almost natural. Maybe even a little bit fun, the way it had been when Brayden was the one who gave her access to Rob's exciting adventures.

Maybe this was how it always should have been between friends like them. A part of Natalie felt an ache that she would probably never know if it was true.

Chapter Eighteen

Harper turned in a slow circle before the mirror in one of the Palmetto Isle Resort's suites, admiring the wedding dress fabric's sheen, and the long train spread around her feet and across the polished wood floor.

"Look at this thing," she said. "I feel like I'm the girl in that perfume ad where the dress sweeps the whole floor. It fits me like a glove." She pressed her hands against the fitted seams of the bodice. "How can somebody make a dress this perfect?"

"With years of practice and experience," answered Natalie. "You look gorgeous."

"She does, doesn't she?" The designer, Nola Gayne, had a mild aspect and a blasé demeanor that didn't suggest she was responsible for the princess gown now gracing the bride. "I think just a little tuck near the zipper's seam, and we will be there." She made a note on her electronic pad.

"I think I might cry," said Harper, who was still gazing with disbelief at her reflection. "Can we get me out of this thing before I spot the fabric with tears?"

"I'll help her," Natalie said to the designer. "Go on with your notes." She unzipped the formal garment for Harper, noting the magnificent tiny hand-stitches along its garment panels, and the perfect ruches along the chest. She could only come seventy percent close to a garment this perfect with her own skills, leaving her in awe of Nola's talents. She'd never handled a Gayne original, even when working a brief stint at a runway show outside Bellegrove just after college, but the garments she had seen showcased on the runway always made her imagine that Gayne was ready to burst onto the fashion scene of New York, or maybe Milan.

"Thank you, Nola," said Mrs. Winship. "I think that dress will be very satisfactory for Harper." She sipped lemonade as she stood by, watching the garment fitting take place.

"I think satisfactory doesn't say it," called Harper from behind her changing screen. "Let's up the adjectives for this thing."

Exactly what the likes of Mrs. Winship won't do, Natalie thought, taking the garment handed out from behind the screen. She thought a tiny bit more steel entered the gaze of Harper's future mother-in-law, who looked staid and dully elegant in a plain cream summer dress trimmed with blue braiding along its collar.

"I'm glad you approve," said Nola, with an equally mild smile. "I'll make some final alterations before the big day, but nothing major." She carefully folded the dress in one of her trademark garment boxes with the dramatic, streaky-style printed letters spelling out *Nola* across the top.

"I sent you those links to the bridesmaids dresses we talked about," Natalie informed Harper as the bride emerged from behind the screen in a colorful spring-green fake chiffon that seemed oddly dressy for today, even with striped canvas and straw sandals and a shell necklace to dress it down.

"Good," said Harper. "I'm having trouble getting the girls together for picking them out, but I'm thinking Saturday. I thought maybe we'd have tea at that English Ivy place that looks so swanky on all the tourism brochures; I've got a whole stack of them at the travel agency." She shrugged on a white blazer with green daisies embroidered on its pockets, and reached for a big straw-weave handbag.

"I spoke to Marsha yesterday," said Mrs. Winship. "She won't be available except on Friday. I think Lilia volunteers at the local amateur ballet society until one." She took another sip of lemonade.

"So when will they all be available?" Harper sounded hurt. She had been looking forward to this day, or maybe she was just eager to get through her first social outing with a group of strangers who would be sharing her biggest day. That's how *she'd* feel about it, at any rate.

"I can call them and try to arrange something, if you like," said the groom's mother. "Perhaps at the club next Friday afternoon? It's conveniently located next to Marsha's and Burkette's offices, and near the showroom for some of the more decent retailers in the city. But the girls have very busy lives, Harper, dear, so perhaps you should consider simply purchasing the dresses and having them altered to size. I'm sure the wedding planner's fashion consultant would happily do it."

"Sure," said Harper. "We can go that route, if that's what it takes. I just thought it might be nice to get together before the wedding. I mean, they are walking me down the aisle, right?"

"At least you'll have your dad," said Natalie.

"Sure." This time, however, Harper's tone was vague. She jammed a floppy white straw hat on her head with a sigh, one that puffed her cheeks out momentarily.

*

From the flagstone platform overlooking the blue sea, Tessa gazed at the future wedding site from the exact spot where the nuptials would be conducted. The breeze fanned the bright canna blossoms and some vivid summer lilies, in the vibrant color shades she imagined Accented Creations planned to incorporate in its three possible centerpieces and bouquet design for Harper.

The beautiful site of lush green and bold colors, the elegant mosaic tiles surrounding the tiered stone fountain with its gentle crystal stream… It really was a breathtaking site. Harper and Brett would be standing with the sea and the first colors of the sunset as their backdrop, every bit as incredible as the posters in Harper's travel-agency windows.

With a sigh of contentment, Tessa snapped photos facing both ways, then crossed the garden courtyard to the hotel's side entrance. Time to gather her thoughts for a presentation on the chef's menu paired with Ama's thoughts on the dessert buffet, which embraced Blake's idea of an ice sculpture fruit fountain wholeheartedly. Both the Winship parents were coming, although there was still no sign of either the Lucas family or the elusive groom.

Maybe Natalie's suggestion that he didn't exist was valid. Brett Winship might be an illusion shared by both bride and family alike, Tessa thought, amusedly.

"We have ten minutes until lunch," she called to Ama, who was sitting in the suite provided to them for the day. A sketchpad lay on the baker's lap, depicting designer chocolate truffles and petit fours decorated with dark-chocolate mirrored ganache and candied fruit peel. Ama was staring out the window as if her mind was far from the proposed desserts.

"Hmm? Oh, yeah. I'll be ready." Ama closed her book and tucked it in her shoulder bag. "Where's Natalie?"

"She and the bride were on their way to the hotel's main dining room," said Tessa, who freshened up by trying to tame the mess the sea breeze had made of her hair.

The door to the Winships' suite was partly open as she walked past a few minutes later, a pair of golf clubs parked just inside, proof that Terrence Winship had returned from his latest tee time. Tessa caught the sound of their voices, realizing they were discussing their son's upcoming wedding.

"She's dreadful, but it could be worse, I suppose. She's not as avaricious as that gold-digger Tiffany that we feared he was going to marry," Myra Winship was saying. "You could see the gleam in her eyes every time he pulled out his credit card at a restaurant."

Tessa halted.

"At least Tiffany could speak French and had a college degree of some sort," said Terrence, dryly. "She had some poise and dignity in public—she could *pass* for one of us, with a little help, which you and I both know this girl will never be able to do. I imagine her parents are ripped from the cast of *Roseanne*. They'll cross the ferry in monster trucks and tip back beers through the whole reception," he mused.

"You have an excuse to be absent for planning it, at least. I'm trapped here the whole time."

Tessa walked on, slowly. She tried not to feel hurt and indignant on Harper's behalf, though it wasn't working. It wasn't her job to be concerned with the personal feelings of the wedding families, so long as everyone behaved in public... but to know that all the worst suspicions she had held about the Winships were true still stung. Harper tried hard to give them the benefit of the doubt, and this was her reward.

Did Brett know that his parents felt this way about Harper and the woman he had previously dated, she wondered? Or did he not care how they felt about his romantic partners?

*

Harper was standing at the resort's picture window with Natalie, chatting about the different cruise packages available for the summer, and about the honeymoon destination for her and Brett.

"He took charge of it, as a sort of wedding gift," she said. "Through this fancy agency that he uses for his yearly vacation, of course. They mapped the whole thing: a cruise around the Cayman Islands, then we fly to Europe for a weekend in Paris, then a trip on the Venice Simplon-Orient-Express. Luxury all the way, and hotels so exclusive that most people don't even know about them." Harper gave a deep and enamored sigh. "I feel like it can't get better than this."

"He must be a great guy," said Natalie. "If we ever meet him, I'll have to compliment him on his taste."

"He's so…" Harper paused. "Attentive. He finds out what I want and he takes care of it. I never had somebody do that before. Sure, I had promises, but no action. Brett's so capable, it's like he snaps his fingers and it's done. Not by him, necessarily—I mean, he has Ashleigh, and a staff that answer to him. And his people. You know—accountants, investment planners, a personal shopper—"

"So, a dozen people run his life?" joked Natalie. "If I had that many people working overtime to run mine, maybe I could be a millionaire with perfect taste, too."

Tessa's approach was eclipsed by another arrival through the front doors of the hotel. Harper glanced casually in that direction, then did a double take. The breath was sucked from her lungs, and without warning, she ran to the hotel's latest guest and threw her arms around him.

"You came!" she said. "It feels like it's been forever since I saw you." She kissed his cheek and released him from her arms as she turned to Tessa and Natalie. "This is Brett," she said, proudly. "Brett, these are the people planning our wedding. Tessa the event planner, Natalie the fashion consultant."

He was handsome, all right. Just like the photos Harper had shown Tessa on her phone. In his tailored suit, he looked the part of a perfect playboy executive, as if he was ready for the cover of *GQ,* or a billboard on the confident executive's choice of Rolex. Light blond hair with a single wave across his forehead, the rest gelled into place by product, charming green eyes, and a silvery gray tie paired with a charcoal-shade suit and polished shoes. And he definitely went to the gym on a regular basis.

"Nice to meet you," he said, and flashed them a confident but relaxed smile. "The wedding plans look great. I couldn't have done a better job selecting things if I had planned it myself."

"Thanks," said Tessa.

Harper's arms were wrapped around his own, her hand holding his as she leaned against him, looking relieved that he was finally here. Brett was in better control of his emotions for their reunion, giving her hand a gentle squeeze now and then.

"Mom. Dad." He held out his other hand for his parents as they emerged from the hotel's elevator.

"Brett," said Terrence, with a brief handshake.

"Hello, Brett dear." His mother kissed his cheek, briefly. The groom's business smile returned afterward.

"Shall we go into the dining room and talk wedding plans?" he said.

"Of course," said Tessa, who couldn't think of anything to say in the face of a real live version of Brett Winship except for matters of business, as if his executive side usurped the scene entirely.

"There's so much to tell you," said Harper, her gaze finding the groom's with an eager smile. "Gosh, I wish you'd been here for the first few meetings. I missed having your voice actually state your opinion, instead of reading it off a sheet of paper."

"Me too," he said. His cell phone rang. "Sorry, honey—I have to take this," he apologized, answering it. "Gary? What's the latest on the new headquarters in Atlanta? Right… send all the details to my assistant. We probably need to move on this quickly, if it's anything above 3 million. Sure. I'll be in touch today, but I'm spending part of it with my parents and my fiancée… wedding plans." He glanced briefly at Harper with a smile as he talked.

Tessa could see the surprise in Natalie's eyes, who mouthed the words *That's him?* as they walked. Harper had definitely landed the whole package, from a Greek god to a finance wizard, and without a single apparent flaw in between.

Chapter Nineteen

Natalie's phone buzzed as she waited in line at the coffee bar. She glanced at the screen to find a message from Tessa:

Harper's maid of honor dropping by at 10AM.

"Finally," Natalie muttered. She had wondered when another member of the wedding party might materialize. She quickly typed back:

What about bridesmaids?

Maybe. Still waiting to hear back from them.

Natalie frowned. Were the groom's friends being this rude to his future wife on purpose? So much for good breeding in elite circles. They had been dodging Harper like a case of the flu, and so far Brett didn't seem inclined to help her connect with them. But then, he had been missing in action for most of their wedding stuff himself, so it shouldn't come as a surprise really.

With a sigh, she typed:

See u at 10.

She slid her phone into her pocket as she accepted the two cups of coffee the barista handed her across the counter.

"Everything okay?" Chad asked as she slipped back into the chair across from him. "You looked kind of worried a second ago. Not bad news, I hope?"

"Just a problem with a client's wedding," she told him. "She's trying to make some plans with her bridesmaids, but it's not going well so far. They keep cancelling on her."

"So are you designing their dresses, then?" he asked, taking a sip of the special Colombian blend he had ordered. "You could probably make the world's first attractive ones ever if you did. Even a prom dress might stand a chance at flattering its owner in your hands."

"Thanks," she said, grinning slightly at this assessment of her talent. "But I'm not making any dresses for this wedding. The groom has a high-society background and a mountain of money, so he can just buy whatever they want for it. Plus, I've got the line for the fashion show keeping me busy, since it's just around the corner. I'll be making adjustments on its designs until the last minute probably."

"That's right," said Chad, remembering. "You know, I feel kind of bad that I'll have to miss that. If I hadn't promised the guys weeks ago that we'd head over to that canyon upstate and go exploring I would totally be there."

Natalie paused, slightly surprised he even bothered to say it. She had known from the start he wouldn't choose her fashion revue over his weekend passion, so she hadn't exactly been shocked by that choice. "I don't expect you to break your plans for my work," she said.

"Still," said Chad. "It's the kind of thing couples do for each other. You know, give and take. I feel like I should at least make the offer."

"You don't have to," she assured him. "I mean, we agreed we wouldn't put that kind of pressure on things between us. It's just not 'us,' right?"

This was all true. She really didn't expect Chad to share her enthusiasm for this, given their arrangement. But... wouldn't it be just a tiny bit nice if he did? If he had been excited for her, say, and not merely interested for her sake? They were really serious enough that Chad would logically be part of her biggest milestone yet. Maybe even celebrate with her, and do something mushy, like bring her flowers on the big day, or take her someplace special to relax that evening. That kind of wishful thinking was probably foreign to Natalie's DNA, but part of her wouldn't have minded for this occassion.

It wasn't Chad's style, and she had no right to expect it from him, either. It was different with guys who were romantics or the "soul mate" type, who would plan on appearing last-minute to surprise her. Something like Brayden was always doing, although in his case the chocolates were likely to melt and the fizzy champagne go flat when he popped the cork.

Despite those truths, it actually seemed kind of sweet when Natalie pictured it. It was Brayden's disarming smile, the quiet sense of humor that would shrug off those disasters. If they were real friends —or if his crush on her hadn't finally faded at long last—he would probably have bought a ticket weeks ago, and come to watch. He'd take photos, and stand by awkwardly and shyly to congratulate her post-show in the presence of all her cooler fashion colleagues. He'd listen to her talk about it for days afterward, and tell her what he thought of it. Maybe with more honesty than she gave him credit for, truthfully.

Hang on. Was she really fantasizing about... Brayden? In the middle of a coffee shop with Chad right across from her? Natalie suddenly imagined that the world had turned upside down, flipping her to an opposite version of herself. Chad seemed not to notice that her mind was elsewhere.

"Should I make a reservation for us at Loco's next week?" he asked, gathering the messenger bag he kept his work folders in. "My friends say it's the hottest new place in town, so I better call early. Their vegetable lasagna platter is supposed to be fantastic."

"Sure," said Natalie. "Sounds good." She kissed him goodbye—lightly—on his cheek, still a little confused by what had happened a moment before.

Then again, maybe Brayden coming to the show wasn't such an unrealistic picture. As a friend and nothing more, of course—just to be supportive, the way he had always been when he was still desperate to get her to fall in love with him, and not for any other reason that would concern her. Gathering up her coffee in one hand, her bag in the other, she made her way onto the morning sidewalk.

*

Right away, Tessa disliked the maid of honor. She was too perfect, and obviously not a friend of Harper's, nor possessing any intention to be one, despite her ingratiating smile that was practiced to the point of charm.

"You're the wedding planner, aren't you?" she said. "I'm Marsha DuMont. I'm a friend of Brett's." Her blonde hair was styled in careless-but-smooth curls, her dress as casual as any designer casual wear retailing for three figures could ever be. She was a stunning Greek goddess only slightly shorter than a runway model.

For some reason, Tessa thought of Mac, though there was no resemblance. And, unlike the phony-sounding maid of honor, Mac was actually nice.

"How nice to meet you," said Tessa. "You'll be helping Harper out a lot, I'm sure."

"Of course," said Marsha, with another pretend expression of enthusiasm. "When Brett asked me, I couldn't say no. We have quite a long history, Brett and I."

"Do you?" Tessa couldn't put her finger on why, but she sensed a subtext in these words.

"She's helping me find the right bridesmaids gowns," said Harper. "It's taken us this long to get together, but after today we should be friends, and come back with great dresses to boot."

"Just as soon as the other girls arrive," said Marsha. "I should check on their status. There's always a chance they've forgotten, they're all so busy." She slipped aside, dialing a number on her phone.

Yep, Tessa hated her. She reached this conclusion in about two seconds. Now the big task was keeping anyone else from knowing.

"Looks like we had a few little calendar snafus," said Marsha, with a pity face, as she rejoined them. "They'll be a little late. Is there somewhere I can wait for them, and maybe call my accountant and my pedicurist? I have to rearrange just a few appointments now."

"You can use our parlor," said Natalie. As she ushered out the maid of honor, she made a face at Tessa—that of someone upchucking after bad sushi.

Tessa hid a smile. Thank heavens Harper noticed none of this but was busy smoothing a horribly plain outfit that only Myra could have chosen for her. Or Ashleigh on a mean day.

"Isn't she nice?" said Harper. "I'm sure we're going to be good friends. Brett just loves her, and says she'll be great for me. And I'm really making an effort to get to know his friends. This should be fun, really."

"I'm sure it will be," said Tessa. She crossed her fingers behind her back. Until now, she thought there wasn't anybody involved in this wedding that she could like less than Ashleigh.

After a minute, Natalie reappeared and gave Harper a reassuring smile. "She's getting her appointments straightened out, so you won't have to wait much longer. By the way, you have my number in your cell phone, right? Because if you need to call me or text me for advice on bridesmaids dresses today… or anything… I'm glad to help."

Normally, she would have accompanied a client to look at garments, but Harper had decided to make this more about bonding with the other girls than fulfilling another task on her wedding to-do list. This time, Natalie would be on standby, and Harper would be left to the mercy of Brett's friends as they perused racks in overpriced boutiques and fashion houses across town. That's how Tessa thought of it, anyway. Harper, of course, had made it sound more like a fun "girls' day out" when she described it to her earlier.

"I might give you a call," Harper replied, punching Natalie's cell number into her contacts. Laughing nervously, she added, "I'm no expert on haute couture, so hopefully the other girls will help me out. But it would be great if I could shoot you a question if I need to."

"Absolutely," said Natalie, who was obviously thinking a little support might keep Harper from being so badly outnumbered when it came to this experience.

Perhaps Harper was thinking the same thing as she tucked her phone inside her bag again. "I should join Marsha in the parlor," she told them, summoning a smile to her lips again. "It's a good chance to get to know her a little before the other girls arrive."

"Of course," said Tessa, who glimpsed the maid of honor through the parlor's open door. Chatting on the phone and tossing her blonde locks as she swung one foot in a bored motion from her seat on the divan. If the bridesmaids were anything like the maid of honor, Tessa decided she would rather spend a day at the dentist than find herself in Harper's shoes right now. "Let us know if you need anything," she told Harper. Perhaps work had kept the travel agent too busy to form new friendships, but she wished at least one of the bride's past acquaintances could have found time to return to Bellegrove and help with her wedding plans.

As their client disappeared into the parlor, Natalie and Tessa exchanged dubious glances. Money could buy a lot of things, but not friendship—and Tessa only hoped the groom would realize that before his friends made Harper feel unwelcome at her own wedding.

Chapter Twenty

Ama sat on the bench in the station as the train rumbled past the platform. Arms wrapped around her knees, she gazed at a pouty-lipped model in a cosmetics ad on the nearby wall as several more passengers walked by to meet the next train, mingling with those disembarking.

She had come here to think this week, whenever she was free from the restaurant and planning the dessert buffet for Wedding Belles. The last place where she and Luke had been together seemed like a good spot to think about her possible future with him. Or without him, if that was the case.

She sighed. Life without Luke seemed impossible to imagine. But a life married to Luke, with her parents' disbelief and dismay on one side, and the unwritten future on the other—did she know that she could survive it? That once she put the ring on, she wouldn't panic and try to rewind that choice, causing Luke and herself deeper heartache than the one wrapped around her now?

Closing her eyes as the train began pulling away, she imagined Luke had disembarked from it and was standing on the platform, waiting for her. She had to give her answer to him now, from the gut instinct within her, the very bottom of her heart, a place she could trust. And that answer was absolutely—

Not coming to her. Ama opened her eyes, blinking against the lights in the station. One of the newly arrived passengers had entered, wheeling along a suitcase, pausing to remove an airline tag clattering against its handle. Not Luke from her imagination, returned home without warning, but a neatly dressed figure in a business suit and a pair of trim, black-frame eyeglasses.

"Tamir?"

He noticed her sitting on the bench now, a look of surprise on his face. "Ama?" he said.

Tamir, her sort-of ex—if someone could be an ex-boyfriend without having been a boyfriend in the first place. The neat, nice, dull Indian boy who had delighted her father through the short period of two dates Ama had reluctantly agreed to before last Christmas. He hadn't changed, except for the frames of his eyeglasses. Still as well pressed and sensible as before, when she had left him in the holiday square for the last time.

"It's nice to see you again," he said. He pushed his eyeglasses back into place on the bridge of his nose, and smiled politely. "Are you waiting for someone?"

"I saw a friend off at the station," said Ama. Days ago, but that was beside the point. She stuffed her hands in her jacket pockets. "How are you?"

"Good," he said. "You?"

"The same." She shrugged. "Can't complain."

Yup. Same small talk as before. Ama glanced down at the laces on her shoes. "Back from a business trip, right?" she said, since Tamir still seemed to be looking for some polite answer.

"Right," he said. "I travel a lot these days. I was promoted at my job."

"Wow. Congratulations," she said.

"Thanks," he said, with another smile.

"I should probably go," she said. "It was nice seeing you again." She turned to walk away but saw Tamir hesitate.

"Do you want to grab a coffee?" he said. "If you're not in a hurry?" He paused. "It's just that I'm hungry, and I've been eating every meal alone for the past week. I'd like some company."

Tamir of old would never have asked her to spontaneously share a meal. Ama felt surprised. "I'm not rushing anywhere," she said. "I'd like a cup of coffee."

Colors Cafe had a very old neon rainbow above their sign, and an equally old painted signboard for five-cent Coca-Colas. The kind of place that Brett Winship's parents would probably call a dump, particularly since it was in a neighborhood with an old car partly disassembled in its alley, and a combination tattoo parlor music store across the street. They were only a couple of blocks from the Blue Moon Travel Agency's exotic posters and from the petunia-draped window boxes of Wedding Belles itself, whose crumbling stateliness was worlds away by comparison.

It was an odd place for Tamir to pick; its convenience must have factored in, Ama decided, because this didn't seem like the type of place he would select after meticulously researching the area's beverage joints.

Then again, what did she know about anybody these days? She didn't even know herself, apparently.

Ama ordered a soft drink and one of the diner's famous mini burgers with summer tomato. Tamir ordered a plain cup of coffee and a small plate of fries with some ketchup and hot sauce on the side. "I think they probably wouldn't have any garlic here," he said to Ama, as the waiter walked away.

"You could ask," she said. "You could be surprised."

"I doubt it. Not much surprises me anymore." He removed his glasses and cleaned them with a lens cloth from his pocket. "Maybe the internet has lowered our skepticism as a society instead of making it stronger."

"You mean like all the talking kitten memes, or like impossible lawn mower stunts?" said Ama. "Some of those don't seem that different from a Telugu movie stunt." She reached for a paper napkin from the dispenser on the table as the waiter set their plates down with a friendly word of advice about the tricky tops on some of the salt shakers.

"You saw a Telugu movie?" Tamir sounded surprised, despite his previous remark on that emotion. When he and Ama had briefly dated, she had admitted to having little knowledge of the popular Indian action films.

"Sure. It came on late-night TV while I was baking a double batch of white chocolate cupcakes for a bridal shower," said Ama. "It was my second one, remember? I saw the one with the elephants."

"Right. You mentioned that," said Tamir. He sipped his coffee. "So... how are you?" he asked. "Since I last saw you. Are you still working as a baker?"

"I'm still at Wedding Belles, yes," she said. "Actually, I'm getting to bake my dream wedding cake in the next couple of weeks," she confessed. "I'm excited." She plopped a straw in the fizzy brown beverage, watching the bubbles rise to the top. "What does your promotion at work mean?"

"Travel, mostly," he said. "I'll be training security teams for my tech firm. Right now, I'm attending a series of human resource classes first. You have to know the correct way to conduct classes, so the firm can't be sued, obviously."

"Sexual harassment stuff?" guessed Ama. "Avoiding offensive jokes?" They really didn't have to worry about any of these things when it came to Tamir.

"More or less," said Tamir. "Not that they were worried about me personally stumbling into one of those problems," he added, as if reading her thoughts.

Surprised herself, Ama laughed. "I was just thinking that," she said. "Not that I was thinking it was because there's something wrong with that—"

"—just that anybody as sensible and dull as me never accidentally tells an off-color joke," supplied Tamir. His smile was different, twisted wryly to one side. A new expression from him that Ama didn't recognize but liked.

"Guilty," she confessed. "Not that there's anything wrong with being sensible."

"You're not sensible," he said. "You do what you want. You say what you think—not meanly," he corrected himself. "But honestly. That's a better way to put it. You were honest about how you felt about me."

"I had to be," said Ama. "I thought if I kept it up any longer, you were going to get hurt. I don't like hurting people. It's the hardest thing for me to do." It had been bad enough to see Tamir's lonely resignation last Christmas, as stoic as he had been in the face of the truth.

Right now, it was tearing her up inside to think she could walk away from Luke in a similar manner. If it had been hard with Tamir, who was barely a friend, it would be impossible with someone like Luke. They had shared too much, so there was no way not to leave a hole if she didn't choose him.

"If it makes you feel better, I wasn't brokenhearted," said Tamir. "Disappointed, a little. I did like you." He confessed this with a sheepish smile.

"I didn't dislike you," said Ama. "If things had been different... if we had been different people with similar backgrounds, and our families were more alike..."

"I'd rather not think about my parents' opinion, frankly," said Tamir, dismissively. Ama's eyebrows lifted in response.

"You don't happen to have a persistent auntie trying to find you a nice wife, do you?" she asked, jokingly.

Tamir blushed—the second time ever, to Ama's knowledge. "I think every family has its aunties," he said. "In some form or another. You do," he said. "I remember your Aunt Bendi from our first meeting."

"Auntie Bendi is one of the world's worst matchmakers," said Ama. "She married me off to half a dozen boys she met in the most random places. Right now, she's unhappy with me for my last—latest—relationship," she corrected herself, as if afraid that this terrible slip was a cosmic sign. "He's very... untraditional," she said. "Sort of like James Dean." Luke the rebel, whom her aunt envisioned sweeping her into the sunset on the back of his motorbike, then leaving her devastated in the next city down the road. She just never imagined that city being Portugal, of course.

Tamir nodded, solemnly. "A friend of mine from Haryana dated an American girl when he moved here—the first person in his family to court someone outside the conventional pool of choices. It was hard for them to accept it at first. But your family is a lot less traditional than his, clearly. They had just moved here."

"Have you ever dated someone who wasn't Indian?" Ama asked.

A sheepish look stole across Tamir's face "I haven't dated anyone, really," he said.

"What about after me?" said Ama. "You still had the matchmaking profile. I can't imagine there was no other girl on there you liked. I mean, there were girls on there way prettier than me. With college degrees, too."

"I didn't try again," said Tamir. "Actually, I haven't been out with anybody since last year."

She was his last, and only, girlfriend. This confession was almost shocking to her, for its symbolic nature as much as for the fact that an eligible boy like Tamir hadn't succumbed to someone's offer recently. Plenty of girls must find him attractive, because he was certainly good-looking.

"I didn't know," said Ama. "It wasn't just me that kept you from it, right?" she added, although not quite sure what way he would take this. Fortunately, Tamir laughed.

"No, it wasn't," he assured her. "It's mostly me. I think… I'm not good at relationships. I'm too reserved. How can you ever know someone in such a short time period? I'm not gifted at it the way you are. You make it seem easy, knowing a person after one conversation or two."

"Ever think that's a facade and not a gift?" Ama asked, wryly.

Tamir trailed one French fry through the hot sauce pool on his plate. "No," he said. "It is a personality type, I know; but it's still the real you. You're an open person. Me, I'm not. Sometimes I think I could date someone a hundred years and still not know them, truly. They wouldn't know me either."

"I don't think it would take you that long," said Ama. "In fact, I think… maybe it's just me… but you seem different from when I met you before. A little looser, a little more casual. Maybe you're already growing more comfortable in your skin and you just don't realize it yet."

"That's what I want to be able to do," said Tamir, gesturing toward her as if her words were physically present. "Say things like that to make someone feel better, and mean it. Granted, we have a history together, and we're not strangers. But that's still hard to do for a lot of people, including me."

"It's not much of a history," said Ama. "I strung you along for a few weeks, then finally confessed how I really felt. In public," she added, as if to remind Tamir that she was worse than he remembered.

"There are worse things," said Tamir, mildly. With a brief smile before he popped another fry in his mouth.

It was cooler than before outside when they emerged, a sign that rain was rolling in. Tamir pulled out the handle of his suitcase on wheels. Above, the rainbow sign buzzed slightly, its blue stripe flickering in the dark.

"Are you going home?" she asked him. "Do you… have a place?" He quite possibly lived with his parents, the same as herself, since it was traditional for generations of Indian families to live under one roof. Then again, if Tamir was trying to appeal to prospective wives, he might have gotten his own place for the sake of a little privacy. She had never asked him about it when they'd met before, since it hardly mattered to her what his living circumstances were while she was trying to escape the matchmaking game.

"I'm going to my parents' house tonight," he said. "You?"

"I'm still living at the restaurant," she said. "That's my final stop for tonight."

He nodded. "Thanks for sharing a meal," he said. "And for listening also."

"Same here," said Ama. "It was nice." She tucked back one strand of hair.

She thought Tamir was debating the possibility of saying something else—there was a slight side flicker to his gaze, and his lips parted to one side as if hesitating to speak. "What are you doing Friday, two weeks from now?" he asked. "I have these tickets for an event at the Bellegrove Cultural History and Arts Gallery. It might be really boring to you, so if you look it up and you're not interested, it's fine. But if you'd like to come, I'd like the company."

Ama's turn to hesitate. "I'm not busy, that I know of," she said. "But... you know that I... I'm not exactly free." He must remember Luke being mentioned, and surely he construed from her remark that it wasn't over between them.

"I didn't mean for a date," said Tamir. "Just to hang out. Would you like to hang out? I'm not at home long enough these days to make time to see many friends. I see more of my parents' friends than my own."

"Okay." She nodded. "I'd like that."

This time, their goodbye wasn't an awkward handshake but a friendly one. She and Tamir walked opposite ways under the streetlamps as a little patter of rain landed on the windshields of the cars parked outside the cafe.

Chapter Twenty-One

Harper's day out with the girls had yielded two choices for bridesmaids dresses: both kinds were elegant, expensive, and very high-fashion… but not special or eye-catching in the sense of style that Harper preferred, something Natalie acknowledged with dismay as she viewed the different snapshots Harper had sent her of the dresses. The bridesmaids and Marsha had definitely carried the day when it came to this aspect of the wedding.

"They're pretty," said Tessa glancing over her shoulder at the images. "Just kind of, you know…"

"Boring?" suggested Natalie. "I agree. But at least they're attractive. I had this terrible nightmare they insisted on something hideous just to embarrass Harper in front of Brett's social circle."

"Oh my gosh, I never would have thought of that," said Tessa with disgust. "That would be twisted. How does your brain even come up with a scenario like that?"

"I'm twisted, too," said Natalie with a mocking grin. "Just be glad it wasn't prophetic."

She emailed Harper her thoughts on the dresses, feeling like a traitor for endorsing either of the garments when she knew their client would have preferred something more in keeping with her wedding's theme. A fiery shade of rose or burnt fuchsia perhaps… or that rich magenta Harper loved so much in her personal wardrobe. Some would call it bad taste, but Natalie knew that bold colors could be made chic with a little graceful design work.

At least the bride was getting a beautiful wedding gown. They would have to have another fitting for it before the ceremony, but it was everything a girl could dream of for her special day. *Not something you'll see yourself wearing anytime soon, is it?* a little voice whispered inside. Silly folder and jokes aside, Natalie couldn't see herself standing at an altar with Chad. She wasn't saving clippings for cake designs or bouquets, despite Ama's prophecy.

But was it because of her age-old words on not wanting to commit—or because she was with the wrong guy?

As if on cue, her phone chirped with a message from Chad about their next date. A reservation at Loco's on Monday night. She smiled. One thing was certain, at least, and that was Chad's penchant for picking quiet places to dine, precisely the places where she could clear her head from all her work and worry. She tucked her phone back into her purse, knowing he didn't expect a reply.

It turned out to be a quiet afternoon at Icing Italia when she covered for her mom on the afternoon shift, with most customers picking up orders to go. Natalie worked on sketches for a new dress design in between filling cups of coffee and dishing pastries into plain white boxes. She tucked the notebook out of sight in her tote bag when Maria returned to help close up the bakery for the day.

"Thanks for minding the store," said her mother, boxing up two lemon tarts. "I know it's an inconvenience with you working so much, but what could I do? Rob had a thing with his firehouse training, Guido couldn't make it."

"It's okay, Ma. Really. I was happy to come," said Natalie. "Don't make a big deal of it."

"Here, take these for you and Chad." Maria closed the box's top. "The least you can do is take extra pastry to make up for it."

"Ma, I don't need them," said Natalie. "Chad doesn't like desserts anyway, remember?"

"Take them anyway. Maybe he'll learn to like them. Doesn't he need calories to climb all those cliffs?"

Natalie surrendered. "Hand me the box," she said. "You know I'm a sucker for your citrus tarts anyway."

"Finally," said Maria, handing it over. "Sometimes I wish you'd just take them without arguing. It's always so hard to give you something, you have to be forced to accept anything. Desserts, help, advice, comfort. Doesn't matter."

"I could be more like Rob and be needy," suggested Natalie, teasingly. "Of course, he minds the store like a wolf watches a pigpen, but who am I to criticize?"

"You know what I mean." Her mother's glance was sharp. "I'm a mother. I want the best for you, that's all." She locked the cash register with tomorrow's change in it, then flipped off the lights behind the display counter.

"We're low on imported flour, by the way," said Natalie. "You better put in an order tomorrow." In the old days, Brayden would have delivered it, wheeling it into the restaurant's pantry. He would have been disappointed to know that he had missed Natalie's workday, too. She wondered if that had changed.

"I'll make a note to do it in a couple of days." With a deep sigh, Maria shouldered her purse and glanced around at the bakery cases veiled in shadows now, and the display window stocked with Uncle Guido's long bread loaves and olive oil bottles.

Something about that sigh distracted Natalie from her thoughts of an old friend's feelings. "What is it, Ma?"

Maria shrugged. "It's nothing," she said. She lifted a couple of bakery boxes from the counter. "You know, I should probably start looking for a buyer for this place," she said. "I'm spending as much time looking after family as I do baking bread, and Guido won't always be around to chip in the way he does."

"Sell the bakery?" Shock was in Natalie's tone. "Ma, you would never do it. You love this place. It's a Grenaldi tradition."

"Who's going to run it someday?" asked Maria. "You? You have your own life now, your design career that will take you off to new places. Rob's not going to leave his job and run the business. And the two of you can't agree on anything, so I don't think you'll work out a solution between you both. No... I think it's better to face the facts on these things."

"You wouldn't." Natalie shook her head in disbelief. "You without this place? That's not you, Ma."

"Sometimes we become different people." Maria's tone was pragmatic. "Sometimes we have to, because that's the way our lives worked out. This is mine now, having a family business but no family who can run it the way it needs to be run."

Natalie was speechless.

Maria held up the topmost box. "Do you want some of this cream cake, or should I give it all to Guido? You know what a sweet tooth he has, but the doctor's been telling him his cholesterol is too high. I feel like I'm feeding the problem."

"Let him have it," said Natalie. "The tarts are my favorites." She could hear the quiet in her own voice, the lack of assertive opinions that any Grenaldi would wield for another's health or passions.

Selling the bakery—her mother made it sound so final. It hit home, contrasting with all her grumbling for getting stuck with weekend or emergency shifts there because Rob was too busy, jarred into a new perspective by the idea of a different name stenciled on its door or, heaven forbid, a dry cleaner's moving in to take its place.

You have your own life now, her mother had reminded her. Natalie sank down on her apartment's couch that evening, one hand propped underneath her chin. What did that mean, exactly? Her eye fell on the stack of sewing books on her coffee table, wound with a pink ribbon from trimming an outfit. That was the part of her that her family latched onto first, the part that made her different from them.

She loved designing, she really did. Both her burgeoning fashion line and her work at Wedding Belles—although she did feel like the weakest link in their partnership's chain sometimes. There wasn't as much for her to do, really, even in their busiest season, unless their client wanted her to design a dress… and with this latest wedding, she'd felt especially expendable, since their agency had taken a hands-off approach with the wedding gown and bridesmaids dresses.

But I could never quit on Tessa. I'd feel like I was quitting on a part of myself, she thought. Although, part of her feared their little trio was drifting apart these days. Between her own work on launching a fashion line and Ama's personal problems it felt like the Wedding Belles were less of a team right now. Did Tessa feel that way, too? Like her dream business was facing a few uncertainties as both of her partners' lives moved in new directions?

This must be how Maria felt about the bakery. The sharp pain in Natalie's chest reminded her how much she loved the parts of her life that everybody always said she took for granted. Her family, the bakery, her home roots: things she had fought against as obstacles, but loved with a fierceness all the same. It hurt Natalie to know her mother believed she wouldn't help save the bakery from closing, join forces with Rob and the rest of the Grenaldi's younger family to keep it alive. She'd abandon it in a heartbeat in Maria's mind, running off to work for Versace's fashion house.

What would Chad say if she talked to him about it? It occurred to Natalie she never once thought about sharing this problem with him. She never thought about sharing any problem with him, really. Not her worries about her Wedding Belles role, nor the tremendous pressure of the upcoming fashion show. Chad never really mentioned his problems to her either, except for the occasional bad day at work.

Maria wasn't selling the bakery. Natalie convinced herself that she and Rob would work something out, somehow, if it took every last fiber of herself, because her family was wrong if they thought she would abandon them.

Who said a fashion designer couldn't turn out perfect Italian loaves a couple of days a week at the family business?

Chapter Twenty-Two

"Do I replace this door or try to fix it?" Blake asked.

Tessa was startled back to attention. Until then, she had been sitting at her desk, envisioning Mac wearing Harper's designer wedding gown, and Blake wearing a tool belt over his tux.

"What?" she said.

"The door. I just told you I need to take it off the powder room and either replace it or repair it. What did you think I was asking?"

"I forgot, actually," Tessa admitted sheepishly. "I'm sorry. It's this wedding. You know, the usual issues when it comes to bridal parties and family disagreements," she added, even though it was a little more complicated than that.

Blake's gaze became more scrutinizing. "So, what's up with you these days?" he asked. "Before you say anything, I've noticed that you're not yourself, so skip the part where you pretend it's not true. I'm just wondering if you can talk about it."

Tessa hesitated. "Not really," she said. "I'm just pondering the conflicts of imperfect matches in romance." Not him and Mac—they were probably a more perfect a match than she ever wanted to admit. It was Harper she was thinking of, and the little clues all was not well for her in the happily-ever-after department.

"Imperfect matches." Blake looked thoughtful. "Personally, I always assumed those turned out the best," he said.

Tessa smiled. "Me too," she said. "But this isn't quite the same. This is more about people settling for something. Call it compatibility, accessibility, whatever. It's depressing when you think it might be happening. That someone is making choices just because they're ready to move on from their past, say."

"So we're talking about desperation here," said Blake, sitting down for the moment on the edge of the desk. "That's not the same thing as compromise."

"I suppose not," said Tessa. "I don't know what's bothering me, really, since it's not my business. It's just me feeling sorry about missed connections." Maybe just for herself, if she was being honest. And with Blake, she had a terrible habit of being honest, except when it came to the attraction she held for him.

"Those hurt," agreed Blake. "It's always lost potential that gets you. In anything in life."

"Sometimes it feels like our collection of regrets end up being the biggest of our lives," said Tessa. The blue feelings were pervading her whole body now, and infusing themselves in every thought which passed through her mind.

"I don't think that's true," said Blake. "I think we just keep regrets around longer than we should. We let good memories be fleeting and get away, but we keep the disappointments like we're afraid that forgetting them means we didn't learn anything from them."

"I learn mostly that I keep making the same mistakes," answered Tessa, wryly.

"I think you're doing fine," said Blake. "Besides, it takes more than a door or two closing to make anything in life impossible. Sometimes you can still find a way when you think all your chances are gone."

Easier said than done for me, Tessa thought. Chasing away Mac to profess her love for Blake would be a dramatic and disastrous way to undo her missed chance with him. But Blake had no idea what they were talking about, so he had no idea what ludicrous notions were in her head, otherwise he'd probably stop giving her advice right now.

"I think I blew this one," she said to him, giving him a better smile than before. "But thanks for the vote of confidence."

"I still think you're selling yourself short," he said. "Be impressed, Tessa. Look at this place, and what you've managed to build. It's been less than a year, and you've defied the odds for small businesses. That's accomplishing the impossible, a lot of people would tell you."

Their eyes met. For a moment, Tessa stopped breathing and felt her heart briefly skip a beat. And then her phone rang.

From behind her desk, Tessa gave a little leap in her chair.

"Want me to hand it to you?" he said, reaching for her cell phone by her handbag.

"No," said Tessa. "I mean, yes. Of course." She accepted it and answered it. "Hello?"

"Ms. Miller? This is Brett—Mr. Winship's—assistant." She recognized Ashleigh's annoying voice right away. "I have a quick question about the changes to the guest list, if you have time."

"Which changes?" Tessa felt annoyed, though there was no good reason for it. Blake gave her a nod of farewell as he exited her office. *There goes my last big chance*, she thought.

"Here, I'll read the list off to you," said Ashleigh, as Tessa settled in for a very boring conversation.

*

Natalie's fork rolled through her pasta and pesto in Loco's softly lit dining room. What was supposed to be a relaxing night out with Chad to clear her head had been anything but so far. Probably because she had chosen to confide in him about some of the stuff weighing on her mind instead of sticking to their usual lighter topics.

"If your mom wants to sell, let her sell," said Chad. "It would leave her life open for new experiences. Maybe she would decide to travel, or move to a new city."

"Ma doesn't even join Aunt Louisa on her Caribbean cruises," said Natalie. "Besides, she'd never leave the city. Move just when there's a chance Rob might finally give her a grandchild?" She realized a second later she hadn't thought to suggest it might be her instead, even though she and Chad were going on six months as a couple.

"It might be good for her. Being stuck in a family business can be the pits sometimes," argued Chad. "You didn't want to be stuck there, did you?"

"No, but… it's different for me," said Natalie. "I wanted to design and come up with fashions that helped people define who they were, and flatter their individual beauty. That didn't mean I didn't love the bakery, I just didn't want to run it the way Ma did, as the one who called all the shots."

"So what's the problem? If she sells, you can still bake. I mean, pretty much your entire family is in the food business. You and Rob could help out with somebody else's business, and your aunts and uncle can do the same thing. Besides, your uncle looks like he's getting too old to be baking bread every day."

"He looks older than he is," lied Natalie. Uncle Guido *not* spending every day in a kitchen would mean he was two steps away from the mortuary. Something Chad probably couldn't understand, since his sole family was his mother and some cousins on his father's side that he barely spoke to.

Her eye was roaming the dining room, and that's when she glimpsed someone she didn't expect to see at a table across the room. Was that *Brayden*? At a fine-dining establishment? A jolt of shock passed through her body. Brayden who only went to burger joints and other casual restaurants for as long as Natalie could remember? That might be a group of friends with him, though Natalie didn't recognize the other people at the table. And the woman sitting right beside him, her fingers briefly touching his arm when she spoke to him…was that his date?

Brayden was on an actual date?

Something odd was happening to Natalie's system, out of sheer shock and amazement. For a moment, she thought Brayden glimpsed her, and she felt the color vanish from her cheeks with the notion he might have caught her spying. Her jaw hadn't dropped open—that was some consolation, at least.

Her hand fumbled into the bread basket, seeking to cover for her momentary distraction. Chad didn't seem to notice, busy with his lasagna.

His phone buzzed, and he checked its screen—they had been past the "phones off" dating period for a while now. "Hey, Trey found an awesome spot for us to go climbing this weekend," he said. "Are you in?"

"Not this weekend," said Natalie. "I thought I'd help out Ma Sunday morning, then work on the fashion lineup for the show with Cal later that day."

"Okay," said Chad. "I guess I'll see you at my place after that?"

"Guess so." They had taken to this routine lately, his and hers takeout boxes at each other's places. Sometimes they Netflixed a travel documentary, sometimes they just sat quietly, answering texts and emails, making a little small talk in between.

"Gee, I'm so stupid, I forgot to ask," said Chad, glancing up from his phone. For a moment, Natalie actually thought he was planning to switch his plans and come with her to the bakery, given how rattled she had been emotionally this evening. "Do you have extra tickets to your fashion show? One of my mom's friends wants one. She used to collect Valentino years ago."

Natalie's heart fluttered back into place with his words. Ones that had nothing to do with Chad offering to help her with an emotional dilemma, it turned out. "I don't," she said. "She can buy them online, though."

"I'll tell her." The phone in Chad's hand rang. "I should get this. It's probably Trey calling about the climb." He answered it, rising from the table at the same time.

Natalie sneaked a glance at Brayden's table. The girl sitting close to him seemed to like him, judging by her body language. She was cute, Natalie decided. And so was her dress, a sleeveless twist-front style in a flattering shade of peach.

Was this a date, really and truly? Was she flirting with Brayden, or was that Natalie's imagination? If this really was a date, this was an amazing milestone for him, so why Natalie didn't feel happier for him was anybody's guess. Wouldn't any lifelong friend be excited that a girl that cute liked him?

"Hey, Nat, Trey's just down the block at the new Brazilian bar and wants me to meet up with him. He wants to introduce me to his new friend, a guide who might be able to lead us to a new spot we've never climbed before in Ecuador—if I don't go now, I'll miss my chance because he has a flight at ten tonight."

"Go," said Natalie. There was no point in saying no since it wasn't as if he was actually asking if she minded being left alone at dinner.

"I'll call you later tonight." He kissed her cheek. "Grab a cab and text me when you're home, if you think of it."

It was only after he was gone that Natalie realized that she had to pay the bill. Her hand dove into her purse, opened her wallet, and discovered no cash. Her credit card was charged almost to its limit with expenses for the fashion show, she remembered. What was she going to do?

"Look, I have a problem," she explained to the waiter, quietly. "My date left before the bill came, and I don't have enough to cover us both unless you take personal checks. Otherwise, I'll have to find an ATM."

"You can't leave the restaurant until you've paid," said the waiter. "And I'm afraid we don't take checks."

"I don't have any other way to pay, though," said Natalie. "My debit card got ruined, and all I have is this credit card, and it won't be enough."

"I can't help that. You have to pay your bill or you can't leave this restaurant. We've had a lot of trouble lately with people trying to leave before their bill comes."

"Can't you trust me long enough to let me walk to an ATM?"

"I'll have to call the manager." The waiter's expression was stony.

She should try to phone Chad, she decided. He would be annoyed by the interruption, but she didn't have a choice, really. Selecting his number, she waited, breath held... only to have it go straight to voicemail. For the first time in months, it seemed, Chad had switched off his phone for a social meeting. What were the odds?

The manager had the same attitude as the waiter, and while Natalie had sympathy for the plight of restaurants everywhere, she was beginning to feel like a criminal. More people in the restaurant were noticing this incident, some of them seated close enough to overhear her embarrassing predicament.

"Scan the card, will you?" said Natalie, hastily holding out the plastic card from her wallet. "If there's not enough, maybe I can scrape up enough cash."

The waiter accepted it and disappeared. "I'm sorry, but we have to enforce this policy," said the manager. "Where's the other person who was at this table?"

"He left," said Natalie. He had taken his car, even though cabs weren't always easy to hail in Bellegrove—if it was a busy night at the airport a city away, for instance, she had a long wait ahead of her.

"You're twenty-five dollars short," the waiter announced. He and the manager waited for what seemed like a painful interlude as Natalie fished every spare dollar and even the change from the bottom of her purse. The waiter's tip came to a quarter. She could feel the coldness of his glare without meeting his eye. She was going to have to ask her neighbor with a spare key to meet her outside her building with the emergency cash she kept hidden in an Oriental jar on her entryway table in order to pay for the cab home.

"I'll bring your receipt," the waiter said. The moment he and the manager were gone, she felt conspicuously alone. Just when she thought she couldn't feel any worse, a host nearly collided with a waiter in a hurry with a big tray of pasta, knocking Natalie's table, spilling the last of her wine onto her lap.

"Great." With a groan, Natalie went to the women's powder room to dab at the red stain. It left an ugly spot, even with the wine's puddle partly soaked up. Pulling her phone out of her handbag, she made her way to a small bench in the restaurant's lobby. On the off-chance Rob would answer, she dialed her brother's number first.

Pick up, Rob. His phone was switched off; he was probably at the movies with Kimmie tonight.

"Are you okay?" a familiar voice asked, and she looked up to find Brayden standing there. Had he seen everything that happened with the payment debacle? Heat rushed into her cheeks at the thought of him witnessing her hopelessly digging through her purse.

"I'm fine," she said dismissively, as if nothing had happened.

His suit was better tailored than the tuxedo she remembered he used to wear. With his tie crooked and his overly long hair in need of a little taming, though, he looked almost the same as when he was in old jeans and a ball cap. A feeling oddly like relief came to Natalie, though she felt prickly and irritated tonight.

"You don't have to check up on me," she said. "I can take care of myself, like always."

"Actually, I was heading that way," he said, pointing in the direction of the restroom door. "But if you need something, I can help. If you need some money…" His hand was already sliding into his pocket. Natalie thought of him paying for her cab ride home from her date with Chad, and felt embarrassment flood her. She could find an ATM and spare herself *that* discomfort at least.

How presumptive did she sound just now when she'd assumed he'd followed her? "No, that's okay," she answered, shaking her head. "I'm just making a phone call." It was the truth at least. "I don't need any help with anything. Don't interrupt your date for me."

Brayden's cheeks flushed red. "It's not a date, exactly," he said. His body language suddenly grew awkward, almost shy. "A few people from work invited me out to dinner, sort of a goodbye present. I've never been to a nice place in the city. Figured since I was leaving, I should give one a try."

"Right," she said, realizing what he meant. "Because you're leaving here soon." This still hadn't fully sunk in, strangely enough.

She gave him a faint smile as he passed by, then brushed absent-mindedly at the stains on her skirt. White fabric that made the Bordeaux look like bloodstains. She sighed deeply as she pressed the number for the cab company and waited for an answer.

To her surprise—and relief—they actually picked up. A thirty-minute wait for her driver, but what choice did she have? Most of her cousins were busy and her mother didn't need more worries. As for Tessa and Ama, neither of them owned a car, relying on public transportation and borrowed vehicles to get around town for the most part. She would just have to sit here and feel conspicuous until the driver arrived.

A shadow fell across her again a few minutes later. "Any luck?"

Natalie started, lifting her forehead from where it rested on one hand. "Yeah," she said. "It'll be awhile, but the cab company is sending someone. I guess they're pretty busy tonight."

"That's good. I was afraid you wouldn't be able to get one if traffic was busy." The concern in his eyes melted a little. "I couldn't have gone back to dinner knowing you were stranded here."

"What could you have done?" she asked. "It wasn't your fault, anyway." Or anybody's really, although she did wish Chad had given her a little more thought before he took off. No need to mention that to Brayden, though.

He shrugged. "I could've borrowed my friend Max's car and taken you home. It wouldn't have been a big deal."

And he would have done it too, she knew. It would be just like Brayden to leave a group of friends, even a date, to drive somebody else home. It would ruin his evening, sending him back to this place just when the party was breaking up, and he would never let on that he minded in the slightest. Especially for her sake, she thought. At least, that's how it had been in the past.

"What happened to your dress?" he asked, noticing the stain on her skirt.

"Just a little accident," she said.

"Shame. Pretty skirt." He paused. "Part of a dress you made, right? The one you wore to Chelsea's wedding?" He looked slightly unsure as he ventured this remark, as if not quite trusting he was right.

"You remember that?" Natalie was floored. He was right—she had cut it apart and refashioned it a few years ago when the bodice cut went out of style for good. "That was five years ago."

"I've got a good memory, I guess," he said. He smiled. "Night, Natalie." He walked on, leaving her to wait for the cab. Natalie lifted her gaze and stared at the wallpaper across from her. Maybe she could make a game of counting the stripes in it to pass the time. Anything besides watching couples enjoying their dinners.

From the dining room came the sound of laughter, which might belong to Brayden's party of friends. She glanced that way and could see a fraction of his table, the girl beside him touching his arm as she laughed. Ever so brief, but oh so telling. This evening might not be a date, but that girl did like him. She was leaning into his space ever so slightly, and Natalie couldn't explain the unsettling feeling in the pit of her stomach.

Was she jealous? No. Just no. Not of this girl liking Brayden, the same guy she'd turned down a hundred times, it seemed. Jealous of something she could've had in a heartbeat only weeks ago if she wanted it. Which she hadn't, and didn't, at least not ever before. So why was she asking herself if that was still true?

"Ma'am?" A waitress's voice roused Natalie from these unsettling reflections.

"Yes?" Natalie said.

"Here. For your dress. Your date said there was an accident with your glass of wine." The waitress held out a white cotton towel soaked in what Natalie presumed was cold club soda.

"Thanks." Natalie accepted it, knowing exactly who this "date" was, although the waitress had erroneously assigned him that part. Feeling confused and touched at the same time, Natalie dabbed the skirt gently, watching the pinkish-red stain begin to fade a little.

Chapter Twenty-Three

It was noisy inside the Blue Moon Travel Agency on Tuesday morning, and Tessa pictured a big party planning their vacation. Something she imagined might not be a bad idea after planning a big society wedding. Maybe Natalie and Ama would like to come, and they could get a cruise package to an island resort, with sun and sandy beaches, or maybe opt for a long weekend in New York. Natalie would love to browse the fashions in the windows, and Ama would die for some of the ethnic bakeries' diverse creations. Maybe a Broadway show at night, a museum visit...

She pushed open the door and discovered there was no happy crowd inside Harper's place of business, only two people engaged in a very heated discussion: Harper and her ex-boyfriend Danny.

"How dare you come here?" Harper demanded of him. "How dare you come here and tell me you love me? I told you I didn't want to see you again. I meant it, Danny, I swear I meant it."

"I can't give up on you," he protested. "I can't forget you, Harper, ever. I want us to work things out—"

"There is no 'us,'" she retorted. "There wasn't since you decided to go weld car parts together or whatever you were doing out in the world, Danny. Not since I told you point blank what I needed from you and you couldn't give it to me."

"When did I ever say that?" he said. "When did I ever refuse to do something for you?"

An incredulous laugh escaped her. "By the way you live your whole life?" she suggested. "By the choices you make, and the fact that you're standing here with two cents in your pockets, begging me to break somebody else's heart for you."

"The love of a man who sends you the same flowers every Tuesday? You don't even like red roses," Danny scoffed.

"What business is it of yours?" said Harper. "Get out! Get out of my place now. I don't want to see you again, you understand?"

Tessa moved aside quickly as Danny opened the door, pausing to face Harper. "You know you're crazy about me," he said. "That hasn't changed. You can't blame me, because I'm not the one who walked away. You made me go—you only had to tell me you loved me and I would've done whatever it took—"

"Go back to your junk metal!" Harper lifted an object from her desk and aimed for Danny. Both he and Tessa ducked as the item bounced off the doorframe and landed somewhere outside. "Out!" she yelled, and Danny exited, the door closing swiftly between them.

Fury colored Harper's face a bright crimson. Her black mane of hair looked teased and frizzed out beyond its usual barely contained style, as if raked in frustration at some point during their argument. She took a deep, rattled breath and straightened her blue uniform jacket.

"Are you okay?" Tessa asked cautiously as she took one step forward from the office corner, though she highly doubted she was the next target of Harper's wrath. The bride-to-be turned to face her.

"Just your luck to be a witness to the big blowup with my ex," she answered. "Pretend you didn't see. We'll both feel better then." She pinned her hair back with one hand, trying to smooth her curls' frizz beneath two sparkly black hair clips.

"What did he want?" Tessa asked, placing her summer jacket and her shoulder bag on a nearby chair. "Is he really trying to break up you and Brett?" She might have been wrong about the mental stability of Harper's ex.

"He's crazy." Harper expressed Tessa's thoughts more succinctly in words. "He thinks I still love him. Like I'd waste my time thinking about somebody from my past who's been gone for years. He didn't have the decency to look ashamed when he turned up here after all that time away. He didn't think I meant what I said just now, but I did."

"You don't love him, do you?" said Tessa.

Harper laughed, as if this was the most ridiculous idea in the world. "I would have to be completely delusional," she answered. "I would have to be a raving lunatic, loving some starving artist who could walk out on his life at the drop of a hat. No—I am happily engaged, happily getting married, and finally having a life that won't be full of crazy notions and saving pennies picked out of ashtrays to buy lunch from a vending machine." She plopped down in her office chair, the force of her emotions becoming kinetic energy now.

"I could be wrong," said Tessa, "but I think his problem is more emotional than delusional." Thinking of the cafe more than the scene that just transpired here. "He might still be in love with you, like he claims."

"He didn't love me enough to make it count in the first place," said Harper. "I can't imagine it's strong enough to matter now. He's just crazy, that's all." She pushed aside a stack of travel brochures, making room for Tessa's folder, which was still in the event planner's hands.

"He said you were pretty amazing," ventured Tessa. "Impossible to forget was implied."

"Look—don't feel sorry for him." Harper pointed, to add emphasis to this command. "Do not feel sorry for Danny Reynolds. He made his bed, all right? You don't know what it was like, loving somebody when neither of you had a future and there was nothing to look forward to except when it was going to come apart. Do you?" She looked at Tessa. "That's what me and Danny had. It was hard, but I did the right thing by ending it then, and that's all. Now, do we talk about this flower appointment or what?"

"Absolutely." Tessa laid the sketches on the table, and the ones that the artist from Accented Creations had emailed her. "If you're ready, we'll leap right in." She arranged them before Harper, who stared at them, but distractedly, so that no real reaction appeared on her face.

"So… if it's not too forward of me to ask… do you want to talk about it?" said Tessa.

"Hmm? What?" Harper lifted her head.

"You and Danny," said Tessa. "You said you don't want me to feel sorry for him. If you tell me the story, that would explain why… and it might make you feel better. But only if it's not overstepping any boundaries," she said. "If you don't want to talk about it, I totally understand."

Harper sighed. She swiveled her chair the other direction, facing a large wall poster of a tropical island escape.

"It was years ago," she said. "We were just kids. Danny says he had a thing for me since he first laid eyes on me. Outside this hall at Brooker College—I was taking a course in business school before I had to drop out, and Danny was studying in the trade program. I guess you could say I had eyes for him, too, that first day. Seeing him standing under that oak tree, chaining his bike to a post, and staring at me like the world had just stopped in place for him." Her voice softened. "He's not bad-looking. For him, it's all in the eyes, though, and the voice. I used to love that voice. No Brett, but then…" She shrugged her shoulders, as if this said more than words could.

Tessa crossed her arms and leaned forward on the desk, assuming her "listening attentively" position. "How long did you date him?" she asked.

"Six years. Seven," corrected Harper.

"That long?"

"It wasn't exactly dating. He says he would've married me at any second, but that's ridiculous. How was I gonna marry him? I worked, I had family who needed every dime I could make and then some—but he's the type who passes on a good-paying career to be an artist. It was already over between us, but he swore that when he came back, things would be better. Of course, he didn't come back for four years, but that's another story."

It was a terrible one, in Tessa's opinion, despite the *West Side Story*-esque romance at the beginning of it all. "He just left after that?"

Harper propped her chin on her hand. "He said it was to make a better life for us," she said. "His one big chance to make something of himself. It wasn't." She shook her head. "You can't live off love, that's what I say. That's all we were ever gonna have. How long does that last?"

There was no good answer to that question. It could last a lifetime or a few years or a few months, depending on the people involved. But being tied to someone who sounded as unreliable as Harper's ex could explain her fury when he showed up again. What timing: her ex walking back into her life not so very long before handsome, charming Brett swept her into a whirlwind romance. Poor timing, as

Danny would probably say, though Harper clearly hadn't taken him back when he returned.

Harper cleared her throat. "Enough about him," she said, dismissively. "So, I think I really like these flowers in the middle," she said, pushing forward one of the sketches. "How do they make the real thing look that grand?"

After the meeting, Tessa stepped outside into the fresh air, the scent of gardenias reaching her on the breeze from a flower stall two blocks away, along with the tantalizing, unmistakable perfume from an old honeysuckle vine creeping from a broken planter up the wall of a former department store converted into a rent-to-own emporium.

On the sidewalk, she saw a twisty, copper-colored shape lying near the trash can. The item she mistook for a snarl of metallic tape was actually a paperweight-style sculpture of a globe. Rough-cut continents welded to its bands, a spindle through the middle adhering it to a two-legged stand in the shape of twin leaves. It was definitely some of Danny's work, although different from the flower he'd given her.

She picked it up, studying it closely. Reaching into a pocket in her bag, she found the folded business card he'd given her. *You can't live off love*, she thought. Danny shouldn't try it, given the force of Harper's feelings on their past.

The studio address belonged to a warehouse near the waterfront— not the part that had become cool Bellegrove restaurants or even hip nightclubs like the Cannery, but the dilapidated part that tended to flood and was filled with condemned buildings and boat shacks. Tessa pushed open the door below the number listed on the card.

It looked worthy of being condemned, this space of gapped boards and iron supports with old rusty hooks and chains dangling from them. The concrete floor was pitted and stained, but it was the perfect zone for a metal sculptor, judging by the size of the creation Danny was now working on: a twisting tower of metal that possessed a vaguely human form in its shape and curves, the smooth luster of steel married to modified ironwork touched with rust here and there.

Sparks flew from a welding torch, a protective shield covering Danny's face as he worked from the third step from the top of a high ladder. Tessa shouted several times before he realized she was below. He lifted the hood and looked down at her.

"Can I help you?" he called down.

"I came to return something," she answered. "I'm the planner from Harper Lucas's wedding—the one you stopped in the street?"

Danny climbed down a few steps. "Come to buy something?" he asked. His clothes smelled of heat and metal; it went well with the scorch and char marks on the floor around his sculpture, as if the whole room exuded heat more crisp and smoky than the summer sun.

"No," said Tessa. "But I brought you this back." She fished the metal globe from her bag.

Danny's face fell when he saw it. "Thanks." He took it from her, turning it over in his hand. "Did she give it to you?"

"She threw it at you, actually." Tessa's smile was halfhearted. "I thought you might want it. I know you sell your artwork, despite giving it away."

He tossed it onto a nearby table, where several more small items of his handiwork were visible, a few resembling the paperweight he had given Tessa. "I sell a few now and then," he said. "At some of the artist fairs and the craftsmen festivals. But I didn't need it back. Probably should've let her toss it into the garbage. It might have let her finish working out her anger toward me."

"It's pretty," said Tessa. "And more conveniently sized than… this." She waved her hand toward the metal man.

Danny grinned. "That," he said, "is my masterpiece. Finishes at twelve feet tall in sections that disassemble at every four feet. When it's finished, there will be a connecting piece between the two hands. Kind of like a lightning bolt, or a music staff," he said. He laid the welder's helmet on the table and unfurled a blueprint-style sketch, revealing a facsimile of the metal man behind him.

"It's very impressive," said Tessa. "But I liked the paperweight you gave me better." She touched a copper rose lying on the table, beautifully fashioned so it almost looked like a real one dipped in metal. "Harper's not a big fan of red roses, is she?"

"She likes flowers that have more pop, more pizzazz," answered Danny. "I used to buy her neon-colored gladiolas sometimes, from this guy who priced down all his flowers at the end of the week. She didn't even mind that half the blossoms had already bloomed. Just plucked them off and put the stems in water. None of that stuff where you put a couple of colored blossoms in a plastic sleeve with an armful of baby's breath."

"She could've changed since then," Tessa pointed out.

He shook his head. "Not Harper," he said. "She didn't change. She might be trying to, for this rich guy who doesn't think flowers like that are good enough, but it's not real. She's fooling herself and she's fooling him." Scorn entered his voice as he dug through a pile of castoff metal junk nearby. Old car bumpers, automobile doors and hoods, even old train track rails, all jumbled with dead lamp stands, toasters, and other metal appliances.

"I think she really loves him," said Tessa. "Besides, you weren't willing to make a real commitment to her, were you? Running off after the breakup for four years?" She laid aside the metal rose, which belonged in a pile of similarly sculpted metal flowers, near a mini sculpture shaped like a flock of birds rising from a tree.

"Did she tell you that?" Danny dropped the fender in his hands, the aluminum clattering loudly against the concrete floor. "Is that what Harper said I did?" He laughed, somewhat bitterly. "Harper, Harper," he said. "Why? Why do you always have to see it like that?"

"Is it because that's what you did?" Tessa raised an eyebrow.

"Look at me. Do I look like someone who would walk away from the love of his life?" he asked. "From the love of a lifetime? That's what she is to me. I didn't leave her—I left 'cause she wouldn't give me a chance. I thought if I made something of myself, she'd finally let us be together. I saw my chance and I took it—it was that or keep hanging around, chasing dead ends, and waiting for her to give up on us for good. I begged her…" He turned to Tessa, his voice building a little passion. "I told her I was coming back. She wouldn't even give me the benefit of the doubt."

"So you didn't, I take it."

"It took me longer than I thought," he said, turning his back again. "I kept working. She wouldn't return my phone calls or my letters. Friends told me she wasn't seeing anybody else. I kept thinking she was going to forgive me as soon as I showed her what I'd done."

"What you've done is put scrap metal together," pointed out Tessa. "It looks great, but I think she was making the point that she's working a real job while you're playing with fire for fun."

"She would say that." He rolled his eyes.

"I said it. I'm just assuming that's her opinion," admitted Tessa.

"I have a good job, okay?" said Danny. "I'm a certified welder. It's a good skill and it pays well. I take jobs whenever I can, whenever I need to, to pay the bills. That's what I've done all these years… while still working on stuff that's just for beauty's sake. I didn't start out to be an artist. I was going to do the practical thing… It just came out of me while I was trying hard to be the other. So I thought, why not try to balance both? It made sense to me."

Not to Harper, apparently. There was a definite fear of risk and open life plans in the bride, maybe entirely because of her first love's career change. Or maybe there was something ingrained in Harper's past that made her afraid of ending up at the bottom forever.

"The big life-changing career opportunity didn't pan out, I take it?" said Tessa.

"Actually, it did, in its own way," said Danny. "I sold a lot of pieces, I built a reputation. I didn't get the grant for the park sculpture, but I got the attention of the guy who hired me to build this piece. For a pretty decent commission, all things considered." He glanced toward the metal man. "If I hadn't stayed, I would've missed the opportunity to do it. But I would've come back in a heartbeat any time in those years if I thought Harper would have me." He pulled off his welding gloves. Deep calluses and burns on his fingers and hands.

"She said you weren't serious about her," said Tessa.

He lifted his gaze, sharply, from a blister on his palm. "I proposed every other week!" he said. "Six long years I proposed to her. I bought a ring—two rings."

"Two?"

"They weren't exactly the Hope Diamond," he admitted. "But I promised her each time that I would be there for her, that she could look to me, always. But it wasn't good enough, because there were no guarantees of anything. Life has no guarantees, I kept telling her. We don't get anything for certain except for this. We can promise to love each other and keep it, no matter what it takes."

He sighed, tossing his gloves on the table. "You think she really loves this guy?" he said. "Brett the filthy-rich millionaire, who makes her wear neutral tones? I saw her in a beige dress the other day, and nude heels. It made me sick." He lifted a hammer from his pile of tools, and a pry bar.

"He seems like a nice guy," defended Tessa. "She seems crazy about him."

"Yeah, 'cause she thinks he can give her the moon," said Danny. "He can solve any problem, pay any bill like Superman with a supersized bank account. He can't give her what matters. He can step up for her when it comes to financial tight spots, but there's no heart in it for him, no real sacrifice or devotion in doing it for her. He can't make her really laugh, and doesn't think she looks beautiful however she looks."

"You said that she made you feel sick in beige," said Tessa.

"On principle only," said Danny. "I don't care what she wears. Even in colors she hates wearing, she's still beautiful." He paused before the twisted car bumper, as if momentarily losing heart for his project beneath this conversation's weight. He turned back to Tessa. "Why did you really come here?" he asked.

Tessa dropped her gaze to the floor. "She asked me to tell you not to bother her anymore," she answered. "She said if I saw you on the street that I should tell you to stay away from her. I thought it would be nicer if I told you in private that she isn't going to change her mind about Brett. She's moved on, and you need to do it as well."

She could see that Danny wasn't accepting this idea. A stubborn gleam was in his eyes before he looked away. "You came all the way down here to tell me nicely that I have no chance," he said. "You'll have to forgive me. I don't buy it. If I only felt half of what I felt back then, I still couldn't do it."

"Please, don't make this hard on yourself," said Tessa. "I'm being honest with you. I don't think she's going to change her mind. She seems happy with her life the way it is now. Or determined enough to make it true, even if it's not one hundred percent."

Danny lifted one of the metal flowers. "Here," he said. "On the house. In case I get famous after this metal guy moves to his new home."

"I can't take it for free," protested Tessa.

"Sure you can." He refused to take it when she tried to hand it back to him. He shoved one end of the pry bar against a twisted bolt in the fender and brought his hammer crashing down in the other end.

Tessa's protests were lost in the ensuing racket. Danny ignored all further comments from her, and his smile proved it was on purpose, leaving her with no choice but to walk out with his gift or leave it on the table.

It was pretty. Tessa twirled the long, coppery stem between her fingers, noting the fine detail on its metal leaves and the perfect droop of its outer petals. It was a shame that Harper didn't like long-stemmed roses that much, or this gift might have softened her better than the globe paperweight. But it wouldn't be enough to change her mind from the perfect future that lay ahead with Brett, Tessa was willing to bet.

Chapter Twenty-Four

"To the left," Ashleigh directed. "Now back to the right again. Stop—right there." She studied the effect, tapping a pen against her notepad in a way that annoyed Tessa more than she could say.

They had been in the Paradise Garden for more than an hour now, staging possible setups for the wedding day's outdoor photography session. This involved moving around a driftwood bench on loan from Blake himself and fashioned by his own skilled hands. He had accompanied his handiwork across on the ferry that morning and was immediately recruited—or wheedled—by Ashleigh to aid the groundskeeper in setting up the props for the photographer's consultation session.

Ashleigh let out a sigh. "Maybe the lighting might be better over by the fountain?" she suggested to the photographer.

Was the quest for perfection out of loyalty to her boss's wedding? Or just an excuse to admire Blake's rippling muscles every time he helped the photographer haul the bench from one spot to another?

Ashleigh had already cornered him again during the photographer's break. "I love this bench," she said, casting a pert smile in his direction. "How did you happen to find it?"

"I carved it, actually. Years ago for a craftsman workshop I attended," he said.

"You made this?" Ashleigh let out a tiny gasp of surprise. "You're kidding! This is fantastic work."

Blake's shrug was modest. "I need a little more practice to qualify as good," he said. "This was kind of like a learning piece at the time."

"Maybe you can tell me all about it later," hinted Ashleigh. "Over a drink. There's a great little pub on the mainland. Not too crowded and very cozy."

Blake blushed, although he didn't immediately shoot down this invitation. Tessa noted this, although she knew it was none of her business. Mac's business, yes, but not hers. Not as anything more than a concerned friend and co-worker, that was.

"Hey, Blake, ready to help move the bench over by the fountain?" The photographer had saved Blake from having to disappoint Ashleigh at this moment. Tessa couldn't summon much sympathy for the girl, try as she might.

The bridesmaids were here this weekend, too, which Tessa hadn't realized until she went upstairs to the bride's suite. She spotted Brett's "friend" through the open French door, the maid of honor who was trying so hard to be Harper's friend, supposedly. They were sharing salads brought by room service, sitting at the patio table on Harper's room balcony while she was out with Brett. Their voices attracted Tessa's notice as she laid the latest quote on the bride's bed.

"… but you have to be incredibly uncomfortable with this, given your history with him," said one of the bridesmaids—the one they called Buffy, Tessa thought. "If he goes through with the wedding, how are you going to feel?"

"I don't think he'll do it, in the end," Marsha answered. "Not Brett. He's in denial if he thinks he's over what we had, because it was so amazing he can't live without it. This is just a rebound for him, dating a girl from the wrong side of the tracks. I can't believe it's lasted this long, truthfully."

Her tone of voice had changed completely: less syrupy, full of the smugness and confidence of someone who always knows they're right. The kind of person who implies that challengers and detractors of their opinions have to be incredibly ignorant

"Maybe he really loves her, and you're both wrong," said the other bridesmaid, whom Tessa would forever label "the nice one" after this moment.

"He's calling my bluff," said Marsha, confidently. "That's all this is. He's waiting for me to come crawling back and apologize."

"Why? Why doesn't he just buy you something really glam and be done with it?" asked Buffy. "Nothing patches things up like a grand gesture, right? And we all know that Brett is great at those. So why hasn't he tried to win you back at least?"

"Because my parents don't approve. They think it's too soon for me to get married, before I've experienced everything I can on my own. They want me to do a world tour. Brett was so ready to get engaged, but he knew they wouldn't approve. We had a stupid fight over it, and until I say that I'll marry him even if they don't approve, he's going to stay mad at me. And pretend he's in love with Little Miss What's-Her-Face, apparently. As if he really cares about her that much." She paused, then giggled faintly. "It's kind of romantic, if you think about it... but it's also completely inconvenient."

"So he'll marry this bimbo, then divorce her after you've traveled the world?" said Buffy.

"Like I said, I don't think he'll go through with it. Why do you think he asked me to be her maid of honor? It's all just a ruse to make me apologize between now and 'I do.'" The maid of honor speared a cherry tomato with her fork and popped it between her lips. She still hadn't noticed Tessa, who was now retreating quietly, although with quiet rage in her thoughts. "But if anybody should apologize, it's him. I'm sure Brett will come to his senses eventually. Even though he's the one who wanted an ultimatum in our relationship when it was too soon."

The maid of honor was likely just an arrogant, bitter ex who was so self-entitled she thought everything was about her. There was probably no truth at all to this suggestion that Brett was still in love with her. Plenty of people have a fiery breakup then meet the love of their life who's the complete opposite of their old flame.

It was time to forget about it. Professionally, it was the right thing to do, and personally it would be the only way she could get through this experience the way she was supposed to: without a trace of doubt or negativity when it came to her client's happy day.

Just one more hurdle to overcome in your assignment, Tessa, she reminded herself.

Tessa was still fuming over what she'd accidentally overheard in Harper's suite as she found herself alone at a late lunch in the resort's dining hall. The bridesmaids had gone to the beach for a swim while Brett and Harper joined his parents for a wine tasting at the gazebo. To Tessa's relief, the maid of honor had stuck with the bridesmaids rather than situating herself close by the groom. One ex with an agenda was all this wedding could handle, in Tessa's opinion.

"Too late to offer you some company?" Blake sat down in the empty chair at Tessa's table for two. "I was hoping to grab some lunch before we move on to the next tropical garden's photo potential."

"I can recommend the roasted salmon with herbed potatoes," said Tessa. "But only if you're in the mood for something gourmet."

She picked at the corner of her menu. "I guess Ashleigh must have been disappointed you couldn't have that drink together. She did ask you in a roundabout way… and probably isn't used to guys turning her down either. She's very cute, after all." She pretended to be interested in the menu's list of appetizers.

"She has an interesting background. She was first runner-up in the Gardenia Blossom State Beauty Competition in 2012."

"I can well imagine," said Tessa, but this time without her careful emotional guard from the previous remark, so that traces of sarcasm crept into it.

"You could've earned the same title," he said, with a laugh. "If you told me that story, I'd believe it."

"I didn't really go in for beauty contests when I was younger," she said, blushing despite her best attempt not to feel flattered by this remark. She tried to control her scorn better this time.

"I don't think anybody applies anymore for the beauty title, do they? I think it's all for scholarships," said Blake. "She said something about an internship with an investment firm. But when I said I would believe it of you, I wasn't talking about the scholarship part, necessarily… if that's not insulting or offensive to say," he added as he reached for the menu.

"I won't ask you to apologize," said Tessa, who was dangerously aware of what compliments from Blake might do to her. Mess with her head and heart when they were already in a tangle over what to feel about him these days. "Though I can't say I think I qualified for the compliment of being a candidate for Miss Gardenia Whatever-It-Was." She managed not to blush.

"You said you weren't offended, right?" said Blake. "Then leave it." He smiled at her, a brief one, before studying the menu again.

It took Tessa a moment to recover. "Anyway," she continued, "I guess Ashleigh won't have trouble finding someone else to take her up on that drink, given all her great qualities. Once she gets over her wounded pride from you turning her down, that is." *Especially if he doesn't tell her* why *he can't go out with her*, she thought.

All these months, it had really surprised her that Blake hadn't talked about Mac or their plans to get married. He'd been silent on the subject despite Mac's multiple texts about menus and flowers.

Maybe he sensed how uncomfortable she was about it and didn't want to make things awkward between them? Tessa didn't want him to feel like he had to tiptoe around her, though. She didn't want pity. She didn't want to end up like Harper's ex, still clinging to some notion of what could have been when Blake was gone. That would just be too pathetic, even for a hopeless romantic like herself.

"Ashleigh was probably just being polite." Blake gave a shrug. "I don't drink while on the job, usually," he said. "It wouldn't be professional to have a casual drink on the job with one of your clients anyway, would it?"

"I guess not. I suppose she's like a client, in a roundabout way," said Tessa begrudgingly, since Ashleigh was practically Brett's mouthpiece in this affair. "It would be a conflict of interest to be personally involved with a member of the party before the assignment was over, logically." Maybe they could make this a rule written into the Wedding Belles' partnership: no fraternizing romantically with members of the wedding party or their associates before the ceremony. Of course, it would only apply to herself, since everybody else who worked there was in a relationship.

"So I thought I would pass on the mainland pub and just grab a sandwich here before I catch the ferry," continued Blake. "No need to offend protocol or hurt anybody's feelings that way."

"Right," said Tessa. She took a breath. "Besides, Mac would obviously have something to say about it, right? You having lunch with someone like Ashleigh."

Way to sound petty, Tessa. And jealous. She should have just kept her mouth shut, or stuffed the last of her pear in it before those words slipped out.

"Mac?" His tone was puzzled. "Why would Mac care who I have lunch with?"

"Because…" Tessa paused. "Because…" It was obvious, really. So why wasn't it obvious to Blake?

Tessa's fingers froze in mid-pluck of a stray fern leaf on the table-cloth. It felt like forever since Mac had shown off her engagement ring and announced that "the most perfect guy in the world" had popped the question. And despite the careful work her heart had done to repair itself, it still skipped a beat for the implication behind Blake's words. "What about the wedding?" she said, confused. "You and her… getting together." A juvenile way of putting it, but she was amazed she could say anything on the subject at all since she was having a hard time catching her breath now that she and Blake were finally talking about it.

Had they broken up? Their engagement come to a grinding halt over some personal disagreement? It wasn't impossible, though she couldn't picture it somehow. Not with Mac texting her every other week with ideas for the ceremony she desperately wanted Tessa to plan for her.

"Mac's wedding?" The handyman was looking at her like she was crazy now. "Why would she meet with me about that? She wants you three to plan it, and that's all she's said to me on the subject. I'm sure she'll stop by once she and her fiancé finally settle on autumn or spring."

"Her fiancé," said Tessa. Her lungs were operating without oxygen now. "He's…?"

"Called Oliver. An accountant at one of the firms downtown. Nice guy." Blake motioned for the attention of one of the waiters passing by. "You'll like him."

"Will I?" Tessa feigned nonchalance. Badly. Her voice wasn't shaking the way she expected it to be, but her hands definitely were, and her heart felt as if it might take flight from her chest. From surprise? Relief? Or was it just plain old shock that made it feel like the room was rocking in those first few seconds after the news was uttered?

Good thing she was already sitting down. Otherwise, she might have ended up flat on the carpet of that very elegant dining hall.

Chapter Twenty-Five

"So Blake's *not* engaged?" Natalie lips formed a low whistle. She had arrived at Tessa's office extra early to go over the bridesmaids dresses one more time and confirm their bouquet arrangements. All details that were temporarily forgotten the moment Tessa confided the reason for her somewhat absent-minded mood.

"That is seriously big news, Tessa. How did you find out?"

"Never mind," said Tessa, her cheeks growing slightly pink. She had been lucky she survived that incident without doing something embarrassing—like blurting out exactly what she had been thinking all this time about him and Mac. Thank goodness the waiter had shown up to take their orders, otherwise who knows what she might have said. She might have confessed her feelings about Blake right then.

Stupid, stupid assumption. How could you be so wrong about everything, Tessa? How can you ever trust yourself again after this?

"I just can't believe it," said Natalie. "All this time, we've been thinking she and Blake are an item while she's been hooked up with somebody else. Talk about mistaken impressions."

"It's true," said Tessa. "Her fiance's an accountant, or something like that. She has an Instagram account with pictures of the two of them." If only Tessa had thought to track down Mac on social media before, this misunderstanding could have been cleared up long ago.

Then again, if she'd just found the courage to confront Blake about her feelings last year…

"So…how are you taking it?" Natalie arched one eyebrow. "Frankly, I would have expected a bigger reaction from you at this point. Something with a little more drama—or, dare I say it, celebration?"

"I'm not a child," scoffed Tessa. But pretending to take this lightheartedly was going very badly, to her mind. "So I was mistaken about Blake getting engaged. It was just a stupid misunderstanding. Those happen, right?"

"This news was completely wasted on you, I can see," said Natalie, with a groan of disgust. "Come on, Tess. We both know you've been carrying a torch for Blake since the beginning of this thing. You're crazy about him, even if you *think* you're not. You've got to be a little excited that he's not really engaged to anybody."

"I'm just surprised," said Tessa, wishing Natalie didn't know her so well. "What do you want me to do? I mean, this has been a wild few months in the romance department. Mac's announcement, Ama's proposal, you and Chad getting serious—" Her eye was on the folder lying among some recent quotes from a florist—the one with Natalie's name on it, and a scrapbook sticker of a wedding gown.

Natalie noticed it, and buried it from sight under a stack of bridal catalogs. "What does that have to do with anything?" said Natalie. "Forget about our love lives. Just focus on the fact that the sexy decorator you were so obviously jealous of has another attachment, meaning the guy you like is free and clear."

"I was *not* jealous of her," said Tessa, defensively. A total lie, as Natalie sniffed out ages ago. Who wouldn't be jealous of a woman like Mac, who was gorgeous, enthusiastic, and probably a perfect fit for Blake… except for being in love with the accountant, that is.

"Please." Natalie rolled her eyes. "As if that wasn't the biggest sign the universe gave us that you have a thing for Blake. Listen to me, Tess—look me in the eye for this one. Blake is free. You're free. There is no time like the present for taking advantage of those two facts."

"I have to call the florist shop about some last-minute alternations to the centerpieces," said Tessa. "Any thoughts about what would be perfect?" Her heart was pounding in her chest, though she tried outwardly to seem unruffled by anything Natalie had said.

Natalie sighed. "Do it your way, then," she said.

"I will, thanks," said Tessa. "Do you want to keep your folder?" A bright tone of voice as she held it out, unearthed from beneath the bridal catalogs. "For the future, maybe? You'll want to be ready for your big day when it comes." The world's biggest commitment dodger could hardly lecture her on spilling her heart to somebody.

Natalie accepted it—but not with her usual disgust, as Tessa couldn't help but notice. "Mark my words, Tessa," she said. "There's no time like the present."

With that, she disappeared into the neighboring office, as Tessa went back to her notes on the centerpieces. But with slower fingers, and a lot of distractions in her thoughts.

There was no time like the present. A part of Tessa felt desperate to let go, now that she had learned that Blake was free. Reckless abandon was calling her, steering her to tell Blake the truth. *You said you would do it, if you had a second chance, Tessa*, it whispered. *The engagement isn't real—what more do you need in the miracle department?*

Maybe it really was the second chance she had wished for. This was a sign for her, a lesson in taking a leap of faith. She could do it this time… if she could find the courage and the right time in which to announce that she thought of him constantly, and had butterflies in her stomach every time she touched him.

It wouldn't be easy. She would have to do it face-to-face, and look into those eyes as she took this leap of faith. And she was taking it alone, if Blake didn't feel the same way, despite all her hopes and wishful interpretation of those old signals.

For better or worse. Wasn't that what every client vowed when they leaped into love's future?

Chapter Twenty-Six

The Magnolia Fashion Revue was packed this year with the region's top designers and a few new faces, including Natalie's. For the first time ever, she would actually see something she designed appear on the runway, the way she'd watched countless of her old boss Kandace's designs appear. For once, she wouldn't be toting the emergency sewing repair kit or fetching bottled energy drinks for her boss.

"This is so exciting," said Cal, in a hushed voice. "How long have we waited for this, Natalie? You, me, no longer slaves to the Wicked Witch of plastic couture," he said, referencing their ex-employer's fondness for using fabrics that were better suited for ponchos and picnic table cloths than actual garments.

"It seems like a lifetime," answered Natalie. "I just hope everything goes great after slaving the way we have." There was a definite chance it could fail—plenty of designers did, even ones more talented than herself. The first runway show was a big pitfall for many an aspiring talent.

"Lorene Swick's latest design is supposedly amazing," Cal was saying as he adjusted the jacket one of the models would wear, a last-minute touch before showtime. "I caught a glimpse of it earlier when we were fitting the dress for good measure, and I can't believe she hasn't designed for three years."

"I only saw part of Van's, and it was good," said Natalie, brushing the summer skirt one last time.

"Can you believe Kandace isn't part of it this year?" said Cal. "She hasn't missed one since the safety pin disaster of 2013. I thought for sure she'd be here to parade some dystopian line of latex and faux fur in a death march down that ramp."

"I'm relieved she's not," said Natalie, trying not to sound uneasy. In truth, she preferred not to encounter her ex-boss professionally—crossing paths with Kandace in the design community would only lead to trouble, since she had taken Natalie's decision to quit poorly.

"You don't have to feel guilty, Nat. You put in good work and more than your fair share of time with her," Cal reminded her.

"I know. But it's weird, you know? The thought of seeing her now that I'm a designer, so it's something I think I'd like to avoid. At least until the reviews are out."

"Whatever." Cal shook his head. "Nella, where are the pins? I need to fix this little issue along the lapel."

"Here you go." Nella hurried over, breathless as she pulled a card of sewing pins from her kit. "It's ten minutes until showtime. Can you believe it?" Her voice became a hushed squeal.

"Let's hustle so this show can get on the road," said Natalie, who seized the jacket post-repair and slipped it on a hanger, adding it to the rack of garments awaiting the runway models.

To the upbeat rhythm of canned modern music and light hip-hop, the models paraded down the runway. Six local designers' creations appeared before Natalie's: the first model who stepped from behind the curtain after Luki's House of Fashion wore Natalie's tailored navy pinstriped suit, stilettos, and a wide-brimmed floppy hat trimmed with a satin ribbon and bud flower, hands on hips as she marched with sophisticated attitude to the end of the catwalk.

The sundress, the caftan loungewear, the cocktail dress, and the stunning evening gown that had cost Natalie several bloody fingertips to perfect its beading. Cal's updated take on the go-go look of the seventies stepped out among Natalie's creations, and so did Nella's "Marilyn Magnolia," as Cal had nicknamed it. He and Nella were snapping photos like mad, Natalie knew, as she watched from backstage, making quick adjustments to each garment before its showcase, helping models with quick tucks and necessary pins—just like she used to do for Kandace's clothes, only without any respect or reward except her boss's picky criticisms afterward.

This time it was satisfying. And terrifying.

The last model wearing one of Natalie's designs returned from the end of the catwalk, replaced by one sporting another designer's boldly striped minidress. Natalie draped the evening gown over its hanger again, and smoothed the pleats of Nella's dress beside it, then stepped out of the way for the next design team.

Surviving was the first stage. With a deep breath, Natalie checked the time, knowing that in twenty more minutes, the last designer would walk, and the main event would be over. It was gossip time afterward, and she would hear the first reactions to her work in that crowd, which was often worse than experiencing a runway mishap. *Brace yourself, Grenaldi*, she thought. *Be thick-skinned and stick it out to the end.* That was the only way to survive in this business, and nobody knew that better than former underlings like herself.

*

"Ready?" said Nella, who was excited by the thought of mingling with the best and brightest designers along the southeastern coast.

"Sure," said Natalie, with a smile.

Plenty of people in this crowd were recognizable to her. Ching Cho Fashions was here, and the fashion podcaster from Couture Revue who had insulted Kandace's creations unfailingly in every fashion show broadcast. There was the writer from the *Bellegrove Herald*, and the elite designer Nastasia, who never spoke to anybody at a fashion show, even the press. Natalie felt intimidated in this crowd—the new kid at the dance, whose name nobody knew, and whom everybody would avoid standing too near.

"I know who you are," said a female voice close by. It belonged to Nola Gayne, the designer of Harper's wedding gown. "You work for the wedding planner the Winships hired. I saw your name in the show's catalog, but I couldn't put a face to it until now. I had no idea you were a designer."

"Sometimes I'm just a fashion consultant for the planning firm," said Natalie, with a smile. "When a designer as good as you is on deck for a wedding, at least."

"I thought your work was very good," said Nola. "You were the designer of that beautiful floor-length gown. I was very impressed by the unique style."

"Thanks," said Natalie. "I was sort of surprised that you didn't have anything in this show." Despite the overwhelming flattery she felt in having this designer actually willingly converse with her, she managed to sound normal, even casual thus far. How that was possible, Natalie had no earthly idea.

"I took a year off," said Nola, dismissively. "I think I'm getting too old for the runway's chaos. I prefer private design work, like I do for the Winships and others. The retail lines, the runway shows, the exclusive seasonal couture, those are for the younger fashionistas, who have the energy and passion still young within them."

"I think you're plenty young," said Natalie.

"That's kind of you," said Nola. "Congratulations on your debut. I look forward to seeing more of your work." She clasped Natalie's hand then moved on in the crowd. From somewhere inside Natalie, a deep breath of relief slowly escaped.

"Was that *the* Nola Gayne?" asked Nella, in awe.

"It was," said Natalie, whose voice betrayed how really un-casual she actually was after such an encounter.

Cal squeezed his way through the crowd to join them. "Good news from distant battlefields, troops," he said. "Sadie Hatterson of Ching Cho Fashions actually *liked* one of our creations. She didn't remember the name of the designer behind it, so she erroneously attributed it to Bill Waters, but still…" He was pushed aside by a design team squeezing their way in the direction of the champagne bar.

"Isn't that great?" said Nella, squeezing Natalie's arm.

Another designer half-turned in their direction. "Are you the new fashion designer in this show?" he said. "The one with the vintage vibe and the magnolia dress?"

"My dress," whispered Nella, who looked ready to faint.

"That's us," said Natalie. "Natalie Grenaldi, Grenaldi's Couture. We just—"

"Traitor!" The scream was so close to Natalie's ear that she thought its drum would split beneath the vibrations. The grip on her arms nearly yanked her off her feet, bending her ankles painfully sideways in her stiletto heels. "You're a sneaking, sniveling liar who's a talent-sucking leech!"

Kandace was here—and furious. The designer's face was red with rage, her synthetically red hair sticking out wildly from its topknot spiked with weird-looking antenna hairpins. Her shirt had a purple-splattered skull eating a butterfly as part of its motif, and as Natalie struggled to free herself, she imagined it might be the designer's intention to rip off her head and put it to similar use.

"What are you doing?!" Natalie yelled. "Get off me! Are you crazy?!"

"You stole from me—you sucked up my brilliance and creative vibes, then ran off, you vindictive little harpy!" screamed her former boss. "I *knew* you were leaving to screw me over. And you do it on *my* turf, with *my* staff?! You didn't think I'd show up to see it, did you? Well, I did—just in time to see you stabbing me in the back!"

"Let go of me!" Natalie yelled again, although her breath was coming in choking gasps thanks to the thick fingers squeezing her windpipe and ruining the collar of her silk blouse. Was Kandace trying to strangle her? Two security guards had seized Kandace and were trying to pull her off while Natalie's fingers pried the designer's from her neck.

"I won't forget this!" With a parting scream of rage, Kandace was escorted from the room.

Natalie sank down on a chair, rubbing her neck. Utterly mortified, utterly bruised, and without a clue as to what exactly had just taken place.

"Nat, are you okay?" Cal rushed to join her.

"Kandace tried to kill her!" said Nella unnecessarily.

"I knew she was crazy, but I didn't think she was homicidal," said Natalie, who realized her hands were shaking as she pushed her hair back from her face.

"Can I quote you on that?" asked another. The writer from the *Herald* was in front of her, smartphone recorder at the ready. "Are you connected with the designer just escorted from the venue? Are you part of Kandace's Kreations?"

"No quote," croaked Natalie. "And definitely not." She buried her face momentarily as several more people snapped mobile phone photos.

*

Perry, the florist for Accented Creations, had created a stunning wedding centerpiece using the huge shells that, in Tessa's estimate, must cost a fortune. The pearly-pink vases held a near-invisible clear plastic tube in the middle of each one to nourish the long-stemmed blossoms of showy gladiolas, bright cannas, and hibiscus blossoms in neon-pink and fiery rose and red hues.

"This one is titled 'Inferno' because of the subtle tiger-stripe blossoms artfully woven here and there in the form of both cannas and a new spotted ruby trumpet lily we've just acquired from our crossbreeders," explained the artist.

"Wow," said Harper. "I love how bold it is. Those colors just pop, don't they?" She glanced at Tessa. "You like it, right?"

"I think it's very impressive, and very fitting," said Tessa. "But I like the one with the glass vase filled with pearl marbles, too." It was a slightly subtler centerpiece offered as an alternative by the artist, featuring birds of paradise in bud form, yellow and pink miniature orchids, and sprays of ornamental grass.

Harper shook her head. "Pretty, but I don't know… I think I like the big one better."

Tessa hid a smile, one inspired entirely by Danny's words, which she had intended to forget all about now that he'd been warned to stay out of her client's life. But he was definitely right about Harper's taste.

"Either one is a perfect match for your potential cake," said Ama, who had her eye on the mini orchid display in particular, despite their client's preference, no doubt imagining those flowers as tiny cupcake decorations. "But I think having birds of paradise for both *might* be a little much, so maybe the first one is better."

"Onto bouquets, then," said Perry, who directed their attention to creations that incorporated the basic colors from both centerpieces, but with a touch more domestic sophistication. Tight bud roses in purplish-pink and yellow-tipped red, surrounded by two-toned blossoms of the pink-tipped white of Princess de Monaco, accented by the delicate shades of mint juleps.

"What about something more… I don't know… tropical?" asked Harper. "That is the wedding's theme, you know."

"For that, I designed the 'Kuliki,'" explained Perry. "Take note of the exotic orchids paired with marbled peonies, tropical pink gladiolas with white hearts, and the bold but delicate trumpet lily from the centerpiece. "

"The bridesmaids' bouquets will be the same?" Tessa asked. Harper had said nothing, but the look on her face as she admired the bouquet proved it was the winner.

"Smaller versions," said Perry "We'll remove the peonies and the glads and substitute a few light sprays of baby's breath for that 'seafoam' touch. We don't want to outshine the bride, do we?"

"Sounds perfect," said Tessa, making a note.

Today, Ama was planning to deliver the sampler cake to Harper's office: a two-layer one in perfect white frosting, with the hand-sculpted fondant and marzipan birds of paradise blossoms decorating it, identical to her original sketch. In the full-size version, chocolate and vanilla layers were alternated, with each tier, five in total, pieced together with a vanilla-pomegranate cream as requested by Harper. It sounded delicious, and Tessa hoped there were a few leftover samples in the Wedding Belles' kitchen.

"She's been looking forward to this," said Tessa, as she shifted the car into reverse and backed out of the space outside Accented Creations' sophisticated downtown headquarters. "She's having dinner with the Winship family tonight, and they'll all taste it together for dessert."

"That's intimidating," said Ama, with a little shudder. "I think I'm glad I won't be part of this tasting, for a change. Even for my favorite design."

"You and me both," said Tessa. She pulled onto the street and turned right, in the direction of Harper's office. "I sometimes think Harper is overestimating the Winships' acceptance of her into their family. I wonder if she's going to be an outsider for her whole marriage."

"What makes you say that?" Ama glanced at her.

"Something crazy. The remarks of Harper's ex-boyfriend, who caught up with me in the street one day. He keeps talking about how he and Harper were meant to be, but fate got in the way. He wanted to leave and chase his dreams; she wanted security. He says that's what she found in Brett."

"Running away with somebody isn't easy," said Ama. "I'm sort of finding that out myself." She twisted something hanging just below the scoop neckline of her peasant smock blouse. Tessa saw the glint of a tiny little stone, a thin circular band between Ama's fingers. A ring, and undoubtedly one from Luke.

"What are you going to say to him?" Tessa asked, softly.

Ama shrugged. "I don't know yet," she said.

"What are you saying when you talk to each other?"

"We don't." Ama sounded sad. "That is… we keep missing each other's calls. He has bad cellular reception, and I've had my phone turned off while I've been working at the restaurant. He told me to take the time I need to think about it, but I know I can't wait forever to answer him. I have to decide which feelings to trust, because if I don't, I could lose Luke over something stupid, like fear. That would devastate me."

"Harper could sympathize," said Tessa. "She waited four years after Danny's last try to enter another serious relationship."

"Four years?"

"Pretty much. He claimed they were so in love that it's impossible she got over him—I think it's more likely she's just a romantic who had a hard time moving on."

"Four years to get over her first love, and she's way more practical than I am. Someone like me will probably die alone if I screw this up," said Ama, glumly.

"You haven't said goodbye to him yet," said Tessa, with a little laugh. Ama's lack of an answer, however, made her wonder if part of the story about her and Luke contained possible holes that needed filling. "Have you?" she asked, more seriously.

"I don't know?"

"Ama, are you serious?"

"It's not on purpose—it's just that he has this offer for Portugal, and I told him before that I don't want to change his life and he doesn't want to change mine, and if I can't or don't go… and if something happens and he doesn't talk to me again—"

"Portugal?!"

"See? I don't know if I'm ready for a spontaneous adventure in Portugal, or to marry Luke, or to make any decision this big," said Ama, frustration entering her voice. "I've never been in love before. I've never faced any of these choices before. Is this what it's supposed to be like? This hard? This… difficult to define or explain?"

"You're asking the wrong person," said Tessa. "Remember? Reformed hopeless romantic? Who never got any relationship beyond the hopeless crush status, either." She turned onto Harper's street, searching for a parking space in her distracted state. "The leap into love is terrifying enough for me. At least you made it that far."

She shifted the car into park and shut off the ignition. "Business smile," she said, to herself and not to Ama. "Time to make the client happy." Time to focus on work, not problems like love old and new. No need to reflect on her many romantic failures in the past, including the one this past Christmas that still made her heart ache whenever movies she watched featured sentimental love songs.

"I hope the cake's okay." Ama unbuckled her seatbelt and stretched to reach the cake box carefully padded between several foam pillows. "What if I was thinking about Luke and not paying attention and left out something crucial to its flavor? It makes me worry about my work—heartache and baking don't go together very well."

"If it tastes as gorgeous as it looks, we'll be fine."

Harper was on a short ladder, pasting up a new giant poster of a Scottish castle as they entered. "Is that my cake?" she asked, looking over her shoulder eagerly before the topmost corner of the poster fell across her view.

"Need a hand?" Tessa scrambled up on the nearest cardboard box, teetering on high heels as she tried to help pin the corner in place.

"Thanks. This just arrived. Bus tours from Edinburgh to the Shetland Islands with a ferry from Aberdeen," said Harper. "I think it'll be a real winner with my clientele. There's a big Scottish community in this town."

She stepped down from her ladder and waited as Ama opened the lid to the cake's box. Inside was the glorious middle section of Ama's "Birds of Paradise" wedding cake. Streaked, peaked orange and rosy blossoms on the verge of opening, jade-green stems, and spiky leaves pressed against the smooth white frosting.

"*Those* are edible flowers?" Harper's eyes widened. "Are you sure?"

"I'm sure," said Ama. "I made them myself. It's all completely edible. There's room for a cake topper, but I was thinking that an edible flower would be a nice choice—even a cluster of real ones with the little bride and groom in the middle." She was undoubtedly thinking of Harper's general taste for window dressings.

"Oh, I don't know. I like it simple like this," said Harper. "I know I'm a little showy... but some things are nice when they don't say too much. It makes them special." She shrugged. "Let's keep it like this."

Ama looked relieved. "I'm glad you like it," she said, closing up the box. "I thought I would bring by the sampler of the chocolates and petit fours next week—the specialty shop won't have them ready until then."

"I can't wait to show the pictures of the centerpieces to Brett tonight," said Harper. "For once, Ashleigh won't have the last word. Sometimes I feel like I'm a parrot repeating everything she texts to him."

Tessa bit back a smile because this definition was perfect. "Do you want to stay for lunch?" Harper asked. "I have extra sandwiches and nobody to keep me company. Have a heart and stick around."

Ama shook her head. "I can't. I have six dozen cupcakes that need packaging for mailing."

"I could," said Tessa. She tossed the car keys to Ama. "Just park the car anywhere outside so my friend can pick it up this evening," she said. "I'll walk back to the office later." She opened her bag and pulled out her work folder to double check some wedding details as Harper removed two sandwiches and some overripe tangerines from her mini-fridge.

Harper moved aside more of the chaos on her desk to make room for Tessa's folder; one of the objects was a metal flower similar to Tessa's, except for the fact it was shaped like an amaryllis.

"Is that your ex's work?" Tessa asked, before thinking.

Harper glanced at it. A brief flush crossed her cheeks. "Yeah. Silly," she said. "He made it for me when we started dating. Just fooling around in one of his metal classes." She lifted it up and tossed it into a nearby drawer. "Let's just put it where it belongs."

Tessa was quiet. "Do you sometimes feel like you can't be yourself around Brett and his family?" she asked. "I wouldn't say anything... just I noticed that lately you dress differently when you're with them. You sometimes look as if you planned to say something, then don't."

It was only a couple of times, so why was she mentioning it, she wondered? One quick working lunch at the resort, and the day Harper and Myra stopped by the Wedding Belles' office to see the wedding favor gift bags assembled—that was all the evidence she had, really. Danny's words were influencing her in negative ways.

"I'm trying to fit in," said Harper. "Doesn't everybody?"

"If they want to," said Tessa. "I guess you would, since you're marrying him."

"It's just a different world, that's all," said Harper. "The loud lipstick, the colloquialisms—that's stuff they don't get. I want to show them that I'm a good fit, so they like me better. So it changes a few things… Stuff changes anyway in life."

She stuffed a file folder in a random drawer, but more for the sake of busy work than cleaning her desk now. Tessa gathered up her folder and placed it in her bag again. "So long as you're happy, that's all that matters," she said.

"You wanna see why it makes me happy?" Harper asked, suddenly. "Do you?"

"Sure," said Tessa, feeling surprised by this. "If you want to show me, I'd love to."

"Come with me." With a sigh, Harper rose from her chair. "It's about time I closed up anyway. Today's a half-day—my lone employee got food poisoning, and I'm supposed to run some tickets over to this eighty-five-year-old lady who's going to Greece this fall. Now's as good a time as any." She lifted her keys from the desk and turned the lock on the door. "Be prepared for a lot of chaos," she warned Tessa.

From the travel agency, they turned left, then right, then entered a small dead-end neighborhood that wasn't familiar to Tessa in this part of Bellegrove. Harper Lucas's home was near the end of it, in a two-story, plain Victorian home that had been bricked over on the lower level, and showed signs of needing a new coat of paint from upstairs siding to porch pillars. It was now a boarding house, Harper explained, with her parents renting rooms to multiple lodgers.

Three old bicycles were chained out front, a faded turtle-shaped sandbox was filled with plastic toys and roller skates, and a shaggy dog barked at Tessa before it slunk beneath a hole in the porch underpinnings.

A child ran out of the house's front door as Harper opened it, nearly running headlong into Tessa before dodging aside to keep running. "Hey, be careful, Vick," Harper scolded him. "I'm bringing company home. Be nice to people, all right? Didn't your mother teach you manners?"

"Sorry," he called over his shoulder. Harper sighed.

The front foyer had two old ladies sitting on a love seat, both knitting as they watched a television set playing an old episode of *I Love Lucy*. The one in coke-bottle glasses looked up and smiled at Harper. "Hi, dearie," she said. "Home early?"

"I am. I got your mail, Mrs. Porticolos," she said, rummaging through a thick stack of correspondence that Tessa had assumed was business mail from the travel agency. "There's a notice from the city about your car license, Ms. Dell," she said, handing the furiously knitting boarder a thin envelope. "You better open this one."

"Yeah, yeah." The lady nodded but didn't look away from the television as her fingers steadily looped yarn between her needles.

A crowd of five dogs of varying sizes raced past them, followed by a breathless man holding a series of leashes attached to them. He looked so old and frail that Tessa was amazed he was actually capable of walking these animals. He disappeared through the open front door, where he narrowly missed tripping over a tricycle on the stairs. In the distance, from an unseen room, Tessa heard the sound of a baby wailing.

Harper kicked some toys out of the way in the untidy hall leading to an old-fashioned dining room. A man was sitting at the table, looking at small metal parts laid out on a sheet of newspaper. A bigger, half-assembled appliance of unknown usage was on a separate sheet before him, with a little pool of oil beneath it that Tessa imagined would ruin the table's glossy finish.

Harper kissed his cheek. "Pa, put some more papers under that. What would Mom say if she saw how you're ruining this place?"

"I put papers down, didn't I?" he answered. He pushed up a magnifying jeweler's lens in a headset so he could see Harper's face normally. "Did one of my answers come?" He gestured toward the mail.

"No, Pa. I checked."

"Twice?"

"Of course I did. There's nothing here but bills and stuff about Mom's medication." She laid the stack of envelopes on an untidy writing desk, which had bills crammed into nearly every envelope cubby.

"Who's this?" The man noticed Tessa now as he wiped his greasy hands on one of the many rags piled on the table. He held one out to Tessa. "Willy Lucas. Harper's pop. How you doing?"

"Good, thanks," said Tessa.

"That's Tessa," said Harper. "I told you about her already. She's planning the wedding, Pa. We were looking at flowers today."

"The wedding." This was uttered in a tone better suited for shifty car sale ads and cockroaches, not for nuptial celebrations. "You and the rich young ruler who can't eat off plastic plates."

"I told you, I'll buy some real dishes—when I finish paying some of these bills—then we'll have him to dinner," said Harper, sounding exasperated. Several of the envelopes she was putting under a bronze paperweight had a big red "overdue" stamp on them, Tessa noticed. "You could have had dinner with us at the restaurant sometime instead of pretending you're too busy."

"I don't go to those fancy places. You know that," answered Willy. "Plastic plates are fine. I don't want your fiancé going through the trouble of paying for anything for me. He's paying enough already to buy my daughter."

"Don't talk like that, Pa," Harper said in a warning tone.

"What? You don't want me to say it, fine. But you know I think it. You know what I said, Harper." He pointed at her with a screwdriver missing part of its tip. "You can't wait for me to make enough to support us, but you go and pick some fancy guy who can do it for you. He could be anybody—he could be psycho killer who targets dark-haired women, for all you know after just a few months—"

"I'm not hearing this again." Harper slammed the desk's roll-top lid. "Pa, I'm past my prime, I work like a dog, and nothing gets better. So a handsome, charming, rich guy asks me to marry him, what am I going to say? When do offers like that come along for girls like me? Do I stay here at the bottom, 'cause I'm not good enough?"

Tessa shrank against the doorway. Should she leave? This argument was getting very personal, and not like something she should overhear. She looked behind her and discovered her way was blocked by a red-faced toddler on a pedal car, clearly the source of the crying earlier.

"Who said you're not good enough? Look at you, you're pretty. Lots of guys like girls who aren't too skinny. If you wait, a good guy will come along who you're not afraid is ashamed to be seen with you and your family, like we've escaped from a leper colony or something."

"You're coming to my wedding, at least," said Harper. "Aren't you, Pa?"

Suddenly, Willy was cagey. He fiddled with his screwdriver. "I think I'll have to take the cord off this thing," he said, muttering to himself as he inspected the appliance beside his parts pile.

"Pa?" repeated Harper. "I'm getting married. Isn't that a good enough reason? Did you ever think the reason I don't bring him around is because I know you're gonna be tough on him, and you won't give him a fair chance?"

"Hand me that can of lubricant spray," said Willy to Tessa.

Startled, she glanced over the rows of possible products, selecting a slightly rusty one with a blue lid that seemed to be what he wanted.

"I'm talking to you," said Harper, not giving up. "Are you coming to my wedding or not? Mom probably won't be there. Who's gonna give me away if you don't come?"

"Maybe I don't want to do it. Maybe it's against principle for me. To see my daughter leave me for people who are ashamed of her." Willy glanced at Harper, chin lifted and eyes clear. This was a firm line in the sand: Willy did not approve of or support Harper's engagement in the slightest. No wonder Harper's family wasn't involved in the wedding plans.

Father and daughter remained locked in combat gazes. Willy was the first to back down.

"Harper, darlin', you know if I thought that it were any other reason than him not deserving you—"

"I'm going upstairs," announced Harper in a sharp voice. Whatever he planned to say, she didn't intend to listen. "Is Mom awake?" Offense dripped from her tone.

Willy shrugged. "Wake her up if she's not," he said. "See if that wedding stuff cheers her up. Silver lining in this thing, I suppose." With a sigh, he sprayed the contents around a rusty bolt.

"You're impossible, you know that?" said Harper. She walked out, Tessa following. The child in the pedal car followed them to the bottom of the stairs, where he crashed the toy's plastic bumper against the bottom step, the ride stopped short by it. A loud wail followed.

Harper's mother's room was dark, with the shades drawn closed. Harper eased them open, revealing a big-boned woman with Harper's features framed by sandy-brown hair, curled on her side. She opened her eyes as Harper sat down on the bed.

"How you feeling, Mom?" she asked.

"Tired." The woman's voice was listless, though she smiled. "You have a good day?"

"So-so. Saw the wedding flowers today. They're so gorgeous." She pulled out her cell phone and showed the woman pictures. Her mother pulled herself into a sitting position. Her summer nightgown was faded; on the bureau beside the bed, three pharmaceutical bottles, a glass of water, and a pile of tissues.

"Look at all those colors," said the woman, somewhere between amazed and drowsy. She noticed Tessa. "Is that a friend of yours, Harper?"

"No, this is the wedding planner, Tessa." She beckoned Tessa closer. "She's the one who's putting everything together. Tessa, this is my mom, Rose."

"Pleased to meet you." Rose shaded her eyes. "Can't see you too well in this light."

"You should come with me next time," said Harper, patting her mother's hand. "Put on some clothes and come out with me, Mom. We'll have lunch somewhere."

"You work too hard." Her mother shook her head. "You buy groceries, you got bills to pay—I'm not letting you buy me lunch."

"I can scrape up a few dollars to take my mom for a bite to eat," coaxed Harper. "You want to see me in my dress before the big day, don't you?"

A weak smile from Rose. "You just be happy," she said, patting Harper's hand in return. "I'm too tired, honey. I think I'd better wait awhile." She closed her eyes and leaned back against the pillows. "The flowers sure are pretty, though. The lady planning your wedding did a good job."

Harper drew the drapes partway closed again, then walked out and closed the door behind her and Tessa, a reluctant expression on her face.

She entered the room two doors down, across from a messy bathroom where a child had recently squeezed toothpaste over the sink and a pile of bath toys lay scattered on the floor. A woman was trying to clean it up while scolding the twin of the downstairs toddler.

"This is my space," said Harper, showing Tessa a slightly larger bedroom than the other one. An old-fashioned wood bureau, a bed with a flower-print coverlet, a series of postcards decorating its faded floral wallpaper. "Home sweet home. Not much, but it's all I have."

Tessa glanced toward the hall again. "Is your mom sick?" she asked.

"Clinical depression. That's what the doctor says." Harper opened the drapes in her room, letting sunshine flood in. "It got worse years ago, and just doesn't seem to get better. They try different medications, some kind of therapy—they say it's just about finding the right thing for the right person. She gets out of bed once in a while but sleeps away most days."

She sat down on her bed. "I guess you know now why she hasn't been around for any of the wedding stuff," she continued. "Pop, too. He's been out of work for the past decade. That's why they started renting rooms to people in the first place. Eight strangers who are now like family, in the fact that you loan somebody five bucks you write it off as gone and buy the kind of jam at the grocery that they want on their toast at breakfast."

"I would have thought your father was a repairman of some kind, judging by his work downstairs," said Tessa. "It looked like he had a pile of appliances on the buffet, all with little tags."

Harper smiled, wryly. "Pop's an inventor—of a sort. He's always coming up with crazy schemes he thinks will make us a lot of money as soon as he sells the patent to a big company. Toasters with timer settings, humidity-proof spice jars. My favorite was the battery-operated lens wiper for car side mirrors. You know, to clear off rain or fog so you can see when you're backing up the car."

"Sounds like a budding genius," said Tessa.

"He could be," said Harper. "If we hadn't been living like starved peasants for the past decade, it'd be fine. But the medical bills pile up, the cost of living goes up. I quit school in the first place because ends were hard to meet around here when he was still working, and I could barely pay for my classes. After he was fired, he wore out shoes walking the pavement, trying to find a new job. And Mom… she can't get out of bed long enough to make a sandwich most days, much less help out."

"I'm sorry," said Tessa. "That had to be incredibly hard. It probably still is." Brett wasn't paying the bills around here, she sensed, only Harper—and he had never seen this down-on-their-luck family of mismatched members, judging from what was said in the dining room.

"Yeah, well, I finally got my associate's degree going to school nights. I went to work at a big travel agency after I quit my old part-time jobs, then I opened my own agency a few years ago after I learned the ropes. I like dealing with old people who don't know how to buy tickets on the internet, or people who don't like the impersonal firms in the big city or online. Plus, I can be near home, in case things get worse and they need me."

She played with a fake flower lying on the bedside table. "You see why I'm the way I am now, don't you?" she asked. "Look at my life. I run this. It takes everything I have to do it, and I'm just barely getting by. I don't want to wake up another day wondering if I can scrape up enough to pay another bill, or hoping in the back of my mind that Pop's right and luck's just about to turn. I'm sick of it, Tessa. Of being alone with all this." She held her hands out, gesturing toward the whole house and not just the room, Tessa sensed.

"It makes perfect sense to me. This is a lot for anybody to handle," said Tessa. "And it makes sense why things didn't work between you and your previous boyfriend."

"Wish he saw it that way," said Harper. "Silver linings. He sounds like Pop when he talks about that. I see the storm clouds first. I see that we can get rained on through our leaky roof, and why take a chance in life that could mean you might not have the money to fix it when the time comes?"

Tessa sat down beside her. "Do you want us to meet here some-time?" she asked. "So your mom can be part of the planning?"

Harper shook her head. "Mom's right. All she wants is for me to be happy. She doesn't care… She can't care in a way that makes her want to help," she amended. "To her, life's all the same color now."

Tess nodded. "I just thought I would offer," she said.

The real reason for Harper turning her down went unstated: that the Winships would see Harper's home of chaos and compare it to Brett's perfect background. What if Willy called them snobs to their faces? Or Myra Winship stepped into a powder room occupied by a diaper-clad toddler playing in the sink? Harper was hiding the truth from them as best she could, just as she tried to conceal more of her bright colors and bold manners underneath nude lipstick and her plainer clothes on recent outings with Myra.

But that was Harper's business, not hers. That's why it was better to keep that obvious point to herself in this situation, and suggest that the next meeting take place in the Wedding Belles' parlor instead. Harper would no doubt find a way to enfold Brett in this situation sometime in the future, in her own way.

But Tessa would be willing to bet, given what she witnessed today, that the Lucas family would not come to the Palmetto Isle Resort for Harper's wedding. The groom's family and friends would occupy most of the seats in the tropical garden and the glass dining hall on that occasion.

Chapter Twenty-Seven

As Natalie suspected, it was there: first page of the fashion section, a story on the Magnolia Fashion Revue, sporting the headline: *Catfight Behind the Catwalk as Local Fashion Maven Attacks Newcomer.* A photo of herself, blurred in motion, with a clearer perspective on Kandace's enraged face as she wrestled with Natalie.

With a groan, Natalie stuffed it out of sight. There were two more online stories about the incident, treating it mostly in humorous fashion. One had misprinted her name. This was not the kind of publicity she envisioned for her debut, her designs eclipsed by Kandace's rage.

My work is still trapped in her shadow, even after a year. How is that fair?

Her phone rang. "It's not as bad as it seems," said Cal, who forewent chitchat to go directly to the subject she knew they were both thinking of this morning. "Any press can be good press, Nat. At least we're getting mentioned in these stories, right?"

"Yes, as a former employee of Kandace's Kreations," said Natalie, grimly. "No mention thus far of any of our designs, our talents, or what critics think of our work. In one, she actually accused me of stealing her designs, Cal. That *she's* behind the garments in our part of the runway show!"

"No one will take that seriously, Nat. They've seen her work—are you telling me that somebody would believe the queen of plastic trousers and tin-foil vests is behind those gorgeous clothes? Please, Nat. We both know that's impossible."

"Maybe somebody will believe it, though," said Natalie. "Their readers don't know Kandace like the fashion community does."

"They will after she does that spot on Channel Six news," said Cal.

"She's doing an interview on the *news*?"

"It's all good, Nat," Cal assured her. "People will see she's a kook, and by then, everybody else will move on to the review part. You know people are going to love our stuff. Already Chic Beat's fashion tweets listed your evening gown among the five 'must-see' moments from the runway. That's a good sign, right?"

"Did they spell my name correctly?"

"Well… I didn't notice, actually," said Cal. "I'll look. Darn, why is every other tweet about Kandace? I'll call you back as soon as I find it." He hung up.

Natalie sighed. Maybe Cal was right. Then again, maybe Kandace would appear reasonable in the six o'clock news broadcast and people would think she, Natalie, absconded with a satchel stuffed full of Kandace's secret designs then sewed them out of silk and chiffon instead of vinyl and upholstery fabric.

Her apartment buzzer rang. She pressed the button. "Who is it?"

"Package delivery," came the reply.

"Come on up." She pressed the button, then realized a moment later to whom the voice belonged. She unfastened the door latch and opened it, finding Brayden on the other side.

"Hi," he said. He smiled. "Sign here and it's all yours." He held out a package and a clipboard with a pen tacked at the top.

"Thanks." She scribbled her name at the bottom of the sheet, aware Brayden was watching her.

After a moment, he cleared his throat. "Saw the reviews for your fashion show," he said.

Natalie's fingers slowed. "Did you?" She tried not to seem concerned about this, even though she winced inside.

"Yeah." He paused. "That lady—Kandace—she didn't hurt you, did she? Your old boss?"

"Only my pride," answered Natalie. She summoned a weak smile as she tacked the pen back at the top. Getting emotional about this in front of Brayden wasn't an option. She might've cried in front of him as a kid plenty of times, but this was different from falling off her roller skates as a six-year-old. She didn't want him to think she was falling apart over one horrible setback to the career she worked so hard to create. Even if she totally was.

At least he hadn't been there to watch. She'd scanned the crowd beforehand and had been ninety-nine percent sure of it. No homely-but-kind smile to be seen.

"I thought your dresses were real pretty," said Brayden. "You looked good up there, Nat. You should be proud." He smiled at her, the same one she had just been thinking of. She almost blushed because of it, though it faded quickly in the reality of the subject at hand.

"I'll feel proud of myself later, after I'm over my initial humiliation," she answered. Lowering her glance, she contemplated these words. She hadn't meant to confide in him. Why didn't she just say thanks and let it go?

Brayden's smile faded. "Why?" he asked. "Nat, that wasn't your fault. It didn't have anything to do with your work, your old boss going crazy—except maybe for her being sorry she can't sew anything that nice."

Natalie's lips twitched at this remark. "I think Kandace prefers safety pins and barbed wire as part of a fashion statement," she said. "However… it's nice of you to say that. But it doesn't surprise me, you being nice. You were nice to me the other night at the restaurant, even though I was ready to bite somebody's ear off when you approached."

He shrugged. "Sometimes a date can go wrong, right?" he said. "It happens."

"At least you were just out with friends and didn't have to worry about those faux pas," said Natalie.

It was the brief, awkward pause that told Natalie that wasn't fully the case.

He and the girl from the restaurant were an item now. For a moment, Natalie's world rumbled with the deep tremors of its shifting tectonic plates. It felt unpleasant.

"So, who is she?" she asked. A smile crossed her lips, though it felt different from usual. Must be the surprise of Brayden actually dating a girl that made it a hesitant one, versus when it was only a theory in her mind. There was a time when nobody would have believed it possible, including herself.

"A girl I work with," he said. He studied the tops of his boots for a moment. "It's not serious or anything. We just went out a couple of times to grab dinner together. She's nice. You'd like her," he added, as if this was an honor that someone should earn, the badge of Natalie's approval. "She's gonna take my route when I leave."

"Lucky her," said Natalie. "On both counts." This earned a modest shrug from Brayden.

"I don't know about that," he said. "But she deserves that route. She's been driving as long as I have, been working a long rural route that gets pretty tiring, especially if one of the trucks breaks down."

"Is she okay with you moving?" said Natalie.

"She knew about it already. We have the same group of friends. Word travels pretty fast in the company when somebody's moving on."

"She looked like a nice girl," said Natalie. "And she's cute." She started to make a comment about Brayden's good taste, but realized who it was coming from and bit her tongue.

"She is," agreed Brayden. "Maybe you two can meet sometime. She won't be at the party 'cause she's got a family wedding out of town, but maybe we'll all hang out some night. You could bring Chad." It was almost an afterthought, this part—maybe Brayden hesitated because he forgot about her own relationship.

Double-dating with her and Chad. Something about this suggestion seemed horrible to Natalie, though she couldn't put her finger on what it was. Her skin wanted to crawl suddenly, over the idea of Chad's arm around her shoulder, cuddling her as Brayden sat across from them, watching.

But what did it matter now? It wasn't as if Brayden could be hurt by seeing someone else kiss her, his old crush flaring to life again, right? Brayden would clearly be holding hands with someone else… an idea that also made her feel intensely uncomfortable.

Suddenly, at this imaginary table, space appeared between her and Chad on their side of the booth. Natalie shut her mind to these ideas as quickly as she could.

"Long-distance workplace relationship," said Natalie. "Wow. I know you said you were changing things, but I never imagined how much you actually meant it. New girl, new job, new city. You've turned over pretty much every page of your life in the last three or four months."

"It ain't that much," said Brayden. "I was doing stuff before, just not as big. We all start out small, like when you first started taking classes so you could work up to getting your degree. You only took two or three that first semester. When you first moved to your apartment, you only took three boxes, remember?"

"Yeah." Her voice softened. Brayden had been the one who carried those boxes for her. Rob had come along as a driver since Natalie's car was in the shop, and he had claimed that he pulled some muscles the day before in a training exercise.

"See? It all starts small." Brayden took the clipboard from her hands. Natalie's signature was an unintelligible scribble on its sixth line.

"You're right," she said. She laid the package on the table. "And... that was nice of you to say. You don't have to try to make me feel better, though."

"I know," he said. "I don't have to, 'cause I'm sure you did fine." He tucked the clipboard under his arm and tipped his cap. "Have a nice day, Natalie." He stepped outside the door so she could close it.

"I'll be at your party," she said, remembering now the invitation he had given her over the phone. "I'll bring something. Anything you want."

He shook his head. "Nothing's fine," he answered. "I'll see you there, I guess." He offered her another smile, but this one was different from old. "Say hi to Rob for me."

"I will."

I'm sorry, Brayden, that I wasn't nice to you, she thought. *And that you've always been nice to me for no good reason.* She wanted to say it, because she should apologize for all the damage she did over the years in trying to escape her past and find herself. She owed it to him as an old friend before he left town.

Instead, she closed the door behind him and leaned against it, thinking about what he'd said about her having done fine. Clearly, he hadn't read the fashion pages too closely this morning. Did he read them because he knew about her show? Or was it force of habit after all these years of desperately trying to keep up with her world from a distance? He didn't have to do it anymore. He never had to in the first place.

Cal hadn't called back, she noticed. That tweet mentioning their gown must be deeply buried in the feed by now.

As Natalie feared, her mother dropped by that afternoon. Sometimes she thought Maria was psychically aware of when she was off work—or maybe she tapped her cell phone to know when she phoned in at Wedding Belles to cry off a day's appearance. The knock on the door was followed by the sight of her mother outside it, holding a pastry box.

Natalie sighed. "I don't need more leftovers, Ma," she said.

"Take them anyway." Maria entered, marching to the kitchen with her burden of canvas tote bags. "Your uncle made double the number of sourdough rolls some customer ordered for a breakfast, then we ended up selling no cream cakes this week, and he made double of those while he was minding the store. I tell you, sometimes I don't know about him." She shook her head. "I should never leave him in charge for more than five minutes."

"Pawn them off on Rob." Natalie closed the door behind her. "I'm really not in the mood for extra sugar today."

"What? You're sulking now?" said Maria. "Your brother told me you had a fight with your old boss at some fashion show, but that's not the end of the world, is it?"

"Ma, it wasn't just a fight. She attacked me. In public, in front of all my peers," said Natalie, who now felt like she was describing a childish playground incident involving bullies and stolen lunch money. "She stole my professional thunder, and I would prefer to be alone while I deal with it."

"You need family at a time like this," scoffed Maria. "Stop doing everything on your own. Come with me to dinner at Chrissy's tonight and tell us all about it. Have a good cry out with the girls instead of doing it in your apartment where it's lonely and unhealthy." She unpacked two more pastry boxes, piling them on Natalie's tiny counter as she spoke.

"I'll pass on dinner. Thanks." Natalie leaned against the door as her mother finished stocking her kitchen with unnecessary baked goods. "I have some work to do for the wedding that's coming up."

"Work. That's your big excuse for everything these days," said Maria. "Someday you're gonna wish you still had a safety net of family wrapped around you," said Maria, shaking her head. "You'll look back on days like this and miss it. You used to love being with your family all the time. Just the other day, I found the paper you wrote back in school about your family being the best in the world."

There was a lump in Natalie's throat, though she managed to laugh. "That must've been a blast from the past," she said, sitting down on the sofa.

Maria didn't know how near to the truth she was at this moment. Natalie's hard shell wasn't covering up the softness she felt for them all, and for the community of food and support the Grenaldi name represented. It was the only thing that countered the ache of disappointment and uncertainty inside her.

"Did you find much else that was interesting?" Natalie was working up the courage to ask her mother what she thought about the Paris and Milan dreams being put aside for a career that involved weekends at the bakery and at Chrissy's brunches. Would Maria laugh? Would she be relieved, or tell Natalie she was crazy not to leap at life's chances?

"I found your baby dresses too," said Maria. "I never could get the tomato sauce stains out of that one your grandmother made you—you were the messiest eater."

"Ma!"

"I did find this, though, and thought you might like it," said Maria, taking a shoebox out of one of her tote bags; its cardboard sides were papered with old magazine pictures, a decoupage of fashion catalog clippings. "One of your treasure boxes when you were a kid. I thought you'd enjoy looking through it."

She laid it on the coffee table. "There are three or four more boxes of your childhood stuff that I need you to go through sometime, so I can clean out the attic. I'm making your brother do the same."

"That'll be the day," said Natalie, popping open the lid on the shoebox. Inside, she spotted a souvenir keychain, a rock, a series of old photographs pried off the memory board in her childhood bedroom. Junk, she estimated, like most of the stuff cluttering up her mother's attic.

Maria buttoned her bag again. "Cheer up," she said. "You'll find your success, Natalie. I hope you'll have more than just fashion shows to make you happy... but I'm your mother, so what do I know?"

"You know a lot, Ma," said Natalie, softly. "I think you're right about more than I'll ever want to admit. But... give me time to say it's true, all right?"

Maria's gaze softened. "You'll always figure things out, baby." She kissed the top of Natalie's head. "Don't let a little moment of weakness take all the fight out of my girl. You're a Grenaldi, and all the Grenaldis know how to be the best at what they do. Give yourself some time and you'll come blazing back in a day or two."

"Thanks, Ma." Natalie rubbed her neck, wearily, as she laid aside a plastic Polly Pocket from the shoebox.

Maria shouldered her last empty tote bag. "If you change your mind, Chrissy wants everybody there by seven, but you know her, you can walk in at any time."

"Sure, Ma." Natalie dropped the lid back on the box, hiding the lucky orange troll with its belly gem from her eighth birthday, and a birthday card that Rob had colored for her when he was three. "I'll try to make it."

It would do her good, like Maria said. And Natalie was lonelier and hungrier these days for old connections, even with a full-time relationship that should fulfill her need for understanding and sympathy. So why didn't it? She wondered why in a crisis like this one that, short of Maria, her best source of sympathy was the boy she had been trying to escape for more than a decade. Why was she so mixed up these days?

Picturing Brayden in a relationship was so hard for her, for instance. Brayden was a good guy at heart, deserving of someone special, so it was not the miracle her past self would have snarkily claimed. That a cute girl had finally spotted that truth was the inevitable, if the world wanted to be just and fair at times. It was good news for everybody concerned, wasn't it?

That girl was lucky, because a decent guy who listens to you and cares about your feelings is hard to find. Natalie herself couldn't lay claim to that fully in her current relationship, even though Chad was a good listener on the surface.

The longtime image in her head of her childhood friend and lifelong hopeless admirer was being disassembled bit by bit, and being rebuilt as a different version of Brayden. It mattered deeply to her that it was happening, as strange as it seemed. If Brayden only knew, he would be the recipient of the biggest compliment her past self could ever pay him.

She reached for her phone. Hesitating, she dialed his number, hearing his voicemail pick up. His line was busy, probably on a call to his new girlfriend.

"Hi, Brayden, it's me. Natalie." She paused. "I just wanted to let you know… if you need any help for the party, you can call me." A lame cop-out to keep herself from telling him the honest truth. She rolled her eyes. "I'll use my contacts to give you a hand. Anytime, just give me a call. Bye."

What a drip you are, Natalie. She fell backwards onto her couch, against its poufy pillows, and buried her phone out of sight. Too little too late in their friendship to tell him how she felt—the new Brayden would never be desperate enough to accept such a pitiful bone of apology for the sake of scoring bulk party supplies.

*

While Natalie was burying old memories under a cardboard lid, Ama was considering the nature of new ones as she sat in her bedroom. Downstairs, the Tandoori Tiger's preparation for the dinner rush was about to begin, so it was time for her to finish cooking the summer carrot *halwa*, dressed with crushed sugared peanuts, Ranjit's latest idea. But she was sitting on her bed, gazing at the ring dangling from the ribbon around her neck.

Moments ago, she had tried to phone Luke. She pushed the button again. After four rings, she heard the sound of a static-ridden connection. "Ama?"

"Luke, hi." She sat upright, her hands actually trembling. "How are you? Is everything okay there?"

"It's good." Something unintelligible followed as the signal cut out. " —you must've been busy."

"I know. I worked extra hours at the restaurant because Rasha had some dental appointments," she said. "I'm designing a cake for a wedding, and it's my dream one, Luke. I showed you the picture of it before, remember? With the birds of paradise? You'd be proud—it's really gorgeous. I dropped the sample off yesterday."

"I remember that picture you showed me," he said. "Photograph it for me if I'm not back before you finish it."

"I will," she said. "Are you coming back soon?" She crossed her fingers tightly.

A pause. "That's the thing," he said. "See, the job will take a couple more weeks at most, but I—" the connection between them crackled, and Ama lost his words "—if you've had time yet to know what you feel," he finished.

"I'm thinking about it every day," said Ama, who was trying to piece together what his missing words might be. "Luke, please, I want you to come back. No matter what, you said that you—"

"—but I would call you," he was saying, across the broken thread of their conversation. "I can't stop thinking—"

"Luke? Luke, are you there?" Ama moved the phone away from her ear and looked at its screen. The call was dropped, the connection having fizzled mid-sentence for Luke. She pushed the redial button and waited. More static noise, then the automated service for Luke's voicemail.

Ama hung up. That wasn't what she'd hoped for, and whatever words she'd missed seemed important. Luke wasn't still thinking about leaving for Portugal from his friend's house, was he? He promised he'd come back, even if it was to say goodbye. Since the phrase "saying goodbye" made her feel slightly ill, even at her most doubtful times, Ama tried not to think about it.

She bit her thumbnail. She could try to call Luke again this evening, of course. But if he had been asking if she was ready to marry him, she still didn't know the answer. That terrifying question, with the power to confirm her and Luke's love or possibly reveal its hidden instability, remained unanswerable for her. Could he understand why she felt these uncertainties? Love was so new for her, so impossible to maneuver in its maze of feelings and choices… and marriage was the ultimate crossroads in its passageways.

Carefully, she tucked the ring out of sight beneath her dress's neckline. Her phone buzzed, and she checked its screen, hopefully, but didn't see Luke's number. It was a reminder for the upcoming museum exhibit, sent from Tamir's phone. She remembered promising to go with him if she was free.

See u there on Friday? If not, ok. ☺

She texted in reply:

See u there ☺.

She laid aside her phone afterward and reached for her apron, draped across the end of her bed. She double-checked to make sure her ring was hidden from sight before she went downstairs to prepare dessert for hungry customers.

Chapter Twenty-Eight

Tessa rushed through the Wedding Belles' door, grabbing her work portfolio from the hall table on her way. "Ama, are you here yet? We're meeting with the caterers at ten." She checked her watch on her way up the stairs, confirming she wasn't late yet. "Ama?" She knocked on the baker's office door, peering inside to find no sign of her business partner. The pile of cookbooks on Ama's table were unmoved from last time, and there was no funky paisley handbag on the coat hook.

She consulted her planner then pulled out her phone. "Natalie? Hey, can you do me favor and check with the company we're renting the chairs from? I got a message from them this morning about not having enough of the bamboo ones or something."

"Um, sure," said Natalie, sounding less than enthused for this mundane task. "I might be running a little late today, but I'll definitely do it."

Tessa bit her lip. "Are you doing okay? Because I know you probably need a little space after what happened." She knew her friend must be down in the dumps about her fashion show debacle even if she was too stubborn to admit it.

"It's not too bad," said Natalie after a moment. "I felt sorry for myself, but I'm getting over it now. Plus I already cried on somebody else's shoulder so that helped a little bit."

"Was it Chad? He probably took you out somewhere to cheer you up, right?" said Tessa, assuming this was the "somebody" Natalie had mentioned. On the other end, silence.

"Chad's kind of busy right now." Natalie's vague tone was back. "Listen, Tessa, I really have to run. But I'll take care of that chair thing, promise."

Great. She dialed Ama's number. "Ama, when you get this, it's just me checking to see if you're going to be late for the meeting today," she said. She hung up then sat down on a trunk in the hallway, sighing aloud.

"What's up?" The sound of Blake's voice startled her. With a jump, Tessa was on her feet again. "Sorry," said Blake, holding up his hands. "Didn't realize you were lost in thought at the moment."

"I'm waiting for Ama," she said. "I think." This last part was tacked on with slight exasperation.

Blake dusted some wood shavings from his shirt and tucked his thumbs into his low-slung work belt. "Is something up with you guys?" he asked. "None of my business, I know, but Ama's seemed kind of weird lately. So has Nat. And you, as far as that goes… at least, I'm picking up on a certain level of stress whenever you're around here."

"For Nat, it's because of the fashion show," said Tessa. "It's making her crazy, all the labor and the… well, backlash. In case you don't read the fashion section."

"I don't," said Blake. "In case you're wondering."

"Ama is… is having some personal problems," said Tessa, who didn't want to go into detail about the secret proposal from Luke. "So that leaves me holding the bag, so to speak. It's not that I can't handle it, but it's hard—this is the biggest wedding we've ever planned. I want it to be perfect, and that means every detail needs care and attention."

"And you can't count on them to share that focus," guessed Blake. "That's new." He seemed surprised.

"There's a first time for everything, isn't there?" said Tessa. She hesitated. "This is crazy, but... it would help if I could lean on you sometimes—metaphorically," she hastened to add. "You've just been so helpful... so amazing... in the past, that I could use that same help again, if we end up falling behind."

His face wore a mild expression as she talked, so he didn't look as if he wanted to escape from the prospect of helping her. But Tessa knew that Blake must have mastered the ability to hide his feelings about the certain level of craziness attached to the Wedding Belles and its events.

After all, he had finally stopped suggesting they duplicate its period wallpaper, or put back whatever banister and rails comprised the original staircase before the metal circular one went into place. He might be equally good at hiding telltale signs of wariness at being asked to provide an extra pair of hands for moving tables or placing centerpieces, and the dozens of other things that Tessa would be doing over the next couple of weeks.

"I don't want to ask, but I feel as if I don't have a choice, in case this wedding needs more than I can give it alone." She sighed. "I don't want to be this honest with you, but I have to be sometimes," she said. "I'm sorry. It's like it comes out by accident when I'm around you."

"Why wouldn't you want to be honest with me?" he asked.

"Because I don't want to scare you away," she said. "I mean, someone who's leaning on you, who's just a friend—I ask too many favors, and I know that one day it will be one favor too many." More honesty—it was just tumbling out on its own now.

"What have I ever said to make you think that?" he asked, sounding baffled. "I say yes because I want to, Tessa. Maybe I like being asked for help." He met her eye. "Maybe I like being a part of this, just a little. Did you ever think of that?"

"Really?" She was surprised. Too surprised to say anything else, actually.

"Is that so hard to believe?" he asked. "Honestly, it's kind of fun sometimes. Crazy, but fun. You haven't asked me to do anything I couldn't handle… yet."

Tessa tucked a lock of hair behind one ear then realized her face was burning with heat inside out.

"Look," he said, gently. "If you need something this time, ask. I'm around. The house over on Keele Pike is nearly finished, and I'm just doing some things here that I didn't get done before I started that project. But it's nothing that can't wait a little longer. It's not like I'm going anywhere, is it?"

"I hope not." Tessa was being honest again. But in a very different tone of voice from before. "I never told you this. But I would really, really miss you if you ever finished working here. I know you have to someday, because you can't keep repairing little things, and we can't afford to pay you for anything bigger—but I dread the day it finally comes to that."

The expression on Blake's face changed subtly, as if he were surprised. "You mean that, Tessa?" he asked.

She liked it when he said her name. Why did it sound different than when other people did?

She nodded. "Call me crazy," she said.

Blake touched her arm, softly. Tessa shivered as his fingers made contact, lightly, with her skin. He looked as if he was going to say something else, then they both heard the sound of footsteps on the metal staircase. *Ama must have arrived*, Tessa thought. They turned to find Ashleigh on the landing.

"I'm so sorry," she said. "Am I interrupting?"

"No, no," said Tessa, quickly, though that was exactly what Ashleigh was doing. She and Blake moved apart automatically, and Tessa could swear that Blake actually looked guilty.

"Is this where we're meeting today?" Ashleigh asked. "I have Brett's—I mean, Mr. Winship's—thoughts on the ceremony all typed up and ready to go, so I thought I would drop them off with just a quick rundown, then pop over to the nail salon before the rest of the gang arrives."

"This is the place," said Tessa. "And I take it that Brett won't be here?"

"Mr. Winship had an emergency meeting in Tampa," said Ashleigh. "So... do I run those suggestions by you? It's just a few little particulars he feels really strongly about."

Although she was talking to Tessa, her eyes were on Blake the whole time, like an eager puppy. Tessa, who felt like physically gagging over the thought of discussing Ashleigh's little "suggestions" from her boss, searched for her customary businesslike smile to see it through.

"You know what? I'll take them," said Blake, who glanced at Tessa's face before he spoke. "Just a quick list of pointers, right?" He raised one eyebrow questioningly, to see if this was all right with her—a signal to jump in if she wanted to. "You can jot them down for me in this office. I'll take charge of that list in your hand, and my colleagues and I will review them while you're getting your nails done."

Tessa smiled at him. Ashleigh looked elated over this suggestion. "Perfect," the assistant answered. Ashleigh followed him in the direction of Tessa's office. At this moment, Tessa was feeling too grateful that Blake was taking this particular task off her hands to even be jealous of the way Brett's assistant kept finding excuses to put her hand on his arm.

But not too grateful to keep from hoping that he didn't make this offer for the sake of getting to know Miss Gardenia Blossom 2012.

Chapter Twenty-Nine

Natalie was taking her turn at bakery inventory when her cell phone rang. For a split second she thought it might be Brayden. He had texted her last night to accept her offer to help him shop for party supplies later this week. Now she wondered if he had changed his mind.

Heart skipping—what was up with that?—she fished her phone from her jacket pocket... and found Harper on the other end of the line.

"Is this a bad time?" the bride asked, sounding apologetic. "I tried to call Tessa but her phone must be turned off. I think she had a meeting with the florist or something."

"No problem," said Natalie. "I'm here to help." She put down the clipboard she had been using to log baking ingredients and reached for the Wedding Belles folder inside her tote bag instead. "Is there a problem with something for the wedding?" she asked. The bride's tone was missing its usual upbeat attitude, she realized.

"It's nothing big." Harper feigned nonchalance badly. "I just need you to cancel the flower wreaths for the bridesmaids and Marsha."

"Cancel them? Why?" Natalie frowned, wondering if something had gone wrong with the order. The wreaths had looked beautiful online and seemed like a perfect choice with Harper's exotic island theme.

"They just don't want to wear them. Not their style, they said. They're more the 'simple flower tucked to one side' kind of girls, apparently. Then they pointed out they don't really go with the dresses they... we... picked out, so I'm thinking we should go ahead and send them back. I'll still wear mine, but we'll have to get them each something a little less showy."

This is just plain unfair, Natalie thought. These bridesmaids were bullies. First, they had pressured Harper into picking dresses for them that didn't go with her theme, and now they refused to wear a simple flower crown just to make Harper feel like her taste was beneath them. She could tell this had hurt the bride's feelings, but she obviously didn't want to make a fuss about it.

"Let me take care of that for you," Natalie told her, biting her tongue before she could say something about the snobby bridesmaids' behavior—although she imagined Marsha, the maid of honor, had probably been the instigator, from what she knew about her.

"Thanks," said Harper, sounding relieved. "I better go now. I have some clients coming in. Honeymooners on their way to Europe."

"Hey, that'll be you in a couple weeks," said Natalie, trying to end their call on a bright note.

Harper laughed. "I'm counting the days," she said. "Thanks again, Natalie."

"Anytime." She hung up feeling discontent. She could send the wreaths back, no problem there. It was Harper's obvious disappointment that bugged her so much. And Tessa would be upset.

She knew the bride's unspoken worries would weigh on her business partner's mind like a sack of stones. Tessa was clearly feeling pressured by their client's emotional dilemma, the underlying friction from the groom's family, and it was beginning to show. Not that Tessa would ever ask for help, especially while Natalie was still reeling from her fashion show disaster—not even so much as a sticky note asking for a favor had been pinned to Natalie's computer monitor. No request for anything since the chair rental check-up, and that had only taken a few minutes.

She was letting them down and they didn't even have the nerve to make her feel guilty over being the only useless Wedding Belle this round. That's what sent Natalie to the only place she belonged—back to her fabric pile and her sewing box. She searched through her bolts for the right color or print, something that declared itself to be Harper without saying words.

When Harper saw it a few afternoons later, it was love at first sight.

"Oh my gosh! I adore it!" Harper clapped her hands together then framed her cheeks as if she were a real-life version of Edvard Munch's *The Scream*. "It's so gorgeous—are you serious about giving it to me?!" She looked ready to sink down on the sofa in Natalie's office.

"Of course I am," said Natalie. "I couldn't make your wedding dress, but I figured I could make something for your rehearsal dinner, and this felt perfect for you. Consider it my gift to you for being our customer. The Wedding Belles are nothing if not appreciative of their clients."

The fabric was a deep, rich maroon chiffon, which crisscrossed at the bodice to form a medium-plunge V-neck, with soft, wide shoulder drapery. The skirt brushed a few inches below Harper's knees, while the low waistline and subtle pleats complimented their client's waist and curves.

"Can I try it on?" said Harper.

"Of course," said Natalie. "Come on, I have to pin this thing if it needs adjustment."

Eagerly, her client shrugged off her work jacket and unzipped the dress's back.

It fit Harper neatly, except where Natalie wanted to make some adjustments. But seeing herself in her favorite color had lifted Harper's mood already. "Gosh, it looks perfect," she said, gazing at her reflection. "I love this color, did I tell you that? It's like red and purple got together and made a love child. After a week of beige and off-white—" Harper paused and corrected herself, "—I mean, after days spent in business clothes, it's nice to wear something that feels more like *me*, you know? And this is so classy, not like anything in my closet at home."

"I'd like to think I know my stuff." Natalie tucked a pin in place.

In the doorway, Tessa appeared, and Natalie smiled. It was good to see Tessa relax, too, and nothing took her stress down a notch like a happy customer. The smile on her face was definite proof.

"I can't wait to show it to Brett," said Harper. "His secretary had emailed me a couple of 'exclusive' deals she thought I might like, but they were both so plain and blah, I hated to pick one of them. He's bound to like this one, though."

"It's always hard to bend to each other's tastes when you're part of a couple," said Natalie. "Me, I'm dating a guy who wants to move to South America. I hate snakes, by the way. I think it's just how things work in relationships."

"Maybe," chuckled Harper. "When it was me and Danny—" She caught herself, and the smile on her lips faded. "With my ex, we used to disagree all the time over little things. But he was always making it up to me. Usually with some stupid little gesture." The snort that followed this remark was convincing enough to Natalie's ears.

"Is he still hanging around?" asked Tessa. She sounded slightly concerned.

Harper shrugged. "Who knows?" she said. "It's Danny. I can't predict what he's doing, because even if you know him like a book, he can still do the last thing you'd expect." She rolled her eyes. "He could be stalking me from the alley outside right now."

"Kind of like your guy Brayden used to be," said Tessa to Natalie.

"What?" said Natalie, sharply. "No, not really. He and Brayden are nothing alike." Danny was handsome and charming, whereas Brayden was… well, Brayden. No fortune, no looks, but something intangible, if you were the kind of girl who could see it.

"I meant the situation," said Tessa. "You're both being stalked by your childhood sweethearts. At least, until recently."

She meant Harper, not Natalie, with the "recent" comment—she didn't know about Brayden's girlfriend. "It's still not the same," said Natalie, shrugging it off now. Her previous reaction Tessa could interpret however she wanted.

"Your childhood sweetheart is still in love with you?" Harper asked Natalie.

"Not exactly. He just had an adolescent crush that lasted into his late twenties," said Natalie. "We were never sweethearts. It was a strictly one-sided affair." Her fingers didn't do as good of a job pinning the dress as she intended.

The last Valentine's card she had given Brayden was signed by her six-year-old self; by second grade, when Brayden's grade-school crush was born, Natalie had avoided giving him anything that might encourage it. It hadn't been nearly as nice as the glamorous birthday card he gave her that inspired her business cards… but it had been heartfelt, at least. It would be the last kind thing she would give him, except for the quiet and fierce episodes of protection she performed in secret on his behalf during the dangerous years of adolescence—and only when strictly necessary.

Harper sighed. "I wish mine would grow up and get over it," she said. "It just makes me so mad. The way he's still convinced that he's the only person who could ever make me happy or treat me decently. Look at the guy I ended up with—and this after Danny decides to run off and make a name for himself, like *that* was going to prove something to me."

"What if he had stayed?" asked Natalie.

Harper paused. A little flicker of doubt crossed her face. "We were doomed," she said, at last. "We had already broken up. He knew I couldn't marry anybody then. I couldn't be with anybody… I mean, I had a lot of stuff to deal with, without having somebody in my life who was chasing crazy dreams. I'd had enough of that already."

"So it's not like his leaving you was the reason," said Natalie. "You weren't meant to be, period."

That's what I have in common with Harper, she thought. *Not the blast from the past sweetheart connection.* Maybe pointing out the obvious facts of this case would help Harper reach the same conclusion she had, which was that youthful love connections pan out with heartache, disillusionment, and complex, mixed-up feelings on both sides. Just when Brayden was sorting his feelings out, Natalie's were beginning to slip into a weird zone of regret and curiosity.

Harper sighed. "I suppose that's true," she said. "If I'd promised him we'd be together, he might've stayed. Knowing him, he'd say that, and even think he meant it… but some other crazy opportunity would've come along sooner or later." Steel had entered her voice again.

"If you feel good about the decision, that's all you can ask, right?" said Natalie.

"At least you found a great guy in the end," supplied Tessa.

"I did, didn't I? Brett is so wonderful. He's so capable and confident and… and just really incredible," said Harper, filling an evident blank with a handy superlative for her groom-to-be. "I just feel so lucky that he walked into my agency that day. Otherwise, who knows?" She shrugged her shoulders.

You would've fallen for Danny again? Natalie's curious half didn't say this aloud, even as a joke.

"I'll let you know when Brett and I are available to sit down with you and look at the latest plans," said Harper, as she changed back into her business clothes. "It should be soon. He's just been tied up with some big business deal."

Tessa's smile looked artificial—it was too bright, for one thing. "Sounds great," she said. "We're looking forward to it."

She wasn't. Natalie wondered why, but now was not the time to ask.

When Harper was gone, Tessa flopped down on the sofa, her face against one of the sequined Indian pillows that Ama had left here, and that Nella adored.

"Feeling better?" asked Natalie, pointedly.

"No." Tessa's voice was muffled. "But it's not my problem, so I shouldn't worry about it. At least that's what I'm telling myself." She rolled over and gazed at the artsy light fixture that Cal had insisted on having installed above his workspace.

"Want to talk about it?" Natalie asked.

Tessa sighed. "I don't want to explain it," she said. "It's none of my business, and I should stay out of it."

"Fine. If you say so. I'll just sit here, pretending I'm not waiting for you to speak."

Tessa turned to her. "How did you know Brayden wasn't the one for you?"

Natalie looked at her as if she was crazy. "What?" she said, with a laugh. She shrugged, pretending to think about it for a second. "It was Brayden. My brother's friend who made sand pies with me at the playground when I was five. I didn't have to know. We knew everything about each other—too much about each other to ever make things work between us. The older we grew, the more we were complete opposites in every sense, except having families who liked each other."

"So? Opposites attract, at least that's what everybody says."

"We just weren't right," said Natalie, firmly. "You know me, you know what I'm like. I can be a horrible person, and he's the nicest guy in the world. Brayden would've hated me if he'd actually dated me."

"Don't be so down on yourself," Tessa scolded. "You make a pretty great friend, so I can't imagine you'd be anything less as someone's girlfriend. And I'll bet Brayden would second that opinion, given how long you've known each other," she said.

"That guy who likes you?" Ama had appeared now, with an armful of fake flowers for decorating fake cakes. "I thought he was sweet. He didn't seem like the type who hates anybody, except for maybe bad people. You know, cold-blooded murderers or animal abusers or something."

"I just mean it would've made him miserable," said Natalie, struggling to explain herself. "So I exaggerated what his feelings would be if we had ever gone out. Sue me."

"Why *did* you dislike him so much back then?" Ama asked, perching on the edge of the fabric-cutting table. "What did he do that was so awful?"

Natalie sighed. "I don't know." It was too hard to put into words, the reasons why she always pushed Brayden away. "He was clingy, and too polite, and always trying to get my attention by doing nice things.

Other boys would swing from the monkey bars or call you a troll to get you to notice them—he was the kind who brought you flowers and tried to share his lunch cupcake."

It wasn't what Brayden did back then that made her run away from him—it was just the typical irrational childhood prejudices at fault. And afterward... well, her popularity versus his passivity, she thought. She was the bold one, while he was always willing to let someone step on him rather than hurt somebody back. He was always patiently waiting while she was always leaping ahead to the next stage of life.

"My first crush stomped on my crayons," said Ama. "Nobody ever offered me half a cupcake."

"It was a long time ago," said Natalie. "I just knew how I felt back then. There was no real reason, I guess... it's just how it is when you're kids. You know how it is," she added, unable to find the words that made it all clear and simple. "Besides, you noticed yourself how nice he was. We're a terrible match."

"You're not a match at all, are you?" laughed Ama. "Not now. You're dating Chad, so you're technically half of a couple. That pretty much closes the door on Brayden's old dreams, unless you and Chad aren't really in love."

That present-tense statement regarding her and Brayden had slipped out on its own. That wasn't what Natalie had intended to say, but there it was all the same, as if volunteering itself from her subconscious.

"Even Natalie must be a bit in love to have been dating somebody for six months" laughed Tessa. "I'm pretty sure it's impossible to go that long without there being *some* feeling."

"That's what everybody says, right?" Something sounded forced in Natalie's tone; they didn't notice, however, which was good. She didn't want to answer more questions at this point about her and Chad's status. She wasn't even sure what it was, truthfully.

Brayden was still Brayden, right? And she was still Natalie, even if she had finally consented to date somebody for more than two weeks, and tried to find a softer side beneath her blunt self. It wouldn't work between them, and that was that. They might become better friends, even good friends, if it weren't for the fact he was leaving. But even if he stayed, nothing would happen, because she simply couldn't become that kind of girl after all these years.

It was confusing her just to think about the idea at all. *Just don't do it*, she told herself. *The only thing changing for you is the fact that you're open to commitment now, sometime in the future.* Besides, Brayden probably wouldn't even be interested if she fell in love with him, since he had started dating other people at last.

See? It was so impossible she shouldn't even be imagining it.

Chapter Thirty

The featured exhibit at the Bellegrove Cultural History and Arts Gallery was devoted to kites painted and designed by various international artists. It was imaginative and interesting, and Ama enjoyed seeing the bright, boxy ones, and the standout projects like the mermaid kite from Indonesia and a multicolored dragon from Beijing. She took a photo of one shaped like a tiger, knowing her father and brother would appreciate it the best.

She probably enjoyed this more than the one Tamir had planned for them last year, an exhibit inspired by Indian tapestries. Then, Tamir would have come equipped with a digital history guide so they could be informed about the cultural relevance of each project, she imagined; but this time, he didn't seem pressured to do anything but observe and comment.

"Did you like the one that was supposed to be an abstract painting?" Ama asked. "I couldn't figure out how it would actually work in terms of flying."

"I think it was only in theory that it works," said Tamir. "It reminded me a little of a canvas I saw in a hotel lobby in New York. It had the same blue squiggly line traveling down its middle."

"Maybe it was the same one. Don't fancy hotels buy real canvases for their lobbies?"

"I don't stay anywhere that nice when I'm on business," laughed Tamir. "The company doesn't pay for five-star hotels. Anyway, I don't remember it really well. As much traveling as I do, it all becomes a blur."

"Is that new?" Ama asked. She sat down on the middle step of the museum's front entrance—a grand classical approach rendered in a modest size architecturally, with a half-dozen steps rising to the glass front doors currently decorated with mini silk kites. "You weren't traveling that much last year when we... when we hung out," she amended.

"I've been shadowing the current personnel trainer since February." Tamir paused one step below, then sat down a polite distance from Ama on her step. "I'll take his place when he transfers to a branch office in California later this year."

"Sounds very responsible," she said. "I'll bet your parents are excited."

His smile was faint. "It's very dull a lot of the time," he answered. "But, yes, they're excited. Visions of my future dancing in their heads and so on." He sighed. "It increases my matrimonial prospects, as my family sees it. You know how it is."

Not in those exact terms, but in spirit, yes. Ama did know what it was like to have your every decision weighed according to how it would affect prospects of a future mate. "Is there someone?" she asked. "Anybody you're interested in right now?"

"Sort of." Elbows on knees, he gazed at his hands, fingers interlaced; suddenly, he looked very boyish. "There's this girl on the tech team in Jersey. She's friendly—we have lunch together whenever I'm there for training conferences. But it hasn't turned into anything. I haven't said anything to her... not that you're surprised by that." He looked a bit embarrassed.

"What's she like?" Ama asked, interested.

"A lot like you," he admitted, flushing slightly. "Maybe I have a type."

This caused Ama's cheeks to turn a few different shades of rose as well. "I think you should ask her out," she said. "If she's friendly, she might be interested. If it were me, and I ate lunch with a guy every time he was in town, it would definitely be because I liked him."

"I'll have to work on my courage," said Tamir. "It was hard enough last December, when I was seeing you. I was dry, dull, and with manners stiff as a board. I'm actually kind of surprised you went out with me twice. Especially to the movie. You really weren't a huge fan of Bollywood films, after all."

"I like some of them," Ama pointed out. "And as far as Telugu films go, you were right—they are kind of hilarious. But... my favorite films from our culture will always be the romantic ones, with their impossible endings. You know, where the match turns out to be the unsuitable love interest from the marketplace."

"You have an emotional stake in that kind of ending," said Tamir. "You're dating a 'most unsuitable boy,' aren't you?" His fingers made a quotation marks gesture for this middle part, and his voice took on the snooty, shrill pitch that made Ama think instantly of her aunt.

She laughed. "Okay, I guess I am," she said. "Maybe that's the happily ever after I need."

"Is it serious? You and the guy you're dating?"

Ama paused. "Very," she answered. "That is... he gave me this." Reaching beneath the collar of her paisley blouse, she pulled out the ribbon with its ring. "He gave it to me just before he left to help out a friend."

"That's a big step, Ama." Tamir looked surprised. "What did you say?"

"Nothing. Yet," she added. "I'm trying to decide what to do. I love him. I just don't know if the timing is right. Or if I'm ready."

"For marriage? Or for love?" asked Tamir. "You seemed pretty sure of what you wanted last December. You definitely knew it wasn't me. I had the impression that love was all you really wanted in a relationship. The guy could be anything, or do anything, and you wouldn't really care."

"True," said Ama. "But I want to say yes and mean it with my whole heart. No regrets, no looking back."

"What would you regret?" Tamir asked, with a laugh. "Not me."

Ama's eyes widened. "No, that's not what I meant," she said. "I'm not talking about specifics—just dreams, ideas, hopes. Everything this ring represents. I always knew I only wanted to fall in love once, and to be sure of it. I'm a romantic at heart; if I put this ring on, I have to be one hundred percent. I don't want to fall for someone else by accident. Or fall out of love because it wasn't meant to be, or because I can't face the challenges it brings."

"Accidents like that don't just happen," said Tamir, still amused.

"That's what you think. You're a practical person," she answered.

"So I am. But that doesn't mean I'm completely practical," he said. "I can still have impulses. You just have to know which ones to embrace and which ones to ignore."

"Again: a romantic." Ama pointed at herself. "I spent my whole life believing that love begins in a second, with one look or one touch. It doesn't have dials or switches to control it."

"Do you also believe it's only meant to be with the one right person?"

"Of course," said Ama.

"Then I'm telling you that the one-right-person part is created in your mind," said Tamir. "The world has billions of people, Ama. We're driven by chemicals to find someone in the crowd to whom we're attracted emotionally and physically, and those same attributes belong to more than one person on the planet, even if we only meet one. We choose, even if we think we don't."

"It's so unromantic when you put it like that," said Ama, wrapping her arms around herself more tightly.

Tamir shrugged. "Is it?" he said. "Look at it this way. You could have hundreds of chances on the planet to meet someone, but you chose Luke and you can keep choosing him forever, no matter who else comes along. Isn't that romantic?"

"Sort of. Only since I never liked anybody before him, it's strictly theory in my case," said Ama.

"It's a shame you didn't like me a little. Then you could say that your subconscious held out for him," answered Tamir. "We could pretend that it was just bad timing. I was wary of dating, trying too hard; you were trying to escape your family's interference in your life."

"I like that better than you saying I didn't like you," answered Ama. "That makes me feel so guilty. You're not an unlikable person, you just… you weren't for me."

Tamir looked as handsome as always, with the cool breeze ruffling his dark wavy curls. He looked casual, less stiff, in his leaning, confident pose beside her on the steps. If he had looked more like this—been more like this version of his personality—back in December, it might have been harder to say goodbye to him.

"What happened to your glasses?" She realized he wasn't wearing his usual prescription lenses, and hadn't been all evening.

"Contacts," he said. "I'm still getting used to them. But someone told me that it was to my advantage to wear them—aesthetically speaking. Basically, they make me look less like a nerd." He smiled.

For the girl on the tech team, Ama thought. He was wearing them in hopes she would find him more attractive, since he was definitely good-looking. "I like it, "she said. "But… don't change yourself too much for anybody else. You want them to like you for you."

"I thought I would try being the version of myself that *isn't* the sensible Tamir software guy," he said. "Maybe if I had made an effort to balance my life better last year, I would have made it past two dates."

He had echoed the thought in Ama's head a moment ago. "Maybe. But I'm not a total romantic, no matter what I tell people. So, what was in my head when we were together was the same thing with Luke. All the realities behind the feeling. Like what other people thought, how other people felt. It's like I can't escape it, no matter how I try."

Imagine what all those people would be thinking if they saw her right now? For that reason, Ama laughed aloud, suddenly.

"What?" Tamir's brow furrowed with puzzlement.

"Nothing," she said. "I was just thinking about what my auntie would say if she could see me right now." Bendi would probably drop dead of shock—no, not her. She'd be crowing with triumph, preparing one of her "see, I told you" speeches about a suitable boy destined to cross Ama's path.

"She'd say that I'm too dark, for one thing," said Tamir, referencing her auntie's rather traditional feelings about the Indian caste system. "A very unfortunate complexion for a nice young man."

Ama caught his eye and discovered a spark of humor burning in it. They both laughed now over this terrible cultural cliché.

"Your family thinks mine is so inappropriate," said Ama. "So loud and overemotional. If we were a couple, that's what they would say, isn't it?"

"Are they really?" Tamir asked. "First impressions are a mistake. Now is your chance to change my mind and break down those stereotypes."

"I can't, because they sort of are," answered Ama. "They live for food, for our business, and for big, noisy family events. But they have good hearts, and they love me, even though they don't always understand me."

"My family are pretentious snobs," said Tamir. Ama glanced at him in surprise. "No arguing it," he added. "It's the image they prefer, the lifestyle they devote themselves to. At least they don't have to be quietly embarrassed anymore that I'm on the bottom rung of my career." He gazed into the distance, across the square. "But they love me and I love them. They mean well when they pressure me, and they're only disappointed by my life sometimes because they want things to work out for me."

"How do you feel about motorcycles?" Ama asked, on impulse.

"I used to have one when I was still living in Mumbai," he answered. "Why?"

"Just curious." She propped her chin on her hands in a moment's contemplation. She moved a moment later to wrap her arms around herself, rubbing her bare skin against the cool night breeze.

"Here." Tamir shrugged off his suit jacket and put it around her shoulders. It smelled of a new kind of aftershave that was unfamiliar to Ama's nostrils, a light, minty scent.

"Thanks," she said.

He drew it more closely around her, then paused. They were close together, their eyes meeting, exchanging a long glance. Without thinking, Ama closed her eyes, feeling Tamir's hand cup her cheek and his lips touch hers. A tender touch, quick and impulsive, but incredibly electric. Tamir was a good kisser, which Ama would never have believed last December.

She opened her eyes as he drew back. Her upturned face caught a glimpse of the stars through the city's twilight haze. The streetlamps of the quiet square below were reflected in Tamir's gaze like yellow diamonds, an expression of surprise in his eyes as they met hers.

It was a perfect kiss. Under the stars, with a summer breeze, in a moment of complete impulse. It was the perfect kiss from her dreams, but the moment after wasn't anything like she had imagined. Something was wrong, something was missing. Luke.

Tamir kissed me. Tamir, not Luke. This thought exploded in Ama's brain in the midst of mingled pleasure and amazement for the actual touch, as a sharp pain pricked her heart.

Her hands pulled Tamir's jacket from her shoulders and placed it in his hands. "I'm so sorry," she said. "I'm sorry—I didn't mean that. I'm so sorry. You're so gentle, so attractive and nice... You're amazing, but..." She couldn't finish, unable to find the words to explain what was so very wrong about this moment between them. "You know, I should go. Thank you—thank you for a nice evening." She scrambled to her feet and climbed down two steps, then a third one as Tamir rose with his crumpled jacket in hand.

"Ama, wait," he said. "I didn't mean it like that. I didn't mean to... I didn't mean to make you go."

"I know. But... I should do it anyway." It was late, and she was confused. She had made a mistake and she knew it. Not in leaving Tamir, she felt, because she knew they weren't right for each other. Her mistake lay elsewhere in this moment.

"Ama," he said again as she turned to leave.

She halted one step lower.

"You're choosing Luke by this," he said. "That's why he's the one."

She glanced back. The tears gathering in her eyes surrounded her view of Tamir with a hazy frame. "You're right," she said. "I guess I am." Her vision cleared slightly as she blinked back the unspilled tears. The first thought in her mind had been of Luke—his face in her mind, the look of concern and trust mingled in his eyes when they said goodbye at the station a few weeks ago.

"I didn't mean to do it," said Tamir, softly. "I did... I would have... last year. But this was more..."

"Wishful thinking?" suggested Ama, equally softly. "Wrong time, wrong place?"

He nodded. "Even if I could rewind time, it still wouldn't work out. I think we both know that." He smiled at her as he slipped his jacket back on.

Ama felt a touch of wryness in her own smile. Like she would not have dated Tamir six months ago, even if he had been this incredible—not with the matchmaking site's profile instigated by her father, at least. She had been ready to rebel against anything to choose her own way.

"Is it too much to ask," he began, "to ask if you'd come say goodbye to me at the station in a few nights? I'm leaving for Jersey City. I don't have a friend to drive me, and my mother has a lecture at the arts center." He tucked his hands in his pockets. "I never like waiting for trains alone, since my job has me doing it all the time now. It's always nice to have a *friend* there." He stressed the word "friend" ever so slightly.

"Nobody likes waiting alone at a station," said Ama. "I'd like to be there. If you'll text me when to be there, I'll meet you outside." She smiled back and waved. "Goodnight, Tamir."

"Goodnight, Ama."

Chapter Thirty-One

"So, which one do you prefer? The cold cuts platter or the chicken strip one?" Natalie asked Brayden.

"I think maybe both," he said. "Or just the chicken? It's what my mom wants that matters—she's the one who's driving this thing, even though I told her it was too much fuss. I just volunteered to pick up stuff so she wouldn't wear herself out running around the city." He checked the list in his hand. "I can't read her handwriting, so I may have to call her."

"We could do a tray of salami, Parma ham, and pepperoni with Italian cheeses," suggested Natalie's cousin Val. "That way you get the best of both worlds. Chicken and cold cuts."

"I think that sounds good," said Natalie, helpfully. "Throw in some of Uncle Guido's sandwich rolls?"

"At family price? How about a dozen, then you buy a couple of sliced loaves at regular price?" her cousin countered.

"Done." Natalie stepped back from the deli case of cured ham, spicy turkey breast, and rich salami as Brayden paid for the platters and filled out the order slip. It wouldn't surprise Natalie if he was covering it out of his own pocket, even though his mom was insisting on paying for everything herself.

That was Brayden all over again. She shouldn't even be here, since he could score every one of these bargains on his own as an unofficial member of the Grenaldi clan, but he had probably been afraid that ignoring her message would be rude. He probably still figured she wouldn't show at the last minute, spending the evening watching Chad sort his climbing gear or something.

"I guess maybe I should get some chips, too," said Brayden, re-pocketing his list. "But I figure I should get the bulky stuff first, like the paper plates and cups."

"Where to next?" Natalie asked him, signaling her willingness to be helpful beyond negotiating for cured meats.

"The corner mart, maybe? They sell that kind of stuff."

"I've got someplace better," said Natalie.

The retailer of Natalie's choosing, close to the indoor shopping center known as the Belleview Plaza, had worked with the Wedding Belles for many a casual wedding reception. They had reasonable prices and Natalie had enough goodwill between them and herself to get Brayden a modest discount on bulk supplies, the extras of which his mother would probably never use. A box of plates, some plastic utensils, some cups, and an army supply of napkins, all of which Brayden insisted on carrying himself in a big cardboard box.

He bought Natalie a lemon slushy at the beverage stand outside the Plaza's main entrance, despite her protests. "My way of saying thanks for your help," he said.

"You don't have to thank me," she said. "You didn't need me along today. I think Val would've given you a break without me standing by."

"Yeah, but she would've felt guilty if it hadn't really been family asking for it, maybe," he said. He sat down at the little iron patio table, beneath its striped picnic umbrella.

Natalie laughed. "You *are* family, Brayden," she said. "How else could I have treated you so horribly all these years and you still speak to me?" This, with a little twinge of guilt. She was thinking of Brayden's hopeful expression when he'd asked her to the prom. Okay, not a family move on his part, exactly, but her answer had been as cutting as any refusal she'd given to one of her brother's requests.

Brayden shrugged. "I just wanted to say thanks anyway," he answered, sidestepping the issue of past incidents. Maybe he didn't think about them that much these days, his head full of the cute blonde co-worker, Natalie reflected. Still, the fact he'd accepted her help made her think the crush was still alive a little, and required careful handling. Just in case.

"Maybe you're just too nice to say no to someone even when you want to," said Natalie. She leaned back against her chair's intricate wrought-iron back.

"Maybe we're just being friends, the way we used to be," said Brayden.

"You have a very different memory of our friendship than me."

"Really?" he said. "Sure, we didn't always get along, but we used to hang out, you, me, and Rob. Not just with the tent in the backyard. Remember movies on Saturday nights, pizza pockets from the freezer? You'd sneak downstairs and steal our snacks if you didn't have any girls to hang out with on those nights. Stay for the whole movie." He grinned. "Even though you claimed you hated the Teenage Mutant Ninja Turtles."

"Those were fun times," said Natalie. "But you have to admit, they were pretty few and far between. Usually when we were little, Rob would try to make me cry and go home. And when we were older…" She trailed off, dancing too close to the issue of Brayden's crush again, something that neither of them wanted to talk about. Not now that Brayden was moving on and accepting the fact that Natalie was meant to be with somebody else.

"That was all my fault, so you can't blame Rob for that," said Brayden, softly. "It was me who made you not like the idea of being friends with me when we were growing up. That crush of mine tended to throttle down the chances of us being good friends, pretty much every time."

"Why not blame me?" Natalie asked. "I was the brutal one."

He shook his head.

Natalie rolled her eyes. "Never blame the lady in the situation, huh? You are such an old-fashioned gentleman," said Natalie. His new girlfriend would love that about him. Brayden was the ultimate peacemaker in any situation, and would probably be a human shield against any blow that deserved to fall on his romantic partner. It was one of the many things Natalie knew about him by instinct, having seen his personality in all stages of its development.

Not many people could say that about their friends. Or anybody in their life, for that matter. The fact that she knew Brayden better than anybody in her life who *wasn't* family—didn't that make it all the more ironic that he had been one of the people she had claimed to like the least? Even though the good qualities outweighed the defects, too.

She sipped her lemonade. "You said the other day on the phone that you'd been trying other new things in life," she said.

"That." Brayden looked sheepish. "It's nothing much. Mostly little things. Like joining the softball team. Oh, and I took some college courses for a while."

"College courses?"

"Yeah. It was just some stuff in case I wanted to try for a B.A. I took a couple of math classes, a class in advanced engine repair, and a refresher science class. And a poetry one for English."

"You took poetry class?" Natalie was amazed.

Brayden blushed. "Mine were pretty bad," he said. "There were a couple of students who wrote stuff that sounded like Tennyson or something. But it was kind of interesting, and it was something new. It got me out of my box, I guess you'd say."

"What kind of degree were you thinking about getting?" Natalie traced a design on her cup in the moisture from her slushy's frosty exterior.

"Maybe something in engineering. I don't know. I always liked working with motors back in shop class. I thought about studying then trying for a mechanic's job when I first started as a driver, but I didn't have the skills. But then I started thinking about learning how to design motors and mechanical stuff, and began liking the idea, so I signed up for a basic class at the college, then for a few others. Maybe I'll take some more after I'm settled at the new job, and see if it turns into a lifelong passion."

She remembered the hot rod his friend was fixing up. No wonder he had asked for Brayden's help.

"I don't know what to say," said Natalie. "I didn't know that. Rob never mentioned you were studying anything." It was probably at a different college than hers, otherwise Brayden would have made strides to "bump into her" in the past, whenever their class schedule coincided. Unless, of course, he had been getting over her the whole time he was making these other changes in his life.

"You knew I was good at math and motor repairs and stuff," he said. "You're probably not really surprised to know that's what I'd pick if I took classes."

"I'm not surprised that you're smart at it or interested in it," said Natalie, quickly. "Just that you did it. I mean—I just never pictured you taking classes again after high school."

Brayden following a passion: that's what she had never pictured. Real friends could picture each other chasing a dream or exploring a new path, but their one-sided friendship meant she'd never given Brayden's interests a second thought, beyond simply remembering they existed.

"Rob never thinks to tell anybody anything," said Brayden. "There wasn't much to talk about, they were just basic classes. Everybody talks about family when they're together anyway, right?"

"Right." Natalie smiled again. A long silence fell between them—was that because they were practically family, or because she had no reply for her evident ignorance when it came to Brayden's life? She wished she could find the words to tell him exactly what she thought, how impressed she was that he had taken a leap like that after so much time had passed.

She cleared her throat. "From now on, maybe you can drop me a line or two to tell me when you're doing something new or interesting," she said. "That way I'm not waiting for Ma to say something, or Rob. They barely tell me the news about family anymore."

"You're pretty busy," said Brayden. "I don't expect you to keep up with everybody you know. You probably don't even talk to all your cousins for months at a time."

She laughed. "No, I don't, but they call me and make sure that I know everything that happens to them, which in a big Italian family probably means a wedding or a baby."

"Is that gonna be you pretty soon?" Brayden asked. "Rob says you're pretty serious with that Chad guy." He didn't look at her but at some flowers blooming in a pot by their table.

Suddenly, Natalie's lemonade tasted sour. "Rob's exaggerating things, as usual," she said. "Most casual romantic relationships take things slow. They don't put a ring on somebody's finger in a few months."

"Your mom had a picture of you wearing a ring," said Brayden. "I saw it on her phone."

By accident, Natalie was willing to bet—Maria would never have willingly shown that picture to Brayden. "A joke," she said. "Just a silly joke. Plastic ring from a Cracker Jack box, that's all."

It would make more sense to let Brayden think it was serious—it would go a long ways to putting his crush to bed permanently. Why was she trying to make him think that Chad was just one more dating experience?

Brayden's body language was awkward, though he was trying to hide it—more so than usual, which was saying a lot. For some reason, Natalie's heart skipped a beat, as if she was expecting something important to happen in this moment. What and why, however, eluded her completely as she sat waiting for the moment, the beat in her chest pounding rapidly with anticipation of whatever he was holding back.

He opened his mouth, pausing before he spoke. "It's not my place to say it," he said. "It's none of my business, I know…"

"Why not?" Natalie asked. What on *earth* was she saying right now? "Maybe it is. Tell me."

"I guess… when I first met Chad, I just didn't think he was right for you. And I'm still not sure what I think of him. Rob tells me stories, things you shared about him, and… I don't know…" He trailed off then took a deep breath. "But if he makes you happy, then I'm happy for you. If you think he's a good guy, then that's enough for me."

She didn't know what to say. Her heart was beating normally again, but not with the relief she expected for hearing this statement from Brayden, which was mature and free of all the usual disappointment with which he often mentioned her latest crush.

"Thanks," she said. "I figured he wasn't the kind of guy you would approve of. So that's nice of you to say." Guys like Brayden had limited respect for the romantic practices of a guy like Chad, who considered each other's family gatherings optional after the introductory period, and thought commitment was a vague, faraway future event. It probably took effort for Brayden to accept that this was what she might want.

"And... Chad is a good guy," she said. For the hundredth time since they'd begun dating. "He doesn't move fast or need a connection—" she almost said "that's deep" but changed it to, "—that's traditional, necessarily. I'm okay with that."

Brayden nodded, a serious expression on his face. "If that's what makes you happy," he repeated, softly. "I'm glad that it's working out."

Something about his tone made Natalie soften toward him as she only had a handful of times in their past. This was the real Brayden, beneath the humble and sometimes fumbling exterior: The man who could lose gracefully, and not just because he had a lot of practice doing it. The man who was humble when he did win, to the point that almost nobody ever knew when Brayden actually achieved a goal or milestone of real significance.

He looked so mature, so serious and understanding, that it was almost like a different person was sitting across from her. She had never let Brayden grow up in her opinion of him, or her mental picture of him, all these years after their childhood friendship grew distant. She was seeing the real him now, and it both humbled and amazed her. *How did I miss it before?* she thought. *I only ever saw the crush, and the way he never liked to hurt anyone. He was always good at masking the pain of rejection, and never showed off the best of himself to anybody. I never looked closely enough to know about any of it.*

"You don't have to say that," she said. "Just to be polite for Chad's sake, I mean."

She was too afraid to look at his face, just in case a little of his old crush appeared because of her words—she didn't quite know what she was going to do or say if that was the case, but she suddenly didn't want to find out.

"I'm just saying it as your friend," he said. "It doesn't have anything to do with him."

The simple gravity of those words actually made Natalie shiver a little, for the second time. Brayden's courteous side tended to mask any confident, masculine statements in thorough politeness, but what was bleeding through now had a tiny bit of steel in it from his hidden side. She didn't know what to think. She made a pretense of checking the time instead.

"I guess maybe we should be going, if we're going to pick up the beverages on your mom's list," she said. Her voice was slightly husky. She tried to hide this fact.

"Guess so," said Brayden, who stood up and hoisted the box of party supplies. "Gotta get you back to your studio before the day's over, too. Dresses don't sew themselves." He held out his hand. Natalie accepted it, though she usually didn't. That polite grip of his was only friendly, not pressing her to return it.

"No, they don't." She felt relieved to be back at a normal level of politeness. Feeling new things about—and for—Brayden affected her strangely, and that made her uncomfortable, like taking a wrong turn and finding the street around you unfamiliar, the buildings and signs all foreign.

But Brayden's words stuck with her, even after they had dropped off the supplies at his mom's house—receiving profuse thanks and cookies from his eager mom—and Brayden had brought her back to Wedding Belles' headquarters.

If he makes you happy. That was the second time someone close to her had made that remark, in addition to her mom, who implied it in dozens of ways, possibly out of desperation for grandchildren.

The list of things about Chad that satisfied her was long enough to surpass her worries about their relationship, surely. Since Chad was the sum of those things, it meant he was making her happy as a romantic partner. Maybe not enough to marry him on the spot, but enough so that they might still be dating by Thanksgiving.

She called Chad's number to see if he was coming by for dinner, but he didn't answer. He was probably practicing climbing at the gym's rock wall, and he never answered his phone when he was in the zone. Instead of leaving a message, she hung up.

Chapter Thirty-Two

The bouquets for the wedding would be delivered the day after an elaborate family dinner party, to be thrown by the Winships at the island just before the weekend of the wedding. The glass dining hall would be rearranged on Friday, the morning after the dinner, as would the ballroom for the reception's entertainment. The chairs for the ceremony would be in place by early Saturday, each one with a special garland of bud roses, pygmy orchids, and tropical leaves draped across its back. Petals from these were to be tossed onto the bride and groom as they walked the aisle hand in hand after the ceremony.

It was all very elegant, all very breathtaking. As Tessa stood on the ferry heading toward the private island, she studied the photographs of the dining room's silk-draped chairs and the gleaming crystal.

She drew a long breath. The breeze fanned her hair and rippled the sea below as the elegant resort came into view. She almost envied Harper for the good fortune of getting to have this wedding site, though part of her still didn't particularly envy her client's relationship. Tessa was still enough of a romantic to sense that the balance in Harper and Brett's relationship was off somehow, despite Harper's glowing description of their connection. She would prefer her partner to be represented by his physical self more often than his signature on a check's bottom line.

Hypothetically preferred, that is. She hadn't had a relationship in years. Things with Blake had brought her too close to those ideas again. But could they open the door to a true relationship? If just this once the stars would align?

A fantasy, maybe. But would it become real, with just three little words spoken aloud?

Tessa disembarked on the island's shore and climbed into one of the golf carts, and the driver motored along the paved path to the resort's main drive. In the distance, the blooms in the garden scene of Harper's upcoming nuptials gleamed like jewels beneath the afternoon sun.

Weekends and random weekdays of short flights had been taking their toll on Tessa's physical and emotional energy and Brett's pocketbook—not that the latter source was complaining. But the beauty of the island's lush, summer self, weeping willows swaying carelessly in the breeze, lifted those feelings away from her like clouds dispersed in the blue. She crossed the walkway to the front entrance and let herself into the hotel's cool, quiet lobby.

"So, we're really down to the final steps," said Tessa, perching on the edge of a chair in Harper's suite. "I know you have a lunch date with the family and a meeting with the minister, and I have an appointment with the chef, so we'll keep this short. Mostly, I need your approval of the candles decorating the tropical garden after sunset, and the bridal party gifts you asked me to find."

The latter was a simple silver compact engraved with each bridesmaid's initial: Tessa had selected them from a mid-price online retailer, since Harper wanted to purchase them with her own money and not from Brett's account. They looked nice enough, though Tessa's brief acquaintance with those women—and the remarks of Mrs. Winship on various occasions—led her to suspect that none of the recipients would ever use any gift Harper chose.

"I like them," said Harper, studying one that Tessa removed from its box to show her. "That's way fancier than the one I carry. Mine has a busted lid, and the only initials on it are for some cosmetic line that they don't even make anymore." She tucked it in the box. "It's plain, too. I think Mrs. W—Myra—would say that's more elegant. Some of these girls are a little picky about that kind of thing. Brett kind of warned me about it beforehand."

Tessa placed the box in her purse again. The papers surrounding Harper on the bed were travel brochures, she realized—for the honeymoon destination, undoubtedly, as a travel site was open to a page on the Venice Simplon-Orient-Express's route.

"How's the planning going?" she asked.

Harper smiled and spread her hands. "Nothing for me to do," she answered. "Brett took care of every bit of it. Ashleigh just sent me the itinerary. I guess the travel agency he used finished all the little details the other day. Lots of walking tours, wine tastings, that kind of thing."

"No random exploring?" said Tessa. "Nothing left to chance or spontaneity?"

Harper shook her head. "Brett's not really a spontaneous type," she answered. "He likes everything planned real well. Probably why he didn't ask me to help—I always leave just a little room open. You know, in case the client wants to try something they didn't think of when they were sitting in my office. People I talk to who travel a lot always tell me it's different when you're there than when you're looking at the books and the brochures at home. Real makes the world something you don't quite get until then."

A rap on the door. Myra entered. "Harper, dear," she said. "Would you mind if lunch is quick today? Terrence reserved the tennis court at the other end of the island for one o'clock, not two."

Harper's face fell slightly. "Okay," she said. "Sure."

"I know you'll be terribly bored on the court," said Myra. "I could arrange some lessons for you, if you'd like. I'm sure the resort employs an instructor of some sort."

"Thanks, but I don't have any sports clothes," said Harper. "I left them at home. I didn't realize that it was going to be such a big part of today. The whole tennis thing."

"My things might be a bit small for you, but I do have spare tennis whites," said Myra. "I'll see you in the dining room shortly." She offered Tessa a polite smile of greeting then disappeared on the other side of the door again, closing it between them.

Harper scowled. "I wish now I'd sprung the cash to buy some of those little sweaters and skirts," she said. "I never played tennis in my life, and all those clothes cost a fortune. But Brett probably wants me to partner with him."

Marsha was probably an avid tennis player, Tessa thought. She probably packed a tiny white skirt and sweater everywhere she went, and awaited an opportunity to relive her and Brett's days of playing doubles as a couple.

"There's still time to change," coaxed Tessa. "You could buy a white skirt from the pro shop, and I'm sure you can borrow one of Myra's sweaters. They can't be that small." While the groom's mother was more trim than the bride-to-be in the waist, she hardly wore skintight garments.

"Maybe so," sighed Harper. "Or I guess I can finish reading this travel plan. I'll have to pack my stuff according to how we're spending our time." She lifted a brochure on a boat tour of Venice.

"I'll catch up with you later, after the chef and I talk," said Tessa, deciding to give the bride some privacy, and time to sulk. Poor Harper would probably be stuck in this room alone for hours with nobody who really mattered here to share her excitement over the upcoming honeymoon destinations.

Chapter Thirty-Three

"I tried something new with the rice tonight," said Chad. "I wanted to try this recipe for a new sauce, but I didn't have all the ingredients." He stirred the pot.

"Smells good," said Natalie, who actually thought it smelled like boiling gym socks. Some of Chad's choices in spices were not her jam. She placed two brown plates on the grass-woven place mats that decorated Chad's table.

"Listen, I forgot to mention it yesterday, but I'll be taking off in a couple of weeks to help Trey prepare for his rafting trip. He's doing an extreme outdoors challenge with some friends. I'm going to help him port his stuff to the river, then follow along the first few days until he's sure he can handle it." Chad tapped the spoon against the lip of the pan.

"I thought you wanted me to come with you to your mom's birthday party?" said Natalie.

He glanced over his shoulder. "I already told my mom I won't be there," he said. "She understands. But if you wanted to go for some reason, I'm sure she'd be glad to see you."

"You're missing your mom's birthday for a friend's river challenge?" said Natalie. She stopped setting the table, sitting down as she watched Chad season his rice. He had been planning to go only last weekend, and had asked Natalie if she would pick out a present his mother might like.

"Yeah. She doesn't mind." He glanced back at her again. "What? What's that expression for?"

Natalie shrugged. "I'm just thinking of what my mom would say if I missed her birthday after saying I'd come. She'd be crushed."

"That's different. Besides, your mom would probably understand if you had something better to do."

Natalie was quiet. "But your mom would like me to come anyway?" She glanced at the birthday card for Chad's mom, pinned to the fridge beneath two new takeout menus and a client's business card.

"Sure. She likes you." Chad sounded as if he was surprised she would ask. "She'd probably invite you even if we weren't a couple. She's like that."

"And if we weren't a couple, what would you feel?" The question left Natalie's mouth before she could resist it.

He shrugged. "Maybe feel a little disappointed. Our connection is a good one. I think we're pretty compatible, and we've never had a major fight. I like an even emotional keel in a relationship." He smiled a little. "My last girlfriend was on a psychological roller coaster a lot of the time. Changing jobs, signing up for night classes. She didn't handle stress well, so there was constant friction in her life."

"Disappointment, huh?" said Natalie. "That's what you'd feel the most."

"It wouldn't break my heart yet, since we've only known each other—what—five or six months?" Chad laughed. "We're testing the waters. We're not even talking about the serious relationship subjects yet." Suddenly, however, he grew sober, an inquisitive look on his face. "Why are you asking what I'd feel?"

"Because I don't think this is working," said Natalie.

Chad stopped stirring his rice for a second. "What's not working?" he asked.

"We're not working. There's something missing, Chad. The chemistry is there, all the right boxes are getting checked… but love isn't just about being a perfect match when it comes to personal tastes, is it?"

"It is to me," he said, frowning. "Not love, but dating, which is what comes first for me."

Not love, but dating. That summarized it perfectly. They were a couple, but not a romantic couple. There were no feelings involved, not even complicated ones. Chad had put his finger on the one thing Natalie had never been able to define, the thing which was wrong with their relationship. Dating wasn't enough anymore.

She waited until he poured his rice into a clay Ecuadorian dish before she spoke again.

"Look, Chad," she said, softly. "I think we should talk."

"Talk about what?" He sat down, placing the rice and chicken dish between them. "Are you serious about this? Because it sounds like you're breaking up with me." He sounded uncertain about this.

"If I was," she said, "what would you say?"

Suddenly, it seemed important to know, to finish this conversation all the way. She wasn't going to Chad's mom's birthday as a casual friend, and she knew he didn't care. Deep down, she knew he didn't care about her enough that losing their relationship would sting for more than a couple of weeks.

"I'd say I'm surprised." Chad sounded floored by this conversation, unhappiness creeping into his voice. "I thought we were doing all the right things. You said you were like me, that you liked things to stay open in a relationship."

"I thought that's what I liked," said Natalie. "I guess I realized that things have changed. This feels too distant to me. I don't see a future for us, Chad. Do you? Would you have still wanted to keep going after our July deadline, or would you feel ready to move on?"

"Maybe. I don't know. That's the future, and I'd have to be there to know the answer." He shrugged. "I just know that I like you, and I like what we have." He raked back his floppy hair with one hand. "Is that what this is about? Whether I would make a grand gesture or sacrifice? If you want me to say that I'd go on my knees, or crawl after you… I'm not that kind of guy, Natalie. I thought you knew that." A tremor entered his steady tone; she wasn't sure if it was one of anger, or frustration.

"I do know it. I'm not asking for that." She shook her head. "I'm saying that I'm not the casual girl I thought I was. I guess… I finally grew up all the way, and this isn't going to work between us."

Chad sighed. "So, this is it?" He sounded annoyed, but Natalie suspected it was the hurt of surprise rejection that was in his voice. After six months, she thought she knew him well enough to be sure.

She stood up. Leaning over, she kissed Chad on his cheek. "I'm sorry," she said. "I think it's time for both of us to move on. Maybe we should've kept to our first agreement."

"You could stay for dinner." He didn't sound like that's what he wanted. His tone wasn't inviting her to stay, at any rate. "You don't have to leave hungry just because you don't want to date me anymore."

"That wouldn't be fair," she said. "I think you deserve your space." A final recipe from Chad's cookbook was not what she needed to make this revelation go down any easier, even if they both knew it was coming.

"All things end, right?" Chad didn't return her kiss before she drew back from him. "Take care of yourself, Natalie." He avoided her eyes. "Maybe we'll see each other around sometime."

"Maybe so." She lifted her bag from the sofa. She glanced back as she opened the door and saw Chad was staring out the window. He let out another deep sigh.

Natalie closed the door behind her.

Chapter Thirty-Four

Tessa turned another corner on the garden's winding path and found one of the hotel's alcoves lined with palm trees. A man and woman were standing beneath the shade of the trees, engaged in conversation. To her surprise, it was Brett and Ashleigh.

Deep in discussion, they hadn't noticed her approach. Tessa started to move closer then came to a halt as part of their conversation reached her ears.

"I ordered the earrings you wanted," Ashleigh was saying to him, "but I thought you should know that Marsha already has a pair just like that, so she'll probably exchange them."

Brett scowled. "I had no idea," he said. "I can't keep up with her jewelry anymore now that we're not…" he stopped himself, switching to, "… since I don't notice what she's wearing at our lunch dates, I mean."

"Maybe you should get her something less expensive for her birthday," said Ashleigh. "Don't you think Harper will be suspicious? I mean, given how much time you still spend with your ex already—"

"But I want Marsha to like the gift, and that's why it has to be jewelry," said Brett, firmly. "Look, I really don't want to discuss my feelings, all right? I just want you to order a gift for Marsha and have it sent to her apartment. If the earrings aren't good, pick a diamond bracelet instead."

Tessa's feet were frozen to the stone pathway as she listened. She had never heard this much drive in Brett's voice, except when he was talking about business.

"I know it isn't any of my business, Brett, but you know I'm right," said Ashleigh. "Maybe you should tell Harper the truth."

"I can't tell her. It's too complicated. She wouldn't understand. Besides, nothing is happening between me and Marsha. It's been made clear to me that I should move on with my life, and that's what I'm doing. It just takes time."

"And what are the earrings supposed to say about moving on?" Ashleigh lifted one eyebrow with a very unprofessional look for her boss.

"They say that I care for her, which is true," said Brett. "Even if our connection has to change. Let's leave it at that, shall we?" A tighter version of his smile put Ashleigh in her place—the assistant resumed a professional version of herself.

"Of course. I'll order the bracelet, then."

Brett's cell phone rang and he answered it; to Tessa's surprise, he actually made the business contact on the other end hold by putting his hand over the receiver. "Oh, and make lunch reservations at her favorite restaurant. I take her there every year," he said to Ashleigh. "No sense in breaking tradition this year."

Blood thundered in Tessa's head, in every vein of her body. She felt disappointment and despair as the negative theories in her head became reality. Poor, poor Harper, being a rebound choice by a man who was still in love with his ex. Finishing second in Brett's feelings to a harpy like Marsha, who was spoiled and simply waiting for Brett to apologize to *her* for insisting that he wanted to marry her someday.

It was disgusting. But what could she do about it? Nothing at all, because it wasn't her life or her choice, or any of her business. If

Ashleigh was right at all, then Harper already had an inkling that Brett was still very close to his ex. Maybe she thought she could simply win over his last doubts, since he cared about her. Maybe he didn't love her deeply, but he did care about her: that much Tessa was certain about.

Harper couldn't know everything, however, otherwise she never would have agreed to let Brett's two-faced ex be her maid of honor. Tessa *knew* her instincts were right from day one on that girl.

Harper was downstairs at the desk chatting with the concierge when Tessa walked into the lobby of the resort. "Hey," she said, smiling at Tessa. "Brett called and said he's almost ready to go over the details for the ceremony. He wants us to move our little meeting to the terrace and order some drinks."

"Great," said Tessa, a little too brightly, unsure how to handle what she'd just overheard in her walk through the grounds.

"He just has to give one of his colleagues a call to check on something first," Harper continued, shouldering her purse. "It'll take a few minutes, probably. You know what he's like when he's talking business."

"All passion," said Tessa, almost sounding bitter. She hesitated. "Harper, it's not any of my business… but do you know that Brett and Marsha were… well, more than friends?"

Harper nodded. "I do," she said. "Brett told me they had a past. But they were friends before they were together, and he said they wanted to try to stay friends afterward. She's almost like family to him, he's known her so long. Plus, his family loves her."

That was the death blow to any chance they would ever love Harper, Tessa felt with certainty. "So long as you're fine with it, it's great," she said. "I guess I was getting the impression it was still a little serious."

Harper shrugged. "Maybe it is," she said. "You've met her. She's nice, but she's pretty persistent. I'm not blind: I can tell she has feelings for him, even though she's helping me out. Brett's trying to be nice, I think, and let her down without shutting her out of his life. It's just one of those things."

This was extremely perceptive. Tessa was impressed, since she had only picked up on half of this from the beginning, and that was with the aid of a few accidental eavesdropping moments. "I didn't mean to pry," she said. "You don't have to tell me anything about it, really. It's professional caution that made me ask in the first place. I never like to think I've picked up on something that could create difficulty for a client."

"I guess we all have complicated relationships in our pasts, don't we?" said Harper. "Look at me and my ex," she said, avoiding saying his name again, as if it might invite trouble. "If people didn't know better, they'd say we still have a thing, though I've been telling him to get lost since he came back into my life."

"That's true," said Tessa. "We can't judge by appearances, can we?"

"I just think everybody's looking for a second chance," said Harper. "Brett and I are each other's second chances. We're starting over in life romantically, building something new together."

Danny had used his chances up, apparently. Tessa felt sorry for him again for a brief moment, thinking of the look in his eyes whenever he spoke Harper's name. If he'd tried a little harder to show her he was serious instead of welding sculptures in old warehouses, maybe she would have given him one more chance.

Toughen up, Tessa, she thought. At least Brett had partly confessed his lingering fondness for his ex. If she wasn't mistaken, somewhere between the lines Harper had uttered was the knowledge that Brett wasn't completely past those old feelings. She had chosen to overlook these things, the way she had Danny's flaws for years. For a woman ruled by passions, Harper had a surprising level of tolerance too.

That, however, did not make Tessa like Marsha even one bit better. All it did was make her worry that maybe Harper was diving in over her head with this "I do," even though she truly cared about Brett.

Chapter Thirty-Five

Brayden's mother lived in a narrow two-story with a bad coat of brown paint peeling on its outside, and a cramped little front lawn of spring bulb flowers with spent blooms. Natalie had been here only a couple of times before to drop off leftover baked goods for *her* mother, and to have dinner a few times when her mother twisted her arm to accept the invitation.

Inside were Mrs. Carmichael's copious collection of ceramic figurines and a lot of guests for Brayden's goodbye party. They were crammed in the tiny living room, in the doorway to the galley kitchen, and in the little TV room, where Brayden's mom kept her houseplants for better sun. Someone had turned on a rock mix CD of hits from the past two decades, the sound of Good Charlotte and Matchbox 20 playing; someone else had accidentally elbowed over Mrs. Carmichael's peace lily on one of the tables.

No sign of Brayden in the crowd. "Hey, hey, if it isn't the elusive Natalie," she heard one of her cousins say. A hand on her arm, a kiss on her cheek from Chrissy. "I saw Rob twenty minutes ago—he didn't say you were coming."

"It's a surprise," said Natalie, whose dry tone failed to be funny. "This place is packed. Is the whole family here?"

"No, just me, Rob, your mom, and Louisa," answered Chrissy. "Most of these people are strangers to me. They must be your old high-school friends." She held a soft drink can above the head of a guest trying to squeeze between her and Natalie. "If you're looking for the gift pile, there's not an official one. But you can give it to Mrs. Carmichael if you want. I think she's in the big easy chair by the window.

There was a cluster of people gathered over there, and Natalie caught a glimpse of one of Brayden's mom's famous ugly sweaters—only worn as serious couture and not a seasonal joke at Christmas, like most people do. "I'll just leave this on the table in the hall," said Natalie.

"Sure. Oh, Nat—I heard about the fashion show. Sorry." Chrissy gave her a sympathetic smile.

"Thanks." Natalie had been wondering how many of her relatives might have seen the article in the fashion pages. She knew half her family watched Channel Six news, so if they missed it one place, they heard it in another.

It wasn't much, the gift in her package: a book on the history of Wrigley Field, because she knew Brayden loved the Cubs baseball team, unless something had changed drastically in that quarter too. She had noticed some other presents on the table by the stairs, including a bottle of Tuscan wine that could only be from one of her relatives. She placed the book in the pile. It was nicely wrapped, at least. She had bothered to tie a bow, unlike that person who added some decorative stickers to a brown paper bag and called it done. Most likely that was her brother's wrapping job.

Conversation drifted from various gatherings, a laugh or two mixed in. "… but I had the route next and got totally lucky because the sheep were gone by then, due to some city ordinance…"

"… you mean Mrs. Frobisher? Wasn't she the worst for history? I flunked her final exam senior year…"

"Natalie, dear, you came."

Natalie smiled as Brayden's mom came up to her.

"I'm so glad you could make it." She put her arms around Natalie in a light, paper-soft embrace as always.

"Hi, Mrs. Carmichael," said Natalie, hugging back with her usual fear that Brayden's mom was somewhat physically fragile. "I wouldn't miss it."

"Brayden will be so glad. He's here somewhere. It's a nice crowd, isn't it? All his friends from work and school… the teacher he liked so much from high school is here. I saw your mom just a moment ago—I think a lot of your family came. Did you see them?"

"I did," said Natalie. "I haven't seen Brayden, though." She had been looking for him, unconsciously maybe. Scanning the crowd for a glimpse of him even as she said hi to the other guests and members of her own family.

"I'm sure you'll see him here," said his mom. "Now, where did he go?" She glanced all around. "I know he's around… I'll go see if he's in the kitchen." She squeezed past a cluster of Brayden's co-workers and disappeared.

Natalie sighed. The hall mirror was an old one with a chip in the glass, but she could see that her face had a sleepless look that could be improved by cosmetic touch-ups, if she had some mascara and lip gloss in her bag.

Losing sleep over Chad? a little voice mocked. She knew that she wasn't. It was something else that kept her up at night sometimes. A dilemma she'd been fighting for longer than she realized and still hadn't fully surrendered to in its complexity. It was more than just guilt involved, she sensed. What was it, exactly?

There was a line for the downstairs bathroom, as Natalie expected. There was another bathroom upstairs, so she climbed the steps to the little hall above.

"Hey, Nat—saw your old boss on Channel Six news the other tonight." Leslie from high school was passing just below the banisters, a beverage in hand. "Is she suing you?"

"No, she's not," said Natalie, emphatically. Kandace better not even *think* of trying it, and not just because lawyers would cost a fortune for both of them. Not that she had any doubts that she could prove to the court that the sketches were her own—all she had to do was present the body of Kandace's work that her fingers had slaved and bled to produce all those years.

"Hey, I saw that in the papers," someone else was saying, from one of the nearby conversation circles. "Was that *you* in that weird chick's headlock, Natalie?"

Natalie had retreated to the upstairs hall now, which was darker and quieter than the rooms below. She bumped against a couple of framed photos from Brayden's school years and a big one of his graduation picture. The door to a dark bedroom ajar to the left, a closed door beside it. It wasn't the bathroom, however, but Brayden's old room, as Natalie discovered when she opened the door all the way to see by the sunset's light.

A twin bed under a plain coverlet, a line of sports figurines on the bedside table, old ball caps and sports posters hanging on the wall. An empty gumball machine on the window seat, and a series of framed pictures on top of the dresser. A definite shrine to Brayden's past, as his mother would probably keep it even when he packed up his grown-up things in his apartment and left town shortly.

"Not what you were picturing, is it?" Brayden's voice was behind her. With a start, Natalie turned around, now finding herself embarrassingly caught in the doorway of Brayden's room, with the friend himself in the hall behind her, holding a red plastic cup.

"What do you mean?" Natalie said. "I was just looking for the bathroom."

"I mean no creepy shrine to you," he said. "You probably figured I had a wall papered with your face by now."

A smile twitched Natalie's lips. "Okay… maybe I expected it a little," she said. "I knew you were taking my photo at parties all those years."

"Check the closet wall too, if you want to be sure," he said. He tucked the thumb of his free hand in the top of his jeans pocket. "But those photos on the dresser are the only ones. Most of the others are probably in some box by now."

She lifted one of the pictures. A photo from her thirteenth birthday party at the amusement park, her and a friend in a whirling teacup ride. She wasn't in any of the others: among them were Brayden and her brother at a baseball game, a photo of a stranger sitting on a hot rod car, and the view of a lake at sunset.

"Definitely not a creepy shrine," she said, putting the picture in its spot again. Brayden smiled. Lopsided and humble in style, but nice in the sense that his true nature was in it—you could trust someone with that smile not to be a jerk or a serial killer. That was one thing she had always liked about him.

When she set it down, the picture frame's back fell open, and out fell two more photos from that birthday party—both featuring Natalie prominently. Behind them, a couple of Natalie on prom night that she had never seen before, in the pink sequin dress she had sewn by hand for the occasion.

She held one up, Brayden's face blushing red momentarily.

"What can I say?" he said. "I was in love with you back then." He shrugged, his smile becoming sheepish now. "Guess I had a few tucked away I forgot about."

The use of "was" caught Natalie's ear, the past tense of it all. Maybe Brayden wasn't in love with her at all now. He had outgrown his childhood crush, just like this room and his job. He used to love this city, and his devotion to family and friends was always strong, but he was leaving it all behind for a new chapter. Why wouldn't he leave behind something as ridiculous as being in love with a girl who'd rejected him since the second grade?

"You should have burned this one," she said, holding up the second prom photo. "I did a hideous job on that dress's back seam, and you can see it here." A ghost of a smile on her lips as she gazed at her seventeen-year-old self, dancing with her date. "I can't believe you actually photographed me that evening after I said no to your invite."

Not just no, but emphatic no—and in front of most of the cafeteria's lunch crowd. Brayden had been begging her for weeks, knowing that nobody else had asked her yet. He had made elaborate plans involving a limousine rental and bought a huge corsage that matched her dress. Hanging on until the last minute, when semi-hunky Trevor Johnson from the track team had halfheartedly asked her out, and Natalie had leapt at the chance.

Suddenly, it seemed terrible. And Trevor hadn't been such a great catch after all, but had spent most of the evening with his buddies in the gym's locker room after dancing with her once or twice. It had been a lousy evening, one of the dullest of Natalie's life. She had gotten what she deserved for waiting for that jock to ask her out.

"I hope you got your money back from the limo deposit." Natalie laid the photos aside again. "I know the rest was a loss." The flowers, the rented tux had all been wasted.

"Nah. But it wasn't so expensive," said Brayden, as if he hadn't worked all Christmas break at the Burger Buddy Shack just to earn it. "You can have the photo if you want," he said. "Do whatever you want with it."

"You have copies?" Natalie meant this as a joke, but it came out badly.

"No. But it's a bad photo. The angle's all wrong—I never was good with a camera," said Brayden. "I wouldn't blame you if you tore it up. Girls don't like unflattering photos, as a general rule."

"I won't hold it against you that you took one," said Natalie. "Anyway—sorry I came in here. It was an accident. I didn't mean to invade your privacy. Or your mom's." Technically, this wasn't Brayden's room anymore, was it?

"That's okay," he said. "I always wanted to get you to hang out in my room. 'Course, it was a different room back then. But the idea's still the same." He grinned, and Natalie realized this was a joke—but not before she felt her eyes widen a little.

"Sorry if I embarrassed you," said Brayden, whose humor sobered a little. "I know you weren't exactly thrilled that I liked you. I didn't mean to mention it like that."

"Oh, well." Natalie shrugged her shoulders. "We were younger. And I was always a little too rude about it, probably. Definitely too rude," she amended. "I made you feel like dirt. Most of your life I made you feel that way, really." Not just for liking her. The worst side of Natalie had always emerged like a beast whenever Brayden was around. He had always seen the worst side of her.

Brayden's turn to shrug his shoulders. "Oh, well," he repeated. His grin reappeared just a little afterward—crooked, but kind. "Life's got regrets for everybody. Don't lose any sleep over it for my sake."

"Thanks." That was the closest she had come to a real apology, though it wasn't enough after all these years. "Am I crazy, or is that Bilbo in one of those pictures?" She glanced back toward the dresser.

Brayden laughed. "That's him," he said, nodding.

"He bit you on the arm."

"Yeah, I know. But I like dogs. I didn't hold it against him, either. He was just defending his yard—he didn't know that was your doll I was trying to steal back."

Laughing like old friends. That's what they were, Natalie realized, even if much of it had been complicated. Like it or not, Brayden was probably one of her oldest friends in the world by now. He had known her almost her whole life, and kept track of its details in a way that the people closest to her had failed to do. She was saying goodbye to a friend, not just her big brother's boyhood pal, or her hopeless admirer.

He cleared his throat. "I heard you and Chad aren't dating anymore," he said. "Rob told me."

"It's true." She glanced downwards, directing her eyes at the carpet. "Things didn't work out. I'm single Natalie again, back to my old freedom." The fact that it was a hollow shell of what it used to be couldn't be explained in this conversation, even if she told him what she'd been thinking about lately. About him… and whether there were things about him she had yet to notice, but should. Was it too late for everything? For a mended friendship… for something deeper, if such a crazy thing was possible?

She scraped up the nerve to meet his gaze now, as if hoping to see something in it—a glimmer of the old hopefulness, the old desire that had burned all through her years of rejecting him. But Brayden himself was studying the floor now as he digested this news.

"I'm sorry, Natalie," he said. "It must hurt. You were seeing him for a while."

"It's not that bad," she said. "We didn't have any really close ties, even after months of dating. It turns out we didn't have enough in common to make it work. I couldn't share his dream, and he wasn't picturing me in his future." She took a deep breath.

"Are you okay?" he asked, softly.

"I'm fine." She put on a smile—bright, artificial, and self-mocking. "You know me, right?" The hurt inside her right now wasn't for letting Chad go, but for whatever had killed Brayden's feelings for her If only something would kill the ones beginning to unfurl inside her, the tenderness that had blossomed in record time for Natalie.

"I do. You're not pretending, so I guess it was for the best." His hand, tucked in his pocket until now, reached out and touched her cheek, so softly and quickly that she almost missed it happening. "So long as you're okay, that's all that matters."

Natalie felt herself tremble. *Actually tremble.* For Brayden's touch, no less. It amazed her and embarrassed her all at once, now that she didn't know where things stood between them.

"Thanks," she managed at last. She was grateful, although the fact remained that she needed to work on feeling less about Brayden, not more. This was goodbye, at least as far as their friendship in the same city was concerned. After he was gone, they both knew that this renewed bond would start to unravel between them.

He shuffled his weight from one foot to the other, an awkward motion in this conversational pause between them. "The door you're looking for is the first one on the left," he said, gesturing down the hall.

"Thanks." Natalie had worn out that word with Brayden lately. But she meant it this time. She just didn't know if it mattered to him anymore, or if he was just being kind the way he always was. She ducked her head and started to slip past him.

"Hey, uh, I saw your boss on Channel Six the other night."

"Did you?" she said. Had everybody been watching Kandace's meltdown to the local press?

"What a nut," said Brayden, with a snort of derision. "Like anybody'd ever believe you stole from her."

"I know," said Natalie. "She's only saying it to soak up attention because she didn't launch a summer line this year. It's really kind of sad, actually. I could almost feel sorry for anyone who has to physically attack someone to feel better about themselves."

"She's not gonna cause you any trouble, is she?" A little of Brayden's old concern was back, familiar to Natalie's ears. Welcome, too, if just for this brief, last goodbye.

"Just steal my thunder is all," answered Natalie. "But thanks for asking." Thus far, nobody else had. It was nice to have someone actually express genuine concern for her career after the post-runway disaster that befell its moment in the sun.

He smiled. "Any time."

Natalie met his gaze, the frank and friendly one that seemed so steady and mature on the threshold of Brayden's third decade in life. Was he handsome to everyone? Maybe a bit these days, she had to admit… but unless that girl was in love with him, then she'd never know how beautiful he was, inside and out. And it wouldn't matter what the rest of the world saw, because she would want him exactly the way he was.

Natalie had never thought of him this way before, though it was true enough. As the subject of his crush, she had never taken the time to notice his best features versus his less flattering ones. But at the end of all those misunderstood feelings, she wasn't above paying him this compliment silently… though Brayden deserved to hear someone say it aloud about him, truly. Among other kind things he deserved to have someone say to him.

He stepped further back into his old bedroom, and Natalie continued to the next door on the left, snapping on the old-fashioned light above the vanity sink.

The bedroom door was closed again when she came out, no light under its door. Downstairs, Brayden had vanished again, and so had his mom. Natalie spotted her own mother near the living room doorway, with Natalie's aunt Louisa. They were both laughing and talking, and when Maria spotted Natalie, she waved to her.

It was a beckoning wave to have her join them, but Natalie's wave was one of goodbye. She descended the rest of the stairs and opened the front door, stepping outside without saying farewell to anybody else.

Chapter Thirty-Six

The chef had sent them away with a complimentary box of the opening course's special hollow radish and mango chutney appetizers. Tessa tucked it in her bag, wondering if Blake was a fan of mangoes, since he liked the resort's food so much.

As she boarded the ferry, someone disembarking brushed past her. Tessa caught a familiar whiff of a cologne resembling fire and metal, then realized it wasn't a cologne. She seized the man's sleeve before he stepped ashore.

"What are you doing here?" she demanded.

Danny met her eye with a guilty grin. "Trying the famous shrimp salad?" he suggested.

"Nice try." Tessa pulled him toward the ferry's deck as Danny braced himself for resistance.

"Listen," he said. "I have to talk to her. I know you don't understand—"

"I understand that the men in Harper's life are *extremely* exasperating people to know," snapped Tessa. "However, it's my job to respect her choices and her relationships, and the one she's chosen for you is that of a stranger, so don't even think of going ashore."

He sighed. "You don't get it. I can't help it. I have to fight for her. Until she says 'I do,' there's still a chance that I can change her mind."

He pulled against Tessa's grip. "She's got to see how wrong this guy is for her—"

"He's making her happier than you are right now," said Tessa. "Do you not care what Harper wants? She told you to leave, she gave back your present. That's the end."

"The day she marries him, I'll know she means it," he said. "But until she does it, I will never believe that she loves him more than me. She may hide it, she may fight it, but we are meant to be."

The ferry's warning signal sounded. Before Danny could go ashore, Tessa gave his sleeve a tremendous yank, causing him to stumble onto the deck. The warning lights flashed as the ramp began to lift, trapping him aboard.

"Look what you did!" He spread his hands in exasperation. He tried to make a run for the lifting ramp, but one of the employees posted nearby pulled him back on board. He gazed toward the shore as the ferry pulled away, a look of disappointment etched deeply in his face.

"Unless you're swimming, you're not joining Harper today," said Tessa. "I suggest you take the sculpture aimed for your head as a testament of her current feelings toward you."

He looked at her. "You really think this is best for her?" he asked. "Her marrying that guy? Cuddling up with his bank account at night instead of a real human being? You and I know that's her fate the moment she's married. He'll never spend enough time with her. He'll never love her enough to make up for it."

Tessa was taken aback by the forcefulness—and perceptiveness—of Danny's words. "It's not my business to decide that," she answered, with less steel in her own voice than before. "It's my job to do what my client wants. What she wants is to marry Brett in a matter of days.

It won't be perfect, but nothing in life is. And he cares about her, and wants to take care of her. That makes her happy."

Danny looked hurt by this. "So you believe everything she told you, too," he answered. "Just my luck that everybody thinks I'd let her get eaten by life's pool of sharks before I lifted a finger to help her with her problems. Must be the starving-artist label, am I right?" A scowl crossed his face. He brushed past Tessa and crossed the deck, disappearing into the ferry's crowds, past the cars parked in the middle.

Tessa chewed her lower lip, watching him leave. She felt that she had wounded him, and she hadn't meant to. Danny wasn't a bad guy. He just wasn't what Harper wanted.

She turned away and gazed at the island slipping away, and the water growing darker as the sun dipped lower. As soon as Harper said her vows, maybe Danny would be willing to move on with his life. Moving on before the chance is gone is always the hardest part. That's why she was so desperate to say the right words to Blake while he was still single; the *what if* made taking a chance on her feelings so tempting it couldn't be denied, even for the fear of being rejected one more time.

Chapter Thirty-Seven

"I'm leaving early tonight, Mama." Ama hung her apron on its kitchen hook, having cleaned the dessert station thoroughly after a night of serving *halwa* topped with candied ginger to the dining room's customers.

"Why?" asked her mother, who was pouring the last of that day's masala into a large food container.

"Luke came back early and they have a hot date," said Jaidev, as he scraped the blackened vegetable debris from one of their skillets. Deena gave him a warning smack on the arm.

"It's nothing like that," answered Ama, cagily. Lately, mention of Luke had drawn mostly silence from her, and she was dreading that someone from her family would notice and ask if something was wrong—and that might bring her dangerously close to the truth. "I just want the evening off."

"Are you going to see that new romcom?" asked Deena. "Don't, Ama. Wait for me." She covered the container of leftover rice with a laundered cotton cloth, in preparation for Rasha taking it home to feed to Sanjay. "I thought we could see it together next week, and maybe try that new Vietnamese place near the mall."

"I thought I would go for a walk," said Ama. "I need some time by myself," she added in case Deena volunteered to come with her.

Her sister-in-law loved an excuse to avoid loading the restaurant's dishwasher or scrubbing its stockpots.

She could feel her family exchanging subtle glances as she left the kitchen, as if her shoulder blades possessed special senses for Bhagut family communications. They could think she was behaving weird if they wanted to. One way or another, they were bound to find out about the indecision that had been plaguing her mind these past few weeks.

Tamir was waiting outside the station, his suitcase beside him. He smiled when he saw her approaching, and waved his hand. "I don't think we have time for a cup of coffee," he said. "Rain check for next time, okay?"

"That's fine," said Ama. She knew her clothes probably smelled of garlic and onion, with a hint of sugar from the sticky dessert syrup. "We'll just talk on the platform until the train arrives."

A crowd disembarked from the train arriving from the east end of town. Ten minutes until the one that travelled to the airport's nearest light rail stop. Tamir sucked in his breath and tucked his hands in his jacket pockets. Ama watched a stray piece of paper dance its way across the platform's floor.

"I had fun the other night," said Tamir. "Thanks for coming with me. And for understanding."

"You too," said Ama. "I hadn't been able to talk to anybody that seriously about me and Luke yet. Everybody told me what I should do… just not why. I guess they didn't think it needed to make sense to me."

"That's because it takes a sensible person like me to try to explain the science of *amore*," said Tamir, but with the hint of a smile. "Your friends and family know you're a girl who tends to take things on faith."

"I haven't told my family," said Ama. "I told my friends by accident. Except for you."

"Wow. You let me in on a secret," he said. "I'm flattered. In return… the thing about me and the girl in Jersey is a secret, too, by the way. My parents have no clue that I'm interested in anyone. I'm afraid they'll push me to pick another match. I'm not ready for that."

"Do you think you'll ask her out this time?" Ama asked.

He smiled. "Who knows?" he said. "Maybe. I think the contacts helped. I feel like a new person."

Ama hid the smile twitching at her lips. "She might like you in your old glasses," she suggested.

"Did you?" he asked. "Or did you think I looked like a tech nerd?" He lifted one eyebrow as Ama's blush appeared. "Thanks. That was the answer I needed."

"Will your parents approve of her?" Ama asked. "More than me?"

"She's Indian—Kannadigas," he said.

"A Bangalorian tech?" said Ama, lifting one eyebrow herself now. "Isn't that pretty on the nose, culturally?" Her auntie always spoke of Bangalore as a modern IT hub—prime real estate for producing a potential successful husband.

He blushed. "Her grandparents were from Bangalore, her parents are from Connecticut," he said. "She likes snowboarding and Mexican food, and joined Oprah's Book Club last month. That's as far as we've gotten in our conversations."

"Tell her you like art," said Ama. "That always impresses women. Tell her about the motorbike in Mumbai, too." The girl would then picture Tamir on one, hair ruffled by the breeze as he rode through the busy city streets, the way Ama pictured Luke sometimes. It definitely wouldn't hurt his image.

"I'll do that," he said. "Thanks again, Ama." Tamir paused then leaned forward and kissed her lips, quickly. A friendly one, this time, and not a real one like the one a few nights ago.

With a rolling noise like thunder, the next train entered the station. A *whoosh* as its hydraulic doors opened, letting out the tide of passengers. Ama and Tamir exchanged glances. He reached down and lifted the handle of his rolling suitcase.

"See you around, Ama," Tamir said. "Good luck with Luke." He walked toward the waiting train compartment. "Tell him I say hello."

"I will," said Ama. "Say hi to the girl in Jersey for me."

"Arika," he said. "I'll tell her." He smiled and waved goodbye one last time before the doors closed. Ama waved goodbye again as the train roared back out of the station.

She sat down on one of the benches. She reached to fiddle with the ribbon around her neck, panicked briefly at its absence, then remembered that she'd left the ring lying on her bureau earlier when she'd changed clothes. She hoped she'd remembered to cover it with something before she'd hurried downstairs to work.

Her hands slid into her pockets. She felt a packet of tissues, a couple of peach pits, a gum wrapper, and a packet of something else, soft with hard corners. The packet of Luke's love letters, she discovered, as she drew it out.

In this time of spotty mobile signals and missed calls, the only words she had about his feelings were these. She had read them dozens of times... nevertheless, her fingers untied the ribbon and lifted the top one, unfolding it. The first letter from Luke, the first love letter ever in Ama's life.

It was as if she knew its words by heart. Luke, who claimed to never be good with words when he wanted to be, had said it all in those frank lines. They were beautiful to Ama, and in this moment, she didn't believe anybody could write ones that would replace them.

Would he write from Portugal? If she was there, he wouldn't have to… but if she wasn't, and she and Luke were still she and Luke…

That's what she wanted, really. It boiled down to the essential fact that she wanted him and needed him. Tamir really was right; the other night had opened her eyes to that fact. Even a kiss under the stars with a handsome suitor—a knight who had given her his jacket against the cool breeze—hadn't erased the essential power of Luke's first kiss, on a random street corner by the market, with a chilly wind that had made Ama cry.

Carefully, she folded the letter again, slowly turning the rest between her fingers. Someday, when these envelopes were yellow and faded, she would still read them with love.

Ribbon tied around them, she tucked them in her pocket again. A crowd of teenagers giggled as they entered the station, and an elderly woman stopped to gaze at a poster for platform safety. Ama slid off the bench as she rose and began walking toward the exit.

She took the long way around, passing beneath neon lights in the neighborhood known for its Hispanic flair, and through a sleepy district with a bakery where Luke liked to buy cinnamon rolls whenever he didn't have any of her pastries handy.

The Chinese restaurant at the far end of her block was closed for the night, although its neon dragon continued to appear and disappear in timed flashes. Outside the apartment building in the middle of the block, a window box of herbs smelled of pungent cilantro and ginger from where fresh roots had been dug. Ahead, she could see the lights from the Tandoori Tiger still ablaze. And… her family in the foyer?

Something had happened, something bad. An accident, a health crisis, a sudden death—that was the only thing that would put lights ablaze in this place at an hour when her father was usually checking his inventory logs and her mother watched sitcom reruns while mending aprons. Rasha should be home with Sanjay, and Jaidev almost never showed up after hours unless it was for a family dinner—or an emergency.

Heart pounding, Ama crossed the street, hurrying though every step felt slow, and the pavement beneath her feet felt nonexistent. She hopped up on the sidewalk, not bothering to look for her keys but pushing against the door, which was unlocked despite the late hour.

Bendi was halfway up the private stairs, having a fierce argument in broken Punjabi with both Pashma and Ranjit, who were standing below with faces white with tension. Rasha was there, sans work apron, and so were Jaidev and Deena, and her brother-in-law Sanjay, who was sitting on a chair by the restaurant's entrance. All of them stopped talking the moment she entered.

"What's going on?" she asked, breathlessly. "What happened? Is someone hurt?" She glanced at all their faces in rapid turn, mentally calculating who wasn't here. Nikhil in a car accident? Nalia's family in trouble?

"Where have you been?" Jaidev demanded, the first to speak. "We've been worried sick—"

"Do not do it," Ranjit said, his hand on her arm, pleadingly. "Don't go, Ama. Stay. Stay and marry him. He is a nice boy, I want you to marry him—"

"How can you even *think* of running away?" said Rasha. "You love him, Ama. You would be crazy to walk away from a chance like this—"

"Listen to your father," said Pashma, who laid her hand on both Ama's arms, as if to hold her attention in this chaos of voices. "To leave is a mistake, Ama."

"How can you be afraid to marry him?" Ranjit sounded bewildered. "First you don't like the nice boy with the good job, then you pick the motorcycle boy, now you are going to lose him, too? We didn't try to drive him away. I will give him my blessing, if you will only stay—"

"Hold it!" Ama held up both of her hands. "What is everybody talking about?" She felt bewildered. "Who is running away? What are you all doing here yelling at me? And where did you get the idea that Luke…" Here, her voice died because she saw her ring dangling from its ribbon, in Rasha's hand.

"I found it on your bureau," said Rasha, slightly meeker than when accusing Ama of running away.

"You went through my stuff?" Ama didn't know what else to say at this moment.

"We were looking for a note. Ama, please—we were worried, seriously worried. The way you've been acting lately, the way you just took off after the dinner shift—"

"Are you planning to tell him you're leaving?" Jaidev demanded. "Ama—cold feet? Seriously?"

"Hold it," she repeated, but this time more quietly and, strangely enough, with the attention of her family in return. "I didn't tell Luke anything because I wasn't running away. I didn't go to hitch a train and leave town, I just went for a walk, like I said. And… yes… that ring is from Luke." She ended it there, drawing a deep breath afterward rather than saying exactly what had happened with him after he popped the question.

Silence from her family. "You're getting married?" Rasha's voice was cautious.

"This is awesome, Ama!" said Jaidev.

"Oh my gosh—there's so much to do! Wedding sari, wedding jewelry—I saw *the* most perfect site for hair jewels yesterday. I have to find it," said Rasha, now frantically swiping through apps on her phone. "My sister is getting married! I can't believe it!" With a squeal, she abandoned her search and threw her arms around Ama instead.

From panic to elation in two seconds. Ama's head was still reeling. She was aware of a smirk on her aunt's face and a remark about her "having sense at last" on the subject of marriage. This for a proposal from *Luke*?

"You must always tell us things, Ama." She felt her mother's embrace with these words, the scent of turmeric and extra-garlicky masala clinging to the folds of her cotton sari. "Never make us worry about you like this."

"I wasn't running away, I promise," she said over Pashma's shoulder, as if her family still wasn't believing her. The only one listening to her was her brother-in-law Sanjay, who waved to her from his seat, a weary smile of indulgence on his face for their family's dramatic antics. Ama gave him a sympathetic smile and wave.

"I didn't think you liked Luke, so I didn't tell you…" began Ama again to her mother.

"He is *so* amazing, Ama," said Deena, who looked thrilled.

"Of course he's great. He's marrying my sister," said Jaidev. "That proves he has good taste and good judgment."

"Where are you two getting married? Are you doing the whole wedding chapel thing? Or are you going to ride off into the sunset on his motorcycle?"

"She is not getting married on a motorcycle," barked Ranjit. "She is going to get married the right way." He spoke begrudgingly, but the look in his eyes proved he hadn't quite recovered from tonight's developments.

Released by Pashma, Ama moved closer to him, seeing the confusion and conflict in her father's eyes. "Do I still have your blessing?" Ama asked him, quietly. "If you don't want to do it, I understand. I don't want you to pretend, because I didn't want to pretend, just for you to be nice to him once in a while."

He couldn't truly like Luke; she knew to her father that her would-be fiancé would always be a wild boy with a motorcycle and a tattoo. The fact that he would agree, even to stop her from running away from a difficult choice, amazed her more than a little.

Ranjit shuffled his feet. "You like this boy," he said. "Enough to marry him?" He looked at her.

She nodded. She hadn't told Luke that in words, but it was true even without them. After tonight, she was more sure of it than ever before, as if those doubts had melted away with Tamir's words on love and choosing it.

Her father sighed. "I know," he said. "I know that he is not a bad boy. Not what I want for you, truly… but I do not get to decide, as you remind me constantly. It would be nice if he would ask your family about it first, but they do not do things the right way here, so I suppose he doesn't know the right thing to do. But… he has given you a promise. I will have to be satisfied with it." He sighed. "Maybe he could at least come and pretend to ask me for my approval?" he suggested, hopefully.

The ring was in Ama's hand. Rasha had given it back to her—Rasha, who was now squealing again, this time over a picture on her phone that she was showing to Pashma and Deena, no doubt from the jewelry site. Ama hadn't put the little diamond on her finger but was still holding it in her palm, as she had the first time Luke had given it to her.

No one asked her if she had said yes, for they all assumed it. How could a romantic like Ama, who loved Luke so deeply, have given him any other answer?

"He would be honored if I tell him that's a message from you." She put her arms around her father and kissed his cheek. "Thank you, Papa," she said. "That means a lot to me."

He shook his head. "Go," he said, waving her on dismissively. "Your mother and sister will plan your wedding without you unless you stop them." Ama smiled at him and stepped aside. Ranjit hadn't accepted it completely… but he wasn't going to hide in the kitchen, either, the way he would if the news was completely unacceptable to him. Maybe he had softened to Luke just a little over the past few months.

"At least you won't end up an old woman with no husband," said Bendi, with mild satisfaction. "Even a poor husband with no prospects is better than no husband at all."

Chapter Thirty-Eight

"Good news," said Natalie. "Cal called me and said that a local boutique wants a couple of evening gowns from our collection for their summer window display. Finally, I'm actually selling something I designed to a retailer! Me, Natalie, slave to Kandace's plastic couture, can now officially see her own designs on display for the general public."

"That's great," said Ama. "Which ones?"

"The white evening gown with the dogwood motif and the blue chiffon and white lace cocktail dress," said Natalie. "Plus, they want Nella's 'Marilyn Magnolia' design, so she's over the moon." She tucked her phone in her handbag. "I really needed this good news after everything that's happened. At least now I have some proof that our hard work wasn't in vain."

They were dressing for the dinner party at the island resort. Several of the Winship family friends had been invited to Palmetto Isle for the occasion, and so had members of the Lucas family, though Tessa knew better than to suppose they would arrive. Harper's mother was probably still lying in the shadows of her darkened room, while her father wrestled downstairs with his concept for a self-cleaning electric can opener.

The Wedding Belles were representing Harper's side of the affair, as well as one or two friends—*or possibly former customers*, Tessa thought—who might not arrive at all. Each time the hotel's private boat arrived at the pier, it brought ashore more members of the Winship social circle, who were greeted with polite enthusiasm at the hotel's dining room entrance by Terrence, Myra, Brett, and—with a smile of complete cluelessness for who these people were—Harper.

Sunset. The dinner hour was almost upon them. With a sigh, Tessa closed the drapes and checked her appearance in the suite's mirror. Her dress was a white silk cocktail one with handprinted hibiscus flowers on its fabric, one Natalie had sewn from her own fabric stash, an early design for the summer runway show. Ama's dress for tonight, a deep lavender chiffon trimmed with tiny silk flowers along its scoop neck and narrow shoulder sleeves, was also Natalie's work, as was the designer's own chocolate chiffon halter dress with a soft pink underskirt.

"Shall we go down, ladies?" Tessa snapped her handbag closed over her cell phone, emergency sewing kit, and stain remover stick: three things no planner should ever be without.

"I'll be down in a minute," said Ama. "I want to try Luke's number one more time. Reception is better in the evenings for him." She unclipped a glitzy Czech crystal earring as she lifted her phone from the bed.

"Then I guess it's just us," said Tessa to Natalie.

"Together again." Natalie held out her arm. "Need an escort?"

"Funny. Let's go."

Dinner was an elegant menu of roast duck in a caper and peppercorn sauce with roasted potato quarters and red peppers. Tessa was seated closer to the family than she anticipated, largely due to the absence of any Lucas family members, and because she was expected to explain wedding details to the family's closest friends. A few seats away, Harper fiddled with her red peppers, gazing distractedly in the direction of Brett, who was busy chatting with his best man, who Tessa was certain was some kind of stockbroker.

"Kill me." Natalie leaned closer to Tessa's ear to whisper this. "I've had more entertaining evenings scraping gum off my shoes after the movies."

"Shh," said Tessa. "Be nice. We're here to be supportive and to chat pleasantly about the wedding."

"Couldn't we do that by text?"

Tessa pretended not to hear this remark as she forked another potato chunk.

Upstairs, Ama listened to the choppy ring of Luke's cell phone before her call connected with a hiss of static. "Luke?" she said, eagerly. "Luke, it's me. Can you hear me?"

"A little. It's great... long time," he said, in the snippets of conversation that reached her end of the connection. "I've been so... the wedding is... you said in your message on Wednesday."

"I've definitely been busy lately," said Ama. "But there's so much I want to say to you. I want to talk to you, Luke. I don't know if the phone is the right place to do this, but..." She paused, her fingers turning over the little gold band and its stone as it lay in her palm again.

"I'll be... later tonight." Luke's voice swam through the static again. "I thought I would... before we do anything... maybe a flight on Monday."

"A flight?" Ama's heart skipped a beat. "Luke, are you leaving?" Her voice cracked slightly. He promised he wouldn't go yet—he promised. "You can't."

"I'll be... midnight," he said. "I don't want..." Here, Ama strained her ears, desperate to catch whatever was missing of this call. "... I want to see you so I can…" The line popped horribly, and Luke's voice disappeared again. "I know you said… I wanted to… but won't be home until then, at this rate. Maybe I could come to the restaurant… you might be home…"

Ama was trying to keep her calm. "Luke, I really need you to know—"

She stopped speaking, aware from the silence that the call had been dropped. Lifting the phone away from her ear only confirmed this fact. Luke was gone, along with whatever he had been trying to tell her. He was coming home, but for how long? And was he leaving because he assumed in all the silence and static between them that she didn't love him as deeply as he thought?

Oh, Luke. There's so much I have to say to you. Please, please don't go to the airport before you see me. Come to the restaurant—please tell me that's what you were trying to say before we got disconnected.

Downstairs, Tessa was circulating after dinner among various dull financial conversations and a few more interesting ones about the history of the resort. Harper and Brett posed for a mobile phone snap on the dining room's red velvet sofa, then for a second photo beside the gilt-lettered sign that would announce the glass dining hall's private reception for the Winship–Lucas wedding.

She sipped her glass of champagne. Where was Ama? Two guests at least had asked for details on the magnificent birds of paradise cake, and Tessa could only provide polite smiles and rough answers regarding its construction. She glanced around, seeing only Natalie chatting away with the dress designer Nola Gayne, who had been invited to this private dinner as a family friend.

Brett was now chatting with a circle of groomsmen, Tessa catching snatches of talk about stocks and bonds. Myra and Terrence were talking with their golfing buddies—and where was Harper now?

Tessa made her way to the other end of the restaurant dining room, not seeing the bride among any pocket of guests. *Maybe she stepped out for some air,* Tessa thought, pushing open the French doors leading to a small patio. Someone was standing there, leaning against its little decorative wall, but it wasn't Harper. It was her former boyfriend, who was wearing a somewhat outdated suit and holding a bouquet of flowers.

Tessa rolled her eyes. Quickly, she closed the door behind her. "What are you doing here?" she hissed. "This is a private party. They'll have security remove you, Danny."

"Very swanky, this party," he said. "I'll bet it cost a fortune. Of course, Harper looks bored out of her mind—gorgeous, but bored. Doesn't he even notice the way her eyes are glazing over?"

"That's none of your business," said Tessa. "Look, Danny. I understand that you care about her, but this is way beyond healthy."

"I told you, I was going to try again," said Danny. "You thought screwing up one little ferry trip would stop me?" he scoffed.

"I thought you would respect Harper enough to keep your distance," said Tessa.

"Would you keep your distance if someone you loved was trapped in a burning building?"

Tessa sighed. "You really are insane, aren't you?"

"He is." This voice was a bit more steely than hers and belonged to the bride herself, who was standing in the doorway to the patio. They both glanced at Harper. Her arms were crossed over her simple white linen cocktail dress, her red nails and lipstick the only color visible since she was pale with quiet fury.

"Harper." Danny's voice was softer now. "I thought I was going to have to come to you."

"Throwing pebbles at the window is childish," Harper informed him. "I could've had you dragged away from here, but I didn't. I thought I'd be nice, because… because I used to care about you," she added, after hesitating. "Maybe you'd like to return the favor and get lost for my sake?"

Tessa stepped aside as Harper took a step closer. She had kept distance between herself and Danny, but the artist covered the rest of the distance in two steps, dropping his flowers as his hands framed her shoulders. "Look at me, Harper," he said. "I'm standing here because I love you more than anybody else in the world, and it's killing me that you're planning to be with somebody else. I can't eat, I can't sleep. I think about you all the time."

She moved his hands aside. "I said it when you came back, I'll say it again. It's over. I wanted a different life, Danny. That's something you can't give me."

Tessa edged toward the door discreetly in an attempt to exit this scene, wishing that Danny would follow suit and exit the grounds before anyone spotted him. But the artist had wrapped his hands around Harper's shoulders again, holding onto her pleadingly.

"I would always look after you," he said. "I would always take care of you, provide for you. If there's anything you need, you can look to me. You know that. You just don't want to trust that I'll step up when you ask me."

"Exactly," she said, with a short laugh. "I don't have to trust Brett to help me with problems because I know he can handle them."

"Love is trust, Harper. You're marrying somebody you don't have to trust, who has so much money that he doesn't even care what it's spent on," said Danny. "You'll never have to ask him to sacrifice anything for you." His hands moved to cradle Harper's face. "Deep down, you know you can trust me. You can lean on me, 'cause I'll be there whenever you need it."

"Trust you? You would've come back from New Orleans if I called to tell you that Mom was sick, right? You would have worked day and night to help me keep Pa from losing his home, right?" said Harper.

"In a heartbeat," said Danny. "I'd do anything for you, Harper, even after you pushed me away and turned me down a dozen times before. I can't buy you an island or a big diamond ring, but everything I am, everything I have, will always be yours. All you had to do was ask."

"I wanted to believe that," she told him. "So many times I wanted to believe all your big promises. But promises only count if you make good on them, Danny. Without proof it's just words. And that's not enough anymore."

"You want proof?" said Danny. He sounded crushed. "You can't believe me without it?"

"What's to believe?" said Harper. "You've said it all before." She sounded tired. "Look, Danny, I don't want to do this anymore."

"I'll prove it to you," insisted Danny. "I will. If that's what you want, then I'll do it for you, Harper. Anything for you." He pulled a slip of paper from his pocket, one printed with some kind of bank number, and held it out to Harper, who didn't accept it. *Is he showing off his earnings from the sculpture?* thought Tessa. It wouldn't impress Harper to know he'd been paid for the opportunity that caused him to leave, if she had any guessing power.

"Will you stop trying to be dramatic?" said Harper, sounding exasperated. "Put away your stupid bank statement or whatever it is—I don't care how much you made in New Orleans."

"Then trust me when I tell you that everything I have is yours," said Danny, desperately. "I mean it. I want you to trust me again, Harper. Just look me in the eye and tell me you can do that, and it's enough for us to start over. If you believe me, then say those words, and read what's in my hand. I promise you, it will change everything between us both."

"Because you promise me you can stick it out?" said Harper, arching one eyebrow in skepticism.

"Because I'm promising you everything," said Danny. "You just have to believe me."

"Nothing," said Harper. "That's what you're offering me. Your potential, your promises—you want me to trust that you would sweep in at the last moment to save things." She shook her head. "I can't. Not when I have a promise from somebody else that gives me a guarantee. How do I know you won't walk away if some better offer comes along to sculpt old car parts in Paris or something?"

"Because you know me," he persisted. "You've always known me. This is Danny you're talking to, and the only thing in the world that remains constant for him is you. All you had to do was call me and I would've come back in a heartbeat, like I said before. We can always find answers together, Harper. You don't have to do this alone, and you don't need a partner who saves you just because it's no big deal or inconvenience to do it."

"I can't listen to this anymore. I made my choice." Harper pushed him away from her as he tried to draw closer. "I made my decision. I chose Brett, and I'm marrying him. If you ever ask me again to choose you, I swear, Danny…" She turned to go.

"Love is a leap of faith," said Danny. "Not a security bond or a trust fund. When are you going to wake up and remember that, Harper?"

"How do you know I don't have both?" Harper answered, facing him with this reply.

The firmness in her reply struck Danny like a blow to the face, checking his passion for a moment. It had never crossed his mind, Tessa realized, that Harper actually cared for Brett, who could probably pay to send Rose Lucas to a special depression therapy clinic in Switzerland as a Christmas present to Harper.

"Is everything okay?" The groom was right behind Tessa, stepping out through the open French door. "Harper, is something wrong?" he asked, with mild concern. He lifted one eyebrow as he glanced at Danny, who looked both guilty and stunned after Harper's last words.

She shook her head. "Nothing," she answered. "An old friend just stopped by to congratulate me. But he's leaving now." Her tone left no room for argument, should Danny want to attempt one.

She accepted Brett's arm as he held it out for her, leaning against him as they walked through the dining room's entrance again. Danny gazed after them with a look of disbelief and crushing disappointment.

"I'm sorry," said Tessa, quietly. There wasn't anything else to say to him. She turned back toward the patio, giving him some space. It was over at long last. Danny would have to take Harper's words to heart and go back to his warehouse studio. It was clear that Harper intended to choose Brett, no matter what feelings from the past might try to assert themselves over her.

She wished she could feel more satisfied about this outcome, but she couldn't. Then again, maybe she was just tired of fielding so many questions about bouquets and cake construction.

She noticed a slip of paper on the ground, and realized Danny must have dropped it earlier, when he had tried to tuck it in his pocket.

Tessa retrieved it, opening it up to see if it was only a receipt, and nothing he needed back.

It was a receipt, but not for any store. It was a bank receipt for a check, made out to Harper for five figures. It took Tessa's breath away for a moment; she hadn't written a check this big herself since the beginning of Wedding Belles. This was probably everything he had earned for the giant metal man he'd been welding for his customer.

Harper didn't have a clue how far Danny was willing to go for her, because she hadn't seen it. Danny had been telling the truth: while Brett could write a check from the excess funds in his account, Danny's had truly cost him everything. Even if Harper refused to take it, he had taken the risk and laid it on the table, knowing there might be no payoff short of relieving Harper's financial struggle.

Carefully, Tessa folded it and tucked it in her pocket. There was no sign of Danny when she glanced over the veranda's railing, in the direction of the garden lit by solar lamps, and the walk to the beach.

She went back inside and closed the door quietly. "Where is Ama?" she asked Natalie, who was sitting on the red velvet sofa, one shoe off, rubbing the heel of her foot.

"I have no idea," said Natalie. "She's not in the suite upstairs, I checked. I think she must've gone for a walk or something. She didn't answer her mobile phone."

"She must still be talking to Luke." Tessa wanted to bury her hands in her hair and vent a little of her deeper frustrations—or bury her face in the nearest pillow and let out a yell. "I really hope she comes back soon because everybody wants to know about the dessert buffet, and I can't remember the complete menu."

"Try her phone. She's bound to answer after Luke hangs up," said Natalie. "Is everything okay?" She scrutinized Tessa with a knowing gaze. "You look as if you've just finished watching *Dying Young* and managed to hold back the tears."

"Everything's fine. Just fine," answered Tessa.

Chapter Thirty-Nine

Natalie had enough of the party by nine and was beginning to think of the last-minute details she promised to wrap up on Tessa's behalf. Plus, the attention of one of the eager groomsmen convinced her that a little fresh air would be good, as well as cutting through to the staircase from the hotel's back patio entrance to circumvent anybody's notice.

She saw the person on the divan, a mere shape at first in the glow of one of the garden's solar lights. Harper was sitting in the semi-darkness, wearing the sensible dress that Natalie had pegged as high-end retail outside of their client's taste and budget the moment she'd laid eyes on it. She wasn't crying, and she looked calm.

"Mind if I sit?" Natalie pointed to the empty cushion on the divan.

"Sure," said Harper, not saying anything else.

"Where's Brett?" said Natalie. "I thought he wouldn't let you out of his sight tonight."

"He's talking with a business associate," said Harper. "I told him I wanted some air. All those numbers make me dizzy after a while."

"Numbers aren't my thing, either," said Natalie. "Unless they're the inches on a tape measure, anyway." She sensed that this wasn't about business deals, but about Harper wanting personal space. This was about the problem Tessa was dealing with.

"I'm sorry I'm not wearing your dress," said Harper. "I meant to tell you that earlier. It's just, I could tell that Myra and Marsha thought I should put on something a little more subdued. They didn't say it, but I didn't want to rock the boat just yet." She rested one hand on the divan's floral cushion. "I figured I'd ease them into my personality after the wedding, give them time to adjust to my more colorful side."

Natalie didn't reply to this, and Harper didn't say anything more. In the garden, a chorus of crickets was chirping while fireflies twinkled here and there among the dark shrubbery.

"Ever think you've made a mistake with your life?" Natalie asked. Harper's body stiffened slightly; Natalie could feel its movement travel through the divan's cushion. "I do," Natalie continued. "And I'm not talking about my job or something like that. It's more about my selfishness when it comes to getting my way in life. And ignoring my family on top of that... and about a dozen other things that keep me awake at night sometimes."

Things like the bakery maybe being sold, and about mistreating Brayden as a friend over the years. Brayden being at the top of the list more and more frequently these days. The memory of her small fingers crushing his flowers long ago actually hurt her now.

"Sometimes." Harper's voice was distant. "I do feel... lost... sometimes. Take this dress—"

"I will," said Natalie, kidding. "If only because it's gorgeous couture, if a little on the plain side."

"Sure. But Ashleigh picked it out, not me. She picks out stuff for me all the time, so I'm always fighting a little to keep myself from getting lost in all those suggestions about how to fit in. Between that, and Pa needing my paychecks to pay off that stupid investment... But we all feel that way, don't we? It's just a normal part of life."

"True," said Natalie. "But—" she hesitated "—lately I can't forget my mistakes. I keep thinking about whether I can still make the right choice, or if it's too late. If I closed all the doors behind me. Things happened that I can't control, even when I see how I screwed up, so it's almost like it doesn't matter that I know. But... it's the *what if* that sticks in your mind. That's what's so hard to get past."

"Pa used to say it's never too late," said Harper. "Of course, he's in debt to his eyeballs, and doesn't care that we can't afford next week's groceries." She rolled her eyes. "But the crazy thing is, I wish he was right. I wish it was never too late to fix anything that went wrong."

"He sounds like a wise man," said Natalie. "Just a little dense with numbers, maybe."

"Well, I've picked a guy who's much better at them," said Harper. "No more mistakes in that quarter anymore."

"You're marrying Mr. Perfect himself," said Natalie. "Everybody says it." How familiar that sounded at this moment.

"They're right," said Harper. "I'm a lucky girl, and I know it. I don't have to regret anything, because I made my choice, and it was the best one."

Her voice gave away that she was dangerously close to tears, though her face looked calm. Natalie felt the urge to lay her hand on Harper's, giving it a gentle squeeze of support.

"Perfection's overrated sometimes," said Natalie. "I've figured out that everybody's taste is different in that department. You have to be sure it's what you actually want. It's complicated."

She felt near to welling up with tears herself all of a sudden. She was thinking of the time she wasted with Chad, all the stupid, pointless relationships she had pursued in the past. None of them had thought about her ever again, and she thought of them with equal indifference. There were never any deep feelings or passion to look back on, like Harper had with Danny in the past. Harper just didn't realize how lucky she was on that score, having it once and having a chance to keep it if she wanted.

Not unless she was anything like Natalie herself when it came to epiphanies.

"What about grand gestures?" said Harper, softly. "Love songs, bouquets of flowers, all the usual dramatic overtures of love? What do you think they're supposed to mean?"

"Romantic passion," said Natalie. "In the movies, at least. Where it's fiction." What it was in real life—that was a kindhearted boy in an outdated suit, holding flowers and chocolate cake for a girl who was ninety-nine percent certain to close the door in his face.

"Pa always said I know my own mind," said Harper. "I don't change it easily when I make a decision. 'Cause if you stick with it, you followed through. Then if it turns out it's the right one, you don't have to look back with regret on it, at least. Right?"

"I suppose," said Natalie, thinking of Chad at this moment, and her breakup. No regrets there.

Harper nodded and sighed. "I should go back inside and find Brett," she said. "I don't want him to think I'm hiding from him, do I?"

A moment ago, Natalie thought she saw a tear on Harper's cheek, but it wasn't visible anymore. The bride smiled at her, tucking a cashmere scarf around her shoulders like a shawl. "Thanks for talking with me," said Harper. "I appreciated the company. It's nice to have someone listen to me for a change."

"Whenever you need it," said Natalie. "Just be happy with your life, Harper. Make sure it's really you standing at the altar."

It was a joke, but she meant it seriously too. Harper gave her a smile over her shoulder before she went back inside the hotel. The calm confidence had returned to the bride's face in the end, but Natalie thought maybe she was just a tiny bit sad. She wasn't completely finished yet with saying goodbye to Danny and facing the prospect of a future battling tan and off-white fabrics in favor of magenta.

Maybe it would take a little more than just some wedding bells for that to happen.

*

Natalie's cell phone rang as she unlocked the door to her apartment. The number on the screen was unfamiliar as she pressed the button to answer. "Hello?" she said.

"Hello. Natalie Grenaldi?"

"This is her." Natalie closed her apartment door behind her and kicked off her high heels.

"This is Nola Gayne. We met again at the party tonight? You gave me a card?"

"Nola. Of course." Natalie was frozen in shock momentarily. "Of course I know who you are."

"I know we've met several times recently, and we've only talked a little, but I've been meaning to tell you how impressed I was with your runway designs. I liked them. Simple but elegant, and the retro touches are very in right now. Have you had any interest in your work since the show?"

"A little." Natalie sat down on the arm of her sofa. "A local custom couture boutique or two would like to sell the evening gowns. But let's face it—my team and I were a tiny bit overshadowed by the post-show show."

"I know. But I think your work speaks for itself, regardless of that incident. Is there any chance you'd be available for a party next

Thursday? I'm giving it at my house for some of the designers stopping by after the big Summer of Love fashion show in Atlanta. I think they would love to meet the newest budding talent in the industry."

"Thank you." Natalie's breath had been sucked from her lungs. "I would love to come. What time?"

"Eight o'clock. I'll text you the details. George Sven is going to be there, and he tweeted something very complimentary about your pinstriped summer suit yesterday, so I think he may want to talk about the possibilities behind your retail launch."

George Sven? As in Sven's, the couture clothing retailer, with no two stores alike and only limited-run garments from independent designers; the "everyman's Vuitton," as the fashion columns dubbed him. Natalie had once spent a weekend in Charleston just to see one of his stores in person.

"I look forward to seeing you there," said Nola. "Have a nice evening, Natalie."

"You, too." Natalie let the phone drop to the carpet after this sign-off, then flopped backwards onto her sofa. *This must be what making the big-time feels like*, she thought. *Like your head is a balloon that floated away on a string, leaving the rest of you far below on earth.* Her tiny studio was on the verge of becoming an actual house of design, if things worked out in the coming months. She'd have to hire more seamstresses, purchase more fabric—she would definitely need more space.

Scrambling around on the floor with one hand, she found her phone to text her mother, knowing this was the night Maria and Louisa went to the movies together.

Ma, exciting news. Call me when you get this.

She pressed the contacts button to call Tessa and Ama, then remembered that Tessa was in bed early before the last-minute whirlwind of wedding prep, and Ama had called to say that she cut out from the dinner party early because of a personal emergency, one Natalie suspected was of the heart.

Too bad there was no one else she could call who would understand how monumental this was for her. None of her cousins would understand it the way they would, and certainly Rob wouldn't.

Brayden would.

The thought sent tingles trailing down her spine. Brayden knew how hard she had fought for this, all the time she'd sacrificed to Kandace's shop and the graduate classes in fashion design. He would truly get how exciting this was for her.

So why didn't she call him? One finger rested above the contact list in her phone, hesitating despite her previous thoughts. After all, he might be too busy to talk with her. He might even be with the girl he'd been dating, since this was his last week in town. She wouldn't appreciate Natalie interrupting their precious little remaining time before Brayden was off to his new adventure.

Natalie turned off the phone and tossed it onto a cushion. She sighed, propping her chin on her arms as she leaned over the back of the sofa, gazing toward the curtains drifting in the breeze. Watching them move, she tried to clear her mind and focus on all the questions weighing on her mind.

First was the Wedding Belles. She would always love designing dresses for their clients and working alongside Tessa and Ama. Maybe she had dropped the ball a few times this round, but that didn't mean she didn't love being part of that team. In the end, they always pulled together and made the most of their collective talents.

But Natalie's couture was her first passion, and she hoped that Tessa would understand if she didn't have as much time for worrying about candles or centerpieces or other more general tasks once her design career began to take off.

I need to be honest with Tessa about that, so she doesn't feel that I've put Wedding Belles on the back burner. If she knows where my heart is, we can work out what solution is best for both of us, and best for the partnership, right?

Her family and the bakery: they would always be a part of her life. The problem with Chad, the big one among many, was his inability to understand that some part of her would always be tied to those things, no matter where she was. Weekends baking bread or making cookies would coexist with fashion shows and model fittings. If she moved, her vacations and holidays would be spent catching up with the same people who challenged her as often as they supported her.

I don't care if I have to drag Rob there and make him work side by side with me to save it. But I don't think I'll have to. I think the rest of the Grenaldis are just like me. Once we close ranks around something we love, it has to happen.

There was no way they'd let a family business slip away, and there would always be a place for her among its staff. They would find a way together.

Those were all things she wanted. But that wasn't the problem weighing heaviest on her heart right now. That was the problem of her feelings for Brayden. It was crazy, her love life actually coming full circle to the boy she had rejected so many times in the past. Her heart was turning rapidly and longingly toward someone who had moved on, judging from his recent choices.

He didn't and she did. Wasn't that ironic? She'd broken his heart dozens of times, now he was getting to break hers. She was devastated to know that the romantic crush that had haunted her since childhood was finally dead. Brayden, the insufferable but faithful friend of the past, now felt like a good friend, an understanding one she would miss deeply. And once he was gone, everything would be different. As she said before, he would come back with new friends, a new life. A new girlfriend, probably.

Rob would laugh if he knew how miserable she was, and that she was kicking herself for all those years of scorn heaped on Brayden. But she deserved to feel it, after being so stupid.

There was only one solution to the pain, but she couldn't bring herself to endure that goodbye. It was the ultimate moment of honesty, one which might cause pain to even Brayden, though she would never intend it that way. If nothing else because it would let him know that she'd been punished for the past. But if there was a chance... just one tiny chance that something else would follow...

She turned her head, her gaze landing on the box her mother had left at her apartment the other day, one that Natalie had intended to shove in her closet as soon as she found the time. Lifting the lid off with the push of one finger, she sat up as it tumbled to the floor, spilling its contents.

Natalie smiled, remembering the pink fuzzy bunny card her grandmother gave her one birthday. That cheap charm bracelet was a souvenir from a trip to Texas with Uncle Guido and his wife for some sort of pasta convention when she was twelve. A photo of her and Rob the toddler in Halloween costumes, and a Valentine's card from Brayden in the seventh grade.

She moved it aside, discovering others below from their grade-school years. A stack of them—she hadn't realized she'd kept them instead of throwing them away years ago. Some had been purchased in what had surely been a tremendous waste of Brayden's meager childhood allowance, while others had been cut from construction paper and decorated with stickers and crayons. Imaginative, really. A stick girl in a badly drawn red princess gown. '*Natalie the princess grown up and wearing her homemade dress*' read the caption in wobbling red crayon letters above it.

A shriveled, papery object fell from inside one of the cards. Skeletal leaves of brown-green, a cluster of spikes the color of dried mustard at the top, turning to dust at the touch of her finger. At first it was unidentifiable until, in her head, the memory surfaced of a cluster of yellow lying on the swing seat, stems crushed by the grip of childish fingers, both hers and Brayden's. Her heart skipped a full beat, the sharp jolt bittersweet in the way only love could be.

Dandelions.

*

Ama had taken the nine o'clock ferry and a cab to the airport, where she changed her ticket to the only flight connecting with the nearest airport to Bellegrove, leaving at ten thirty. A half-hour by cab brought her to the light rail station between her home and Luke's, where the latest train from the airport's station was just arriving.

She pushed her way through the tide of passengers entering to catch the next train, and the ones exiting. She hadn't had time to change, only throwing on a light summer jacket over the lavender dress, and she stumbled occasionally over pavement pockmarks and steam grates in the fawn-colored high heels with ankle straps that Rasha insisted she borrow for tonight. She searched the faces of everyone disembarking, a sea of strangers flowing away from the platform.

Then she saw him. Luke, shouldering his heavy duffel bag, his leather jacket slung over one arm. Incredible, perfect Luke, with his tattoo and the need for a shave. He didn't see her as he walked away from the open train doors. Not until he paused to shift the weight against his shoulder, and noticed her standing there.

"Ama," he said, with surprise. "I didn't think you heard me. I thought you were working."

"I skipped out." She shrugged. "I had something more important than a client's dinner party." Here, without further ado, she threw her arms around Luke, holding him in a fierce bear hug. He stumbled backwards then dropped his bag and his jacket, wrapping his arms around her, too.

"I missed you." Her tone was fierce, her face buried against his shoulder.

"I missed you, too," he said. He drew back slightly, so they were face-to-face. "I couldn't wait to come back. Only I didn't know if I was coming back to anything. Except maybe goodbye." A little sadness entered his gaze as he met her eyes.

"Do you not want to marry me anymore?" she asked.

"Of course I do," he said, looking astonished that she would even think otherwise. "Do you think I'm crazy?"

She shook her head. Her left hand moved from around his neck to his shoulder. On her ring finger was the slender gold band with the tiny little stone on its end. She wiggled it slightly to get his attention and saw the expression on his face completely change in one second's time, from possible disappointment to sheer surprise and happiness.

"I want to marry you, too," she answered. "I don't want you to ever think otherwise. I realized that I'm the luckiest romantic in the world because I found exactly what I wanted in you. Most people don't believe they're going to find their fairy tale, but I know that I have. I won't ever forget it."

A jubilant yell came from Luke's lips, becoming laughter that was as much relief as it was joy. His embrace tightened around her, lifting her feet off the ground, ignoring the stares of other passengers gathering for the next train. "Ama," he said, in a single word that held everything.

She blinked back a sudden wave of tears. She touched his cheek, and his lips reached for hers, pressing against her mouth for a kiss in return.

They stayed like that for what felt like forever to Ama. No stars, no moon, no fairy-tale scene, only the view of a vandalized cosmetics ad and a surly-looking woman with multiple piercings who was adjusting the strap on a guitar case. Like always, however, it was just as it should be.

"Let's go see your family and tell them." Luke released her, gently, and lifted his luggage. "Would that be okay?"

He had no idea that they knew already. But there would be time to fill him in on that, and on Ranjit's begrudging blessing, before they reached her home. Even at midnight, there was bound to be a Bhagut or two up late with the inventory book or a last-minute recipe prep. And a word like "wedding" would bring missing family members out of the woodwork in ten minutes flat.

"That would be perfect," she answered. Her arms hugged him close, his free one around her shoulders as they walked out of the station together and into the summer night's breeze under stars of neon and the streetlamps' light.

*

Telling her mom the news about her big fashion career break wasn't as easy as Natalie envisioned. Mostly because their conversation ended up being about a very different kind of break—the one between her and Chad.

"I'll find someone else in time, Ma, trust me," said Natalie. "It may take me awhile, but eventually I'll be ready. If Brayden can do it, so can I."

"Brayden isn't dating anybody," said Maria.

"Sure he is. He just didn't tell you," said Natalie. "It's a girl from work."

"He went out with her, but he's not *dating* her," corrected Maria, with a scoff. "Brayden's a nice boy who wouldn't string a girl along. They had dinner a couple of times and that was it. Two people sharing dinner, not even holding hands, probably. I think he was trying to be casual in dating—much like somebody else we all know."

Brayden wasn't dating his co-worker anymore? Natalie was floored by this momentarily. "Let's not talk about my love life again," she said, although she was short of breath over this recent development. "I think we've beaten that subject to death."

"I didn't bring it up," said Maria, cagily. "But since you did, all I'm saying is that I wish you'd rethink a few of your choices."

"I know, Ma."

"I'm not saying I loved the idea of you and Chad together, but at least it meant you had someone in your life."

"The wrong someone," said Natalie.

Maria sighed. "Only you can know that, baby."

"That sounds like doubt for what I did." Natalie shifted the phone from one ear to the other as she reached for her measuring tape. "Ma, you keep doing this to me. First you want one thing, then another. You didn't like Chad, so I thought you'd be glad I saw the light."

"I am. But I hate to see you alone. You understand that. And I can't change it."

"So leave me the bakery in your will," said Natalie. "I'll have customers to keep me company. If you sell it, I'll die alone in an apartment full of cats, with only posters of my glory years to comfort me."

"I thought you'd want me to sell it," said Maria. "I didn't think you'd want to be burdened by a business that would keep you from moving on to New York or something."

"Burden me, Ma. If nothing else, Rob doesn't deserve to get off that easy. You know the fire department will dump him someday for trying to be a hero without his fireproof gear or something equally stupid."

"Be nicer to your brother."

"I don't have to," said Natalie. "He's not nice to me. The only person who ever was…" She stopped before she could refer to Brayden again. "Anyway, don't talk about selling the bakery yet. Please, Ma." She hesitated. "Grenaldis stick together. They don't let each other lose what's important, or let go of their passion."

A long silence, in which Natalie couldn't tell if Maria was possibly crying. "All right," said Maria, her voice struggling a little. "We'll talk about it. Maybe at the next brunch. Bring that casserole that was your grandmother's recipe, everyone likes that one. I'm having to bring the potato latkes because your uncle is behind on baking rolls." She sounded more like herself when talking about food once again.

"Okay." It occurred to Natalie how smoothly she'd just agreed to this, without argument. Everyone took it for granted that she would be there, for once. No danger she would cop out in the manner of Rob, hide and lick her wounds after she and Chad broke up. Or jet off to Paris with Nola Gayne to meet the crowd from Versace, either.

"Ma?" It was on the tip of her tongue to ask how Maria knew for certain that Brayden and his co-worker weren't romantically serious. Or seeing each other at all.

Laura Briggs

"What is it, baby?"

Natalie paused. "Nothing," she said. "Just wondered if I should bring the butter sauce for the casserole. That's all."

"Good thinking. It's too dry without it," said Maria. "See you Saturday."

"See you then, Ma."

Chapter Forty

Tessa's finger followed her to-do list for that morning as she shrugged on a cardigan sweater over her white blouse and blue slacks. The day before the wedding, the big day of preparation and fine details before the crunch leading to the ceremony itself, and Tessa had an hour before she finished her errands and caught her plane back to the coast.

She slipped her portfolio and notebook into her carryall bag, then heard her phone ringing inside it, muffled by the fabric. She pulled it out, seeing Natalie's name on the screen.

She answered it. "Hello?" she said.

"Tessa, it's me. I need to tell you something. Well, more like ask your permission for something."

"Okay," said Tessa, sensing this was something important. Downright urgent, judging from Natalie's rattled tone. Natalie was almost never rattled.

"I need you to let me miss this wedding. Just this one time, and I'll be forever grateful, I swear, Tessa. I can't explain it right now, just know that it's big, and I wouldn't bail on you otherwise and I'm sorry—"

"Nat, slow down. It's okay." Tessa paused then let out a sigh. "You've got my permission… but you didn't have to ask for it, technically. I mean, we're partners, right? Equal shares and all that."

"We are," Natalie agreed. "And that's why I feel so bad not being there today. I don't want you to feel I'm letting you down. I've worried about that lately."

"Because you need a little more space for your biggest dreams? Don't apologize for that, Nat." Tessa almost smiled, though Natalie couldn't see it. "And don't think you can't talk to me about this stuff. I know things have been crazy lately—for all of us. But we're going to sort stuff out when we're ready. You, me, Ama—we're a team, right?"

"I know," said Natalie. "And Tessa… thanks. For understanding."

"Go do your important thing," Tessa ordered. "Take care of yourself. And tell me what this was all about when I come home, okay?"

Tessa called Ama's number as soon as Natalie hung up. Straight to voicemail. Her other partner might be having an emergency too, based on her hurried departure from the island last night. Tessa slid the phone back into her pocket.

Lifting her bag, she stepped into the hall. From the next room, she heard the sound of a handsaw rasping through lumber. Hesitating, Tessa pushed open the door to the former bedroom undergoing renovation and found Blake at work on replacing its rotten floor trim.

"Hi," she said, as he looked up.

He pushed his safety glasses above his forehead. "I'm just hanging out," he said. "I had a free morning, so I thought I'd putter around here with some projects while I mull over future ones." He noticed her bag. "Is this the weekend of the wedding?" he said.

"Yup," answered Tessa. "Actually… if you're free…" She hesitated. "My partners are unavailable due to circumstances beyond their control," she said. "I can handle things. I know I can…" She paused.

"I know you can, too." Blake stretched his tape measure across the board and made a new mark with his pencil. "But that's not the point."

Tessa sighed. "I hate to ask," she said. "I don't even know if I'll need an extra pair of hands. But I don't want to take a chance on being shorthanded for a wedding like this one. If you're truly free, I would love for you to come. It would mean a lot to me to have somebody else there who has my back."

He finished making his pencil mark then tossed aside the tape measure. "All right," he said. He reached down and unfastened his carpenter's belt, draping it across the sawhorse's end.

"I don't have a suit on hand," said Tessa. "If you don't want to go home and pack, that's fine—you don't have to be at the wedding itself, or we can rent one using the expense account the client—"

"Ta da," he said, opening a nearby closet and gesturing toward a garment bag inside with a tuxedo label.

"You keep a suit on hand?" she asked.

"As many last-minute calls as I get to appear in one, I figured it made more sense to keep one around," he said. "Besides, my closet's too full at home anyway." He lifted it out. "I know I'm not one of the Wedding Belles, but I'll do my best impression," he said. "Without a dress, that is. Give me twenty minutes to put up the rest of my tools."

"Of course." Tessa's voice was soft, as was her smile as she stepped aside for him, meeting his eyes so briefly in passing—was it different from before? Blake's smile seemed different, too, but she thought she was probably imagining it, it had been so brief. The pressure mounting for this perfect wedding was getting in the way, but maybe it was real. Maybe if she told him the truth...

With this thought, she sucked in a deep breath then glanced behind her, watching Blake disappear downstairs, his tux's garment bag slung over one shoulder. Her heart skipped a beat just once for the fantasies that had never left her head, not from the first moment she'd laid eyes on him in Wedding Belles' hall.

I wish it had been different with him from the very beginning, and that I had never let those first chances slip away. I'm always going to wish that it was different. And if I don't tell him the truth soon, I'm going to burst... or die of crushing disappointment, knowing I missed my last chance when he finds someone else.

And if she told him and his feelings were not the same—well, it wouldn't be the first time it had happened to Tessa. But, somehow, a part of her believed it would be different this time. She wasn't imagining all the little signs between them, the little clues that maybe Blake was still attracted to her after all these months.

With a hopeful sigh, she closed the door to the unfinished room and texted Harper to change the name on the third plane ticket from Natalie Grenaldi to Blake Ellingham.

Chapter Forty-One

While Ama was making a mad dash to catch her flight after a late night with her family and Luke, and Tessa was catching a ride with Blake to the airport, Natalie had been trying desperately to reach Brayden for a real last farewell. The trouble was, nobody knew where he was. He had the day off from work, his mother wasn't answering the phone, and the only other person Natalie could think to call was Rob, who was perversely not answering his phone either.

At one o'clock, as she finished off a tub of cherry-chip ice cream and a sketch of a black-and-white business couture dress, her phone balanced on her knee with a number being autodialed by her every thirty minutes, she heard her brother's voice on the other end of the line. "What is the deal with calling me three times?" he said. "Is the house on fire? Did Ma pass out in the kitchen?"

"Nothing like that," said Natalie. "Why don't you ever answer your phone when I call you?"

"I'm busy, sis. Have pity on me. I'm changing jobs next month when the new station opens. I need a period of adjustment."

"Is that the sound of digital gunfire in the background?"

"And I need CGI violence to see me through it," he said. "I'm playing *Call of Duty*, okay? It's my time off, sis."

"Forget it. Do you know where Brayden is?" she asked. "I need to talk to him. His phone is turned off and his mom's not home, so I don't know how to reach him. I thought you might know where he is."

"Umm, let's see. He had some kind of seminar thing this week, with aptitude tests and stuff," said Rob. "He told me exactly what it's for, but I forgot. He'll be home tomorrow, though. He plays on the company's softball team and they have a game on Saturday morning."

"Thanks, Rob." She hung up.

She tried Brayden's number again around five, then at seven, then stopped with the realization of how ridiculously desperate this seemed. How would it look when Brayden noticed he had four missed calls from her number in one day?

She hid her phone under a pillow and watched a DVR marathon of *What Not to Wear* instead.

Saturday morning, Natalie rolled out of bed to an alarm far earlier than usual.

She pulled on a fitted silk blouse that flattered her curves, then made herself take it off in favor of a loose, casual cotton shirt, then changed it yet again for her best one.

Was she crazy to be doing this? She would have to explain to Tessa why she wouldn't be at work on their client's most important day...if she found the guts to go through with this, that is. Her hand shook slightly as she applied her makeup, her heart fluttering at the plans inside her. She shook her head, then reached for a pair of light-colored ankle boots.

Nice ones with spike heels. Too dressy, right? She reached for her sneakers, had them in hand, then put them back. She was reaching for them again as her door buzzer sounded. That was her cab.

Natalie reached for an old ball cap on a hook by her hall mirror, then withdrew her hand. She ran her fingers through her hair, smoothing it a little. A hint of mascara around her eyes—it could use a touch-up but she was in a hurry.

Natalie stepped outside her apartment, locking it behind her.

The shipping company was playing on one of the community sports fields just outside city limits, traveling northwards toward civilization. As the cab deposited Natalie in its parking lot, she discovered only a handful of cars remained, an empty field of green with baseball diamonds behind its chain-link fence.

Rob had texted her the wrong time. The game had ended already—practically nobody was here. Natalie walked swiftly in the direction of the gate on the opposite side of the field, a set of concrete steps leading down to the dugout. She passed a guy carrying a gear bag, who gave her a curt nod as he passed by. His baseball jersey had the logo for Brayden's employer on it, however, which meant some of the team was still here.

And there was Brayden himself, packing a couple of softballs and a mitt in a gear bag on one of the dugout's benches. He was wearing a pair of dusty jeans and a baseball jersey, and an old cap with the company logo pulled low on his brow, his overly long tawny hair sticking out from beneath its rim.

Natalie slid her hands in the pockets of her leather jacket—one which was too warm for today, even with a cool front moving in with some summer rain, but it flattered her figure and played nicely with her blouse's fabric. The heat must be why her palms were sweaty right now. "Hey," she said.

Brayden looked up. A look of perplexity appeared on his face. "Hey," he answered back.

"I came for the game, but it's over." She shrugged her shoulders. "Guess Rob gave me the wrong time."

"I didn't know you liked softball," he said, zipping closed his gear bag.

"I really might've come for another reason," she admitted, feeling her heart race as she considered all the implications of those words. Was Brayden considering them, too?

"I felt bad that we didn't really say goodbye the other night," she continued. "So I thought I should catch you one last time before you go. You know, to say a real goodbye." She managed to keep her voice controlled and steady at this point. Tell him the truth. That's all she had to do.

He hoisted his bag and stepped closer. "You didn't have to, Natalie," he said. "I knew you meant it the other night. You didn't have to say it, since I knew that's why you came in the first place."

"Yeah, well, that's why I came now, so deal with it," said Natalie. "I wanted to say... to say I was sorry for all those years. I wasn't a nice person. I've never been nice to you. And I don't know if what I really hated back then was you, or if it was myself. If I was really pushing *me* away, 'cause of all the Grenaldis, and all the food and the traditions, and the fact that nobody in my family knows what paper taffeta is—"

"It's that stiff shiny fabric," said Brayden. "It's got that kind of glow to it in the light."

"Yes, but that's not the point…" Here, Natalie stopped, aware that she had wandered off on a tangent that had nothing to do with anything. And Brayden knew what paper taffeta was? Really?

"The point is… I owe you one." Natalie sucked her breath in after this pause. "You were always loyal, and you stuck up for me when other people pushed me down. I never said thank you, but I should've, a long time ago." She swallowed hard. "So I want to say it before you leave town. Who knows. You may not come back."

"I'll come back," said Brayden, softly.

"Yeah, well, I might not see you then," she said. "I mean, I'll be at fashion shows, and busy working my tail off sewing dresses. And then there's all the family stuff. And you have your mom, and… and you'll have a new job, new friends. Probably a girlfriend." She didn't say she would have a boyfriend, since that wasn't as obvious as it would have been back when she was carefree in her dating life. "So it might not matter to you to see me anymore. I want to do it in case that's how it is in the future."

"I know," he said. "That's okay. You can say it now, then if we don't see each other again, it'll be all right." He put a hand on her shoulder. "I don't hate you, Natalie," he said, softly. "I know that you just wanted to get away from things. But I liked you, and I just wanted you to know that—I never expected that anything had to happen, so there's nothing to apologize for."

She was seeing that humble smile for the last time. Brayden's free hand was in his pocket, his eyes meeting hers now and then with a glance. A new confidence in them, a kind of acceptance and resignation. Brayden of old, always hopeful, always wishing… he had grown up at last and gone out into the world. And where was she now, the girl who had begrudgingly invited him to her parties, and put his Valentine's cards in a drawer?

Her eyes burned. "I couldn't like you then," she said. "I just couldn't. I don't know what it was."

"I was ugly," said Brayden, without mincing words. "You were beautiful. Everybody knew that. I ain't exactly a real charmer, am I? And... being honest... there's nothing that drives somebody away like clinging to them. I guess I always thought I'd take any part of you I could get, even if I had to crawl for it."

"Don't say that." Natalie blinked, fiercely. "You're not ugly. You're no Ryan Gosling, don't get me wrong, but you have your points. And you have the best heart of anybody I know. You care about everybody, and there isn't anything you wouldn't do to help someone if it's the right thing."

"That doesn't count for much anymore," said Brayden, softly, and with a rueful smile. He squeezed her shoulder—Natalie had forgotten all about Brayden's hand being on her person this whole time. "You take care, Natalie." He started to walk past her, Natalie turning around before he was even halfway to the steps.

"I didn't want to like you," she said. Her voice choked. "But I do. I do like you, Brayden. Really like you."

He had stopped. He turned around and was staring at her with a look of disbelief, as if Natalie had just announced that she was a secret government agent, or been nominated for an Oscar.

"I don't know what it is about me that I couldn't say it," she continued. "I don't want to date anybody else, not Chad, or anyone. I don't like anybody else that I meet or that I knew before... There is nobody who understands the real me, except for you. There is nobody who makes me feel like I matter as a person—except for you."

Brayden dropped his gear bag and walked a few steps closer to her, closing the gap between them. Natalie had begun to cry, the first few tears escaping her eyes. It made her angry, but there was nothing she could do to stop it from happening, just like she couldn't stop herself from shaking.

Crying always made her feel helpless—and Natalie was never helpless, not even when she was with her family, which should be the safest place in the world for her. But she was crying here and now, as Brayden lifted one hand and brushed away the tears flowing quickly down her cheeks.

"You have no idea how long I wished you'd cry over me, Natalie Grenaldi," he said.

A smile twitched Natalie's lips, faintly, despite her tears. "Pretty crazy, isn't it?" she said, although her voice betrayed how deeply she knew it was true.

A tender look entered Brayden's eyes, a spark of determination deep within it. His hands slid around her cheeks—the same ones she had slapped away at thirteen for trying to pick popcorn kernels from her hair—and he bent closer to brush against her lips with his. Then he kissed her, with a passion that surprised Natalie, as if all those years of being in love with her had comprised themselves in one kiss that he might never again experience.

She should push him away by instinct and run for the door now. But Natalie wrapped her hands around his wrists and kissed him back, more earnestly than she ever dreamed possible. The first droplets of rain began spattering the baseball field outside and through a leak in the dugout ceiling.

Brayden was a good kisser. A really good kisser. This fact alone kept her rooted right there, until all the insanity in her mind had begun to settle, and a new reality was born.

She leaned against him afterward, feeling his arms slide around her. "I feel crazy for doing this," she said, weakly. "You can't possibly believe

I mean it. I don't know if I'm losing my mind or if I was just blind all those years. You think I'm crazy, don't you?" Her arms slid around him now, finding that holding onto Brayden felt better than she would have imagined, had her mind not spent years avoiding that thought.

"It's okay," he answered, softly. "I don't mind a little craziness."

Natalie rested her head on his shoulder, swaying gently in his hold as the curtain of rain streamed past the dugout's view of the world. He felt strong and steady beneath that soft cotton jersey, his arms around her shoulders holding her without holding too tight or leaving her feeling unprotected.

Just right, actually.

Chapter Forty-Two

"Thanks," said Tessa, accepting the little bundle of lavender sprigs, a roll of cream-colored ribbon, and an emergency pack of sewing pins from the clerk at the local "everything" market and bistro on the mainland, not far from the ferry. Outside, the morning fog rolled over the water, disappearing as the sun rose.

She lifted her cup of coffee. Errands complete—time to go back to the resort, have a complimentary breakfast croissant, and head to the ceremony's site in the tropical garden to oversee the placement of guest seating. Only thirteen hours to go before Harper and Brett exchanged vows before a rosy sunset horizon, and Wedding Belles' official entry into society weddings pulled itself off to perfection.

The morning ferry had several cars on board for transport to the resort and surrounding islands—mostly vehicles belonging to people who worked on the surrounding islands, she imagined, at the bed-and-breakfasts, markets, and souvenir sites that tourists loved to visit.

The one that caught her eye, however, was an old van with rust spots, and an unusual, funky design of swirling wind curls and small flowers painted on one side. It looked as if it was crammed full of stuff—specifically, metal items like fenders and old radiators. More importantly, it looked familiar, as if she had seen it before.

Danny Reynolds drove one just like it, in fact.

He was leaning against the rails of the ferry side facing the resort's island, waiting expectantly for Tessa. There was a look of grim determination in his eyes. He wore the same suit from the other night, his face relatively clean-shaven, his appearance modified from the scruffier version of himself at the warehouse studio.

"I know what you did," Tessa said to him.

Danny glanced her way. He realized what she was talking about now. "You do," he said, in a reply that was more of a statement than a question. "I shouldn't be surprised, probably."

"You were telling Harper the truth," she said. It was your best chance, if there's any chance at all." She didn't want to say it would change Harper's mind after what happened the night of the dinner—most likely, it would just end with her tearing up the check, since Harper was determined to stand by her feelings for Brett.

He shook his head. "No," he said. "That wasn't the point of it."

"What was?"

"I wanted her to trust me first. That's all I wanted. To believe without seeing—then I'd show her the proof that I was everything she believed. I didn't want to buy her trust, I wanted to prove to her that it was still there, and that it was placed in the right person." He released a deep sigh after these words, as if accepting the fact that hope for this was dwindling.

Tessa gazed at the water. "Where did you leave the check?" she asked. "In Harper's room?"

"I mailed it to her," he said. "I want her to have it. I'll let it rot in the bank if she won't take it. Besides, I prefer being a starving artist. It makes the next job more challenging."

"Harper doesn't like to starve," Tessa reminded him, with a tiny smile.

"I know. For her, I'll weld industrial jobs until the cows come home if I have to," he said. "That's different. That's about giving her what she needs, while the art is about feeding my creativity. But none of it matters if Harper won't listen to me."

"You just don't know when to give up, do you?" she said.

"I told you before. Until Harper marries him, I'll keep trying," he said. He gazed at the island. "Looks like today is my last day."

"What will you do after that?"

"Go on with a broken heart." He shrugged. "Everything I own is in that van—I don't have to go home after today. I could hitch a ride, buy a plane ticket to anywhere with my last paycheck."

"What about your sculpture?" asked Tessa.

"It's done. It's on a freight truck to its buyer and I've already been paid," he said. "The warehouse was just a cheap worksite, but with Harper leaving for some rich neighborhood, there's nothing to keep me around the city. With a set of skills like mine, I could go anywhere. Find a place to bury myself and my troubles. Send her a postcard now and then in hopes that she's doing well. Be bitter and lonely for the rest of my life."

"At least you have a plan," said Tessa.

A brief flash of a smile from Danny. "I do," he said. This smile was not for her joke, she sensed.

"Danny," she said. "Don't ruin Harper's day for her. Don't make her upset on the day she wants to be a happy one. Please—I'm asking as her friend, not just as her wedding planner."

"You have my word," he said. "I won't go near her. I won't bother her, or try to call her. I want one shot—one final chance before goodbye—and that's all. I don't have to be the one who delivers it."

Tessa's heart sank. She knew what he was going to ask, even before he took the box from his pocket.

"I know I can trust you," he said. "I'm counting on you. All you have to do is give it to her. I don't want it back, so she can toss it in the trash if she's through with me. But if she's willing, even just a little, to trust that I truly love her, then she can come find me. The two of us can start a life together, however she wants to begin. I'll marry her anywhere, live with her anywhere—even in that boarding house her pa runs. I'll weld as a contractor by day to make money, and weld sculptures in the backyard by night. Anything for Harper."

"You already told her that," said Tessa.

"I'm telling her again," he said. "There's a letter inside this box, offering her me and everything I own and will ever own. I'll be on the island until five o'clock. I'll wait at the pier. If she doesn't come find me, then I'll go back to the mainland, and that's the last she'll ever hear of Danny Reynolds' love for her." He put the box in Tessa's hand. "Just give it to her. That's all I'm asking. I'll stay away from the hotel, I promise."

Tessa sighed. "This one favor is all I'm doing for you," she said. "You had better keep your word." She put the box in her pocket and gazed at the resort, which she had begun to wish she'd never left this morning. Then again, Danny might have made a scene at the hotel, and that would have been worse than having a private word with her.

Danny sighed. "What time's the wedding?" he asked.

"Six o'clock," she said. "That's when Harper walks down the aisle." She glanced at him. "You won't try anything else, will you?"

He shook his head. "By then, I'll know she meant what she said," he answered. "I just have to know she means it. There's no moving on if there's still a question unanswered for me."

In sympathy, Tessa reached across and squeezed his arm, gently. "I can understand," she said. She drew away from him and left Danny on the opposite side of the ferry as she watched the shore come closer, and the blue water surrounding it glittering in the morning sun.

Why had Danny asked her to do this? Wouldn't it be better to toss the box in the water while he wasn't looking, and save Harper the trouble of opening it and feeling angry all over again? The happiest day of her life, and her ex was still begging her to trust his love over Brett's solvency and security.

Not that Tessa believed this was solely about Brett's bank account. Harper loved him. She had to care about him, as passionate and devoted a person as she seemed to be. She must have really loved Danny once, before harsh realities about life, money, and goals nipped their romance in the bud. So maybe that love simply transferred itself to Brett, who was more compatible.

But not because of money and security alone. She repeated this to herself firmly as she climbed the path to the resort's perfectly mown grounds, where the willows rustled softly in the breeze. The hotel's staff was unloading chairs from a van and setting them up in the tropical garden, leaving a red carpet path between the two seating sections. The catering staff would be arriving soon, too.

Tessa walked through to the dining room, stowing her emergency supplies in her bag. On the other side of the kitchen's door, she found the chef overseeing the preparation of the evening's stuffed pears and the vegetables for the main course, and Ama with a frilly apron over an orange taffeta cocktail dress that was surely the work of Natalie, paired with a chunky wood-bead necklace from Mexico.

"Are you ready to set up the dessert's buffet table?" Tessa asked. "The flowers are in the cooler with the bouquets. I think the photographer said he'd like to get started around three o'clock to be sure he has ample time."

"I think so," said Ama. "I'll need some help assembling the cake, obviously. And the trays for the truffles are on the counter over there. I was thinking lots of passion flowers and bright hibiscus around the cake's platter, then fan out with the small orchids and the mini spotted lilies. What do you think?"

"Sounds gorgeous," answered Tessa. "Nola's here already to fit Harper in her dress, right?"

"I think so," said Ama. "That's Natalie's department, though. Where is she today?"

"Personal business," answered Tessa, who hoped her voice didn't sound tight. "Blake's helping out if we need it."

"Blake?"

"He's helping with the sound system in the ballroom right now," said Tessa. "I guess there's nobody like a dedicated contractor and craftsman to make sure there's no scuffed woodwork or marble while concealing cables, right?"

"Harper's upstairs in her suite right now, if you want to check on things with her," said Ama, as she unpacked boxes of truffles from a shipment box by the stainless-steel table. "We still need to put the gift bags in the sitting room by the ballroom, and make sure the staff sets up a second table for the wedding gifts."

"I'll wait to see Harper, since she's probably being fitted into the dress," said Tessa "I still have to meet with the photographer first, then take care of those things you mentioned. Plus, I still have to garland the chairs and see that the centerpieces are in place in the dining room."

The florist had delivered the much-hailed tropical bouquets on time. Big triton's trumpet-style shells with a baby-pink complexion disguised hidden tube vases and burst from the topmost opening with vivid spikes of color. One was placed in the center of each table, with the biggest one reserved for the long bridal table at the head of the room.

"Did you look in the left bureau?" Ashleigh said. "No, the left one, Mr. Winship. Yes, I'm sure that's where you put it. Right next to the stock option estimate, that's right."

Tessa didn't roll her eyes, although she wanted to. Brett's assistant was helping her decorate the chairs at the ceremony's site while talking into her Bluetooth phone. Apparently, the groom's best man had temporarily mislaid the ring.

"It is the one you picked out. Well, no... not the exact one. You told me to use my judgment, so I consulted with the jeweler, and he said the oval cut would be much more tasteful. Plus, the filigree band was a tiny bit too *gauche* when I inspected it up close, so I chose something a bit simpler... yes, I know she doesn't like simple things, but I really felt..."

Tessa adjusted the flowers on the back of the chair to straighten them. She accidentally snapped the head of a miniature orchid, which fell sadly to the ground below.

She reached down to pick up the flower, then changed her mind. Something about it seemed appropriate, lying there alone. It reminded her a little of Harper at this moment, who was rather lost in this conversation's perspective between the groom and his assistant.

*

The photographer planned to snap photos of the bridal party on the willow walkway, at the old gazebo, and at the tropical garden's fountain. The wedding party was supposed to be dressed and ready two and a half hours before the wedding for the photos at the ceremony site, with transport by golf cart to the scenic natural backdrops provided by the resort's grounds. A lush and lavish portfolio was promised by one of the region's premier photographers.

By now, the gift bags were waiting for guests to collect as they departed after dancing and champagne in the ballroom, and guests were beginning to arrive early, bearing expensive gifts for the table reserved for costly packages professionally wrapped and trimmed with perfect ribbons, which they left behind before strolling the resort grounds or enjoying the picture window view from the main dining hall. A short distance away, in the glass dining hall, Ama's cake was assembled: five layers of pure white, garlanded by fondant birds of paradise flowers that looked so real that Tessa almost forgot they were Ama's creation.

Lush tropical-colored blossoms of nature's making were scattered across the white tablecloth, around the platters of delicious gourmet truffles that Tessa restrained herself from sampling again. They decorated the base of a three-tier ice fountain filled with fresh strawberries, pineapple chunks, and sweet kiwi and starfruit slices sweetening the flowing chilled champagne.

Now, between the finishing touches of the ceremony's site and the photographer's session, was the time for consultations with the bride-to-be and the groom. Brett was already gone from his suite when she knocked on the door—Terrence, who answered it, informed her that the groom and his groomsmen were in a private phone consultation in the resort's conference room.

"His assistant is downstairs with the photographer, if you need to speak with her," he suggested.

"No, thanks," answered Tessa.

In her suite, Harper was sitting at her dressing table. The designer gown Nola had created fitted her perfectly, pooling in an elegant train at her feet. She was fastening tiny pearls in each ear, a string of simple pearls around her neck. Her wild black curls were pinned up in a perfect chignon, and her floral hair garland lay on the dressing table, with two pins to hold it in place.

Myra wasn't here, and neither were any of the bridesmaids, strangely enough. They were dressing in a suite down the hall, where Tessa had heard voices and the occasional sound of laughter from a partly open door. They sounded like they were having a good time; in Harper's room, however, it was quiet.

"How do I look?" she asked, turning to Tessa. "I feel elegant. I know these pearls are cheap, but I didn't want Brett to buy me real ones. We're not married yet—and these were my mom's. If she were here today…" Harper paused. "Well, it's nice to think of her."

She glanced at Tessa with a smile that was wistful, nervous, and hopeful all at once. "Guess I've got a case of wedding jitters. But everything's perfect. I couldn't ask for better. I wanna thank you for that."

"I'm glad you like it," said Tessa. "The photographer is ready to start as soon as the bridesmaids are all dressed."

"Good," said Harper. "I can't believe it takes that long to take some wedding photos. Sheesh, my parents were happy with a half a roll of Kodak taken ten minutes after their vows. But Brett says this guy is the best—he took photos for one of the Rockefeller's weddings."

"The locations he chose will look wonderful," said Tessa. "Everything is in place and ready to go. All that's left is for you to be ready for your big moment."

Harper's bright smile appeared. "I guess I just have to pin the flowers in place and grab my bouquet," she said. "Brett's probably already waiting, isn't he?"

"Sure," said Tessa, not mentioning the conference call.

"It's the big day. Deep breath, dive in, start living a new life," said Harper, who lifted the wreath and adjusted a sprig of lavender. Tessa foresaw several of the delicate spikes breaking throughout the long day, hence the extra bundle in a water glass in her room.

Tessa hesitated. She shouldn't say anything about what happened on the ferry. Her professional self was screaming at her not to do it, while there was a smile on Harper's face and her makeup was perfectly brushed in place. *Take that box from Danny and toss it in the sea.* He would believe Harper at last, and she wouldn't have to think of him on her happy day. She would start her new life without any thoughts of her past.

"One thing," said Tessa. Her hand drew the little box from her pocket after a hesitant pause. "I have to give you this. I promised—and I feel like I have to keep that promise. You don't have to open it, if you don't want to. Tell me to throw it in the trash and I will."

She didn't have to say who it was from; the look on Harper's face, the way her smile dwindled then vanished as the box was removed, said it all. The bride took the box from Tessa and untied its ribbon. Under the lid was a scalloped seashell, its bowl facing upwards. Two rings lay in it: a thin, silvery-gold band and a slightly prettier one with a filigree design and a tiny little row of three pearls.

"I don't believe it." Harper slammed the box on the dressing table. The two rings bounced out, landing on its polished surface. "I can't believe he would do this. It's my wedding day. My wedding day—and all he thinks to do is send those to me?!"

"What are they?" Tessa lifted the plain one. It had been resized recently, its band cut and a new metal strip soldering it back together, widening it so it would fall off Harper's finger if she tried to wear it.

"My rings," said Harper. "The ones he gave me when he proposed. Both of them, both times he tried with a ring—the other dozen times he didn't bother with one." She shook her head.

"Why is this one big?" said Tessa. Then she realized why. Danny wasn't presenting them as engagement rings but as wedding rings. One for him, one for her.

Beneath the shell was a folded note addressed to Harper. She knew it probably said much of what Danny had spoken about on the ferry. Harper didn't bother with it, leaving it in the box. "When did he give this to you?" she asked, arms crossed.

"This morning," said Tessa.

"You saw him this morning?"

"I did."

"Don't tell me where." Harper held up a hand, as if to stop her from saying anything else. "I don't want to know where he is. I told him how I feel. So he can't deal with it—how is that my problem?"

"It isn't," said Tessa. "I can throw all this away right now and you'll never hear from him again. That's what he told me to tell you when I delivered the box."

"He did, did he?" said Harper. "I'll bet he told you to tell me that he was going to do something stupid, like jump off a cliff if I didn't call off the wedding."

"Actually, he didn't," said Tessa. "All he said was he packed up everything he owned today, and that he wouldn't go back to Bellegrove if you wouldn't be part of the real city anymore. He said he would go anywhere and live anywhere with you if you were willing to change your mind… and marry him instead," she added. "Which is what the rings are for, unless I'm totally misreading things."

Harper picked them up, noticing the changes to the plain band. A sigh which might be frustration or exasperation escaped her. She put it back in the box. "Idiot," she said. "Why does he do these things?" She rested her forehead on her hand. "Why does he always have to be such a crazy fool? Time and time again, no matter how many times I told him…" She pushed the lid back on the box. "If you see him again, you tell him I… You tell him that he needs to stop being like this." Her words thickened and stopped coming altogether. She wasn't angry. Tessa could tell the difference, having seen Harper both truly angry and truly emotional.

Something inside of Harper was coming unglued at this moment, as Tessa had imagined it would all along when this box was opened. For what reason and why, she couldn't be sure, but she could guess. Tessa knew she had to tell Harper the rest, despite the bride's warning from before… and her own better judgment. "He says he'll wait for you at the pier until five," she said. "Then he's leaving."

Harper's back was to her, so Tessa couldn't see the bride's reaction to this news. The look on her face when she lifted it to the mirror was a stubborn, determined one, although the look in her eyes was desperate enough to make Tessa wish that time could rewind itself and fix whatever had gone completely wrong in Harper's life up to this point. Nobody should look this unhappy minutes from their dream wedding. Or their dream life.

"I don't care," said Harper. "I don't care." She put the flower wreath on her head—jammed it there, more accurately—and reached for one of the hairpins.

Tessa nodded. "I'll see you downstairs in a few minutes," she said. She stepped outside as Harper reached for her second hairpin to hold the wreath in place.

The wedding party was assembled downstairs. Brett was on the phone talking with someone—it was clearly business, judging by his body language. The Winships were sitting stiffly on a nearby sofa, gazing with boredom at the view of the lawn through the windows. Chipper Ashleigh had cornered Blake near the door and was leaning into him as she chatted away. Tessa didn't blame her; even in an off-the-rack tux, Blake managed to outshine even perfect, well-heeled Brett Winship in the looks department.

"The bride will be down shortly," Tessa announced, joining them with a bright smile.

Polite smiles in return from the Winships, a minor groan of disgust from one of the bridesmaids, shockingly enough.

"Finally," said one—Didi, Tessa identified her. "She really is taking all day to dress. I was hoping to see the manicurist before the ceremony. My nails look as if I've been doing manual labor or something."

"It *is* her wedding day," conceded Marsha, with an oh-so-patronizing smile.

"Do you think I have time for a quick call to my broker before we do this?" Brett was asking the photographer, in confidential tones. "It's really important. I just need this quick word about a possible stock tip."

This was Harper's future, collected in this room: dull, bored people made happy by investment brokers and small talk about exclusive couture and vacation houses at Martha's Vineyard. She would always be the noisy, loudly dressed one, trying to hide it beneath tennis whites or sensible tweeds, while her former bridesmaids made jokes about her being one of *Jersey Shore*'s rejects.

In a moment, she would come downstairs and join this party for life. She would marry Brett in a wedding that was perfect on the outside only. Was it worth it to never have to worry about her parents' future, or financial security? To have the last bit of color in her life be the photos from her tropical paradise wedding and her worldwide honeymoon tour? She had a feeling that it wasn't... and that Harper knew that too, even if she couldn't admit it before.

"Are we ready?" the photographer asked. "I'd like to get started as soon as possible. I'm sure you ladies would like time to freshen yourselves afterward before the ceremony."

"Let's all go outside to the garden where the ceremony is taking place," declared Tessa. "That's where you wanted to begin, isn't it?" she said to the photographer. "Come on, everyone. The bride will be along in a moment." She ushered the bridal party in the direction of the door opened by the photographer, the groom's parents prying themselves off the nearby sofa.

"Where are the bride's parents?" asked the photographer as he removed the flash from his camera. "I was under the impression when I spoke to her last week that her father might be here, although her mother was under the weather."

"Not coming," said Tessa, who wasn't surprised that Willy was sitting at home with Rose, grieving what seemed like the permanent loss of their daughter to upper-crust society. "But don't worry about that. I don't think they'll be missed."

The photographer looked at her like she was heartless for this remark, but Tessa didn't care, nor did she care to explain why this was the case. The rest of the wedding party was moving in the direction of the tropical garden, Tessa falling back slowly in the ranks until she was behind all the rest.

Four hotel golf carts were parked near the shade, reserved to drive the wedding party to the next photography site. Tessa approached one, leaning down to speak with its driver.

"Wait by the terrace door for the bride," she said. "I just have this feeling she'll be coming out in a moment, and she will need a ride."

"Where?" said the driver. "Everybody's going to the garden with the overlook, right?"

"Just wait for her," said Tessa. "She'll explain when she comes out." She turned and walked in the direction of the tropical garden, turning the bend in the hedgerow and passing the ornamental fountain, where lucky pennies glinted beneath the rippling pond.

The photographer positioned the bridesmaids and groomsmen, and put Brett in place. The Winships were seated in the front row, a frail woman beside them, dressed like the British Queen Mother, who was apparently Terrence's mother and extremely cranky about being outdoors. A dry-looking uncle who, too, was busy texting someone, and Brett's former nanny, who was the only person who looked remotely happy in the family party.

"Where *is* she?" asked the impatient bridesmaid Didi. "Obviously, this is why her people never got anywhere in life—they were probably always late for everything."

Ten minutes passed. Someone phoned Harper's mobile phone, all of the party beginning to fidget and look annoyed. One of the bridesmaids whispered loudly that maybe it was time that *someone* went back to the hotel to check on the bride, her eye pointedly on Tessa.

"I'll go," Tessa volunteered.

The photographer gave her a grateful smile. Brett adjusted his cufflinks then checked a message on his phone.

Harper's suite door was ajar. On her dressing table lay the flower wreath, and Nola Gayne's gorgeous dress was draped over its chair, carefully. The bride's casual clothes were gone, and so was the little box that Danny had left her.

A lone miniature orchid lay on the floor by the dresser. With a faint smile, Tessa picked it up and laid it carefully beside the other flowers on the dressing table.

Chapter Forty-Three

Controlled chaos descended in the minutes after Tessa discovered the bride was not in her suite. Brett looked shocked. "How could she do this?" he said. "How could she? I did everything, I said I could deal with everything she needed done—how can she leave me at the altar? I can't believe this is happening!" He looked helpless and angry, his face turning red. "This has to be a mistake."

"And after all you put up with, and with a family like hers," said Myra, sounding outraged. "I knew we couldn't trust her. How dare she treat you like this? It's completely unbelievable."

Behind him, Marsha was smiling as if she had just won the lottery. Tessa imagined that Brett's confident ex had felt a twinge or two of worry that her soul mate was actually going through with the ceremony.

"No one jilts a Winship at the altar," said Brett's father. "This is what always happens whenever one associates with people like that. I warned you something like this might happen, but you proposed anyway."

"Where's the cake?" demanded Brett's grandmother. "I'm getting tired of sitting here, waiting for everyone else to arrive."

Marsha embraced Brett now, trying to comfort him in his shock. Her relief was palpable; Tessa's only comfort was the fact that Ashleigh looked torn between dismay and jealousy as she watched her boss in the post-Harper chaos. Tessa couldn't help but notice that Brett returned the maid of honor's embrace like a lover and not a friend.

His cell phone rang, and he disengaged reluctantly from Marsha's arms. "I have to answer this," he said. "Winship here. Do you have those numbers, Tony?" He sniffed back his emotions, composing himself for this call. His ex hovered at his elbow, the look on her face an appropriate one of sympathetic indignation that did an excellent job of disguising her relief for all this, which Brett would probably never notice.

It was proof positive to her that Brett and Harper never would have lasted after saying their vows. Brett was going to be fine without the woman who just jilted him for the love of her life.

As the groomsmen and family rallied around Brett and the remaining bridesmaids began whispering among themselves in shocked tones, Tessa knew it was time to step up.

She laid her hand on Myra's arm. "I'll speak with the kitchen and with the band," she said. "Most of the guests are in the main dining room enjoying the complimentary lemonade. If you want, I'll deliver the news that the wedding isn't taking place, as politely and discreetly as possible."

"Please do," said Myra, dryly. "I have the most exhausting headache after all of this." She took hold of her mother-in-law's arm, who attempted to shake her off as they walked toward the terrace doors.

"Isn't Brett ever going to choose some woman who *isn't* a disgrace to his family?" the elderly woman demanded.

"What a disaster," sighed Ashleigh. "I knew she wasn't good enough for him from the start. When he went to lunch with her and she was wearing that awful pink suit and heels, I thought to myself that he only went out with her for novelty's sake, like a fascination with some weird, exotic culture."

She adjusted her phone earpiece. "Until he's ready for my assistance, would you like my help?" she asked Tessa. "I can speak to the guests, if you want. I'm... well... fluent in their language, if you know what I mean."

"I think I can handle it," said Tessa, crisply. "It's part of my professional training to be socially bilingual." She didn't want assistance ever again from the snobby runner-up Miss Gardenia Blossom.

By the time the ceremony's hour was half past, the bustling affair at the private resort had been reduced to a ghost version of itself, beneath a sky turning gray for an evening rain. The guests had trickled away on the next ferry and the hotel's private boat, leaving the foyer and main dining room empty.

In the glass dining hall, the cake was a sober reminder of the abrupt Winship–Lucas split, and members of staff were collecting all the truffles and putting them in boxes again. The gold-rimmed place settings awaited guests who wouldn't be dining on the stuffed pears this evening. The Winship family had departed for their private plane already: when last seen, the groom was still engaged in his business conference call.

Tessa dangled her feet in the tranquil Caribbean-blue waters of the hotel swimming pool, her shoes beside her on the ornate Grecian tile courtyard. No gorgeous sunset in this waning yellow light of day, dimming with each passing minute that left behind the perfect society wedding that wasn't meant to be. Soon, the wedding cake would have to be disassembled, and her things would have to be collected from the suite upstairs so she could catch the ferry. She had decided not to stay, even though the room was already paid for by the Winship account, and probably nonrefundable. No more weekends at the paradise resort.

She heard footsteps in the courtyard behind her. She expected it to be Ama, asking whether they should collect the cake or donate it to the kitchen, since the Winships clearly didn't want it anymore. *We'll cut the cost in half when we bill them*, she thought. It was the least she could do, for having been the catalyst in Harper's final decision. She hoped wherever she and Danny were, that it was worth it.

"Do you want to be alone, or do you want some company?" The voice belonged to Blake, not Ama. He crouched down beside her near the edge of the pool, on the opposite side of Tessa's high-heeled shoes.

"Company's fine," she answered. "I'm just doing a little thinking before I leave."

Blake paused. "It must have been pretty hard," he said. "I know that this wedding was pretty important. Big society affair like this." He glanced around them at the urns of tropical-shaded cannas and the large palmetto fronds forming the lush green stand nearby. "It would've been pretty perfect in this place."

"It wasn't perfect, though," said Tessa, softly. She was not talking about the clouds gathering overhead, and the missing coastal sunset that was supposed to grace the moment of vows. "They didn't really love each other. Harper still loved someone else... and I think Brett just liked the idea of being connected to someone as unique as her."

"Is that why she left?" he asked. "I heard some of the gossip back at the hotel," he said. "I should've stuck around after the garden chairs were arranged, clearly." He smiled at her.

"You might say I gave her a push," said Tessa.

"You?" He raised his eyebrows.

"Yes, me," said Tessa. "I... I probably shouldn't have. But I couldn't let her go through with all this without stopping to think one last time whether her past love was really over. I guess it wasn't." Not that she was all that surprised that a torch still burned within Harper for her old flame. Harper's fury wasn't the cold anger of a woman scorned, even when aiming that paperweight at Danny weeks ago.

"You broke up the society wedding that would put your business on the social map?" clarified Blake.

"I'm not heartless, you know," said Tessa. "I can't encourage my client to go through with a decision that's wrong for them, can I? It's not in me. I'm in the business of making people happy, not just making wedding days perfect."

"I know," said Blake, softly. "But I'm still impressed."

Tessa glanced at him. She was far too close to the contractor right now, to those blue eyes and the hint of a smile that still lingered on his lips. At this moment of feeling good and terrible at once, she wasn't sure this closeness was such a good idea. It was making her shiver, and the rain shower hadn't even begun yet.

"So much for our society debut, huh?" she answered.

The first few droplets struck the ornamental tiles around her and the toes of Tessa's leather shoes, dappling the pool's tranquil crystal blue with dozens of little impressions. From his pocket, Blake drew a travel umbrella and snapped it open over Tessa's head as the rain began pattering in earnest.

"I thought you might need this," he said.

"Thanks," she answered. "That's the perfect ending when you think about it. Rain washing away the last of today." It would sweep aside the stray petals that fell from the garlands of the rented chairs now stacked for collection tomorrow under the service entrance portico, and the accidental confetti spill from the final goodbye the groomsmen had planned for Brett and Harper's midnight departure by boat.

At least she had remembered to cancel the fireworks.

"We wasted your time," she said. "I'm sorry we dragged you all the way out here for nothing. Even if it is a luxury resort… you had other things you probably planned to do today."

"I don't know about that," said Blake.

"Why not?" she said. "You had other things to do with your time. I've been eating it up unfairly lately, haven't I?"

Blake didn't answer. Tessa felt his hand cup her cheek, turning her to face him. In surprise, she let it happen. Their eyes met for a long moment; then, without thinking, Tessa leaned toward him, feeling his body shift toward hers as well. Their lips met, the kiss a real one that deepened in a few seconds' time. Tessa put her arms around his neck, and Blake let the umbrella drop to the courtyard tiles as he put his arms around her, pulling her closer.

Sparks lit, fireworks ablaze—the whole package of incendiary passions lit themselves inside Tessa with this touch. Even the cool rain didn't dampen it as it sprinkled on her skirt and blouse, and the shoulders of Blake's suit jacket.

They drew apart and caught their breath. Blake's fingers were buried in her hair, which was clinging to his hands, wet from the rain. "I've been waiting to do that for months," he said.

"You have?"

"What? You're surprised?" he said.

"I didn't… I wasn't sure you liked me that way anymore," said Tessa. "Not after I blew the last few chances. Then there was Mac, then there was the would-be Miss Gardenia Blossom—"

Blake's expression was incredulous. "You really thought I was interested in anybody else? What kind of signals did you need to figure out that I've liked you since we met?"

She exhaled, deeply. "Ones from inside me," answered Tessa, softly. "Telling me that I wasn't being stupid for believing there might be something between us."

Blake's gaze softened. She leaned across and kissed him again, lingering a second longer before she drew back to meet his eyes again. "You really mean the part about liking me from the start?" she asked.

Blake laughed. "Honestly, Tessa," he said.

"It's not important... I'm just asking for curiosity's sake," she answered. Her hands encircled Blake's as he cupped her face again. "But there are other things that I'm more interested in right now, so you don't have to answer right away."

His arms slid around her again, pulling her into his embrace, Tessa settling against his shoulder. A breeze fluttered away the umbrella, tipping it upside down, where the rain gently filled it like the basin of a fountain.

*

One of the five beautiful tiers of Ama's wedding cake sat in a box on the table in the Wedding Belles' parlor. The rest was boxed up in the kitchen of the Palmetto Isle Resort, where the kitchen staff would enjoy it in consolation for all their hard work now being served as the dinner special on the hotel's dining room menu.

"We'll give Brett a half-price discount on our services," said Tessa. "It's the least we can do."

"At least they can probably recoup some of the expense," said Natalie. "The honeymoon maybe. The hotel will probably give Brett a break because he's a friend."

"Of course, our profits will be pretty slim for a wedding that didn't take place," noted Ama. "On the bright side, though, we didn't have many personal expenses, did we?"

"Except the spa at the hotel," said Natalie, who pulled off her leather jacket and tossed it on the floor. "Which was amazing, in my humble opinion. Why is it so hot in here?" She pushed up her shirt's sleeves.

"Because nobody's been in the office in the past twenty-four hours, unless you stopped by," said Tessa. "Which I'm assuming your personal business didn't require?"

"Not exactly," mumbled Natalie. That was all the information she volunteered on the subject.

Ama snapped on the central air, a cool breeze flowing from the vents. "Better luck next time, I guess," she said, plopping down on the sofa. "Our next wedding doesn't involve old flames, I hope?"

"We finally have an appointment with Mac and her accountant fiancé on Monday morning," said Tessa. "So probably not."

Natalie slid a knife through the cake's layers, lifting out a perfect two-layer slice of vanilla with pomegranate cream. She laid it on a plate in front of Tessa.

"At least Harper made the right decision," said Ama. "Imagine what would've happened if she and Brett had gone through with it? Both still caring about other people, with their hearts not in the marriage one hundred percent."

"I think Harper would have tried to make it work, but she couldn't talk herself into it," said Natalie. "It wasn't strong enough, what she felt for Brett. She couldn't have been happy about his ex being around, either."

"Do you think she'll be happy with Danny? Really happy?" persisted Ama.

"He's everything Brett really wasn't," said Tessa. "Devoted to Harper through and through." She could say that with confidence, and with the secret of Danny's check in her mind. Harper would see the proof of Danny's love when she came home from their honeymoon, if she didn't already know the truth through love itself.

"Monday," said Ama. "Do you need me there? Or can I skip?"

"Why?" asked Tessa.

"I sort of... promised my sister I would go look at wedding jewelry in a shop," said Ama. "No promises. I'm not sure yet if I want a traditional Indian wedding as far as the dress is concerned."

"You *decided*?" Natalie froze in mid-slice.

Ama held up her hand, revealing the engagement ring she had put back in place now that food prep was finished.

"Ama, this is so great!" Tessa hugged her. "You told Luke, right?" She drew back for a second to confirm this.

"He came back the night of the dinner party and I told him then my mind was made up," said Ama. "A good friend helped me see that the truth was right in front of me, and that I would be crazy to miss my chance."

"So when's the wedding?" asked Natalie. "Have you picked a good planner yet? Because I know this *fantastic* firm in the historic district that does wonderful work. And with a seamstress that knows a thing or two about sari fabric despite a completely different cultural background."

Ama blushed. "We haven't gotten that far yet," she said. "But he did get my dad's blessing, sort of."

"Hey, that's a big step," said Tessa. "Wedding dates and cake flavors—that stuff comes later." She stuck a fork into the slice of deep chocolate beneath the vanilla frosting. "Mmm... this is heavenly, Ama."

"It should be," answered the baker. "It was my best cake ever. Too bad it didn't make it to the wedding." With a sigh, she accepted a plate from Natalie. "Maybe next time, right?"

"What are the odds that our next couple will plan a tropical wedding?" mused Natalie.

"What are the odds our next couple could be Harper and Danny?" challenged Ama. Tessa had told her the complete story aboard the ferry, and the reasons the bride had vanished.

"They're eloping," said Tessa, with uncertainty. "I think their wedding will be an impulsive affair. And Danny's pocket money will buy them two tickets to a beach hotel for the weekend."

"I think he'll make her happy," said Ama. "It'll be paradise, even if it's not the world's most exclusive hotel. He sounds like he really loves her. If you have to run away from life, it's better to run away for true love."

"Says the girl who almost chickened out at the thought of eloping with her James Dean boyfriend," said Natalie. "A Renaissance man who's good with his hands *and* artistically sensitive."

"It was a really tough decision that had nothing to do with Luke himself," protested Ama. "I had to be sure I wouldn't break his heart. Plus, my parents weren't going to be thrilled by the news." She dug into her cake with a touch of exasperation "Everything will change because I said yes to him. I had to be mature enough to realize and accept that."

"Does 'everything' include your role at Wedding Belles too?" Tessa hinted. "Because you know we can talk about changing up your work schedule if we need to. I just hope we won't be losing our favorite baker on a permanent basis," she added, quickly.

"Same here," Natalie agreed. "Your version of happily ever after still has room for our crazy business, right? Because it wouldn't be the same without you. And I'm not just saying that because your baking is some of the best I've ever tasted."

"I'm not leaving forever," Ama promised. "But Luke and I will be in Portugal for a few months. Maybe even a year. Still… when we get back, I should have lots of awesome new recipes for my portfolio," she told them.

"And until then, we can always Skype to get your advice on stuff or make recommendations for clients," Natalie pointed out. "Whatever works, right?"

"Right," said Ama, who wore a smile of true contentment as she dug into her slice of cake again.

"We really would love to plan your wedding, if you'll let us," said Tessa. "Don't let our latest disaster color your feelings about our work." She added this part playfully as her fork swept through a pile of rich chocolate crumbs on her plate.

"It wasn't our disaster," said Ama. "I think we'll be just fine. We have future clients, other big moments to plan. This was just a reminder that perfection isn't always what we picture it to be."

"You said it," said Natalie, in an odd tone of voice that attracted the attention of Tessa's sharp ears. Something was different, but she expected nothing but caginess from Natalie if she asked her directly.

She laid aside her empty plate. "So if we can't all be present to meet the client on Monday, what about Tuesday evening?" she asked. "I could ask them to move the appointment."

"I'm available," said Ama. "My family can cover for me at the restaurant if I'm late to the dinner shift, especially if I precook the desserts."

"Not for me," said Natalie.

"Big fashion party?" queried Tessa.

"Romantic rendezvous?" teased Ama.

In response, Natalie's face flamed red. "I have a… sort of date," she said.

"A date?" scoffed Tessa. "Can't you move it?"

"No, I can't," said Natalie. "He's got a lot of other obligations, so time's kind of pressed for him to ask me out."

"A date with who?" Ama asked, curious. "You haven't mentioned anybody new lately. What's he like?"

"You've met him before." Natalie's tone was dismissive, but the look on her face was killing the casual attitude.

"Who is it?" persisted Ama. "Is it with Chad? Are you back together?"

Natalie had told her partners about the breakup with Chad as casually as possible, making it clear that no one had gotten their heart broken in the process. But she hadn't mentioned the reason it didn't work out. The reason she was so on edge right now as they waited for her answer.

"With Brayden, actually." The scarlet in her cheeks deepened to full flame with this admission. If it were humanly possible for jaws to drop to the floor, both Ama's and Tessa's would have done so, if only for a second's time.

"Brayden?" echoed Ama. "You're going out with him?" The impossible had clearly just occurred in the universe.

"He asked if he could take me to dinner that night, and I said yes." Natalie studied the grain in the coffee table with extreme dedication. "I know how it sounds, but it's not a pity date—"

"He's so *cute*," said Ama, in the voice she used for puppies, kittens, and couples holding hands on the street. "Natalie, I think it's great."

"He seemed like a great guy when I met him," said Tessa, gently, sensing that Natalie's discomfort wasn't for what they thought of

Brayden, but of what they thought of *her*, Natalie, saying yes after years of fierce protest toward even a hint that she could like him. "He was so nice. Honestly. In five minutes' conversation, he seemed pretty adorable."

"And he must be a little brainy, since he's landed a promotion—" continued Ama.

"All right, all right," said Natalie, holding up one hand to ward off any further compliments. "You don't have to sell me on him, I know what he's like. And he's not the same clingy teenager who tried desperately to date me for ten years."

She tucked aside a strand of hair and smiled. This was a new side of Natalie: romantically confused and actually concerned about love.

"This isn't pity, right?" clarified Tessa. Her eye searched Natalie, waiting for the first telltale cracks in her flippant attitude. It couldn't be, she knew, but she wanted to make sure.

Something in Natalie's expression was new—no romantic cynicism, no jaded humor for this one, or at least only a ghost of it. "No," she answered. "He is—" she drew a deep breath "—everything I should have wanted from the start, if I'd had any sense. He's sensitive, and he listens. He's what all the guys I've dated weren't. I just wasn't grown up enough to see it until more recently."

She really meant it, and wasn't pretending. That much Tessa divined was true about her friend's answer.

"I think it's great." Ama hugged Natalie. "You deserve someone that special."

"No, I *don't*," said Natalie, with a disbelieving laugh. "And he definitely doesn't deserve somebody as horrible as me. But since he's held out for twenty years, he obviously doesn't care about those facts." And with this remark, Natalie's old humor had returned. "I just hope he doesn't regret it after we have dinner together."

"I still can't believe you said yes to him," said Tessa, who couldn't help this admission. "Remember when you were dodging his phone calls in college? When you told him you had strep throat so he wouldn't come visit you that open house weekend on campus? I thought at the time he must be a total troll if you were so desperate to escape him."

"I was a terrible twenty-something. So sue me," Natalie answered, grinning sheepishly. "How was I to know that shallow relationships with hot guys pretending to be sensitive would turn out to be so unfulfilling?"

"You dating your childhood sweetheart. Me with the love of a lifetime," said Ama. "It's actually been a pretty good summer, when you think about it like that. If we can only find somebody for Tessa, it would be perfect."

Tessa looked slightly flustered in return—but only briefly. "I'm just glad we didn't end up with anybody's heart being broken. Even the jilted groom only suffered some very minor cracks in his own, I think."

"Maybe he'll find somebody who's only in love with him next time," said Ama.

"How about his assistant? Miss Whatever Blossom," said Natalie. "She's available, unless she succeeded in snagging Blake's number after all."

"I don't think so," said Tessa, vaguely.

"Then it's perfect all around," declared Ama. "You know, I think this occasion calls for something special. I have a box of those gourmet truffles in the fridge. Plus, there's a bottle of champagne that our last client gave us." She rose from the sofa. "Anybody else want a snack?"

"Me," said Natalie.

"Not me," said Tessa. "I think I'm going to go upstairs, get out of these clothes, and call it a night. But you two stay and celebrate as long as you want."

Tessa stepped from the parlor into the darkened foyer of Wedding Belles, seeing the street glow illuminate her beautiful summer wedding window on the other side of its filmy cloth backdrop. Natalie's white strapless wedding gown and Ama's model cake—featuring pink and green carnations and miniature daisies to match the bouquet and silk floral arrangements—cast faint shadows across the framed poster of Paolo and Molly's perfect moment beneath the shower of blossom petals. The handiwork of all three Wedding Belles making each one special.

Someone was standing on the sidewalk, a vehicle parked in the space outside their building. Tessa pushed open the door and stepped outside. Blake was waiting there, in his ordinary work clothes of denim jeans and flannel shirt.

"I thought you were going home," she said. "I mean—I assumed—you said you would catch up later, which I took to be—" She stopped herself, calming her flustered emotions a little before she met Blake's gaze.

"I thought maybe you'd like to grab a bite to eat," he said. "If you're not working."

"I'm kind of finished with my latest wedding," she answered as a smile tugged at one corner of her lips. "And the next one doesn't begin until Monday. Or Tuesday."

"Back to the grindstone for the three of you," he said.

"Maybe," she said. "I don't know about my partners on this next one. They kind of have their hands full—or their hearts full—right now." She glanced toward the building again. "I'm not sure how much good either of them will be at handling somebody else's big romantic moment."

What the future held might be a different story for them: Natalie's fashion career was taking off, and Ama now had her own wedding to plan. Which meant, she, Tessa, was the last Wedding Belle whose head was in the game. But not her heart, which belonged to someone else.

"You have a fourth partner you can ask for help," he said. "Maybe not quite as skilled at dresses and cakes and flowers, but he's not too bad at the rest."

Tessa met his eyes. "Is that an invitation to ask?" she said.

"To spend time with you, sure," he said. "If there's room to move up on the partnership, I might consider it. A way to fill the time between jobs… an excuse to hang around this place when I'm not refinishing fireplaces or putting up new wall trim." He shrugged his shoulders. "But in the meantime, do you want to go to dinner somewhere? If you haven't eaten… or if you have."

"You're not wearing your tux anymore," she said.

"I'll wear one for the next client's meeting, if you want," he answered, softly.

"No." She put her arms around his neck. "The way you look now is perfectly fine." She pressed her lips against his tenderly, feeling the reassuring warmth and strength of having Blake in her arms. His own were around her, holding tightly as he returned her kiss.

She heard a whistle from above, followed by a catcall. "Do I spy a romantic incident below?" called Natalie, mockingly.

"Is *this* what you've been busy doing whenever our backs were turned?" demanded Ama. Both girls were leaning out of the upstairs window, directly above Tessa and Blake.

"How could you not tell us?" demanded Natalie. "We've been trying to matchmake you since last fall, even if it *is* a dirty word in Ama's book. And after you *swore* you were a reformed romantic who would never fall in love with anybody—"

"You look so cute together!" said Ama. "I'll go inside and tell them to stop," Tessa said, pulling free of Blake's embrace, only for his arms to tighten round her.

"Let 'em," he said. "I don't mind." He pulled her close and kissed her again, despite the cheers from above.

Shaking her head, Natalie observed, "Maybe it's true, that old saying: 'Love conquers all.' Even someone as determined to run from it as Tessa has been for the last few years."

"Or you," said Ama, with a mischievous grin that Natalie pretended not to notice.

But it was true, wasn't it? Nobody had dodged love longer or harder than Natalie. Yet it had found her anyway, and even she couldn't resist it this time.

Her lips tugged into a smile as Brayden's name suddenly popped onto her phone's screen. It unleashed a feeling an awful lot like butterflies in her chest as she answered it to hear the warmth in his voice.

So maybe there was some truth to that old saying after all.

A Letter from Laura

Thank you so much for reading *If You're Not the One,* my third book about the trio of friends known professionally as the Wedding Belles. I hope their summer-themed story swept you away to both an exotic island paradise and the southern sidewalks of quaint Bellegrove. Be sure to sign up for all the latest news on these books at the link below—your email address will remain private, and you can unsubscribe at any time.

www.bookouture.com/laura-briggs

If you haven't read the previous two books featuring Tessa, Ama, and Natalie, I hope you'll be sure to check them out. I also hope that if you enjoyed this story, you will leave a review sharing your thoughts about it with other readers. To learn more about the Wedding Belles, join me on social media using the links below—I can't wait to share more with you about these plucky wedding planners' adventures!

Thanks for reading,
Laura Briggs

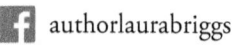 authorlaurabriggs

 PaperDollWrites

🌐 paperdollwrites.blogspot.com

www.ingramcontent.com/pod-product-compliance
Lightning Source LLC
Chambersburg PA
CBHW071732110726
47908CB00006B/1575